THE JAILER'S WAY

By Vivian Lark

This book is a work of fiction. Any resemblance to persons living or dead, or places, events, or locales is purely coincidental. The characters are productions of the author's imagination and are used fictitiously.

The Jailer's Way
www.vivianlark.com

For my husband, who is not averse to whims.

CONTENTS

Chapter 1

Mahtap's Smile

"**W**hen I was a little girl? What do you mean?" I blurted out loudly.

My questions always seemed to come out wrong, and once again Mrs. Griggs was flaming with irritation at me. I didn't mean to irritate her, it was a legitimate question...I thought.

"Theorie Jailer, why are you always overthinking everything, and why must I explain everything to you twice? Girls!" She raised her voice drawing the attention of all twenty-six classmates. "Theorie is once again lost, daydreaming! Can someone give her an idea of what they will use as their essay topic? You are to think back to your childhood, you *were* a little girl at one time Theorie. Think! What is your fondest memory? Lina! What is your fondest memory as a girl? What will your essay be on?"

Lina, a quiet girl with big round eyes mousily squeaked, "My first ice cream."

"See!" Mrs. Griggs cut her off. "A vacation, a favorite food, a present, a simple happy memory. 100 words, proper English grammar, and I am grading on spelling and punctuation." Mrs. Griggs slipped back into her desk chair rolling her eyes. "Theorie, a '*real*' memory," she warned. "I am sick and tired of your bald-faced lies. I will check with Emma if I have to." She nudged her nose up indicating to me to get to work.

An uncomfortable feeling started welling up inside of me. I knew I wasn't going to cry, I just did NOT do that. Both my parents died within days of each other just last year, and I held it together then, so what was happening to me? The already humid sticky air of the Tanzanian spring was wrapping around me, squeezing the life from my lungs. My classroom was like a cage, and I was like a trapped bird. I felt like I needed to measure up to all the pairs of eyes I imagined were staring me down. I had done it this time. I would definitely be alone at lunch tomorrow, choking down my rice and beans. Just when I believed the other girls were liking me too. Now, with my one stupid question they saw my lost side again.

My classroom was filled with twenty-six girls, who had dark creamy skin, and an artwork of chocolate sauce braids over their heads. They were so much better than me. This was a private girl's school, and these students were the daughters of diplomats and resort owners. The girls in the Primary school were from a wealthier side of Tanzania. They were expected to excel and take education seriously. There wasn't a single girl who saw me as anyone important or interesting. They were not to blame, I had no fortune or legacy, and I was out of place. I shouldn't have been sent to this school.

When I first came to this school nine months ago, the girls fell for my far-fetched stories and bald-faced lies. They thought I was neat because I was from New York. That part was true. But, by the end of the month and a few stories that went too far, they passed me off as a liar and gave up on me.

Every day came another opportunity to feel naked and desperate for clothes. I would swallow the pit in my throat and join their cliques. I would try to join in on the conversation and be super excited over what they were talking about. They let me tag along most of the time and would correct me when I was acting like an obnoxious puppy by trying to get away from me. They would turn their backs and speak in only Swahili, forgetting that I had been raised in Tanzania and was as fluent as them. I just wanted to be liked by them. I just wanted to feel normal and have more than our blue and white school uniforms make us similar. I wanted a friend that would help me feel less awkward and would accept me.

I was nothing special to look at either. My mahogany hair was dry and unappreciated, and my body was made all wrong with short legs and long arms. My skin wasn't glistening and smooth chocolate like the others, it was pale peach and a line of freckles dotted across my cheeks and nose, making me stand out in this classroom as misplaced and strange.

I at one time thought I had a nice blue-green shade of eyes, like my father, but when I really examined them, I found a light brown colored streak in the right one, breaking the teal blue with a mudslide. I was plain and awkward, and boring. I wanted to be interesting. I wanted a simple happy memory like the other girls.

The concept of a *simple* memory made no sense to me. Isn't the fact that food, or a single day that impressed your mind make it NOT simple? A memory that imprints is meaningful and important, or it would have been forgotten. This was an irrational assignment.

The girls busily wrote down their favorite memories. Most of them with smiles and smirks peeking from the corner of their mouths exposing their glistening white teeth. As they wrote of a stupid vacation, or food they once ate. I wondered if I could copy someone's memory. Could I steal someone's childhood moment and make it my own? Could I make up a story?

I could make it seem very real, but Mrs. Griggs said she would check with Emma. My brain hurt now. I thought hard for what seemed like hours. I had memories, clear memories, but my assignment was to write of a simple memory, and that's where I overthought everything and came up with nothing. I sat in the smoldering classroom, sweating and nauseous. The slight breeze from the open window brought dust that stuck to my drenched brow, and the chanting rhymes of the younger children playing carefree in the lot made me envy their young age.

My eyes wandered and dragged my thoughts off. I ran the side of my pencil over the six markings on my left wrist. Maybe I could write down the story I made up of how the strange marks got there in the first place. Six pea sized symbols. They had been there my whole life, but I didn't know why or who had tattooed me. I didn't know what the symbols meant because it did not match any language I had ever seen before. They were just shapes or markings, similar to Arabic in form but not recognizable.

I started to write about the story I made up in my head years ago about pirates tattooing me and branding me before they sailed across the Pacific Ocean to collect the reward due for a missing Princess who matched my appearance like a twin. With only those six marks given to me at birth to identify me. I was brought to the palace, the pirates collected their prize, and I lived the life of the missing princess before coming to this awful school.

I had told my father this story when he was still alive, and he liked it very much. He said I should write stories and that someday I would know what the symbols on my wrist meant.

My father! That's it! A good childhood memory. I could write of all the times my best friend Jace and I strapped into his small bush plane, and we would fly to wherever on the earth. Sometimes India, or Europe, Asia, or Russia, Egypt, or Ireland.

My father, Morgan Jailer was a photographer, who had a burning passion for his work and for traveling. His work brought him all over the world to snap flickers in time that he saw as mesmerizing stories, or to capture the desperate eyes of a person otherwise forgotten in history. People's stories were his fascinations, and he chased opportunities to see their joys, their calamities, and their determination to survive and love.

When I was four years old, and my mother couldn't care for us anymore, my father brought me, my twin brother Tobin, and my older brother Gideon to Tanzania to be raised by his friends, Joseph and Emma Taralock.

The Taralocks owned a 400-acre thriving coffee plantation in the lush valleys of Arusha, Tanzania. They had a large home, farm, and cottages scattered throughout their land that housed the hired help.

The Taralock's son was named Jace, and he was my best friend in all the world. He, my two brothers and I had run rampant over the fields and forests of Taralock Estates for the last ten years. We played pirates or climbed up the hills pretending to scale Mount Everest. We learned dances and played football and other games with the Maasai children. Each day was new and exciting and full of mischief.

My father's work had him always on the move, and he knew we would be safe in Tanzania with his dear friends. He would often bring Jace, and I along on assignments though around the world, and we were filled with an understanding of cultures and the trials of people. He loved having Jace and me along. He would say it was nice to have a girl's perspective and a guy to hang out with. Jace's face would light up making him feel ten years older and two feet taller.

Jace's own father, Joseph had more concern over the color of the coffee cherries, or an ailing heifer than his own son, so Jace idolized my father and dined off the attention he dished out. I loved those times, but they were gone now, so was the little plane, so was my father. The memory felt more like listening to your favorite song that is suddenly interrupted by a loud heart stopping weather alert. It would be a betrayal to write of those adventures, and besides, they were too precious.

So, not my father. What about my Mother? No, she had died just two weeks after my father, but I only have one memory of her. It was simple, but could *not* be described as "happy, or fond."

The pressure of finishing this stupid 100-word assignment was choking me. All twenty-six girls had their pencils dancing over their papers. Little girlish giggles could be heard now and then just adding to the distraction. It was expected in a classroom of twelve to fourteen-year-olds. I hate being thirteen, I hate seventh grade, I hate being forced to capture my thoughts. I hate sitting still in this room. I don't want to do this!

"Time is running out Theorie," Mrs. Griggs barked.

She had no patience for me, never did. She liked me briefly, and I mean for about two days when she first met me. The school year started, and I was a new student. I was one of only three white girls in the entire Tanzanian Primary School. When I first arrived, she took an interest in me and wanted to be my friend. But after several incidents of me questioning why she was teaching a subject of no consequence or use to anyone on the face of the earth, her appreciation of me vanished. The original sentiment of wanting to be friends became a disgust for my presence, and she could barely tolerate me.

She asked what the mysterious marks on my wrist meant, and because I did not know or remember how they got there, I told her a previous version of my story that included coordinates to Atlantis. She was not convinced or amused and from that moment on, made it her goal to shut down my imagination and force me to keep my mind on the real world. She would question every word out of my mouth and put me in my place in front of all the other girls. I disliked her immediately, and within two school days, she realized her Tanzanian students outsmarted me on every subject.

I wasn't stupid, I just didn't perform well, while surrounded by a group of intimidating peers. Mahtap, my caretaker and friend had taught me well, and I scored pretty high on the entrance exams. From the time my two brothers and I arrived onto Taralock Estates, Emma Taralock handed our education over to Mahtap.

Mahtap was hired to work at Taralock Estates two decades earlier and moved into one of the little cottages on the land with her husband and two sons. She had been a school teacher before coming to the farm, and Emma entrusted our education entirely to her.

Just a quarter of a mile from the main house where my brothers and I slept, Mahtap's small white cottage became our classroom each day, where we were taught about letters, math, and geography. She taught Jace how to play the piano, and me how to write stories.

She had been our teacher and mother for as long as we could remember. She taught us sign language and how to communicate with Tobin. She taught us how to care for plants and which ones could hurt, and which ones could heal. She showed us the ways of her culture, and how to love God through his creations. Every day we were captivated by her lessons often about animals, often about the earth and its inhabitants, or a story that brewed empathy and forgiveness.

She read to us for hours in the afternoons. Fiction, adventures, love stories, even tragedies. When I listened to her stories, I lived in those worlds and had a hard time coming back to reality. The characters were my friends and enemies, and I felt such a connection, it consumed me. I preferred to push reality aside and live my entire day in my own imagination, it was just so much more enjoyable, and made so much more sense than the real world. I used these stories as a foundation and told farfetched, fanciful lies about my birth, my childhood, and about being remarkable.

Mahtap could paint a picture and compose a song with her words in your mind and you would have a longing to know what happened next. It was a gift of beautiful creativity, and we were honored to be in her care. She would call Jace and me her babies because from the time we were small we longed for her attention and guidance.

I needed to get through the day to be at home with Mahtap, listening to her stories, or to her playing the piano. I wanted to help collect the honeycomb, or help water the coffee trees, and do our daily check for infestations on the priceless plants. She was the only teacher I needed, and I was able to breath when I was with her and be myself. In Mahtap's care, I never needed to escape with my imagination, I liked being real with her. There was no competition or begging for acceptance with her. She loved me and let me be myself.

Mrs. Griggs gazed at my paper. Her hair was black with gray threads here and there, trimmed in a man's short style. She had shiny pink skin and black pebble eyes. She was only about four foot ten inches and shaped like an apple with legs. Her brow always pinched together with a look of disapproval. I would focus on her tiny mouth that was bent in a permanent frown. I never saw her smile.

That's it! Mahtap's smile! Finally, a memory came to me. My memory struck me as the other girls began turning in their papers and started to chatter. The end of the day had arrived, and my mind was just waking up. My hand wrote so fast, the words were barely legible. Spelling, punctuation, grammar...whatever. I just needed to get out this memory while it was still flooding my brain.

My words flowed of Mahtap's smile on the first day I arrived in Tanzania when I was four years old, scared and tired from a very long journey, all the way from New York along with my two brothers. I don't remember a plane or a boat, but I remember the drive to the estate. It was a rickety, rusty, white, open top all-terrain vehicle.

My older brother Gideon, my twin Tobin and I bumped and jostled for a long time. We went over hills, and small creeks, and arrived with bugs in our teeth and wind slapped cheeks.

I was lifted over the sidebars by the strong, dark arms of the driver Rubin Gambre, who was Mahtap's oldest son. He was in his twenties and seemed like a giant to me. He plopped me on the ground, and I was so unsteady from the vibrating ride, I almost toppled over.

Mahtap took my arm and set me straight. With her hands sliding over my tattooed wrist, she gracefully took to her knee matching my eye level. She didn't speak, she just cradled my little hands in her dark palms. Her long fingers were coarse and rough like tree bark. My curiosity drove me to look up, and her eyes were so full of love and so elegant in shape. One eye was dark as ink, and the other was a milky gray.

She smiled and didn't break her gaze, making me feel something brand new. It was a pull towards something I needed. I couldn't look away, I was mesmerized by her. There were sounds of dogs barking and voices from every direction. My two brothers were excitedly trying to get my attention. Tobin was pulling on my arm, trying to make me look at him but I just couldn't stop looking at Mahtap. I wanted them all to go away just so I could have more time to study her face and understand what I was feeling. My happiest childhood memory flooding my school paper was so vivid, so simple. It was the first time I saw Mahtap's smile, *the first time I felt loved.*

My paper looked like it had been written by a two-year-old. Oh well. I was just so happy that I had found a happy memory, I didn't care about the criticism I knew was coming. I had a warmth in my heart that I remembered how Mahtap told me with just a smile that she would be my mama and love me. I was so little and was desperate to feel safe. The beautiful smile she gave me almost ten years ago, had awoken my heart and soothed my soul. Her beautiful smile was my moral guide, builder of confidence, and the key to opening my heart to her for the last ten years.

The excitement I felt as I handed Mrs. Griggs the completed assignment was because I had such a feeling of relief. I *was* like the other girls, I did have a special memory. It was simple but for me the most profound sense of comfort. I felt confident it was a fair compromise between Mrs. Griggs' shallow request and my wild brain.

"This is unacceptable!" Mrs. Griggs screeched, breaking into my pleasant thoughts. My dumb glare enraged her to yelling the same words again. "This is unacceptable!" Her piercing voice matched her expression.

"Why?" I asked as if I didn't know it was written atrociously. I sympathetically asked, "Can I rewrite it with the correct spelling and grammar tonight? It's just that it took me so long to think of a good memory."

"NO!" she snapped, "NO!" making me jump back about three inches. "You have mixed languages again. This school is taught in two languages," flying up a gesture of two fingers very close to my face. "Swahili, and English. This assignment was to be in English, I told you this, repeatedly!" She slammed the paper onto the desk. "You have mixed English, Swahili, Russian, and what is this, Arabic?"

"It is Hindi," I scoffed, scowling so intensely because she was just so stupid. She looked at me biting her bottom lip about to burst. Her breathing became louder, and I swore I saw smoke flaring from the top of her head. Did I just call her stupid out loud without realizing it? She took a moment, but regained her composure and repeated,

"ENGLISH. Not Russian, French, or Arabic, Hindi, or whatever else is filling your untamed head. As for the memory, the few words you do have in English are describing someone's smile. Your memory is a smile. Really?"

"YES! Mahtap's smile," I yelled back as I inched closer, leaning over her desk slightly. "Mahtap raised me, she takes care of me. I call her 'Mamahtap' because she is a mother to me, and she has the most beautiful smile!" My voice raised, and I inched even closer in a standoff. "When she smiles her eyes go up in the corners, and she almost looks like she will cry because she loves me so very much. No one can help but love her, and all she has to do is smile!" I was yelling now.

"That is an idiotic memory, Theorie. The other girls wrote of their first kiss, first tastes of their favorite food. Here one girl wrote of when her father returned from the army. Janine wrote of when she won first prize at the spelling bee. Those are all happy, simple things that they *experienced*. This is JUST a smile."

My hate for her was mingling with feelings of sadness for her. Mahtap's smile was better than all those other girls' stupid memories put together. Mrs. Griggs knew it too. Nothing I wrote would have pleased her, and maybe she didn't understand. Perhaps she was still waiting for a smile like that.

"It may be just a smile to you," I firmly replied. "but, it is MY smile, and it is when I first knew I was safe and loved. That is so much more important than ice cream, or a first kiss. I should not have told you about it now that I see you are shallow and despicable. I am sorry for you because you would understand if you were loved by someone...Anyone!"

I grabbed the paper from under her clenched fist and trotted to the entrance with the biggest grin on my face.

Chapter 2

Taralock

I boastfully dashed to Rubin's truck with my head held high. He was parked in the usual spot near the side of the building with the violets. He was not there at first, so I wedged my satchel in between the crates that were puzzled together in the back seats and covered it back up with the canvas. I knew I was in trouble, but I didn't care one bit. I climbed into the front passenger seat and waited for any sign of him.

My mind was anxious to get home to the farm with the smell of roasting coffee in the air. It was May, and the harvest was complete, the last of the crop was being dried and roasted for local sale and personal use. The storehouses were full and waiting for international sales. The Maasai children would be ready to play a game of football before supper. I wished it didn't take so long to get home.

Rubin's appearance eased my anxiousness, and as he hopped into the driver's seat, he weighed down the truck and tilted it. He chuckled, nodding his head, and in Swahili asked,

"Ni shida gani ambayo Theorie ilifanya leo?" Meaning, "What trouble did Theorie cause today?" I couldn't help but leak a smirk at his question, his voice was so jolly, and he knew me well.

He continued his contagious snicker sporadically for the next mile or so. His plump cocoa cheeks were dimpling from his broad smile. He was always amused by me, and I enjoyed making him laugh whenever I could. He had a genuine catching belly laugh, that was so marvelous even Mrs. Griggs, if she had the honor to hear it would be caught away. He would start off as a low grumble, then melt into an all-out chuckle. He would take one hand and rub it over his bald shiny black head and then slip his hand down to his belly, fold his two hands together and rub his round abdomen as if the laugh had fed him a meal.

Rubin Gambre was Mahtap's only living son. He had always lived with Mahtap in her little cottage, and while she was a one of a kind teacher, healer, and cook, Rubin was the hardest working man on the farm. He knew precisely how to run things smoothly and knew more of coffee and the Tanzanian countryside than anyone we knew. He was older now, ten years had passed since the day he drove me to Taralock Estates, and I always felt safe with him.

The speed Rubin was driving at made the wind blow my hair right out of the braid it had been held hostage in all day. I always looked like an unkempt mess by the time I arrived home each day. I pinched my eyes closed to keep the dust cloud we were creating and the gnats from blinding me. We rumbled and shook as we peaked the hill that made Taralock Estates tuck into a lush green valley. It had been my home for ten years now, and my guardians Joseph and Emma kept it a thriving coffee farm despite lost crops and civil unrest.

As the immense powder blue house came into view I suddenly remembered…the other side of the hill. It was so much worse than it looked. Everyone assumed it was as calm as the ride up the hill, but the wind was not able to dry these trails, and water paths carved out deep trenches. There was a main road that was much less fierce and was a smoother ride.

They would use it for the large transport trucks, but Rubin always chose this path saying, "It was quicker."

Bumping, and Jerking and nearly flipping the vehicle over I clenched the window frame and dug my heels into the floor. We finally made it to the acacia tree that stood halfway between the main house and the first large storage barn. A cloud of dust caught up with us as Rubin abruptly came to a stop. I was about to run off when he grabbed me by my shirt tail.

"Wait, Miss. You must give this to Emma." He held out an envelope clearly marked from Mrs. Griggs. That must have been why I had been waiting for him at the truck. She *caught* him knowing if she had given me the notice it would have been lost purposely on the dusty road we just came from. I wrinkled my nose and sneered at him.

Rubin had been gone all day getting supplies in Tanga at the coast. He was anxious to check on his mother, then he could get the shipment unloaded. He still chuckled at me as he walked down the path towards his home.

I was less than excited to see my brother Gideon come around the side of the barn. He was three years older than me and was not forced to go to school. Instead, he helped Joseph run the farm. He cared for animals, watered crops and trees, and harvested coffee. Gideon enjoyed his work, and I was jealous of him. He had been on the farm working all day enjoying the outdoors, and he looked so glum and serious as usual. He would not even make eye contact with me today. He paused for a second and slowly wandered back into the barn that sat to the West of the house. He was such a hard person to understand. He was quiet and kept his thoughts to himself. He had dark brown hair with even darker black roots and the same solemn facial expression that my mother had when she was alive.

Gideon woke up and came to life when he worked with his mentor and guardian, Joseph, who had taken him under his wing and trained him in all the ways of the estate. Joseph was pleased to have Gideon as an apprentice because he took his work seriously and was the most responsible out of all the children living at Taralock Estates.

Emma Taralock was Joseph's wife and Jace's mother. She owned the estate and ran it with harsh rules, and a strict schedule. She came out onto the porch wiping her hands on the skirt of her peach apron. My twin brother Tobin followed behind her, his arms were covered in flour. He let the screen door slam behind him. He didn't have to go to Primary school either, and he and Emma had been making tomorrow's bread.

Emma's salt and pepper hair, streaked with the remnants of a blonde past, was in a wispy unruly ponytail and was sweat marked. I could tell she had a rough day and was not going to be happy with whatever Mrs. Griggs had to say about me in that notice.

Emma looked much older than she was. She was in her forties but the African sun and working on the fields day after day had aged her fair complexion. Her temperament was as old as she looked, and her disagreeable attitude made her unlikeable. She was not a warm embrace. Instead, she was a task-driven chill. Her only son Jace, had a hard time breaking her shell and they had never had a warm relationship, and her husband Joseph humbly ran the farm like a docile puppy. He never questioned her methods or strict order.

Her patience for strong minded wild children was very little. She may have been my guardian, but she was *not* my mother. I wanted to get the scolding over with, so I could go to the cottage and tell Mahtap and Jace about my happy memory. I prepared myself to be respectful as I waited for the typical Emma lecture on how a kind, uncle had paid for my education and how I should appreciate the opportunity. How I take for granted the kindness people have shown me and without her and Joseph and the Taralock farm my two brothers and I would be orphans. Or, that I had working ears and should be grateful I wasn't born deaf like my poor twin Tobin. She did not start in on a lecture though. She put the notice in her apron pocket, wiped the sweat from her brow, and without expression stated,

"Go to Mahtap's cottage right now."

She motioned for Tobin to go inside and watched me start on the path. My regular skip to Mahtap's was this time, a confused wonder. Emma never wanted me to go to Mahtap's. She saw Mahtap as hired help to teach us what she herself was incapable of, and she couldn't understand why we loved her so much.

Something was wrong. When I got close enough to make out Mahtap and Rubin's little cottage tucked into the long vines and moss of the forest, I saw Rubin first, standing in the doorway. Moments ago he was cheerful, but now his expression was clouded over with sadness. His round black cheeks looked dull and deflated. He stood motionless gazing at the forest. I knew it was Mahtap when she did not step outside with her smile to greet me.

I saw Mahtap only…had it really been three days? I had been so busy with my schoolwork. I needed to know, I needed to confront whatever it was. Jace was where he always met me each day, sitting on the second step up to the small wrap around porch. His expression matched Rubin's. His brow was drawn together, and he gazed at the ground in pain. What could have happened?

My impatience pushed me up the stairs. Jace stopped me as I tried to pass him, grabbing my elbow. Jace was three

17

years older than me, and at sixteen, he was not much taller or bigger than myself, but from the day I met him when my brothers and I arrived in Tanzania, we had been inseparable. He was fiercely protective of me and I of him.

I met his smoky blue eyes that were glazed over with tears and swollen with sorrow. He never had a problem crying, and it irritated me sometimes how emotional he was.

Jace's expression protested my impatience. If I hadn't caught sight of his face I would have run into the cottage head on to face whatever it was and suffered a shock, but I saw him, and I knew. It *was* Mahtap, and I knew I was too late to say goodbye. In that split second my rush to go in froze and stopped my legs from moving forward. Jace could sense my fear and pulling himself up with my hand said,

"Together."

I nodded in agreement and let him lead me through the door. I saw Mahtap's lifeless body across the room lying neatly on her bed looking so peaceful. Her black skin reflected the afternoon sun shining through the window, making her skin look like golden bronze. Her beige head wrap curled loosely around, pillowing her head. It twisted at the side of her neck and lay over her shoulder creating a tail of fabric. Her short, wiry black and graying hair was barely peeking out. Her life was gone, but she looked like she was just sleeping. She had a content expression of rest and satisfaction, and I could still see a small smile in the corner of her mouth.

She was over eighty years old and had gone through the death of her husband and infant son at one point yet did not age. It was not hard to envision her as a youthful woman, she had so much vibrant life in her face. We never once thought of her as aging or ending her time on earth. She was taken for granted because she had an eternal personality.

"She never got up." Rubin's deep voice cracked from behind us at the door. "She was tired when I left early this morning, she said she needed a little extra rest today. She just went back to sleep. Mama- Samahani, nisamehe, please forgive me."

Seeing Rubin's great strength give out and being unable to do anything was the first time I felt utterly helpless. Not the last, but the first. There is nothing so empty feeling as the inability to heal the pain of someone you love. I stood motionless unable to move. My legs felt so heavy, and the gravity of the earth thickened and weighed me down. I held onto the bedpost like a crutch and stared at my beautiful mother lying there.

Jace's pain streamed down his jawline. His navy-blue shirt soaked up his tears. He wiped his face and ran his fingers through his moppy light brown hair, making the windblown mess it had already been even worse. His pain made this unbearable to me. Everyone was falling to pieces, and I wanted to make it stop somehow. If I could hold the hurt for all our hearts, I would have, but I also felt like I was broken in two.

Jace must have caught the frozen in time look on my face because he cleared his throat and took both his hands and placed them on my face. He pushed my loose hair behind each ear and lowered himself matching my height, looking right into my eyes. He took hold of my hands and without a word steadied my trembling.

Rubin covered his sweet mothers face with her lime green quilt as the local doctor arrived. Joseph had fetched him earlier and arrived with him on foot through the overgrown greenery leading to the cottage. With 4 children, workers and animals all needing medical assistance at some time or another, Dr. Korie was very familiar with Taralock Estates and had been a trusted friend of Joseph and Mahtap's for many decades.

He often in an innocent, playful way teased Mahtap for her herbal remedies. They compared modern treatment with herbs and roots that Mahtap's people had used for centuries. As he looked down at his old friend, he stroked his chin and pulled from his shirt pocket his round gold glasses. We stepped outside to wait while he checked Mahtap over. Neither of us wanted to leave without answers. Jace and I sat on the step waiting for any news.

"I knew you would be right here," I spilled out to Jace. "I was so excited to get home. I knew Mamahtap would be making something for us, maybe a mango orange drink. She would have the biggest fresh smile and say,

"Ah, my baby girl… tell me your day's story."

We both allowed a smile for just a second before I bit my lip. I didn't want Rubin or Jace to see me cry. They were in enough pain already. The color drained from my face, and I was gripped with extreme fear. My mama was gone. My friend. My forehead pounded, and my lungs felt like they were filled with rocks. The pain was so real and so sharp, I felt I would die along with my Mahtap that evening. How could she be gone? It wasn't real. Rubin came from the house and said goodbye to Dr. Korie.

"She was fine yesterday. What was it?" Jace asked.

"Age," Rubin replied, "Her heart was eighty-one years old, and worked hard every day of her life. It could not beat any longer, it needed to go to sleep." Rubin stepped down from the porch. "She will be buried on the hill near my father and brother tomorrow. I cannot stay here tonight." He passed us and turning back said, "She had these tucked in her arm." He showed us two envelopes. One was addressed to "Rubin," the other to, "My two babies." He held his letter to his chest, "I will read this alone." He turned and walked toward the creek as the evening sun started to set.

I leaned on Jace's tear-soaked shoulder. His arm curled around me pulling me closer to him as he tilted his head on mine. Mahtap had been a far better mother to Jace than Emma Taralock was capable of and the only person who deserved that title from me. We left a small piece of our hearts in the cottage that day. I felt numb, and a crushing pain bounced from my heart to my head, back and forth. I was racing with questions and fears. What would we do without her?

We walked to the hill overlooking several of the Taralock coffee orchards. We often would meet Rubin and Tobin, occasionally even Gideon would join us for a breezy picnic here. There was an enormous tree with branches low enough to climb on and tall enough to lounge under. The evening was cooling, and the sky was painted with warm oranges and ambers. The breeze brought the smell of roasting meats and spices. The harvest of blood red coffee cherries was over leaving the orchards picked clean and empty of workers. Jace and I could be alone to savor our letter.

He opened it and began reading. I could hear Mahtap's voice as clear as if she were reading it herself in her thick Swahili accent.

My Dearest Babies,

I wrote this knowing that I am an old lady who won't be here forever to guide you or to tell you stories. I never had a lot of money, but the two of you made me so rich, I could not ask for better hearts to share my life with. You have made my life big and beautiful, and I thank you for every time you walked down my path.

Gideon and Tobin will be fine men someday. They will quickly find their path, but I know in my bones that you will need more. I stay awake at night thinking of how to guide you when I am not here. I am worried, I cannot protect you.

Rubin does not know how to keep you safe, I have told him very little. You are both young and innocent. I tried to shield the two of you for so long, so that you would have a beautiful beginning.

Things will be changing soon. There will come a time when you will have to remember all the things I taught you, all the things your father taught you. You will break, and when you do, I want you to remember the stories, the places, the people, and the music. Remember, that the music will set you free, it will heal you.

You have always had a way of understanding each other and helping each other, and I don't doubt this will keep you safe. It may be all you have. Cherish it. I only wish you could both have a normal life and the stories were just that...stories. I love you both. I loved you from the day I met each of you as if you were my own. I know you are sad that I am gone, but I will see you again one day soon when peace fills the earth.

Love,
Your Mamahtap

Chapter 3

The Puff Adder

The crashing sound of glass and metal triggered the menagerie surrounding Taralock Farms. The two Aussie Shepard farm dogs Wilbur and Mansfield whipped around the porch and clawed at the screen door to get in to investigate what had caused the commotion. An orchestra of mooing, clucking, neighing, and squealing broke out from the nearby barn.

The Estate was primarily coffee orchards with just enough goats, cows, and chickens to help the family thrive, but together they made quite a ruckus. Emma stormed from the house slamming the screen door, shoving the dogs aside. Jace and I stood dumbfounded at the sudden destruction. Tobin hurried to start the clean up as Joseph came up the porch followed by his shadow Gideon.

"What in the name of God!" Joseph hollered.

"It was Mom. She dropped the dishes, it was an accident. It's okay, we'll clean it up." Jace scurried trying to calm the atmosphere.

Joseph didn't say another word. He knew right away that it was no accident and his short-tempered wife had been triggered by something. Joseph also knew better than to ask further because he would never be able to get the truth. He knew Jace, and I would not betray each other as the cause of Emma's fury, and that Tobin was our sidekick. He muffled

23

under his breath to be careful with the broken bits of glass, and to not let the dogs in until it was cleaned up, then went back to his barn to settle his riled animals.

Gideon stood for a moment until he gave in to the bellows of frightened cattle and scurried off following Joseph back to the barn. Tobin was focused on his task of sweeping up glass shards, as Jace and I collected pans from the floor and restacked them. It didn't take much to tip Emma Taralock over. She had come from a wealthy family in New York and made it quite clear that a farmer's wife was *not* what she bargained for. She had never liked animals or coffee and scarcely offered any affection to her only son or husband.

She lived in each moment for the task that needed to be accomplished. When her day was complete, and she had fulfilled all her obligations, she would sit on her special rocking chair in the screened part of the porch facing the West. She would focus on the darkening sky quietly by herself.

Jace and I were *never* to bother her there. Joseph and Gideon knew better and didn't have to be reminded that it was her solitude. The only life force that could be allowed to interrupt her on that porch was Tobin. Emma had one square inch of emotion, and the only time it showed was when she had Tobin beside her.

Other than his green-blue eyes Tobin's looks were different than mine, and we were never taken as twins. Our personalities were just as diverse. Tobin had an innocent youthful manner and reflected my father in looks and mannerisms so closely, that sometimes I would observe him just to be reminded of my dad and how much I had loved him.

His fair skin was free of any freckles, and he had platinum blonde hair, with ginger red highlights. The same red highlights that would pop up on my dad's jawline when he didn't shave.

Tobin was small, and frail being born six minutes after me. He had suffered in his delivery and almost didn't make it. He could not hear the world around him, but he didn't mind. Tobin was a follower and let Emma mother him, so she took to him and treated him like a baby bird. He allowed himself to need her and his lighthearted patient manner calmed her.

She permitted him to love her, and he soaked up every bit. He followed in her trail like Gideon followed Joseph. It was kind of nice, Joseph had Gideon, Emma had Tobin and Jace had me. One Jailer for every Taralock.

Often, she and Tobin would watch the sunset on her porch and I would see Emma's mouth moving, as if she were telling Tobin a story. Maybe she was confessing a grave dark sin or explaining how she got the strange drastic scar on her wrist. Or perhaps she was telling the story of how she went from a wealthy American family to a farmer's wife in Tanzania, somewhat unwillingly. Either way, she was talking because she knew Tobin could not hear her.

Our playing around with her favorite, was precisely what set her off that morning. Jace, Tobin and I had been goofing around. I was ducking under the massive butcher block kitchen island, so I could jump scare my brother.

Jace had chased Tobin all the way to the kitchen and was play wrestling with him. They would wrap their arms around each other in a head-lock and try and overpower one another in a manly attempt at dominance. We knew better than to get in Emma's way, but we got caught up in hearing my brothers cracking laughter. She scolded Jace, pausing our playfulness and from the corner of her eye caught Jace's hand gesture. He motioned for Tobin to tiptoe around Emma.

Jace was really named James, but the 'M' was quickly dropped by Tobin who couldn't hear it and made up his own version of the name James. The name Jace stuck, and everyone other than his mother called him this.

"James Taralock! He is not an animal. Stop using those hand signals. He doesn't need your jumbled signs. I hate when you play like this! Go out and help your father and Gideon. Make yourself useful for once and leave the boy alone!"

"Sorry. We're just fooling around, I like when I can make Tobin laugh."

"It is childish. You are sixteen years old. Too old to be wrestling, behaving like a toddler. Grow UP! Go!" she screeched.

As Emma turned back towards the stove, her foot caught my leg from under the table. She stumbled forward nearly smashing into the sink. The island shifted and revealed, me, the other culprit. I don't know why I have the knack of being the last person someone lays eyes on before they've hit their last nerve, but that's what happened that spring morning.

In all calmness, she picked up the pans of cooking eggs and meats and slammed them to the wood plank floor. Next came the stack of breakfast plates, and the large basket of utensils. Calmly, and deliberately thrown with a mighty force onto the floor, she threw half the contents of the kitchen. Her last move was to aggressively shove the island that was my shelter several feet towards Jace, exposing me crouched underneath. I was sure she would hit me this time, but I heard the screen door slam and knew I could open my eyes.

"Are you alright?" Jace asked helping me up from the floor. "She's just overwhelmed with today. She doesn't like having people here, you know that." He weakly defended his mother. "Sorry Tobin," Jace signed, making a 'T' with his fist and drawing it across his brow.

Tobin's sign name was given to him by Mahtap, who first taught us how to communicate with him. At four years old and no real mother yet to manicure him he had such floppy blonde hair he was constantly pushing it out of his eyes with his closed little fist. Mahtap would mimic the gesture with a letter 'T', and it soon became his identity.

Tobin signed back, "Emma OK." He was trying to console Jace to say not to worry, Emma would be alright, and Jace was grateful to see Tobin as usual, was unharmed and lighthearted.

The morning passed, and all the preparations for Mahtap's memorial were put in place by the three instigators. We were determined to behave like adults and be on our best behavior for the day. We didn't want to chance Emma having another fit and ruining Mahtap's memorial. The tables were set in the yard, with freshly pressed white cloths blowing in the wind. A rainbow of flowers from the garden adorned each center. The sun tea was simmering in the large glass pitcher, and a cooler of cola cans was filled to the brim.

Joseph had changed into his one pair of dress pants and a clean shirt and waited to greet the arriving guests. His white hair and cracked cured face looked out of place in clean dress clothes. Emma was still nowhere to be found, and I was hoping it stayed that way for the remainder of the day. The less she saw me, the better it would be for everyone.

Many of the guests were Mahtap's friends and extended family from Arusha. She was known in the community and loved for her wisdom and gentle nature, so the garden and yard were filled with admirers. We greeted Dr. Korie when he arrived, but aside from the Maasai workers we were in a crowd of strangers.

Everyone arriving had some bowl or plate of food that was handed off to myself or Jace. We scurried around finding room on tables and covering plates with towels to keep away the flies until Jace was called off to play a piece on the piano that had been rolled onto the porch.

I was glad to be kept busy. I refused to accept why we were all here today. Everyone was laughing and carrying on as if nothing had happened. The people were here for the food, not to celebrate the life of our Mamahtap, but even though I felt disgusted by the crowd, I knew she loved people and would have loved this party. So I slapped my attitude and readjusted my outlook on the day. I took a deep breath and determined to make it an enjoyable day, for Mahtap.

Chopin's "Spring Waltz" was resonating from the porch. It was a piece that Jace played beautifully. He had played since he was five, and at sixteen years old now played with precision and soul. The upright piano was perfectly tuned, and the song rang like bells. Jace played, letting his fingers express his great loss. I knew his heart was hurting, but he would not cry in front of strangers. He didn't need to, the Ivory keys cried for him. He always played with his heart, but today was different. I knew his mind danced with memories of Mahtap, and playing was healing him, key by key.

"Do you know where I can find Emma Taralock?" A balding man of about Joseph's age maybe a little older stood closer to me than was comfortable. He stood with his hands behind his back looking refined and opulent with a manicured dark brown beard that was flickered with silver. A tightly trimmed mustache painted his top lip. He was handsome for an old guy, maybe he was a relative of Emma's. He looked distinguished and influential, but something in his manner sent a chill down my spine. He stared at me awkwardly with an unusual smirk, that made me wonder what devious thoughts he had.

He was beginning to frighten me when I spotted Joseph, and I eagerly pointed him out. As he approached Joseph, the corner of the picnic table caught his attention. The cloth had wrinkled and folded a little. He paused and straightened the fabric as well as the bowl that was weighing it down. I scurried off and decided that whoever that man was, I did not want to know his story.

There were people in all areas. Tobin and Gideon were at the piano, and that's where I first saw *her*. I didn't see *her* arrive. What was *she* doing here? Allison Cade leaned on my front porch like she owned it or would someday.

I couldn't hear her from where I was, but I knew whatever she was saying it was flirty and sickening. She had a pale-yellow flowy dress draping her perfect curvy shape and a matching ribbon in her more than perfect flaxen curls. Jet black long eyelashes batted and made her caramel brown eyes sparkle. Her father was a neighboring Ranch owner with a successful cattle farm that he ran from the comfort of his million-dollar yacht. She hadn't worked a day in her life and was treated like royalty by whoever met her. She walked with an air of being owed admiration. She was wonderful, and she knew it.

Tobin and Gideon awkwardly tried to pose themselves at the porch as she gawked and giggled and twirled a long dangling curl. She was closest to Gideon and Jace's age and flirted with both of them. Allison would tease Gideon for his strong, rough hands, and round cheeks, and then with a twinkle in her eye point out how handsome Jace was and how he was getting so tall and broad-shouldered.

She was too good for the local school, or even the Primary or Secondary schools in Arusha. She had just returned from a private school in France and was talking about how rude the waiters are there. Even her French was perfect.

She refused to speak Swahili and only spoke in English and treated anyone different than her as inferior. When she talked to you, her shoulders spoke with her, and she would draw you in closer acting like she was about to give you a secret only to make a shallow observation, all in an attempt to seem mysterious and more interesting than she really was.

I pretended to need to check how many sodas were left in the cooler, so I could hear what she was gabbing about this time. She didn't acknowledge that I was near, she ignored me most of the time and only spoke to me to gain back the attention of one of the boys.

The boys gave the appropriate "Ooh's" and "Aah's" as she tapped their arms and giggled. She seemed focused on Jace and tried to draw him from his waltz. She didn't even care to understand why he played with such passion. I couldn't wait for the evening to be over, so she could leave. Her perfection was captivating though, and Jace couldn't help but blush at all the compliments she was spewing at him.

I started to leave, I didn't want to watch these idiot boys drool over Allison anymore. I was going to the cottage where it was quiet. As I walked away a resonating screech of terror shrilled from Allison Cade. It captivated everyone's attention, and all focus was turned towards the porch. Jace had stopped playing the piano, and the whole group of kids on the porch stared at the ground. I was about fifteen feet away, but I could see what startled them, and why they were so frozen.

A snake. A Puff Adder. It was coiled in an 'S' and puffing loudly sending out a warning. Its inflated wide body warned of its danger. It was twisted at the bottom of the porch that I had just walked down. It faced the group of children paralyzing them with fear on the porch.

Allison was the closest to it. Her bare ankle only about three feet from its open mouth. The whole crowd was still, afraid to move. No one was doing anything. They were terrified to move and make it strike at pretty little Allison. The snake was clearly scared and looking for water or shade. I knew how poisonous it was. We were accustomed to seeing them and avoiding them on the farm. They were thought to be slow and sluggish, but Rubin taught us from day one that they were quick, robust and able to kill three men with the venom of one bite. Why did it have to be here today, with all these people? It must be desperate and maybe even sick.

I was in the best position to do anything, I had the advantage. Slowly and with stealth, I moved to my right and picked up the empty bowl on the table. It was my only weapon. I held it upside down, like a shield and inched closer and closer. Jace saw my actions and knew what I was up to. He knew that he needed to keep the snake's attention on him.

"Don't move Allison," he warned. "No matter what, don't move your leg."

"Ya think, Jace Taralock, I'm not stupid."

Jace was slightly to the right of Allison and higher up on the porch. He made distinct small moves with his hands. Just enough to keep the snake's attention on him and not Allison, or me. I inched closer. Voices from behind started whispering for me to stop.

"She's going to get killed. She's going to get Allison killed". I heard quiet mutters from over my shoulder.

"When I say three, pull your leg back," Jace instructed.

"Are you kidding? He will strike me!"

"Just trust me" Jace assured. "One, ...Two, ...THREE!"

Allison pulled her leg up and backed into Jace as the snake lunged for her. The metal bowl went down with force pushing the snakes crown to the ground, pinning it to the earth like a guillotine. I put my weight onto the bowl and felt the writhing body slinking and flopping beneath its metal dome. The mouth was propped open, detached, laying next to the bowl with its fang's extended.

Rubin pushed through the crowd of stunned onlookers and quickly wrapped the decapitated head in a tea towel. He had to pull me off of the bowl because even though I knew the body wasn't dangerous I could still tell it was wriggling to death underneath and I didn't want to see it suffering.

Rubin lifted me into his big bear arms and carried me up the porch steps, sitting me on the piano bench. People ran to Allison to check her over and assure her that she could stop trembling. People were all over her checking if her ankle was okay. They sat her on a lounge chair and started showering her with lemonade and shading her from the beaming sun. Rubin, Gideon, and Jace followed by Joseph surrounded me.

Joseph scolded me, "Stupid, stupid girl," in a ruffled anxious voice.

"What is wrong with you?" Jace asked, still looking stunned.

Rubin nodded his head and wiped his brow looking at me with relief. He defended me, "This girl knows very well the risk she took," still nodding his head trying to process what had just happened.

Tobin stomped up the steps triumphantly and handed me a lemonade. The crowd thought I was insane and reckless, but at least Tobin thanked me and made me feel appreciated with nothing but a cold drink and a silent smile.

People mingled and went on with the gathering. They spoke of memorable Mahtap moments. I hated all their memories and didn't want to hear them. It meant that they knew her, and she had been in their lives, and it was making me mad at her. How could she make a mark on someone else's life other than ours? I didn't want to share her, she should have known that.

Allison thanked Jace for his bravery in distracting the snake and repeated how she would trust him with her life any time from now on. It was nauseating. She said nothing to me, and I was glad. She made me sick. I spent the rest of the evening helping Rubin chop up the snake for soup and burying its fierce head. Being away from the crowd was good.

By the time the yard was empty of people, it was dark. Allison and all the other fakeness had gone home. Joseph and Gideon had gone to put the animals down for the night, and Tobin and Jace were cleaning up the last tables and folding chairs. I thought I would have the house to myself for a little while and I wanted to just sit in my room and process all the day's happenings, so I tiptoed up the front porch steps, and silently slipped into the kitchen. I didn't want to be spotted and be asked to help clean. I was on my way up the hall steps when I heard voices coming from Emma's porch.

"It was the coward that got him killed, nothing more."

As I edged towards the door, I heard a steady deep voice. Emma was standing up facing the yard. The tall man who had been looking for her earlier was sitting in her special rocker with his fingers clasped at his chin resting on his perfectly trimmed dark beard. I hadn't noticed him all day other than for our brief encounter and I was mad that he was still at our home. Emma did not turn to respond to him, but I could see the side of her face and a solitary tear spilled down to her neck.

"Is there anything else?" she uttered, with a quake in her voice.

"No that will be all Mrs.Taralock." As he got up from the chair and came in my direction, I scurried back under the kitchen island.

"I will be in touch regarding the children. You will be notified and told when to put into motion what we have discussed. You know better than to disagree with the arrangement. It is simply... 'The Jailer's Way'... Goodnight."

Emma stayed the rest of the evening on her porch. Joseph did not interrupt her. Jace and I were still reeling from our run-in with her that morning. Tobin sensed he would be unwelcome that night as well and went to his room pouting.

I told Jace all that had happened and bugged him for his theory. He juggled through a couple of possibilities even suggesting it was an old friend of Mahtap, or maybe the uncle who paid for my schooling. Either way, this was the first time this man had been on our farm, and he made Emma cry. As a woman who showed only two emotions, auto-pilot or eruption, this intrigued me, and I wanted to know who he was.

Jace knew my impatience would not let this rest and was sick of the questions he could not answer, so he drove the conversation in a direction he knew would make me leave him alone.

"Allison just got back from France. She really has changed, hasn't she?" he asked. I knew his trap, but I fell into it anyway.

"What is wrong with you guys?" I exploded. "What's so special about her anyway? Is it her looks, the way she walks? What? It's definitely not her brain. I thought you liked smart girls."

"I like how she talks. She's refined, and thanks to you, she still has nice ankles, with no fang marks."

He won... I went to bed scowling.

The next morning my patience ran thin. Emma was making tea while Tobin collected the ingredients to make pancakes. She often made pancakes for him as an apology in her own way. I knew, either way, I would irritate her that day, so I might as well try to get some answers. I sat on the tall stool as she dunked her tea bag into her mug in sort of a trance.

Emma had a scar on her wrist that had been there since I first met her. It always intrigued me, and I pestered her many times to hear its story. She would always refuse and say that scars were unfortunate reminders of times past and should be ignored. This morning, however, as she dunked her tea bag, it was hard to ignore. A cloth was bound tight around her wrist covering her mysterious scar.

"What happened to your arm?" I asked. She stopped her mindless tea dunking and suspiciously replied, "I Burned it this morning."

"Who was that man in the beige suit? The one with the dark beard? He was looking for you."

"Felix," she said after some thought. "He's an uncle." I knew she was lying.

"How come he has never been here before?"

"He had no reason to come here," she snapped.

I knew I had maybe one more question before she lost her patience and pushed me out of the kitchen.

"Did my father know him?"

"No!" she hollered.

With that, I ran out before she could spew lava at me. I spent the next two hours wandering through the knee-high tree orchard and weaving through the farm's paths and hills. I needed to arrange my thoughts, and there was never any better way to do that than being in the outdoors, walking. I finally found my way to our favorite acacia tree on the hill, just overlooking a small graveyard where Mahtap's husband and baby son was buried. I leaned against the stump and watched the goings on of the farm.

The cows were out to pasture, and I could see Joseph and Gideon's four-wheelers far in the West field. They had gone out early to repair the fence. The air was warm and smelled like fresh grass and coffee. Tobin met me with a broad smile...he sat beside me and leaned against the tree.

"You miss her?" Tobin signed.

"Yes," I nodded my head.

"Me too...Remember climbing this tree? Jace got to the top first, and you were so angry. Mamahtap got very mad at you and Jace. She told you not to take risks. The tree was too tall. You cried because she was mad at you...but you do not cry when you are sad because you miss her. Why?" he asked.

I thought for a minute..."Because when everyone else is crying someone needs to be strong. Sad people are scared too, and need someone to be strong, so they will know that everything will be okay," I signed, answering him.

"That's you? You are strong for all of us?" he questioned.

"Yes... I guess so."

"I think you should cry. I cried, and I felt better. Crying does not mean you are not strong. I am strong...but I cry." Tobin smirked his shoulder, and his eyes pooled with sadness.

"We can cry...or we can climb this tree..." I offered, smiling.

It stopped his sad thoughts, and a smile spread across his face. I saw my father's sparkle return to Tobin's eyes, and we jumped into action. We raced to the top like monkeys. We could...We had no mother to scold us or warn us of the danger, no mother to watch over us. We climbed to the top over two stories high and risked our lives as we clung to the branches like sloths.

At noon, Tobin took the stone path back to the house to see if Emma needed help making lunch, and I trotted down the overgrown path to meet Jace at Mahtap's cottage. The white paint on the stucco exterior walls was peeling, and he and Rubin were giving it a fresh coat to brighten it up. They were finishing a section and getting ready for lunch.

"Your mother lied to me," I spurted out as I picked up a brush.

"What?" Jace questioned.

"She said that creepy guy was an uncle, an uncle Felix, but he called her Mrs. Taralock. He's *not* her uncle. She wouldn't answer my questions."

"Miss, you need to forget it," Rubin cut in.

"I can't. I need to know who this man is."

Rubin sighed, he knew there was no arguing with me. "Some things are safer to let blow into the wind. It is like seeds. If you dig them up and take them apart, no beauty can grow from them, no life. If you let the seeds alone or blow them into the wind, they grow and make everyone happy."

Rubin was right, and I knew that, but I couldn't let this go. It ate at my heart and mind.

"Well, why did he say that he will let her know when she has to put things in motion with the children? What children? Me, and Tobin and Gideon? And what is the Jailer's way? Do you think we will be taken away?"

My voice was louder than I realized, and it made Rubin put down his work and break for coffee. I think it was the first time anyone imagined this possibility.

"Jace, I want to know...Why are me and my brothers here? Why did my father leave us here when we were so little? Why did he take you and me all over the world with him? Why do I have hardly any memories of my mother? And what are these stupid symbols I have on my wrist? Don't you wonder? Am I the only one who thinks this is not a normal family?" For a moment Jace looked consoling, like he would agree with every word I said and would help me get some answers.

"Let's just work on getting the cottage finished," he smirked.

For the next several hours I focused on putting the best coat of paint on Mahtap's cottage. She would have loved it being fresh and clean looking.

Around four o'clock, the sound of the dogs, Wilbur and Mansfield running down Mahtap's path distracted us. They were jumping and sniffing around us, wagging their friendly curled tails into the wet paint. It was only then that we noticed they were leading Emma, who stopped and scolded them for being so rowdy. The cloth I had noticed earlier where she blamed a bad burn, was now bloodstained.

"Are you okay?" Jace questioned looking at the cloth.

"I burned myself," she replied, quickly tucking her arm into her waist.

"What does the Mrs. need?" Rubin stood ready to help her, shocked to see her in this part of the estate. His curiosity was as intense as ours. What was Emma Taralock doing on the path to Mahtap's cottage? In all the last ten years, not once did she stop in to visit Mahtap and Rubin Gambre. She saw them as nothing but employees. The only time she even mentioned Mahtap was when she was complaining that Tobin spent too much time with her. Emma's large farmhouse homestead was nearly a half mile away from the cottage, and a path of winding hills and thick trees and foliage separated the two homes. It was as if the foliage and trees were the barriers between two opposite worlds. She was so out of place in this part of the estate; it made everyone uncomfortable.

"I just wanted to see the cottage. It has been so many years," she mourned.

"Does Mrs. want some tea?" Rubin started to scramble.

"No!" A sharp burst from Emma cut him off freezing him awkwardly. Her voice trembled, but her face was stone as she declared faintly,

"I came to inform you ...Tobin is gone."

Chapter 4

The Thieves of Kolkata

I lay in my bed listening to the sound of the storm rolling in. It was still far off, and I wished it would hurry up and get here. The stagnant thick air just began to move, and waves of wind crept through my screen window, making my curtain dance.

The storm would finally cool things down. It had been so hot for the last five days that no one even felt like moving. Everyone on the farm, even the animals were grouchy and sticky. The heat had smogged in on the morning after Tobin had gone, and his departure halted everyone's will to carry on with their regular routines.

Emma explained that a message had arrived unexpectedly, and a car came to pick Tobin up. He had gone to a school for deaf children in New York, where he could be taught to communicate. She said, that she and Joseph had been corresponding with the school and had planned it for quite a while. A place opened up for him, and they had to send him quickly so as to reserve the spot. She had no answers when we asked why we were not told or even allowed to say goodbye. It was just how it had to be.

I hated Emma more than I ever had before. How dare she separate us, and how dare she not give us the chance to say goodbye. It wasn't fair. I had lost my Mamahtap, and within a week, my twin brother was sent away. What mother would do that to someone? But as I lay on my bed, I remembered, Emma was not my mother. Just my guardian and she had always made that very clear.

Emma genuinely cared for Tobin though, and the quickness of him being sent away confused me. She seemed to slug around feeling the loss just like the rest of us. It seemed unlikely that she would want to send him anywhere, and unlikely that she would want him to learn sign language at a big school. She had made her opinion of the language very clear. Emma always had an angry sadness about her, but the moment the words came from her mouth that "Tobin was gone" her entire being sunk like a cannonball dropping to the ocean floor. Emma was the Marshall of Taralock estates, so I knew Joseph had nothing to do with Tobin's move. It had something to do with the man that was here, Felix.

Jace made no excuse for his mother this time. For the last few days, he played the piano with anger and resentment. Emma didn't tell him to stop playing, as she often did. She knew her son was angry at her. He was fond of Tobin and his carefree manner. He was our companion on so many adventures through the orchards, and the idea of him being so far away was just not acceptable. For some reason, my twin brother had to go, and I was going to find out why. Then I was going to get him back.

My room was about ten feet squared and had only one window, but I thought it was the best window. It had a great view of the giant acacia tree in the yard, and a breeze even on the warmest days. I had a small rolltop desk that I stocked with charcoals and graphite pencils. On the top sat three medium mason jars holding every color seed bead you could imagine. I would make strand after strand of necklaces or bracelets with as many colors as possible. I would sell

them for a few dollars in Tanga when Rubin went for
deliveries. I was good at pestering tourists just like the locals
and often would sell out in a short time.

I ran like a feral child through the fields most of the
time, but then there were days where all I wanted to do was
stay in my room and make jewelry or bring a face to life in a
charcoal drawing. I would pick the face of a gorgeous Maasai
woman, or the bright eyes of one of the children from the
village and with charcoal and my forefinger for blending
would bring them to life on paper. I tried to draw what I
remembered of my parent's faces, but each rendition turned
out slightly different and seemed less and less like them.

Mahtap's sketch was my masterpiece. I only drew her
once because I knew her face so well that it was imprinted on
my heart and it wasn't possible to draw it inaccurately. I
treasured this smiling drawing.

A small bookshelf three shelves tall was opposite my
desk, holding all the worlds I would be a part of as I read.
Each book was precious to me. I had Dickens, Austen,
Verne, and many others. On the bottom shelf was my sailor's
box. It was twelve inches wide and made of dark old wood. It
had slices and scratches from age and I thought it was
magnificent.

I pulled it from the shelf and sat on my bed with it on
my lap. I kept a few things in this box that were most special
to me, and I only brought them out once in a while. I guess
with Tobin being sent away I was feeling a bit lost and
needed to remember who I was. There was nothing secret in
it, just some memories, but it had an old key that I had
attached a Maasai women's bangle and thread earing onto the
end. It added mystery to my box and made it look like a
treasure was kept inside.

I kept a few things in my box. One particular treasure
was my ugly beads. My father gave them to me on one of our

expeditions to India. They were small stones of teal, pink, and black, and looked like tiny bits of chewing gum. I would wrap them around my wrist and listen to the stones clank against each other while making up a grand story of their history.

In my box also was a small Atlas. It was just a little book with a page dedicated to each country around the world. Bright, colorful pages showed the country's flag, and national monuments or wonders. It had population totals and a list of things the country was known for producing. It was a simple World Atlas that my father bought me on one of our first trips to New York.

I had looked through it so often, the binding loosened, and I had to cover it with a paper bag book cover with a small piece of twine inserted so I could tie it closed. I used colored pencils to draw a little earth of blue and green on the cover. I liked it so much better with the paper cover because it looked ancient like it had a million stories to tell even though it was just an Atlas. I had drawn in tally marks for every time I visited each country with my father and Jace. Some pages had tally after tally, others had none. I knew someday I would fill each page.

There was also a black and white photo of my mother which is the only memory I have of her. The background is dark, making it hard to see what color her bobbed hairstyle actually was. She sat in a chair wearing a long wool coat. Her left hand propped her chin up as she gazed at the ground. She was such a pretty woman but looked like she had lost all hope.

I loved to imagine stories of who she was. I pestered Emma for stories and details, but she had none. All I knew of her was that her name was Rose, and my father told us she was Romani. I remember her kissing my cheek to say goodbye to me the day I was sent away. She was crying, and it frightened me. My father told us she was not able to care for three little "Jailbirds" and New York was just not a good place to bring us up, so we were given to Emma and Joseph. He often teased us calling us his Jailbirds. It was a funny nickname for the Jailer kids.

I knew that when I was twelve years old, and only two weeks after my father's death, Emma apathetically stated to my brothers and I at breakfast that our mother had taken her own life in her New York apartment.

I was content to have these few things in my box. I would lay them all out, and occasionally, a memory would come back to me. There were such few memories of my life before the farm, I was just too young when I came here. Gideon had other memories being three years older than Tobin and me, but they were still so few.

One memory added to the story in my head a few years ago. One summer afternoon, I was about ten years old, Gideon had joined Jace, Mahtap, Tobin and I on our picnic hill under the tree and out of the blue had a memory he had to share. We had been arguing over who had been given the largest mango, and Jace accused me of being the fortunate one, and that I was favored by Mahtap. It must have triggered a memory because Gideon broke out in a story that captivated us.

"Mother once said to the three of us, that I was the lucky one," he stated. "She said Tobin was unfortunate to have been born deaf and that she was worried about him, but I was the only one that would have a place."

Gideon was piecing together a conversation that had taken place before we moved to Tanzania. Tobin and I would have been too young to remember, but he went on,

"Mother said *you* Theorie, *you* were the unlucky one. She said, 'She is the strongest, out of my three little Jailbirds, she will be the one. The *unlucky* one.'"

After quite a moment of silence from all the captivated listeners, I released a howling, "What does that mean? You can't tell a story like that and leave out the ending. What was she talking about? Tobin is fine, he was born small and deaf, but he is strong now. You can have your *place*, it sounds boring, but it suits you. Besides, I *am* the strongest, and I *did* get the bigger mango for lunch today."

I was mad that he had this memory and that a mother who never loved me or knew me, could judge me as unlucky. Mahtap scolded me for being unkind to Gideon, and I scowled at him. Gideon always had to prove he was better than me. I didn't like when he played games with Jace, Tobin, and I. His competitive nature and excessive need to be adored as the best irritated me. From a young age, I had settled in my mind that I would not help or care for the animals on the farm. I would let Gideon be the best at that. If I backed off and stroked his ego once in a while, showing him that I wasn't a threat and that he was the best in Joseph's eyes, then he would leave me alone and not battle me on the things that really mattered to me.

He still knew how to get under my skin though. This memory of my mother that he had, and I didn't, instantly flared competition and resentment in me. Mahtap told me to change my face and stop using my eyes to growl at my brother, but Gideon's blithe arrogance at proving me unlucky would not allow my snarl to release. Why couldn't he just go back to the cows and chickens and Joseph, and leave us alone on our hill?

These memories rolled in like the incoming storm. My curtain was wild with rage now, and I had to shut the window. Lightning shot through the sky and thunder rumbled closer to the house. As I closed my window, I caught a glimpse of what I thought were lights. The dogs were barking so someone was here. Who would be traveling way out here with a storm brewing?

The moment I was in earshot of the sitting area, I heard his voice. It would be etched in my mind from that moment forward. It was Felix. "Uncle" Felix according to Emma Taralock, and apparently things were being put into motion. Felix stood in the corner of the living room near the fireplace. His hands were clasped behind his tailored suit, and his expensive leather shoes were perfectly shined. Everything about him was customized and quintessential.

"We will leave now. Storms bring change, and morning come when the clouds break you will see it was for the best," Felix's low steady voice explained.

Emma and Joseph sat on the floral sofa as far apart from each other as they could get. Emma's eyes were humbly cowering to the floor. Joseph's cracked, dry hands pressed against his forehead, and his expression showed that he was confused and helpless.

"Is it possible to wait until morning so we can let them say goodbye?" Joseph cracked. "So they can say goodbye to the Maasai children, or Theorie can say goodbye to her classmates," he lamented.

"The school is no longer necessary, she has passed with highest scores. It has served its purpose. We will be leaving now. Emma, go collect the children. You know what to do."

Felix had such an absolute, commanding way that Emma was helpless. She did not even try to defend Joseph or even care to fight for us. We were leaving with this man, this stranger, and Emma Taralock was powerless to stop him.

She found me frozen on the steps wide-eyed and gave no explanation other than that an opportunity had arisen, and it was time for me to go. I was to pack my duffle bag with two changes of clothes, and personal items. No photos or memorabilia, no books, no journals. Just what was needed to survive for several days.

"What about my box of things, and the stuff in my room? My drawings?"

"It will all be left as it is, just like Tobin's room," she replied dryly.

I did what I was told, and before I closed my door, I saw her go down the hall to Gideon's room next. My worst fears had come true. We were being sent away from here. We were leaving Taralock Estates. My first instinct was to run to Mahtap's cottage, but she wasn't there to protect me anymore.

I had every intention of doing what Emma instructed while this sinister NON-uncle was downstairs, but at my first chance, I would run away and hide in the orchards. I had it all planned by the time my duffle bag was packed with two extra pairs of jeans, and thermal tops, socks, underclothes, my hairbrush, toothbrush, and my hunter green canvas jacket. I packed my cream knit scarf and put on my steel-toed work boots.

I tucked my ugly beads deep into the toe. A piece of who I was, hidden deep in the leather boot. I locked up my sailors' box and slid it under my bed, so no one would touch it while I was gone. I slipped the key within the pages of "The Secret Garden" and placed the book back on my shelf.

I was met in the foyer by Joseph and Emma who stood motionless. I needed to find Jace. There was no way I was leaving without saying goodbye to Jace. I would have exploded like a two-year-old who had its blanket pulled away if they didn't let me say goodbye to my only friend in the world.

Gideon came down the stairs next carrying nothing. Jace followed behind with the bags. Did he really make Jace carry his stuff? Gideon made me so mad sometimes. It took me ten seconds more to realize that Jace was carrying his own bag, and had his boots tied and jacket already on. What was he doing?

A breath of hope and a smile broke on my face when I realized that it was Jace that was leaving with me... Not Gideon. I tried to hinder my happiness that my most loved friend would be going with me. I didn't care where we were going now. It went from utter dread to excitement. Maybe this would be like our old adventures with my father. Maybe Felix wasn't so bad, and we just needed to give him a chance. My content acceptance was knocked over by Felix's low deep voice again. Something about his voice was able to change the atmosphere in the room.

"My name is Felix. Gideon will be remaining here to be trained on the farm and be given *a place*. He's a very *lucky* boy." The storm outside was passing, and the room was cool with a frightening haunting feeling as Felix made his next statement.

49

"James Taralock, and Theorie Jailer, you will be accompanying me along with my 'assistants.'" He motioned towards the porch where two previously unnoticed men in gray suits were standing. He continued,

"You are flying to India. You will have some schooling to complete, and many opportunities will be opened to you. I will state my philosophy now, and you are to remember it. There is a motto I have lived my whole life by, it is called 'The Jailer's Way.' You may have heard of it.

The 'Jailer's Way' knows that like the elements that make up our world, some create while others destroy. All people have a 'place' in the world, and the Jailer's Way helps determine *who* belongs *where*...The weak will bring down, the strong will advance. Associates are chosen very carefully based on this. I will not tolerate weakness, it disgusts me. Any unnecessary rebellion will be seen as weakness. This system has worked for centuries and has been perfected. As long as I have made myself clear, we can be on our way."

Felix ended his statement by snapping his fingers alerting his men at the door. I was ready. I heard the words travel, school, and opportunity and I was craving adventure. I didn't understand what he meant by elements, but I knew I wasn't weak, so I knew I would do well.

Felix's men collected our bags, and we turned to say goodbye to Joseph first. Jace had his father's smoky blue eyes, and as they hugged each other goodbye, their expression was identical. Joseph was a kind man, and even though he had spent seventeen years unable to connect to his son, he still held him tight as he said goodbye. Joseph had love, he just didn't know how to show it, or he was not allowed to.

Jace melted into his father's broad shoulders and pulled away to give Gideon a warm embrace. I followed Jace in his order of goodbyes, hugging Joseph and Gideon tight.

Gideon had a hard time letting go of me. I knew he was happy to stay on the farm, he felt home here, but maybe the older brother in him felt a little longing to keep me nearby. With Tobin gone, it would be so quiet here, but I knew he would dive into his work and occupy his days taking care of the animals he loved so much. I wanted to taunt him with the fact that I had been picked to go to school. Even though Felix said that Gideon was 'Lucky,' It was really me.

I finally came to Emma, who gave me an embrace unlike any before. It was still stiff and awkward, but it was more than I had ever been offered previously. I took it. She held onto me tight as if she was trying to convey a message, but from the day she became my guardian, Emma was so closed and introverted, I had no idea why she was holding onto me so tight or what she was trying to tell me.

Joseph, Gideon, and she watched us as we followed Felix and his assistants into his white SUV. The windows were blacked out, and when the doors shut on us, we were blinded from our home and the only family we had ever known.

The ride pulling away from Taralock Estates was freeing and terrifying at the same time. My dreary friend next to me had nothing but dread on his face. I knew he was not seeing this as an adventure of any kind. It was dark, and the rain began fighting the wipers, as the SUV fought the rough terrain. The hour and a half that it took us to get to Kilimanjaro International airport was torture to Jace, and each mile closer to the airport, he withdrew more and more. It looked like it was going to be a quiet flight. I was kind of excited about what lay ahead. I was sure Emma and Joseph knew we would be safe with Felix, or they would not have allowed us to go with him. I hoped anyway.

Felix had a private plane ready at his command. It was bigger on the inside than it looked and had white leather reclining seats and a kitchen. I was sure I was going to enjoy the ride. It was nothing like my father's small bush plane that we would cram into on our trips with him.

It was so late, and the day had been so hot and exhausting that when I was told our destination was Kolkata, India, I remembered traveling there with my father and that the journey would be about thirteen hours. So I settled into one of the large soft seats and was asleep within thirty minutes of us taking off.

We arrived in Kolkata India in the peak of the day. The sun blinded us as we stepped from the plane. The air was dry and hot and full of dust and about a million smells. It was only a moment that I was off the aircraft before I settled in and remembered the air. We had breathed these winds before and the scent of a million human beings and just as many spices flooded my memories.

The crowd filled in as soon as we reached the airport entrance where we would be picked up. We pushed away from the scammers offering to carry our bag and quickly tucked our wrists in our jackets, so the peddlers couldn't force jewelry on us and demand money. There were people everywhere, it would be so easy to disappear, but the security of Jace's company and the unknown adventure with Felix ahead made me ditch my plan of running away. I loved it here, I always had. It was crazy and loud, and bright and smelled mostly awful, but it was full of life. I couldn't wait to meet the other children at our new school. I hoped they would like me and that I would find a true friend.

Jace and I had been here many times with my father. His little plane packed with photography equipment would pick us up at Taralock Estates, and we would be off within the next day. With my father by our side we would wiggle through Hogg Market and point out anything to him we saw as photo worthy. We carried his extra lenses and tripods and were happy to be his helpers. Many days we would just stand at Howrah Bridge to watch the people board the ferry or just carry on with their day. My father insisted on mingling and photographing the people of everyday life, not just visiting the "touristy" parts.

Aside from Russian, Swahili, English, some French and other languages, we spoke fluent Hindi at Dad's insistence. He said that we could not truly know a person's story unless we spoke the language of their heart. It only took a minute or two to collect ourselves and settle in.

We were picked up by a white caravan with similar dark windows and brought to the Oberat. It was the grandest hotel in all of Kolkata. My father had photographed its large ornate steel gate many times, but we had never stayed in its fancy rooms. We had always slept in rented apartments or small cabins on our childhood trips. I felt so important, it was exciting to be passing through the massive gate, in a vehicle with tinted windows this time.

The lobby was enormous, with a chandelier hanging in the center of a sitting area, enlightening the room with a vibrant ambiance. Green marble floors and comfortable couches welcomed the guests. Fresh yellow sunflowers brightened up the already glistening entry. In the corner of the room sat a grand piano. It was breathtaking and of the most exceptional quality. It immediately caught Jace's attention, and for the first time, I saw a look of hopeful possibility pass over his face.

We were escorted into the dining room and introduced to Yuri, our waiter. He would be taking care of all our needs while we stayed here. He was in his thirties and clean cut, with lighter skin than the locals. He seemed friendly and must have been of a different caste to be offered a job here as a waiter. As we sat in the Grand dining room of the Oberat Hotel, Felix had his meal of boiled potatoes and lamb, delivered plain with no spice, as Jace and I were presented with a masterpiece of spice and flavor. I scoffed down a much-missed dish of chana masala and naan. I loved the spice and flavor. It melted in your mouth and sent a surge of signals to your brain. The food here was unlike any other place on the earth.

I loved Ugali and beans and Mahtap's mango dishes, but the flavors here were savory and unforgettable and reminded me why I loved food so much. Jace ate his food slowly. He was still less sure than me about this trip. Felix must have ulcers to refuse these flavors, or he is as uptight as his pallet. I seemed to be enjoying my meal a little too much because Felix cut in to give us a rundown of tomorrow's activities.

As we sipped our golden milk and the warmth of the honey and turmeric slid down our throats, we were told we would be starting our class tomorrow at 6 am. I had been hoping to explore and visit some of our favorite old locations, but it seemed we would be thrown directly into schooling. Our first lesson would be ...Lockpicking.

"Wait, What?" I snarfed, "What was that?"

"You will be meeting with Elias Kamir. He is a master and to be respected. Yuri will wake you at 5 o'clock for breakfast. In the meantime. You may not see me, but I will see you, remember that."

His demeanor was so overpowering, it made me feel like a preschool child, not a thirteen-year-old. I hated the feeling of fear, I hated being trapped and not allowed to leave. I made it my mission to figure this guy out. He clearly was not Emma's uncle, and he boasted of "The Jailer's Way." He was shrouded in mystery, and I wanted to figure him out like a Sherlock Holmes novel.

"What kind of schooling is that?" I blurted out. Felix ignored me, and Jace intensified his gaze, shooting me a warning.

We had a shared room with two suites attached overlooking the city. It was the fanciest room we had ever seen and weren't quite sure how to act. Beautiful satin bedding and tufted furniture. Detailed Persian rugs in blues and reds were placed in the centers of the bedrooms and the shared sitting room. Brass fixtures and cashmere blankets added to the ambiance of the room. There was a folded pile of clean new clothes for each of us. Mostly black tops and jeans, a few jackets, several pairs of boots and underclothes. Everything we would need for personal care and all our meals and laundry would be taken care of. It felt like trapped royalty. I grew more and more suspicious and less excited about this trip around every corner.

The first night in the Oberat was comfortable but lonely. I was sort of afraid of starting our class on lockpicking, but at the same time, it sounded kind of fun, and I hoped that we wouldn't be the only kids. Jace was of no help. He had no ideas on why we needed this type of schooling and was in a bad mood and went to his room. I drifted asleep to the mumbled sound of the other guests chatting in the halls, as I tried to picture myself with my father and Jace piled into a small shanty room the size of a closet. It always felt safe when I was with them, never cramped. I'd prefer to be there than in this grand room.

In the morning, after putting on our new clothes and having a short breakfast, we left the massive steel gate of the Oberat Hotel and walked through a wash of people being led by Nico. Felix had employed this oversized human with deep-set green eyes and an overpowering brow, as our guard. The crowds grew the farther we went from our lodging and the chaos thickened. We were to start locksmith lessons promptly at 6 am, so we scurried along as quickly as we could.

The building that we finally arrived at looked abandoned from the outside like it had been hit by bombs in an air raid. Nico led us through damp cement hallways with exposed brick and the smell of must and sewerage in the air. Through several winding turns we were brought to a closed solid door. A light showed through the bottom. This was not what I was expecting but had no choice other than to comply with the direction to enter.

We were met surprisingly by a very cheerful person. Elias Kamir was a short man, with thick black hair extending down his jawline. He greeted us and said he was expecting someone older. Jace immediately seemed at ease with Elias and greeted him with a handshake, remembering to tuck his left hand behind him, and only offer his right. Jace seemed to want to make an excellent first impression. I was not as eager to be friendly. I was not fond of school teachers, and I didn't see any other students. I played shy and nodded hello.

Fluorescent lighting hung above a table spread with a brightly covered red and gold cloth. A woman in a teal saree stood arranging and perfecting the spread of multiple large platters. Each platter was labeled in Hindi, three through seven, and had a pile of various types of locks.

Elias began by easing our curiosity. "You will learn how to open these in seconds. It takes practice, but by the end of these lessons, you will open a locked door so quickly it will seem as if it was always open to you. Like a wind blew it open. These platters have been numbered one through seven. Three for a three-pin lock and so on. But first, we will look at the tools."

The woman in the beautiful saree pulled the cloth away from a special tray. It looked like an array of torture devices. Small thin metal picks, some like bread knives, some bent in an angle. "You will learn each of these tools," Elias explained. "However, you will also learn when you do *not* need these tools. Let's begin by dissecting this lock and understanding how it works."

And so our lessons went on day after day, week after week. We lived in Kolkata's Oberat hotel with green marble floors and glistening chandeliers. In the evenings we snuck away from the luxury and cattiness of the palace hotel and mingled with the *real* people.

We knew Felix was watching wherever we went so we couldn't go very far from the hotel. On some evenings we were allowed to explore under the watchful eye of Nico and be out with local people though. This made me feel more human, and I looked forward to our classes ending so that I could go wander the area. I watched the other girls in their sarees shopping in the market or trailing behind their husbands. They were so elegant and graceful. The faces of the people fascinated me, and I wondered why some people looked so sad, and others walked with pride. I wanted to know the people and their stories.

I felt so sorry for the beggars, especially the children. At the Oberat we were given curried goat and unlimited bowls of rice. I could not justify filling my belly each day when some of those people ate only a few times a week. In the mornings I tucked away some of my roti and paratha and saved it for after school when I could give it to the homeless people begging by the bridge.

Each morning we would be brought to the hidden school for lockpickers to meet Elias and his array of things to unlock. We were tested weekly on speed and accuracy in tool selection. We learned what a bypass tool was, a ball pick, a rake, and curtain picks. We learned how to feel the slightest release with speed and accuracy. We fumbled and heard the thrilling click of success on four, five, six, and seven-pin locks. We moved from padlocks to deadbolts and doorknobs to safes and finally car ignitions. We learned how to make it look like the door had been unlocked all the time, and we had been invited in.

Each challenge was presented as a puzzle to break, and it was fun. Jace met every challenge quickly and efficiently. I, on the other hand, let myself be distracted and distrustful. I would have been able to surpass Jace, but I couldn't get passed WHY? What were we doing? Why haven't we seen Felix since the first few days of our arrival? I was starting to get bored and wondered if this was where we would be stuck forever. I would be fourteen soon, and I was anxious to get some answers. If I could answer some of my mind's questions, I could let them go and excel, but no one would talk to me.

Jace was busy showing off his picking and safe breaking skills. I'm pretty sure he forgot who he was and was enjoying this whole weird experience. I assumed we were in training to be locksmiths, but nothing made sense. Felix seemed far too diabolical to have gone through all of this training, taking us to India, providing us with a royal hotel room, all to train a couple of locksmiths.

Felix eventually did show up on a rainy day. Monsoon season was in full force. We had been left to stay at the hotel for several days because of flooding. Garbage was washing down the streets, and Kolkata smelled like it was getting a much-needed wash. We were going to brave the water and go to the market when Felix, in his familiar beige suit invited himself to sit alongside us at the back-corner breakfast table. I was stunned at first.

"Mr. Taralock, Miss Jailer, I am told you have done well. You will be moving on to your next subject."

Felix's mannerisms took some time to get used to. He was like Emma in the way that when they spoke, you moved. You didn't ask questions, you just did what they commanded. At least Jace did. I struggled with this relationship. Jace nodded in acceptance and asked nothing. I knew he wanted me to keep my mouth shut, but he knew that it was virtually impossible for me.

"Why are we learning to open locks? What kind of schooling is this, and WHAT is the new subject?" I spat out.

Felix did not answer, he just huffed through his nose, condemning me. I didn't care anymore, I was going crazy, I was anxious for a change, and even though I loved India, and had fun learning to open locks, I was hoping we would be on the move again. Much to my surprise, he answered me.

"We are moving on to the quick of hand. You'll be instructed where to go tomorrow morning."

With that, he snapped his fingers for Yuri who scurried over and cleared our untouched plates of food that had arrived simultaneously with Felix. His removal of my much-anticipated samosas and golden milk made me want to attack him, but I knew it would be useless. He picked up a shining butter knife. Sliding the knife deliberately and slowly inching over my left exposed wrist and remarked,

"For the girl who asks so many questions, do you know what this means?" referring to the six strange symbols staining my arm.

"No, I want to know though," I replied. "It is my life's mission to find out, the one thing I truly desire." I mocked him dramatically with a false air of pride.

He was not amused because his response was cold and punishing. "As do I. It seems we both have questions. We will have to find the answers together since we have similar inquisitive minds."

He intensely studied my wrist. I pulled it close to my lap, hiding it under the table. No way was I allowing him to compare himself with me. These were my marks, my mystery, how dare he be concerned over them. They meant nothing to him, why did he have to try and frighten me all the time?

Jace's was stone, staring me down, trying to tell me to stop speaking. If only he could have frozen my lips shut or made me brain dead, but I couldn't resist, and I hatefully spit out,

"I do like questions. Your greatest hatred is a weakness, you said it disgusts you. I don't know the meaning of these marks on my wrist. Do you see it as a weakness? Why do you care about these marks? They are mine and aren't any of your business. Someone wanted me to be marked for a reason, and I think that scares you. We scare you. That's why you are controlling us. Why are we being trained in 'the quick of hand?' What is all of this for? I want to know who you *really* are."

I tried to sound terrifying, but it didn't rattle him. He put me in my place by holding the butter knife to the under part of my chin, tilting my head up uncomfortably, and pushing it into my skin.

"Like two little Jailbirds, in a cage," he said menacingly. He twisted it slightly into the bottom of my chin, just enough to pinch.

"Go back to your rooms now," he said coldly. He was threatening me, and I knew better this time than to disobey. He was very effective in his intimidation and the ability to strike fear into someone.

Back in our suite, Jace scolded me, "Your middle name should be 'In-a-rush.' Why can't you read my signals, when I'm telling you to be quiet? Why does it matter to you what is happening next? It's not like you can control it," he barked.

"Jace, maybe you can let it all go and push it out of your mind, but my questions are drowning me. We've been here for almost six months, and we can break into a car or a building. Why is that important? I want to leave, I want to go find Tobin. How can you just sit there and not try to find out what's going on? Don't you see that there is something bad in Felix's eyes? AND I DON"T CARE IF YOU CAN HEAR ME FELIX! I want to know why…everything!" I yelled assuming our room was bugged.

I was so frustrated and boiling in my tone that Jace caught on and changed his scolding brow. The change in his facial expression settled me instantly. I knew he was finally hearing my voice, but of course, then I had nothing else to say.

"I have questions too. I want to know why Tobin was sent away, and why my parents let Felix take us here? But rushing into tomorrow doesn't get answers. I can't stop him from hurting you Theorie, I'm useless against him, and when you charge at him..." he paused, and lowered his voice to a whisper, coming closer to me to avoid being overheard. "We can't go anywhere yet. I just wish I could understand him. If I knew who he was, I could understand why he has so much control over people. He has all the power right now and he knows it. I don't want you to get hurt because you need answers yesterday. We just need some time. I don't want your mouth to get you killed."

I felt terrible now and needed to lay off. I needed Jace to feel like he still had a friend and that he wasn't alone. I was irritated but arguing with him was pointless. He was right, we needed more information to get away.

I signed the letters "OK," and with just the breath in my lungs and no actual sound, I mouthed the words and partially signed,

"Fine, I'll go to the new lessons, I'll learn what Felix wants. I'll try to watch what I say… I'm sorry." I signed circling my heart with my closed fist.

The corners of his mouth curled up, and his smile let me know that we were okay, and he wasn't angry at me anymore. He was seventeen now and in the last six months had gotten so serious. It was good to see his smile.

Chapter 5

The Art of Perception

What does it mean to be broken? Mahtap in her final letter said Jace and I would be broken. Those words plagued me, and I wanted to confront them, to do battle with them. How did she know that we would break, and by what? Mornings seemed to be the hardest. I always woke up too early, and my mind would race before my body wanted to move. I couldn't stop thinking of Africa, of Mahtap and Rubin. Or wondering when I would see Tobin again. I missed them so much and would lay in my bed looking at the screened canopy above me wondering if I would ever be able to go home. I kept thinking of what Jace said, to be patient and wait, to give it some time.

I loved India when I was a little girl traveling with my father and Jace, but it was not the same now. We were not here to wander and explore or to take photos of people. I wasn't even sure why we were here. Everything was a mystery, and we were not allowed to question Felix or his ways. Any time I asked a question, I was either ignored or threatened. There was obviously something bigger involved in why we were here, and I was torn between wanting to solve that mystery or escaping home to hide with Rubin in the cottage. Jace made it very clear that he wanted to wait it out and look for clues casually, and I tried every day to comply despite everything inside of me telling me to get away somehow.

I had an hour before our new lessons would start, so I escaped the theatrical atmosphere of the Oberat hotel breakfast buffet and walked down Sun Yat Sen Road to buy a pork bun. I reflected on Mahtap's words. She often told me the story of a boy who was impatient like myself. He was an orphan boy who knew he was not meant to be an orphan, he could feel it in his bones that he had an unknown story. He was not raised with wealth and struggled to eat. He went through life in an unsatisfied state trying to find answers and fighting those that wanted to love him.

He one day met a boy on the street that mirrored his appearance in every single way other than his clothes that were of fine silks with jewels sewn in. He knew right away they were the same boy at one time, and in their mother's womb they had been twins. The orphan immediately followed this wealthy boy and admired all he had. However, his twin was arrogant and cruel to everyone he met. He was angry and bitter and unliked.

The orphan boy spoke to his wealthy brother and asked why they had lived such different lives, but he was pushed aside like a beggar and humiliated in the street.

Mahtap would tell me this story and remind me to be patient and enjoy what I had been blessed with and to stop chasing what I did not know. Contentment was so hard for me though. I knew there was more to my parents than just having three children and being a photographer, and my questions drove my mind into a wind storm. Everything around me made me wonder and added stories and details to my imagination.

The sun was barely awake, but workers were buzzing around, and every second the street filled and got slightly louder. Copper skinned men wrapped turbans on their heads and pushed and shoved their way into the market for work. They only earned 5 Rupee a day, but it meant life for their families. They fought for the right to be the man chosen for the task of lifting tied bundles the size of baby elephants over their shoulders and onto the top of their heads. The massive package would nest into their turban, and they would be off to deliver the shipment to the buyer. The weight must have been overwhelming sometimes taking four or five men helping to lift it onto the chosen trucks. The worker's knees would bend with the weight, but he would soon straighten his back and get on his way. He was not *broken* by the weight of his parcel or the importance of feeding his family on so little. He took whatever job offered and did it with a smile.

My Pork bun was steaming hot and perfect as I wondered how heavy a load it would take to break those men. I looked for what vendor to buy my Chai from when the sound of a bell broke out. A woman caught my attention, she was ringing the bell to awaken the Gods in a custom-made shrine, and she had just lit the bit of cotton soaked in ghee lighting several little bowls with tiny flames.

The lines on her forehead and the corners of her eyes did not change. She was completely expressionless. I knew she was Hindu, and the maroon stain dot between her brows told me she was religious and known to be wise. She wore an inexpensive linen saree that was dyed yellow. I watched her as she closed her eyes, and after minutes of speculating, I was about to leave when I saw a silent tear running from her eye. She made no attempt to wipe it away.

It was not the typical tear of a person in pain or feeling loss. This woman was numb, with a look of hollow emptiness. She was void of emotion, other than the single tear escaping down her copper skin. Her tear said to me that this woman had suffered more than words could describe and that she had endured an injury that was more than flesh and blood could stand. That's when I understood... this woman was broken.

I wanted so much to speak to her and help her heart. I wanted to make her feel better. My curiosity and impulse to approach her was flaring, but as she knelt, I was jolted out of my thoughts by the Rickshaw bus pulling up along the road beside me, shooting exhaust into my face, choking me. The bus line had started.

It must be six o'clock, and now I was late! I ran as fast as possible back to the Oberat. Jace stood at the gate, and even from a distance, I could see him pacing.

"Where on earth were you?" he hollered as soon as he saw me jogging towards him.

"I went to Sun Yat Sen early. I'm sorry, I just... is Felix here?"

"No, Prajna is here," he answered, sounding so irritated with me.

He pointed to a woman standing at the back door of the white caravan. The windows were tinted black, but there seemed to be other life forms inside. Prajna had dark tan skin and stern thick brows that without a word drew me towards her. She was demanding of respect and as I traipsed towards her Jace passed me getting into the van. I stopped at her side. Her saree was brick red and of fine linen, decorated with golden weaves.

"I'm sorry for being late," I apologized.

"I am Prajna. You will not be late again." Her tone was stating a fact, and her brow drew together. I knew from that intense moment I was *not* to disappoint her, or there would be consequences.

As the van pulled away, I settled across from Jace, who was sitting between two other boys, both Indian and young, only about ten years old. They were each playing with a Rubix cube and oblivious to the other passengers. The set of six seats faced each other making it more like a shrunken limousine. Jace looked at me like he was trying to send me a message.

"Theorie," the boy sitting next to me confidently asked, "It's Theorie right? It's hard to remember who's who. I am Arlo. I've heard a lot about you from Felix. He says you have a lot of potential."

Arlo was not a boy, he was a man who had to be over twenty. From the second I saw his face I was taken by him. My heart raced, and I tried to control my blushing, but it was useless because he smiled coyly and made his charm even more entrancing. He had perfect features with a sharp jawline and thick brown hair waving over his head in a clean-cut style like a movie star. His eyes were caramel brown and familiar, but I couldn't quite place where I had seen his face. I had never felt so awkward before, I felt all nervous and strange.

"What does that mean?" Arlo asked touching the symbols on my wrist, making me blush more.

"I'm not sure," I replied."

"Did you design it?"

"No, I'm not sure what it means."

"Well, we will be working with each other, so maybe we can figure it out together," he said with a flirty smile, gawking at me with his light brown eyes and such confidence in himself. I was sure he was fully aware of how attractive he was.

"Maybe." I stupidly replied. I was so obvious, I couldn't even look at Jace because I already knew he would be disgusted. I did catch him crossing his arms tucking them into his sides, leaning back and looking somewhat irritated at our new company.

On the other side of Arlo was a girl. She was about my age, maybe a little older, who looked sort of harsh with dark high-arched eyebrows and a thick pouty bottom lip. Her bright unnatural yellow hair was in a bun, and she wore similar khaki cargos and a tank top like me. I tried to make eye contact, so I could meet her, but she just gazed forward purposely avoiding me.

"What is your name?" I asked. She looked up at me without raising her chin, and from the look of disgust, I knew she wasn't going to answer me.

The van stopped behind a building down an ally. I thought as we got out that we would be led into another dark, damp hallway, but we were told to stand around the van. Prajna exited, and the two boys on either side of Jace, Arlo, and the snobby mysterious girl all formed a semi-circle around our new teacher and waited for instruction.

"You are to do nothing but follow me today," Prajna ordered. "You will watch me closely. As you do this, you must act like you are simply shopping. You may not purchase anything though. You are to act natural and behave like tourists," she instructed.

The two young Indian boys beside Jace were introduced as Aarav and Jag. They began the expedition and were to help us blend in. But they caused more of a distraction with all their mischief.

Obeying her instructions, we rounded the corner, and I recognized right away where we were. It was the Mullick Flower Market. I loved this place. My father brought us here many times to take photos and watch people. We would sit in a shady spot, and he would ask us to close our eyes and tell him what types of flowers we remembered, or how many people were wearing hats. Usually, when we were here it was late though, and the flowers were picked through, and vendors were headed home leaving the streets smelling of a good and bad mix. Sweet smelling sunflowers and roses were twirling with the stink of old orchids and zinnias. How could such beautiful things leave such a stench in the air?

Today was different though, it was still early, and the market was fresh and thriving. Strands of bright orange zinnias and barrel after barrel of roses and hibiscus were spilling out of baskets in every corner. Buyers and sellers bantering over price and the chaos of arguments over quality made our job of following our instructor and looking like tourists very easy.

Wreaths of every color were tossed into our faces as we tried to focus on Prajna. I struggled with keeping her in my sight and for a moment I thought I saw her swiftly pocket a small gray pouch and tuck it into her saree, but I couldn't be sure.

We wiggled through the market trying to keep up with the quick pace of our leader. The day was going quickly because there was so much to look at. I loved mingling with the people, it reminded me of being with my father. It was natural for me to weave in between people and carts. Even though I was a fair-skinned awkward girl, my travels and adventures as a child made me behave like a local, and no one seemed to notice my hair or my freckles. Jace, and even Arlo, and the new girl all seemed to fit right in as well. I wasn't sure what our goal was for the day, but I was content being out with people.

The whole experience made my mind flood with wonder. I loved the chaos and seeing the people in their everyday life. I noticed people's faces and tried to figure out their story. The sight of a mother gripping the hand of her daughter who was about five years old drew me into a daydream about a poor mother who sold lotus flowers, and this lone daughter was all that was left of her once sizeable royal family.

After several hours, it was getting tiring even for me, so when we circled around to the alley back to the van, I was very relieved. The two Indian boys were given some coins that they earnestly inspected and ran off. Prajna was obviously done with them for the day.

The ride back to Oberat was as awkward as the ride from it. Arlo, randomly glanced at his four other companions in the van and smiled curiously. He seemed very pleased with himself by nature, and everything about him screamed "too good to be true."

"Your brother seems kind of quiet. Is he a mute?" Arlo broke the silence, inquiring of Jace.

"No," I replied, "he's not my brother." Jace shot a look at Arlo like an arrow to a target, but it just made this arrogant comrade snicker at him in a challenging tone.

"Oh...I see..." He raised his chin and nodded.

"What was the point of today?" I asked, changing the subject. Arlo just shrugged and gave the same suspicious smile he seemed to hide behind.

We returned to our hotel, and Prajna instructed the four of us to go to room 111. This was new. Jace and I had only ever been to our suite. Prajna opened the door to room 111, and we entered into complete darkness. The blinds were pulled, and the lights were off making us entirely vulnerable to whatever lurked around us.

"The dark is not good for you Sir," Prajna said as she flicked on the light. What seemed like a single room was an entire apartment. It was fully equipped with an open kitchen, and doors to various rooms. We were standing in just the entrance. Prajna moved towards the sitting area revealing our host, Felix.
He sat in an upholstered chair in the corner by the window. His elbows rested on the armrest, and his hands clasped and pushed into his bearded chin. He looked at us waiting for a report as Prajna lined us up in front of him.

"Move that one," pointing to me. "She should be over there."

Prajna obeyed and pulled my shoulder making me switch places in line with the mysterious girl. Now we were to Felix's liking, lined in order of height, me, of course, being the shortest and Arlo the tallest. Prajna walked to the table near Felix and turned on the small lamp. "Do you understand the purpose of this day?" she asked.

No one wanted to answer, even Arlo who I believed was the bravest of us all kept his mouth shut. My impatience dragged my mouth along with it.

"We were to watch you steal from the vendor's and tourists." I blurted out, instantly regretting my choice of words.

I saw her steal things, but I didn't know if she meant to be seen and exposed. Prajna fixed her glare at me as she emptied her saree of all her bounty. She placed each item one by one onto the table. Wallets, coins, paper money, jewelry, and several watches all laid on the table in a neat row. Felix seemed pleased and overlooked the items from the corner of his eye, still wiggling his index finger through his beard.

"You are wrong," Prajna replied.

How could I be wrong? I knew I wasn't supposed to see her snag a gray coin pouch. I knew she was trying to teach us how to steal.

Felix spoke up. "Did you pay attention to *who* Prajna took these items from? Was anyone able to keep their minds focused enough? Arlo, Andrea, James?" He didn't include my name because he already knew I failed and been unfocused. At least I knew the mysterious girl's name now. It was Andrea, or at least that was what we were supposed to call her.

Jace spoke up after clearing his throat. "The silver watch was taken from a tourist, an American in his sixties with gray hair and a short wife who was trying to blend in by wearing a saree over her jeans. The black leather wallet with the embossed J.P. was taken from an Indian man who looked wealthy. He had two bodyguards and walked like he owned the market, and the red garnet bracelet was taken from a girl in her twenties who was with her sister, they were from Ireland."

"Well well, Mr. Taralock that is impressive. A mind is a powerful tool," Felix complimented. "It is one thing to spot a master thief at work," he stated as his eyes met mine, "It is quite another to spot the thief and understand *why* she chose those particular people. You can't understand *why*, unless you know their story," he finished, letting Prajna continue.

"My targets today were wealthy. The ones who have plenty to give. The older tourist was wonderstruck by the market. He and his wife were throwing money around like it was nothing. The wealthy Indian man was the owner of the market and was inspecting his profits. He is a greedy man who has hiked the rent of the booths to such a cost that the vendors sell for three weeks to afford the cost of feeding their family for a few days. The Irish girls were daughters of a wealthy travel agent who makes people pay high prices, so his daughters can flaunt their money and boast of their travels over martinis."

"Like Robin Hood," Jace interjected. "robbing from the rich to feed the poor?"

Prajna collected all the items and put them into a bag one by one, not answering his question. She finally broke the awkward silence,

"No, Mr. Taralock. Robbing whoever it takes, rich or poor, to make the world go around. There are many reasons people buy flowers in Mullick," she continued. "The training you will receive in the next several months will teach you, or perfect you," as she glared at Jace, "in the way of human nature. Why are these people here in India? Why are they in the market? Why are they in the Oberat? You will learn *who* to target, and how to harden your heart and conscience in the process. You will learn how to be unnoticed by the world in order to fulfill your purpose. You will learn the value of a properly timed distraction. You will learn to obey without question." She flared a look my way.

"Our purpose?" I questioned out loud. Maybe we would get an understanding of why we were here, but once again Felix cut in and spoke vaguely from his chair.

"You will learn how to act as a member of The Jailer's Way." He concluded by standing and signaling Prajna to remove us. She obeyed and escorted us out of the glamorous apartment and sent us to our rooms.

The next day began like every other, having breakfast with Jace in the restaurant of the hotel. There was no sign of Arlo and Andrea and I wasn't even sure where they had gone after Prajna's lesson. Our waiter Yuri brought us our usual.

Despite the colorful tastes of India, I was starting to miss the flavors of home, of Africa. It was mornings like this that we would be meeting Mahtap for our breakfast. Tobin would tag along dawdling, soaking up the morning air. He would play with the plants and overgrowth of greenery along her path, using his hands to hear the world. We would help Mahtap with her chores, and she would tell us a story or two, then we would head to the small cleared field at the bottom of the hill to meet up with the local Maasai children to play football for a while until the sun got so hot we would have to hide until evening. We had been away for nearly nine months, and until recently I had taken for granted how peaceful and carefree our childhood was.

Jace chatted away to Yuri, who religiously had our tea prepared even on the days I would sneak away to Sun Yat Sen for street food. He spoke of his duties at the hotel and of his uncle's restaurant several blocks away. He told us that he had been married for four years and he was grateful for the work he was given. He was a timid man who was obedient and highly valued at the Oberat.

By the time Yuri finished the rundown of his week's events and how he had waited on the Vice President of the United States, we were uneasy and anxious to start our new lessons. I wanted to understand our purpose a little better. I felt awful about stealing things from people, even the wealthy ones. Jace was even more apprehensive. I remember the story of Robin Hood, and what he did in the name of honor, but neither of us were sure if we wanted to join the Merry Men. Jace and I had agreed to learn what we could from our lessons and see what happened. We had no other choice, we had no money or means of getting away. As Yuri cleared our dishes, he slipped a small sealed letter onto the table. Jace opened it and read to himself.

"We have to go find a motorbike." Jace handed me the note.

"Bridge at 8 am. Use the motorbike." I read quietly. "What motorbike?" A sleek, black motorcycle with polished silver trim was parked just inside the gates of the Oberat.

"I assume it's *that* motorbike?" Jace said with a crooked smile.

It was too obvious that he was excited about this assignment. There was no key to be seen but that was not an issue. Both Jace and I knew how to start it in a second. It didn't matter if this was someone else's bike, or if it had been intentionally left for us, we knew we were to use it to get to the bridge, and it was nearly 8 o'clock, so we had to get there fast. Jace had more experience riding so he drove, and I held on to his waist as we escaped the gate and screeched into the busy Kolkata streets.

There were no rules of the road in India, you just entered and exited the streets when you saw your opening. Jace zig-zagged and ripped through streets and alleys until we arrived at the bridge entrance.

We left the bike at the foot of the bridge and looked for our next clue as to what we were doing there. People were already gathering to bathe in the river, and dogs were jumping in and out of the water playing. The activities of the people were distracting, and I just wanted to know what was going on, as the familiar white caravan pulled up and we were met by Prajna and the others. Arlo and Andrea exited the van and were less than impressed with our motorbike. They didn't even ask how we got it, or where it came from. It was a... Motorcycle...and we drove it here...but those two didn't think it was as impressive as I did.

Prajna instructed us that she would be watching nearby, and we were told to find a spot and just observe. It seemed like an unusual request, but at least we were not asked to steal anything. She detailed our mission. "There are two people here who have a story to tell. At the end of the day, I want you to tell me *who* they are and *why* they are here. They are your minds targets for the day."

"How do we know who we are supposed to watch?" Andrea voiced.

"You will know, that is why you have been chosen. You have been primed for this assignment your whole lives." Prajna replied. She drove away to watch us from afar.

"Well, Theorie and I can sit on the dock by the ferry. Do you two want to go across the bridge?" Arlo suggested to Andrea. Jace defensively straightened his shoulder and looked at me with uncertainty, but quickly followed Andrea who had already started up the path. I made my mind up to keep my observations to myself. We were being tested, and even though Arlo was curiously charming, I was not about to let him steal my thoughts.

We sat on the dock in the baking sun, and I envied the people cooling in the river. Not much was catching my attention other than a man who seemed out of place on the bridge. He was muscular and in touristy clothes but was far too comfortable to be a tourist. He leaned on the bridge seemingly doing precisely what we were doing, watching.

The other sight that caught my attention was a beggar at the foot of the path. He was skin and bones and so opposite the American looking man on the bridge. His beard was long, and his left leg was twisted and looked like it had broken and healed in the wrong way. He had a walking stick and a plastic bucket that he outstretched to passersby.

Arlo had tried to pass the time with meaningless chit chat, and I quickly realized his best feature was his hair, not his mind. I drowned him out until my ears picked up the words,

"Have you killed anyone yet?"

"No!" I yelped, zoning in on his question.

"Figures," he scoffed at my inexperience.

His words made me so uncomfortable, but I passed them off because he was so nice looking that he could not possibly be serious about murder. He was shallow and arrogant, but he had an alluring charm that undeservedly captured me. There was something familiar in his eyes that was puzzling, but I just could not piece it together in my mind.

"Why would you ask that?" I pressed.

"No reason...It just tells me what Felix thinks of your abilities. It helps me to see who I am playing with," he answered.

"I'm not sure what you think I am. I am not a murderer, and Felix doesn't know me at all."

Arlo passed over my comment. "Those marks on your wrist, how old were you when you first remember them?" he pestered.

"Why do they matter? They're nothing."

"Really...That's what you believe, huh? I think you know more than you're telling me, but that's fine. You know you can trust me...I'm just as confused and wondering why we are here as you are," he confessed.

"How much longer are we going to bake in this sun?" I tried to defer his focus from me.

"Don't know..." He smiled. He watched me like I was about to divulge a secret or admit that he was mesmerizing to look at. He was studying me.

"What's your problem? Focus on the crowd, find the targets. Don't you want to impress Prajna with how clever you are?" I awkwardly asked.

"Sure...but I already found who I was looking for."

I looked around the water, the bridge...nothing stood out. I was going to fail again and be the stupid weak one.

"Who?" I pleaded in my the most charming voice I could muster up.

"Uh-Uh...Not telling you. I know this is a competition, and I'm not coming in second. By the way, your eyes are really cool. I've never seen two different colors in one eye. It's like a ..."

"A mudslide." I cut him off.

He smiled. "No... It's pretty...You're pretty."

No one had ever told me that before, and my embarrassment showed. "I'm not...I think our target is the man on the bridge in the blue collared shirt, he's looking for someone." I changed the subject.

Arlo looked up at the bridge and shielded his eyes from the sun. "Maybe...Not telling you...No matter how pretty you are."

By the end of the afternoon when the white caravan reappeared, I had several stories in my head but had found no real information. I had failed and knew I would be a disappointment to Prajna. Jace and Andrea reappeared from the beach area, and I was relieved to see him. He didn't even notice me though and just hopped into the van.   Andrea followed behind him throwing me a look of arrogance and lordship over me. The bun her hair had been tied in earlier had been let loose exposing her dark black roots and showing her bleached blonde hair to be a mask. She was far more comfortable and relaxed now than I had ever seen her. Her usual distant, angry daze was more human and pleasant.

"You two had a good day?" Arlo obnoxiously inquired.

Jace refused to meet my eyes, and I quickly pushed aside any feeling of what I thought was jealousy because it was not a feeling I liked at all. Jace was my friend, not hers. Was this a set up to divide us? Suddenly, I was suspicious of Arlo for suggesting I be paired with him and putting Jace with Andrea. Maybe the two of them planned this all along. How dare she treat me like a plebian and make me feel inferior to her, she couldn't be more than a year older than me. She knew nothing of me and had barely been in my company. But Jace spends three hours with her at a bridge, and now they're comrades?

Right then it clicked, and my satisfaction of figuring out Prajna's assignment stopped all feelings of jealousy. I knew exactly *who* we were to study that day. I knew our targets.

Prajna sat in the back seats with us and turned facing her four students. "What have been your observations?" she inquired. I looked at Arlo, waiting for him to divulge his arrogant assumption, but he was silent. Jace mentioned the American man on the bridge, he had noticed as well. Several other people caught his attention.

"You did well Jace Taralock," Prajna expressed. "You are observant. Your memory for details is impeccable. Theorie?" She turned her attention to me. I cleared my throat and took a deep breath. I looked at Jace wide-eyed, I hated being called on and expected to put my thoughts into words.

"Two people you said. We were told to observe two specific people. It's Arlo and Andrea. They are brother and sister, and Arlo and Andrea are not their real names. I thought they were students like us, but they are both already trained in what we are being taught. They have secrets, and petty theft is the least of their crimes. They are fully engulfed in The Jailer's Way. They believe in it. They are a diversion to strengthen the skills of Jace and I. They are meant to challenge us. They are meant to test us."

Prajna said nothing in return but glanced at Arlo and Andrea who seemed slightly startled at my speech. Arlo smiled, curling in his bottom lip. I couldn't tell if he was proud of me, or if he found this all funny, and I had just humiliated myself again. Either way, the ride back to Oberat was silent, and I was left worrying about what trouble my words would get me into this time.

Chapter 6

The Studio

It was nearly June and was the hottest time of the year in Kolkata India. Of all the seasons, even monsoon season, I disliked the scorching summer months the most. We had spent two full cycles of seasons in India and spent day after day in the training of Prajna. Arlo and Andrea would sometimes be with us, but for the most part, it was just Jace and I. Our training had continued in pickpocketing, and breaking and entering, and observing people every day. We worked out distraction plans. One of us would divert attention while the other struck at just the right moment to attain the goods.

We targeted people that didn't notice we existed and reported to Prajna with our stolen items. My conscience bothered me, I didn't like taking from people. When I expressed my uncertainty, Prajna reminded me of The Jailer's Way philosophy and justified my actions in a twisted logic. I felt pity for anyone who was my victim, and Prajna knew this, so she would belittle my conscience.

We were told every day that we had an obligation to The Jailer's Way and were helping people with our actions. If we didn't understand Prajna's question or failed to see the way out of a situation, Prajna would criticize our intelligence. I felt useless sometimes, and foolish for failing the task, and I would apologize. Later, when sense returned I questioned what I was apologizing for.

I felt like I was going insane. Prajna would convince us to feel guilty and that we had failed The Jailer's Way, and failed Felix. She accused us of not seeing how important he was to the chemistry of the earth. She praised and admired Felix and put him on a pedestal and expected us to do the same.

We were given our location assignments in a sealed note at breakfast by Yuri. It would instruct us to work in a specific area where many tourists would make easy targets. In a couple of minutes, we were able to assess the crowd, know who was a local, who was a thief, or a tourist. We knew who to target and why we were choosing them. Our movements were quick, subtle and natural. My confidence grew as my conscience weakened day by day. I consoled myself in knowing that I wasn't really harming anyone. It was just money anyway.

After several months of petty theft and being Robin Hood's Merry Men, we were told the scope of our training was again changing. We were given locations or targets, same as usual, but now our plunder was documents, or files, or packages. Clearly, we were going after the more significant game now and our petty theft days had passed. Many times we had to go to a location and pick up an envelope or package and swipe transportation to deliver it to a marked drop-off. We were to be ghosts, never to look in the envelope, and we were never to ask questions. At the end of our assignment, we were to return to the Oberat hotel.

Several times a week, we were told to meet at a random location, where Prajna would have various exercises for us. We would learn to tie knots, how to get out of locked confined places, or how to make no noise at all when moving. Many of Prajna's lessons were riddles and mind exercises. We had to be observant and witty, as well as quick and invisible.

One lesson involved being innocuous in the high-pressure environment of the ER department. We had to have nothing but fleeting eye contact and be lost within ourselves. I took on the persona of a concerned relative of a patient. I walked briskly but with slight worry in my eye. My job was to enter the hospital, steal three bottles of Insulin, and leave without any authorities even batting an eye, and I was successful.

We did drop offs without question at hospitals, museums, markets, and even police headquarters. Once we were told to do nothing but stealthily enter the United States Embassy and collect the names off the tags of the workers. We got names of guards, receptionists, even janitors. All unnoticed and without drawing suspicion. We acted like we were there for a purpose, walked in, got the names, embedded them into our memories, and walked out.

We learned that it was all about confidence and body language. If we didn't feel suspicious, we didn't look suspicious. We had to control our emotions and remain entirely calm under any circumstance. I figured out that if I didn't make eye contact, my job was nothing but obeying an order like a machine. I could remove myself from the human element. If I slipped up and made eye contact, the boulder in my chest would cower me and my heavy conscience would give me away as a thief.

Whenever a moment of weakness was seen, Prajna would punish me by withholding basic human necessities. Mostly food and water, but at other times it would be human contact altogether. She would seal me in my room for several days so that I could not talk to Jace or Yuri. She knew I craved human contact and that I despised loneliness. The tasks slowly became more strenuous and demanding. Many times we barely escaped without being noticed, but we always fulfilled our job.

Day after day we would have breakfast in the hotel restaurant, waiting for our next assignment. Yuri would wait on us and sometimes keep us company. We grew fond of this waiter, and even though we knew he was tied up in Felix's plan, we liked him. He had a genuine smile and was honest when he spoke. He may have been under Felix control, but we were certain he was not fully aware of what we were doing after we left the breakfast table. It took a while for him to trust us enough to mention his family, but after the nearly two years of eating breakfast with him, he felt comfortable enough to bring up his wife and children.

They were a young family and very proud of their toddler who was quite beautiful and intelligent. He beamed with fatherly pride when mentioning her newest achievement or milestone. His infant son was brought into this world quickly and earlier than expected, and he thanked Allah every time the tiny boy's name came up. He was a hard-working, good father and had great respect for his wife. We never met his immediate family, but we felt like we were a part of it because he trusted us with little pieces of their ordinary lives. Many times we met his uncle who often met Yuri for lunch at the Oberat.

Yuri's uncle Rohit owned the Balan Sings Restaurant. The famous local eatery was over one hundred years old and had a central kitchen used by the well-known cooks of Kolkata, and then it had the back hidden kitchen which was for personal use. Uncle Rohit invited us many times to watch him cook and would make us the most delicious authentic dishes to try. Yuri would take us on the random days we did not have assignments.

Nico would stand in the entranceway to the back kitchen and oversee the visit, like a troll guarding a bridge. Uncle Rohit would have all the ingredients placed out, and I would spend my time watching him make authentic Indian dishes. The spices were familiar to me, I had been eating them since I was a child.

Watching him cook captivated me. He was like a conductor of a great orchestra, and his facial expressions would change a thousand times with every spice added. His bushy salt and pepper eyebrows twitched and bent. His dark brown aging eyes glowed with the flame of the ghee hitting the searing pan. His arms moved quickly but with purpose. He loved what he did, and I enjoyed watching his enthusiasm. I looked forward to the days we didn't have assignments, so we could come to the restaurant. One morning however, uncle Rohit asked to make roti. It is a bread, rolled thin and cooked with ghee on a cast iron flat pan.

I was told to use the small velun, a thin tapered rolling pin to make perfectly circular shaped pieces of dough. Uncle Rohit demonstrated and with the fastest and most precise wrist movement made each one exactly like the one before. They were perfection. I was very excited to try.

My eagerness quickly became torture, when every batch, day after day was not to his standards and the misshapen roti and masala was tossed into a metal garbage can. I tried to improvise and use different spices or amounts of ghee to cook them, and repeatedly they were not acceptable. In Africa food is precious. If you made it incorrectly or even dropped it into the dirt, it was still picked up, brushed off and consumed. The way of not wasting was how we were raised, and we valued the ingredients because we knew, even here in India people were hungry.

The waste of perfectly good food was mentally tormenting. I saw the faces of hungry children outside on the streets every day. What was wrong with this man? He threw out food just because it was slightly off in shape or thickness, or a spice was a tinge to strong? He would yell, "Trash! Rubbish!" and throw it away.

Jace and Yuri would snicker and sigh sarcastically at me. I would get so furious at Jace for not seeing the seriousness of my cooking. I wanted Yuri's family to like me. I wanted them to be impressed with me, but instead, I just kept looking foolish, and Jace would pal up with Yuri and tease me, treating it like a joke.

I worked on this wrist movement over and over every time I had the chance. The heat from the stove with the hot Kolkata summer made it nearly impossible to maneuver in the small kitchen. Uncle Rohit was looking for perfection, and I wanted so much to make him happy. He was the only person not connected to The Jailer's Way that was allowed to know that I existed. His real life and flavorful personality grounded me. I was determined to get it right. I tried different spices and measurements of salt, but each recipe failed his expectations. I tried to roll the dough quickly and impatiently to impress him, but the roti was all different shapes, too thick or chewy and deemed garbage.

It took weeks in between assignments for me to succeed in making something edible. I decided finally to self-discipline myself and did not allow myself to eat uncle Rohit's food until I got it right. It took two days, but I finally submitted to my own stubbornness, because I was so hungry.

It was not about trying spice, or my own ideas of creativity. It was a lesson in perfecting my obedience and strictly adhering to the smallest of details, including *taking my time* to roll the dough. I had finally mastered the movement of uncle Rohit's wrist and created a perfectly symmetrical roti. I obeyed the measurements and tamed myself. In this area, there was no room for variation. I was to follow, obey and perfect my obedience. I was to be patient with the spices and allow them to pop and bloom.

With my growling belly, I presented uncle Rohit with a meal fit for royalty. His satisfaction in taste and appearance showed on his face, and the relief of being able to eat my perfect creation was the best reward. When we left that day all he said to me as we exited the kitchen was,

"Now you are ready. There is perfection in obedience and patience."

I was happy to have finally gotten it right, but I didn't understand why he insisted that I needed to be perfect. I didn't think perfection was due to obedience. I wanted to tell him that his recipes could have been changed and still have been acceptable. I wanted to tell him that his way was not the only way to do things, but he was a respected man, and I was grateful he showed me any attention at all, so I kept my mouth shut.

That was the last time I went to the Balan Sings restaurant. The seasons changed once more, and cooler dry days were moving in for the winter. The next morning we were picked up by the white caravan driven by Arlo with Andrea in the passenger seat. Arlo met us with an arrogant smirk that still caught my eye. I don't know why I was attracted to him, he did nothing to deserve my attention. In the last two years, Arlo hadn't changed at all, other than his ego had swelled. He made my stomach feel all funny, and I would get girlishly nervous around him. I felt so stupid and would try to hide it, but I knew Jace could see right through me.

Jace did not like Arlo at all, and I could tell, he felt very intimidated by him. Arlo could read this and would purposely look for subtle ways to humiliate Jace. Arlo always had several more pieces of jewelry, or a couple of extra wallets more than Jace to present to Prajna on her weekly inspections. Arlo's conscience did not get in the way of his theft, and he obeyed the rules of targeting certain wealthy people not because he was afraid of Felix, rather because he enjoyed his job.

Jace from the first day struggled with this task and Arlo seized on his uncertainty and exposed it as a weakness. Felix met with us monthly to inspect and collect the stolen inventory, and to let us know where we had fallen short in his expectations. Arlo used these meetings as opportunities to show Jace's faults and throw him in front of Felix as the *weak* one. Everyone knew of The Jailer's Way, and that weakness would not be tolerated by Felix.

Andrea accompanied Arlo many times, and after watching them together, I was convinced that my theory of them being brother and sister was correct. They had the same familiar arrogance in their eyes and many matching mannerisms. Andrea was small, but she was solid and disciplined. Her bleach blonde was gone now, and a tight ponytail of jet-black hair fell just above her shoulder.

That early winter day, Arlo drove us to a large building that looked newer. It seemed twenty stories high. The elevator ride up to the 17th floor took less than a minute, and we walked in to meet Felix. His suit was darker than usual making him look more sinister. He was standing across the large open room as we entered. The floors were glossed hardwood that glistened in the sunlight. The ceilings were tall with white painted ornate tin designs of flowers and swirls, and large fans hung strategically in between the patterns. The room was naturally lit by the morning sun through floor to ceiling massive windows overlooking the busy streets of Kolkata. It looked more like a fancy dance studio than a classroom.

I had always expected Felix to be more of a mentor and give us attention and training, but every time we met only a few words or sentences would be provided, leaving us to half wonder what he meant. He could never be forward with his meanings. This morning was no different. As we reached the opposite side of the room and stood before him, he walked passed us back towards the door. I suddenly felt trapped and remembered his threat, calling us "Jailbirds in a cage." I hated being powerless against him.

"Your skills will be put to the test today. I have been watching you, and I now understand your strengths and weaknesses," he remarked. "Theorie, you need harnessing, and James my boy, I need to know what motivates you, what puts fire in your fists. I will leave you with your new instructors."

As he left, I searched the room for our new teacher, or if Prajna would appear. However, the door shut behind Felix leaving Jace and me alone with our comrades Arlo and Andrea. I was quickly caught up to speed when a gut-wrenching exhale blew from Jace across the room. Arlo with all his might socked Jace directly in the stomach leaving him bent over trying to catch his breath. I instinctively tried to go to him but was fist stopped across my shoulders by Andrea.

"That's not fair Arlo," Andrea condemned. "He wasn't ready, it's his first day."

Arlo just grinned and walked to the center of the room. Obviously, he had been waiting a long time to have free range on Jace. He started pointing to each station in the order of a clock.

"Three o'clock, strength training," pointing to a weight bench, with various weights and ropes. "Nine o'clock, speed," pointing to an area that looked like gym equipment. "Twelve o'clock, weapons," directing our attention to a wall with several outstretched shelves.

The shelves were lined with items we were entirely unprepared for. Arlo stepped forward a few feet indicating that where he was standing was "The Studio," he stated, smiling like he was in his glory as the center of attention, and the master of the room.

Jace was still trying to compose himself after the blow he received to his stomach, and with a short breath questioned,

"Are you telling me we are being trained to fight?"

Arlo seemed pleased to respond, "Combat, and defense. You need to work on those pitiful biceps," he judgingly mocked Jace. "I've been waiting for this day since I met the two of you. I've watched you closely, read your body language. You two have a chemistry that I need to break down. Let's see if that chemistry can ignite a fire, or if it fails and produces useless gasses? Felix would like to see you both as disciplined physically as you are mentally. You have to be prepared for whatever comes at you." He winked and glanced at me.

The first day of combat training was mild compared to the days that followed. For the next seven days, we were smashed and crushed, trapped and flung in every direction. We would have breakfast with Yuri in silence because our ribs ached, and our knuckles bled. Yuri didn't ask any questions, but his solemn face showed that he was concerned for us.

Arlo had given Jace "special attention," and would continue to knock him down day after day. Jace was not a fighter. He was strong and self-disciplined, but he was so confined by honor and his conscience, he could hardly fight back.

Andrea was bent on blocking me in every way from stepping in to help Jace. If I couldn't take it anymore and stepped forward to intervene, she in some way would confine me, even binding me at times to the metal support beam in the center of the room. She would weaken me with a punch to my stomach or jaw. Arlo fought me with every bit of force that he did Jace, and Andrea matched Jace's strength and fought like a rabid Tasmanian Devil.

Andrea would belittle my physical appearance and weakness. Arlo would cut down Jace and make him feel like a child. I wished Jace would fight back. I didn't care if he killed Arlo, I just wanted this phase of training to end. I didn't want Jace to be seen as weak, or Felix would in some way eliminate him. I had a feeling that we would not move on from these lessons until someone was dead.

When we were not in the fighting ring, we were learning how to calculate the distance of a target and the length of each knife, so it was not a question of *if* we hit the center, but how quickly we could make the adjustment in our mind to hurl the knife accurately. We learned how to hit a moving target with the use of cardboard cutouts attached to expensive remote-controlled cars, and how to be accurate from great distances.

We learned the function of weapons we did not even know existed. The Bennett M82 .50 caliber rifle, suppressed pistols, and a K90 personal defense weapon that had been created for the military. We were tested on what silencers to use, and what bullets and ammo would be used for silent attacks. Many times I imagined hauling off and killing both of our opponents and running away as fast as possible, but I knew we were being watched.

After three months of learning how to choose and use specific guns, we began target practice. I was able to shoot accurately from the start. I had always had a steady hand, that had been useful when doing my sketches. It also helped to picture Felix as the poster target.

Jace and I would be locked in the training facility and given safety gear and watched behind protective glass as we shot off hundreds of rounds. We learned how to defend ourselves if we were ever taken by surprise, and how to quickly choose which weapon would be most effective for the situation. It was out of control, and an anxious desire to get away from anything associated with The Jailer's Way grew each day. I hated this training.

We were raised to respect others, to be empathetic, and hold other people's pain in our own hearts. We were raised to see the struggles of people's lives, and that each person had a story, and a human to love them. Now we were expected to toss away all those things my father, and Mahtap had taught us. We were expected to callously attack and destroy all in the name of a philosophy that we didn't even agree with. I didn't know what to do, or how to have enough strength to stand up for who we were, to stand up for Mahtap, and live up to her honor.

Our strength training continued day after day. I got quicker, and Jace got stronger. It seemed one-sided and unfair. Arlo and Andrea were callous and raw. They laughed at injuries and pain and were forcing us to harden and ignore our conscience.

The suite of the Oberat was now our hospital in the evenings. It was a haven that gave us only until morning to recuperate. I would swipe ginger and garlic, clove and honey from the market to help make anesthetics and tear up the sheets of our beds into strips to bind our throbbing arms and ribs. Every day we were in a worse state than the one before. After a particularly rough training and seeing most of my friend's torso bruised and blue, I had to say something.

We had been silent in our evenings because neither of us knew how to handle our situation and were breathless from having the wind knocked out of us, but I knew we couldn't go on like this and I had to speak up. I showered and washed the blood off my lip where Andrea had taken a swing at me, put on clean clothes and helped Jace with the bandage around his ribs.

"Jace, I know you are hurting, but will you come with me on a walk?" He looked at me knowing I had a reason to want to leave our makeshift hospital.

As we entered the market and headed past the busy vendors, I led him cautiously down the way to the Potter's colony. We knew Nico was following us at a distance, but in all honesty, we were too beat and sore to try and run away, so he laid off and watched us from several yards away. Men were working and molding statues for an upcoming festival, and several tourists were eyeing smaller sculptures and haggling over price. Large wooden scaffolding held drying pots, bowls, and medium-sized clay gods.

We walked slowly and carefully because I knew that my friend was beaten, and sore. We reached the small tables set up for men to play their daily chess tournaments and took a seat at a back table out of the way closest to the drying pottery racks.

"See those men playing chess? We are like the pieces they're moving around," Jace remarked, as if he was giving up.

On the table where we rested, a fading chessboard could barely be made out. Several cheap plastic pieces were lined up, with most of the characters missing. It was a forgotten table. Men often played on this street and spent the hot days in the shade of the buildings battling their knights and pawns. Several other tables with fresher paint and complete sets were being used, and men were deep in thought trying to figure out their opponent's next move. I lowered my voice and leaned closer to Jace, who looked so defeated sitting across from me.

"Even among the chaos of buying and selling, these men are able to focus on their next move Jace. They block everything else out and think five steps ahead of the game to predict their opponent's next move. The sooner they know the play, the sooner the game is over."

He looked at me with desperation, but he knew what I was plotting. "Where Theorie? Where would we go? How would we go? We have nothing. Felix is a dictator, he is the queen of the game. He can go in any direction and is everywhere. He's crueler and smarter than we think. He doesn't in any way let us know his next move. I know he would kill us." He was sounding so desperate now.

"Jace," I went on. "Felix told us in the beginning that the weak will not be tolerated. If we don't get away somehow than we are stuck here, trapped, and he will kill us. He's making you weaker and weaker every day. Why don't you fight Arlo? Don't let him beat you. You're strong enough!" I raised my voice, but quickly corrected myself and spat out to a whisper.

"I hate seeing you being treated like an animal. It has been three months of abuse. Arlo is out to kill you, and Andrea blocks my every move, I can't even help you."

Jace knew my desperate plea and reached across the chess board pushing my chin up making me look at him. "You've taken a few hits as well," running his thumb on the side of my lip. "Felix wants us to be like them. He wants us to be aggressive and to be the ones to take the first swing. You know that I am not a fighter," he admitted.

"I can't watch you be a sitting target. We have to run away, or you have to FIGHT! It hurts me that you are in pain. I hear you yell and have your breath taken away when Arlo hits you, and I can't stop him. He's a monster," I cried.

"You mean," he smiled changing to a sarcastic tone. "Arlo, doesn't impress you with his muscles and perfect hair? You seem pretty taken with him. He seems to like you." His attempt at lightening the situation and trying to make me blush was useless.

"Why do you joke about that? It's not funny. I hate him. I hate that what we are repulsed by, makes him light up. He loves stealing, and fighting and running drop-offs for Felix, being his dumb pawn." I flicked over a chess piece in front of me.

"That was a knight you killed, not a pawn, and I see how you look at him, it sure doesn't look like hate in your eyes." Jace corrected me with a smile. This time I couldn't resist his attempt and for a moment felt like I was home again looking at his familiar grin that always made me feel better. I gave into him and smiled.

"Arlo doesn't like me. No one ever will think of me in that way. I'll just be a loner. I'm not the type guys would want to love."

"I don't know," Jace shrugged and smiled, "You have a mysterious tattoo on your wrist that might intrigue them, and you can cook Indian food really, really well."

I couldn't help but smile. "Jace...We need a code word. Something both you and I know. We'll know that when we hear it, that it means we are leaving, *now*. We can set up a meeting place, and no matter what, we just go...We don't question each other...We just go." I explained. "Felix is escalating his expectations. We can try to plan, but what if we don't have enough time? What if we have to go quickly?"

"The song," Jace offered. "We don't need a word, we can use the song. Mahtap's song. The one she and I worked on and wrote together...You know..." He started humming the notes.

"That's perfect," I agreed.

"It's something only you and I would recognize," he added.

"And now we will know...If we hear Mahtap's music, it means that we have to go...It's like her letter. Remember? The music will set us free," I said.

We walked back to the large black gates of the Oberat slowly with Nico just out of earshot and agreed that we would actively search for a way to escape the clutch of Felix. We needed money and a way to be truly invisible. When we were in the hotel, we would speak only of how well we were doing, or what we learned in our training, and pretend to be turning to stone. We would play the part and pretend to enjoy our training. We didn't know how or what move to make next, but we knew we needed to get away and try to find Tobin. We knew we needed to get to New York.

The next day held mixed emotions for me. I was in terror of what Jace would be put through, and I was still aching from yesterday's pounding. I was hoping to go through my day looking for any way out. I would store up any clue or idea and Jace, and I planned to walk in the evening to the Potter's colony or the chess tables to plot our getaway.

At breakfast, we were given a note from Yuri. Before we went to the studio, and before the sun was up, we needed to make a delivery. The motorcycle was left for us, and we had to leave the attached envelope at the Artemis hospital. As usual, we were to leave the bike several blocks away and weave through the streets until we were unnoticed. This time the envelope was to be left on the roof in the air vent. It was not unusual, and we knew we had to follow orders. We quickly picked the padlock to the stair shaft and made our way up the stairs to the roof.

It didn't take long to tuck the envelope into the metal frame of the hospital air vent, and we were off the roof, back to the alley where we had left our bike. We zipped through the streets and finally made it to the studio's neighborhood. We left the bike a half mile from the building so that it wouldn't draw attention to the studio and we walked the rest of the way.

Arlo and Andrea were waiting for us, and it became evident they were irritated with our delay, by coming at us in a flash. Jace was grabbed and thrown several feet across the room by the powerful arms of Arlo, making him slide into the radiator near the window. Andrea boldly stepped in my path to block my view. She grabbed a spear and corralled me into the corner, pushing me to the wall, then forced me to cower to the floor on my back, and pinned me at the chest. She was so strong and forceful that I could hardly catch my breath. I tried to push the spear from my breast, but she was not breaking her dynamic grip. Her brown soulless eyes lasered into mine, warning me of her desire to cut me in half. I was glued in position, laying on the floor helpless, and at her mercy.

From across the room, all I heard was the sounds of skin being slammed, and bone hitting the floor. Repeated pounding of a fist against skin. The smell of fresh blood filled the room. I couldn't see, but I knew Jace was down, as Arlo fought to keep him in submission. Was Jace even trying to fight back? I wish Andrea would move so I could see what was happening. Groans and thuds could be heard and finally the sound of glass shattering. It must be the window behind the radiator. A wind blew in making the fans turn, giving me a much-needed wave of fresh air. I yelled and broke free from Andrea's spear and twisted my body in order to crawl away, but I was stopped short by Arlo's boot on my neck. I got just a second to observe Jace, face down across the room. Blood was slowly trickling from his left ear.

"I don't think so...Jailbird. You can't help him. He's in the way now. Maybe you and I can find a new *element*," Arlo said flirtingly, looking down at me with a devious grin.

He went back to Jace, leaving Andrea to hold me captive and helpless on the floor with the spear at my throat again. Glass shattered, and the sound of a body being beat to death was pounding in my head, but I couldn't see. This stupid wretch of a girl wouldn't move her titanium twig of a body to let me see my friend's last breath.

All I could picture was Jace bleeding and dying. I knew I had to find an inner breath of life deep within me. I needed to forget reason, forget my conscience, forget Mahtap's smile and fight! I had told Jace to fight for his life just the night before, but if he could not because he was too broken, or because in his soul he could not kill a man, I would do it for him!

The rage inside of me built up so strong, and the breeze of the broken window gave me life. With a mighty force, I lifted my knee plowing it into Andrea's groin. In an instant, I twisted my wrists inward and in precise movement swirled the spear in my palm. I grabbed tightly at just the right second transforming what was holding me hostage into my own weapon. I turned the spear on my captor and forced her back against the wall.

She had not been expecting the agility and precision and was left defenseless as I swung my leg around pulling her feet from underneath her. I jumped to my feet and leapt on her like a lion on prey. I pinned her at the neck with the spear, forcing her hands to try and push it off. Just a centimeter more and her blood would paint the hardwood floors. It pierced her throat slightly making a roll of dark crimson blood drip slowly from the blade. She was pinned on the floor, and her eyes were in a traumatic helpless state of fear. I wanted to kill her, and she knew that I was capable. I would have pushed the spear through her pale neck until her life gave out, but the sound of clapping shook my focused rage.

It was Felix. Standing at 6 o'clock, near the door to the studio. He was clapping slowly and deliberately and angering me with every step he took as he walked closer to the center of the room. Jace was standing near the radiator and broken window looking torn and shattered, breathing heavy.

It was Arlo laying in a pool of his own blood. He was swollen, his brow was pushed against the floor, and his mouth was open. Several crooked and jagged teeth mixed with his own bloody saliva. His eyes were partially open and empty. He looked like a piece of roadkill. Had Jace killed him? I began to panic. I was near killing my own victim, when Jace yelled,

"Theorie!"

I looked down to see the bluing face of Andrea beneath me. I released my hold and pulled my boot up off of her lungs, leaving her to roll to her side and desperately gasp for air, clenching the sliver of warm blood on her neck.

Felix stood at the center of the room now like the dial of the clock and did a semicircle inspection of the scene. His hands went into his suit pockets as he said with a grin,

"Well done. Your strengths have been exposed. You work well together when the other is in *real* danger."

From the floor, Arlo made the guttural sound of an animal refusing to give up its life. "He will be fine, he's had worse. Andrea tend to him," Felix commanded. Andrea crawled quickly to her demolished brother and helped him to his feet while still holding pressure on her neck. Felix seemed quite pleased with us and smiled. "Your strength is exactly what I anticipated." He left the room following behind his two broken trainers, leaving Nico to escort us back to the Oberat. Jace and I tried to understand what had just happened.

We both stood to adjust our sore muscles and breathe deeply. Two little birds flew in the broken window, landing on the exposed pipes from the floor above. They were so small and pretty. The male's bright yellow wings, and shiny black belly made him captivating to look at. They chirped and explored the room. They weren't trying to escape. They just hopped from pipe to pipe, content to make the studio their new home.

It was in that moment, I was reminded that Mahtap would point out little birds, and we would watch them on our hill. She told us that the birds didn't need anyone to feed them, that they were cared for by the Earth and God. They were given what they needed and provided with instinct, so they were happy. She told us that *we* were more valuable than little birds and for just a second as I watched the freedom of those little birds, I had hope.

Back in the suite I tore the sheet and made binding for Jace's snapped ribs. He was the victor in this battle but had wounds from a compatible opponent. A slice on his right temple where the window had broken and caught him from falling seventeen stories had crusted over. I knew I had some peroxide in the bathroom cabinet and ran quickly to get it. The pain winced his face as I tried to clean the wound. I hoped he would have time to heal and Felix would not be expecting us to go into training the next day. There was no way we could go back to that.

"I thought I killed him Theorie. I thought I killed Arlo. He came at me, and it was so quick, and I was thinking of what we talked about, to fight. I just couldn't let him hurt you. When I heard him talk about finding a new *element* with you, I knew he was going to hurt you. I knew that I was the only thing in the way. I don't know what came over me, but I would have killed him if I hadn't seen Felix enter the room. Felix saw me, and he'll expect me to fight now. I should have let Arlo kill me."

He broke down nearly sobbing now, dropping his bloody head into my neck. "I should have let him kill me." I held my finger to his mouth, to quiet him, and then pointed to my ear to remind him that we were being listened to.

"What would I do without you? Where would I go?" I questioned. I pushed him off my shoulder. "You fought for your life, how is that wrong? Arlo would have killed you, and Felix would have let him. Felix wanted to see what would push us, and he did. All we can do is see what tomorrow holds."

He calmed down knowing we couldn't talk freely here, and gave in to me helping clean his injuries, finally falling asleep from sheer exhaustion. He had changed so much in the last few months. He had gotten stronger and taller. He had gone from a boy to a man in the time we had been in India. His hair had darkened, and his face no longer looked so innocent and young. His scruffy jawline had been slashed and scratched, and his gray-blue eyes seemed wiser against his tan skin. My poor friend. I hadn't seen him break down since Mahtap's death, and I had forgotten that he was so sensitive. I felt guilty that I had told him to fight, I forgot his gentle nature. Why did he listen to me? I hated myself and felt so stupid for once again jumping ahead.

I remembered the attention I would try and stir up from the girls at my Primary school, which seemed like a lifetime ago. I begged for people to pay attention to me and ended up embarrassing myself so many times. I always regretted my impulsive behavior in hindsight and would swear I would never behave that way again.

Now, I was in the same situation, only this time it wasn't just me that I embarrassed or drew the wrong kind of attention to. My dearest friend in the world was in danger now because I impulsively pushed him to be something he wasn't. I wanted to run away and hide just like when I would make a fool of myself in school, but I was stuck, forced to see what tomorrow brought.

Chapter 7

The Value of Human Life

The several times in my life that I woke up and began living my day, only to figure out that I was still dreaming was always a strange experience for me. It was always so real. The sounds, smells, colors and feelings were so vivid that throughout the day I would still question if what I dreamt was true or not.

I had been dreaming of scurrying off to the book market early and was fighting feelings of deep guilt and a fear that I was being chased. The sound of a piano was playing in the back of my head, and it took several minutes of fighting that drunk feeling of altered reality before I decided to go with the piano sound and try and fight myself awake.

As I came to, the piano sound remained, I hadn't been dreaming that part. I was not at the book market, and no one was chasing me, I was still in my bed. But I was sure I heard Jace playing the piano. Where was he? I had to be still dreaming because he was always in the next room when I woke up, and this morning I was alone.

The speed at which I searched my room and threw on my clothes was chaotic. I only had one of my shoes on when the sound of the piano playing became clearer. I opened the door to my room and peered down the hallway. Often in the evenings a player was hired and sat behind the velvet rope playing elevator tunes and classic rock songs. It was never played in the morning though, and this was no ordinary entertainer. It was Jace.

What he played sounded familiar. It was the piece he and Mahtap had written together, and they had played it many times at Taralock Estates. It started off thunderous and slowed down to a trickle only to end in a sad, forlorn tone of single notes.

It was the song!... The signal!... We had to leave now! I dressed quickly and quietly. I pushed my stone necklace deep into my boot and threw a few things into my backpack. I didn't question what was happening, or why we were leaving, I just knew it had to be right now. Jace was near the end of Mahtap's song when he stopped abruptly at catching sight of me coming towards him.

"You scared me, I didn't' know where you were," I scolded.

He raised his brow. He took my hand and sat me next to him on the piano bench. Nico sat in the lobby center, overseeing Jace and me from above his newspaper. He slowly sipped his coffee.

It was still early in the morning. It had been two days since we heard from Felix or had been given an assignment from Yuri. Perhaps Felix was rewarding Jace for his win, or maybe he was planning what to do with us next. I knew that we had to leave right now, Mahtap's song had alerted me, and I was ready to go. Jace switched to playing a Mozart Piano Concerto? What had happened?

I watched his fingers flick over the keys and saw in his movements that no matter what the danger was, the piano always transported him and led him to a different world. I felt the vibrations of the piano on my knees and was dragged along with the delicacy of his playing.

As he filled the lobby of the Oberat with tranquility, I glanced at the other guests and hotel staff that had begun their day and started going about their business.

In an instant, Jace abruptly stood, took my hand, and led me right out the front door.

As I followed Jace with a growing paranoia, I looked over my shoulder for Nico. I saw him still sitting in the lounge chair, unmoved by our departure. He wasn't stirring or even noticing our walking away, he seemed to be sleeping soundly. How could that be? He was our captor and Felix's hawk. How did he just let his prey waltz right out of the main gate of the Grand Oberat Hotel?

The Holi festival was being prepared for, and as the sun rose higher in the sky and peaked over the buildings in the distance, men arranged baskets in rows of colorful chalk powder. The streets were outlined with magenta, turquoise, and golden yellow bowls laid out for the day's customers. The sun began to encroach and sparkle on the colors setting off a flurry of activity.

Today Spring would be welcomed, and as we walked through Kolkata the streets began to be painted. The music got louder, and the voices became more jovial. The powder started to burst, and children mischievously threw buckets of colored water on tourists and cars, and anything else that moved. People began filling the streets celebrating and setting up food carts. Water guns were being filled with colored powder and water, and people chased one another around staining clothes with bright springtime pastels. The number of people populating India did help us merge into the population and be undetectable. People were happy and playful and loud. It was the perfect time to escape unnoticed.

As we ducked and skirted in between the activity, we stole what we would need to survive and get away. It added up to about 130,000 Rupees, enough to get us started. I walked by a stand and swiped a tan saree and threw it over my clothes as we turned the corner. Jace disguised himself in stolen local clothes and blended in with the rainbow of people. We snatched water bottles and packaged food and tucked it away, as we made our way to the edge of Kolkata. We walked quite a way and tried to vary, and zig zag our path.

Large idols were being crafted from clay and paper in the form of various Gods for the Holi festival. Enormous crates were being filled and stuffed with hay and sculptures. They were being loaded into large covered trucks to be sent to different train stations or shipyards for delivery. Our means of escape literally opened right up to us. We found a truck that was being loaded.

"I'm going to cause a distraction. Get into the back of that truck," Jace ordered.

"What about you?"

"I'll be right behind you." He skirted off behind the crates, and in a moment, men began shouting and running towards a crate that was bellowing with smoke. Men began drawing buckets of water from wells, and attention was diverted from the jolly festival to putting out the fire that Jace had started. I ran into the truck, and glided into the far back, adjusting the crates slightly to make room for two of us. The truck ignition turned, and a man approached and shut the left half of the door to the truck.

"No!" I scurried to get off. "Jace!" I began sweating under the suffocating saree and I tripped over the loose fabric. I fell forward onto a smaller crate just as Jace hopped through the open right door, silently passed me, took my hand and pulled me behind him. We fell to the ground creviced between the back crates and the truck wall. I fell half on top of him, and we both froze as we heard voices. I knew if the truck driver had looked hard enough, he would notice my boot. I hadn't pulled my foot in entirely out of sight before freezing. The man quieted, and in Hindi said,

"No more! I have no more room." He shut the truck door. A sense of relief released the air in my lungs, and I realized I was squishing Jace who was still holding his breath. His brow was soaked with magenta and turquoise sweat.

"You can breathe now," I whispered. The truck began to pull away, and we made our hideout more comfortable. I tried to pat and brush the colorful chalk from my clothing, but I was too stained. The cramped quarters, and stifling heat made me feel close to dying. I used the saree I had stolen to make cushions for us to rest our backs on. Jace winced in pain from his injuries as he propped himself up against the bouncing truck wall.

We weren't even sure of where the truck was destined but we didn't care, we just needed to try. Once the rumbling of the truck was steady, we had a moment to stretch. After an hour or so, the evening fell, and It was night time now. The cool fresh air whispering in through the cracks of the truck was a welcome relief.

"What happened?" I finally asked.

"Felix was here, and I heard something I know I wasn't supposed to hear," he explained. "I went down to breakfast, to meet Yuri. It was about four in the morning, still pitch black out. I just couldn't sleep well last night; my ribs are killing me. You were still sleeping. I sat at our usual table in the corner, but Yuri didn't show up. It was earlier than he was used to seeing me, so I went into the kitchen just to tell him I was there, and I was going to order chai to bring up to you, but I saw the white van with the tinted windows. Felix was talking to Yuri from a lowered window. Nico was parking the motorbike at the gate to be left for us. So I ducked behind the delivery truck and laid on the ground underneath to hear what they were talking about.

Yuri was told to give me an envelope with an assignment in it. *Only me*, Theorie." He paused and looked at me, studying my face to see if I understood him. I knew right away.

"What is he doing with you? Are you being sent away? Am I being sent away?" I cried.

"I was to go on this assignment, and Arlo was coming to get you. You are to be given to Arlo, as a partner. I don't know what happened to Andrea. Felix felt your skill matched Arlo's, and because I lo… care for you, it interferes with his plan."

He held my hand trying to stabilize the tremor creeping up on me. In the past few months, I had learned what my strengths were, but I also learned what my weakness was and that it was a fear of being alone. I couldn't be sent away with Arlo. I hated him. I wasn't matched well with him, he was immoral and had a deal with the devil. I needed to be with Jace, at least until this was all over and we could get home.

"Yuri later gave me the sealed envelope," Jace paused and looked so sorrowfully into my eyes. "Theorie, Felix assigned me an assassination," he stated. I forgot to inhale, I was so stunned. I knew Felix was a thief, but murder? Was this what all our training was leading up to?

"I am supposed to travel to Delhi and go to the Renson Valley School. There is a boy there, only about thirteen years old. An important boy. I am supposed to make it look like a tragic accident on his lunch recess."

My expression was of shock. Did he mean the Prime Minister's Grandchild? I knew he was in Delhi at a school. It had been in the newspapers. Who else could he mean?

"Are you speaking of..." I started but was cut off.

"Yes," Jace announced. "I won't do this. We have done Felix's bidding long enough. This crosses the line of human decency, and I'm not stooping to his level of sickening. I don't know what his ultimate goal is, but do you know what killing that boy would trigger? That boy is protected by bodyguards for a reason. His death would set off international responses. Do you see? Do you understand now what this was all for?" he pleaded.

"I think so," I responded. I still had so many questions though.

"I would rather die than live in shame anymore, and I am not killing for him," Jace mourned.

"We have to stop him. We need to get away, but we can't run and escape without exposing Felix? He will just continue to hurt people. How do we destroy The Jailer's

Way? I can't live with myself knowing he is killing innocent people. He's an evil man. I'm sorry Jace. I'm sorry I told you to fight, you're so hurt and broken. You listened to me and fought Arlo. I'm sorry I told you to fight. Now Felix wants you to be an assassin!"

"I didn't fight because you told me to," he assured, "I fought because of what Arlo said to you, about you and him. I could have lifted a train with my bare arms at that point. I'm not letting Arlo find any kind of *element* with you. I would have killed him. You are not going to be his partner, in any way."

"Why did Nico let us go?" I asked.

"He didn't...Yuri bought us some time by putting an opium sleeping powder in his coffee."

"No! If Felix finds out...Yuri's family!" I anxiously worried.

"He wanted to help us, and he had a plan. He had an excuse, and uncle Rohit helped."

"Uncle Rohit?"

"Yes, Yuri told me that his uncle would help him. He trusts him. We can't worry about that now...It's done. We didn't have time. It would only be an hour or two before Nico woke up with a splitting headache and symptoms mimicking a stroke, and Arlo would come for you."

"Will Nico be alright?" I asked.

"Yes...Really? You're worried about that oaf?"

"Yes," I answered annoyed at his name calling. "I sort of thought he maybe just had a crunchy exterior. I don't know, I just..."

"He will be fine," Jace reassured. "Instead of worrying about our guard's headache, why don't you think of a masterful plan instead."

I jumped in. "Okay. Let's go. I have a plan."

"Really? That was quick. Okay, let's hear it."

"Well, it involves stealing a fire truck and possibly breaking into the science institute and releasing all of the white mice."

"I don't know why I ask." He rolled his eyes.

We were just beginning to get feeling back in our tingling legs when the truck came to a quick stop. We were pretty sure we were near the water because we could hear seagulls. We picked up our bags and ducked behind the crates. The truck would need to be unloaded and we had a small chance of escaping unnoticed. In one swift movement as the gate to the truck opened and six men focused on getting the first crate out without destroying it, we slithered out and curled around the side of the truck parallel to the sea.

Our legs were not fully working as we escaped and looked around for a sign to tell us where we were. Not far from where we were crouching, we noticed signs for Bangladesh. We had ended up in Chittagong, at the West End Marine Shipyard. Ships were not just loaded and packed for delivering internationally here. We had landed ourselves in the middle of a shipbuilding city. We hadn't gotten as far from Kolkata as we had hoped, but at least it was somewhere we wouldn't be noticed. We might have a few days before Felix caught onto our trail.

We took my saree and Jace's top shirt that had been stained with chalk and crouched by the dock. A heavy piece of scrap metal laying in the sand helped us sink our colorful disguises into the Karnaphuli River.

As we crouched and scurried and tried to be invisible among the massive steel structures, we snuck into a forty-foot-high metal building. Its enormous doors were wide enough for a cargo ship to pass through. "Bonding Warehouse" was printed in black letters above the massive entrance. We knew we could hide here for the night, and we looked for any signs of surveillance equipment that we would have to avoid. The shelves were tall metal structures that had stacks and rows of parts, wires, and welding equipment.

We slid in without being noticed and hid in the shelving. As we made ourselves a little shelf apartment behind the large boxes of supplies, I felt like a little kid hiding under my blanket from monsters.

Jace looked pale. He had taken a beating just 48 hours earlier and should have been in a hospital. His head wound had started bleeding again, and I was worried about it getting infected. We snacked on our packaged nuts and bars that we had packed away and had a little water left. Men in white coverall suits and white hard hats holding clipboards wandered about, taking inventory and speaking to other workers wearing safety gear. The sharp shrill of metal being cut down pierced our eardrums and the dank smell of the river and sweaty workers made my stomach ache and yell at me. We watched the workers running around like termites pulling parts they needed from the shelves. It was like watching television. They worked until well after the sun had vanished and when the loudspeaker finally announced the shipyard was closing we were disappointed that the show was over, but grateful for a chance to stretch our legs.

After the warehouse doors were closed and locked, we waited for any sign of a night watchman. As quiet as possible we escaped our shelf apartment. We found the security guard laughing away sipping tea, watching cartoons in a small office. He seemed relaxed, totally unaware we were scouting about. The employee medical cabinet had enough supplies and water to clean ourselves up and tend to Jace's wounds. We were anxious to return to the shelves though, so we would not be accidentally seen. We quickly gathered some supplies and headed back to our hideout tucking into our cozy hideaway and adjusted some of the boxes.

"Remember when we were kids?" Jace started. "We would make forts and hide in the shipping crates for the coffee after the harvest. We really were wild kids, always getting into stuff. Mostly your ideas. You would get me into so much trouble with my father. He wanted me to work in the barn, but I'd see you running around with Tobin having made up adventures and just want to be with you, to have fun with you. My parents were so serious all the time, but you, you were always fun. I miss those days."

"It can be that way again someday. We will get home," I replied.

"It can't be the same," he said so mournfully. He looked so sad like he'd lost something valuable to him.

"Why not?" I asked. "I know we'll get away from Felix. It just has to work out. Life can't be like this. Everyone else gets to be free to live how they want. I can't let myself believe that we will be running forever."

"That's not what I mean. Even if...when we get back, it won't be the same. You're sixteen, not seven or eight. People get older, that changes everything. Arlo saw you as a grown-up, not a little girl."

"Arlo doesn't matter. He's a deviant. We left the farm when we were still kids, I feel like part of our childhood was taken away, and I want it back someday," I demanded.

"We can't climb trees and run around the orchard. You were thirteen when you left, I was sixteen, we were kids. Wild kids. You're older than lots of girls getting married. Remember when Prajna told us we were being trained to 'help make the world go around'?"

"Yes," I answered sounding baffled, not really knowing where he was going with this. He spilled out his theory. "Felix would have given you to Arlo as a partner or sold you to some wealthy dignitary. We wouldn't have ever seen each other again. You're a woman now, Felix will do what he wants with you."

"Do you mean, he would have *made* me be Arlo's partner? I wouldn't accept that, I wouldn't go."

"Theorie, since when has Felix ever asked you if you wanted to do what he says? He doesn't give his associates a choice. We obey or be eliminated. He trades, sells, steals, and maneuvers people. He has operations all over the world. His hand is in everything. What he has been teaching us, is how to be his pawns. We steal for him, we make mysterious drop-offs or pickups. We're never allowed to look at what we're delivering. It all makes sense now. He has some control over people, like a blackmailer. It's not just threats either."

I had no response and looked like a dope because he had to continue to explain it. I understood his words, just not believing that we were a part of such a complex operation.

"We're thieves. We take from the rich to make the world go around, to balance it," I said, confused. "But, if it's assassinations too...Do you think that's what all of this has been leading up to?" I asked.

"Stealing is only a fraction of what he has done. We only just started our training. It's only been two and a half years. But he is growing us, molding us to be so much more than just thieves. I think we were only assigned what Felix was certain we could accomplish. He only gave us what he knew we could handle. He is too controlled and orchestrated to have us debauch a mission or jeopardize The Jailer's Way. I think everything...even when we were children, was all part of this training."

"The languages, the cultures we had to study. All of it prepped us for this phase of our training?" I pondered out loud. "My dad...was a part of this?"

"I don't know...maybe." Jace acknowledged. "Remember the drop off in the hospital, the day Arlo and I fought?"

I nodded yes.

"The news two days ago said there was a mysterious breakout of Legionnaires disease. It killed fourteen patients and sickened dozens more, at the very same hospital. Children died Theorie...Children! We leave manila envelopes and packages in random spots, and we never ask why. Then something will be in the news that is somehow connected to those deliveries. It's happened too many times to be a coincidence. I've tried to see if I could get any information from Yuri, and he tells me that Felix meets with diplomats and dignitaries from all over the world. He is the only waiter allowed to serve them. He isn't allowed to talk about it though. Isn't that strange to you?"

"Yes, but I don't understand Jace, stealing was all to make Felix rich. Why would he want to kill people? Like the Prime Minister's grandchild? Why would his death benefit Felix? Is it really so much more than money?"

"If I had gone through with the assassination of that boy it would trigger a global response. It could start civil wars or worse. Who's to know who Felix would plant as the perpetrator. It would be blamed on someone, some country would be accused, and there would be a reaction. When tragedy hits, people band together and want revenge. I don't know how many other people Felix has in place, but I know we are not the only ones. He has a network, and people are afraid of him."

"But why us? Why does Felix believe he can maneuver the world like that? Are you telling me you think he is playing God?"

"He thinks he is," Jace answered. "When Yuri gave me the envelope, and I read what my assignment was it all made sense. Yuri doesn't trust Felix, but he is afraid of him. He told me he was afraid for his family and that I shouldn't ask questions. I asked him why he was so scared, and did you know what he said?"

"What?" I begged, even though I was terrified of the answer.

"The chemical plant," Jace stated.

"What chemical plant?" I was so confused. "Yuri's afraid of a chemical plant?"

Jace rubbed his eyes trying to compose his words and explain to me the significance of this factory. "When we were just little, there was a factory near Mumbai, that was surrounded by slums. Poor families living on nothing, and starving. They were looked down on as nothing but a burden to the economy.

The plant had five safety measures in place which included reserve tanks that could be filled with the poisonous liquids in case the main tanks ever malfunctioned or leaked. The workers realized that Methyl was leaking into the facility and into the neighboring area, they started to utilize the safety tanks to transport the Methyl and repair the leak.

The warning system *mysteriously* failed, next the loudspeaker that would have alarmed the neighboring community failed. Two other safety measures shut off and malfunctioned. They couldn't contain the gases. In Minutes 4,000 people living immediately around the factory, as well as the workers within the building were suffocated by the invisible gas. They died such horrible deaths. Children with burning eyes. Their mouths foamed, and they vomited because their lungs burned and blistered so badly. People didn't even know what was happening, and within minutes they burned from the inside out and died.

The ones living slightly further away suffered even more because their death was not as quick. They suffered burned eyes, and lungs, and as they gasped for air, chemical burns crawled up their legs and arms melting and blistering their skin. More than 20,000 people died in the following months, and to this day India is plagued with cancers and birth defects from the incident."

I felt my heart pounding beneath my chest. I could almost feel the tightness as I imagined the pain those poor people went through. I imagined the mothers as they watched their children gasp for air and their eyes swell with poison, not knowing why it was happening or what to do to help them. My head nodded no, in disbelief and I tried to halt the image I drew in my head.

"No No No, please stop! I don't want to imagine this happening." My throat tightened, and I swallowed hard trying to hold it together.

"They never found out how the reserve tanks got water in them. There are many theories including sabotage, but it could never be proven. To this day it's considered to be the world's worst industrial accident. It triggered an industrial crisis and the entire government suffered. Entire family lines were obliterated."

"Felix?" I could barely finish my sentence. "Felix does away with weak people," I finally stuttered.

"Felix judges, manipulates and maintains population control," Jace exposed. "For whatever reason, he needed to demolish the Indian population and economy. I think there are many other things in history that if we investigated, Felix would have some part of. I believe Yuri, and I think he was warning me."

As horrible as the thought was, I knew Jace was right. I remembered the genocides in more recent years. So many lives were lost, in such a short amount of time because hatred was stirred up. Anger led to people killing one another in the most horrific ways. I wanted to know what else Felix destroyed, what else did he stir up and throw into his cauldron?

A fierce desire for justice was traveling up my body. If he was capable of these things, and he wanted us to be a part of it, I was going to fight. There was no way I would be associated with that murderer. A putrid feeling tightened my throat. It was hate. I hated Felix so intensely I would have killed him if I could. He had to be stopped. What right did he have to play a merciless God? What right did he have to decide who would live and who would die? He didn't see people as we did, as my father had taught us. He didn't see the beauty in the human race as a whole. He measured the value of life on race, money, status, and power. His backward perception of people made me want to throw up. Why did he see himself as so superior, so entitled? I must have been huffing like a fire breathing dragon because Jace had to grip my thoughts again.

"Theorie!" he snapped at me, startling me. I had already started to plan how I would kill Felix and was imagining scenarios.

"For some reason, you are a piece Felix needs to move right now. He told Yuri that Arlo would be coming to get you that afternoon, so to make sure you were in the hotel. Yuri wanted my assurance that I wouldn't cause trouble for his family and that I would cooperate.

"We have to stop him. We need to get away but how do we expose Felix? How do we destroy The Jailer's Way? I can't live with myself knowing he is killing innocent people and destroying entire cultures and communities."

"He has too much power and too many connections," Jace pondered. "People crumble under his threats. We have to have a plan, but it's impossible to map it out. I am not killing anyone! And you are not being given to Arlo or being anyone else's partner!" He got loud, but quickly remembered his surroundings and pulled himself closer to me, lowering his voice, "You can't be sent away, it would be…" his words trailed, and he took a deep breath catching his words.

I was afraid of Jace's thoughts and wouldn't allow myself to imagine where I would end up if Felix had his way and sent me to Arlo. He was not using me as a payment or a bargaining chip, I wouldn't allow him to use me like that.

"What is our plan? What do we do next?"

He explained his layout, "Tomorrow, we watch, we listen for which ship will get us closest to the US. Maybe not New York but as close as we can get. We wait until dark and board. We have to steal and lie, but it's the only way. We need to make it to America and go to the police, the FBI even. We tell them what we know, and we ask them to help us find Tobin in return. We can get different names, and hide, the three of us. We know how to be invisible." It was a plan full of uncertainty and what ifs.

"What if we can't find Tobin? They're not just going to believe a couple of people with a conspiracy theory about an international murdering mastermind. What proof do we have?" I asked.

"I don't' know. That's all I've got, but at least it's something. We just have to wait and see. One day at a time.

One step at a time. We will be patient and careful," his voice cracked with uncertainty.

"I always need to hurry up to the end of the story. I hate not knowing. I don't know anything anymore, I've just been mindlessly following orders, and people have died because of me. I tried to force you to be a fighter and nearly got you killed. I want this to be over, I want to find Tobin and be back on the farm with Rubin. It all changed so fast after Mahtap died. It drives my mind crazy. Why can't we just be normal? Like Allison Cade. She has everything, she has parents, and money, and freedom, and she's perfect to look at. How is it fair that she lives that life, and I live mine?"

"It is fair," he retorted. "It is because her story is not over, just like our story is not over. You think she has it all, but maybe you should look and see what you do have. It's not all horrible, is it? We've had so many adventures with your dad, and we were loved and taught by the kindest woman on earth. We were raised in Africa on a beautiful estate, and we had a pretty carefree childhood. And you are wrong, I *am* a fighter. When I need to be, for the right reasons." He paused and moved some boxes to make himself more comfortable as he yawned.

"I'm just saying, we've had a pretty exciting life. Allison spent her childhood in fancy boarding schools, with her whole life planned and decided for her. You might wish you had that kind of 'normal' but I know you, and you would not be satisfied. You have more than you realize." He leaned back nesting into the boxes using his backpack as a pillow.

"I don't know. I'd like to try normal for a while. Maybe a day or two. And I do appreciate what I have, I just don't say," I pouted. "I appreciate having you as a friend," I assured him.

"A friend," he mumbled as his adrenaline gave out and he passed out asleep. I reached to my side and took my boot off, tipping it upside down. My beads slid into my hand, and I tucked them into my palm and clenched them tightly. They really did look like bits of chewing gum. I fell asleep, feeling as secure as I possibly could that night. I was surrounded by shipbuilding equipment, in a strange country, running from a murderer, but it only took Jace's friendship and a few stones to remind me of who I was.

The sound of metal scraping metal shook us awake early the next morning. The warehouse doors screeched open rapidly. The sun was already up which meant we missed the opening announcements for the workers before dawn. The commotion was rushed this morning, something was off. The workers hustled in a panicked state and scurried around straightening boxes and cleaning off the large countertop with the computers. Even the janitors were sweeping in a nervous rush. We were solidified. I was hoping that we would not be seen as long as we didn't move. I tucked my hands tightly into my sides trying to make myself as small as possible.

We were suspended by the sound of barking dogs. They sounded vicious and alerting. Their bark was constant, aggressive, and getting closer. I peeked over the wall of boxes and saw two dogs being held tightly on leashes and pulling their trainers in our direction with a fierce determination.

The dogs pulled and inched closer and closer until their snouts were ruffling through the boxes right at our knees. Maybe they were drug sniffing dogs and we would be passed by.

The boxes protecting us began to rattle and be pushed aside. We sat helpless and exposed. Light filled our hideout and hands rushed in to grab us by the front of our shirts.

There was no explanation for how we had been caught so off guard. We had checked, and we were sure there were no surveillance cameras. We were confident we were not heard by the night guard who spent his evening watching a small TV in the back room. He had been blissfully oblivious to our hiding spot, and we were meticulous in our movements to keep hidden.

Black Italian leather shoes came into view. The feeling of utter helplessness was numbing. We could not move to the right or left, and our backs were pushed up against heavy unmovable boxes. I closed my eyes in disbelief that we had been found. The truth was crushing, and as we were held against the boxes by Felix's men, my legs gave out. Why help them by walking? I melted into the cement slab floor and became dead weight. Jace was more cooperative giving into his body being pushed towards the exit doors. It was then I realized why. We had guns aimed at us, ready to be triggered. Nico held my arms behind me, a second man held a gun to Jace's back, and a third man stood off to the side pointing a gun at the whole procession.

I dragged my legs and wiggled to break free from Nico's grip, so I could duck and try to swing at the brute when a force stopped me. Something had hit me, but I couldn't understand what was happening. Had Nico hit me? Had I hit my side on the corner of the shelving?

My mind was still in my escape plan, but my body wasn't cooperating. Why couldn't I walk? I felt a deep burning heat on my right side. It didn't hurt, it just felt like my body was hit by an invisible wall. I was paralyzed. I watched the ground below me become blurred and discolored. My feet tried to grip the floor, but my legs had no power.

Jace yelled and tried to break away but was stopped by the third man. I saw Jace trying desperately to come closer to me, but the room was spinning. My body felt so heavy, and the earth was pulling me down.

I woke up dizzy and blurred to the familiar smell of leather and cigars lingering in the upholstery of Felix's van. Nico held a gun towards Jace like a robot. A second man held the door open as Felix entered and sat in the passenger's seat in the front of the caravan. His leathery smell thickened as the door shut trapping us in his cage. Jace's hands had been bound behind him, and he stared at me with worry and panic.

"You're awake...Good," Felix stated, looking at me from the fold down mirror in the passenger seat. "The bullet went straight through. We will have you stitched up shortly."

My side throbbed from deep inside, and I awkwardly turned my head down and saw my blood-stained shirt. A warning for sure. If Felix had wanted me dead, I would have been killed point blank. I was shot as punishment for trying to escape and for being stupid enough to get caught.

Felix was silent for the rest of the van ride tormenting us with fear. As I regained the memory of the last half hour and my brain settled, the pain worsened, and I became sweatier and more anxious. The bullet went through, but it felt like it was still burning within me. A band of cloth had been tied around me to stop the bleeding. It was so tight it hindered my lungs from fully inflating, and blood was soaking through. Maybe I would bleed to death before we got back to Kolkata. I pressed hard onto my shirt to help limit my bleeding. Blood covered my fingers, and the pain of the injury snatched my breath from me, but I had to keep pressure on it. Jace watched me with an unbreaking eye, but I was so tired and confused from gaining consciousness and then blacking out in a loop, that I couldn't make eye contact with him.

I tried to piece together what had happened as a sinking feeling of loss fell over me. I realized I must have dropped my beads. I remember them being in my hand as I fell asleep, and in the rush of our capture hadn't seen where they had fallen. I hoped they fell between the shelves and would be safe. They were stones and beads of no actual value, but they were all I owned that were real, and I felt their loss deeper than it made sense to.

We reached the airport after a torturous half hour. Felix's plane was already running and ready to take off. We were pushed out of the van and lead to the plane. The sound of the blades and engine deafened us. The closer we got to the plane my hair whipped into my face, and it felt like tiny splinters. We were forcefully dragged into the aircraft and placed into the seats. I was able to brush the hair from my eyes only to see Arlo in the chair across from us. He looked smug and overconfident as usual. He had healed only slightly from the beating Jace gave him, and his jaw and cheekbone were looking bruised and swollen. I was placed in a chair that had been covered with plastic to keep my blood from staining Felix's precious plane.

Felix joined him and took the seat to his left. He sat, crossed his legs and placed his arms into the familiar position of resting his elbows on the armrest and folding his fingers together at his chin. He looked like he was contemplating over the way he would dismantle us, as he finally broke his silence.

"There is so much to tell you since you've been gone. So much has happened." His fake forced jolliness was maniacal and mischievous. "Yuri and his family received a better offer in Dubai, they have moved on...to a better place."

His cryptical pause made me confident that he definitely had killed Yuri. He had been punished for Jace and me running away, and uncle Rohit had not been able to help him. I pretended in my mind that he and his family were safe and together. He seemed like a good father and a kind man who had been caught up in the wrong job at the wrong time.

"We have big plans." Felix went on, "Since your failed mission in Delhi, we have since had to reassign certain positions within 'The Way.' To make the world go around in the way it has for centuries, we need to instigate a large scale of events. We are headed to our new mission right now. It will be a long flight so please relax. Prajna will stitch you up Theorie."

Felix snapped his fingers and Nico came to his side, pouring him a gin and tonic, dropping in a single green olive. He lit his cigar and sat back in a relaxed satisfied state. Felix loved holding our fate in suspense because it meant for the moment that he was back in control. So many uncertainties and ideas flooded my mind. The plane took off moments later. Nico laid my chair back, and Prajna appeared from the rear of the plane with a medical kit to mend me.

I was determined not to let them see me crumble in pain as the needle punctured through my raw wound. I would not allow them the satisfaction of seeing me writhe. After all,

I had been beaten and broken so many times before I could handle this. I focused on Jace's blue eyes and his grieving brow as the sting of antiseptic and the first stitch went in reconnecting my bleeding flesh. He was the last thing I saw as I felt the second stitch pierce and with a gasp of breath, all went black.

Chapter 8

"Rummaging in our Souls…"

"**R**ummaging in our souls we often dig up something that we ought to have lain there unnoticed." Tolstoy's words slapped me, I believed those words, I just wish it was easier for me to live by them. But, with Russia beneath us, I dug and scraped for any memories I had of traveling here with my father as a child.

The sun was shining, and whispering clouds looked like the wind was carrying a tune through them. The memories of traveling with my father here were not as warm as the ones in India. My father did not like Russia. He seemed to struggle with those trips from the moment his plane landed. He appeared in a hurry to complete his task and be off to another location. I was very young when he started taking Jace and me here, and we spoke Russian very well. Mostly our trips would include Saint Petersburg and Moscow.

My Father told me one time that he found no joy here. I didn't understand what he meant. We spent hours searching for people that would catch his eye. No one smiled here, smiling was reserved for family and those who you were closely associated with. For the most part, tourists were easily identifiable and overly enthusiastic about everything they saw, but the locals walked with a mission and ignored their surroundings. We would see the frustration in my father's face over the lack of a good story in this country. They were a people oppressed and afraid, severe, and stern, but my father insisted on returning several times a year to search for the person whose photo would show the world that the Russians were passionate, romantic, jovial and cynical. He knew there was more to them than the icy glares they threw.

I had woken up in a frenzy, remembering the last twenty-four hours, but quickly realized I had nowhere to go, we were defeated, sunk. My shock and fear of our capture were numb now and I looked out of the plane window trying to fight fear and despair. I had an IV line running to my arm and Prajna explained that the bullet had clipped my liver only slightly and gone straight through. My side throbbed, but the stitches felt better than a bleeding hole. Felix was across from myself smoking his cigar and swirling gin around in his glass without drinking it.

"How are you feeling, Miss Jailer?" Felix dryly inquired.

"Great! I have this look of pain and anguish on my face because I love having a bullet burst through my liver," I sneered back at him.

"Miss Jailer, you can choose to treat me like I am your enemy, or you can be agreeable and at least try to be pleasant. It would make your journey easier. I have watched you too long to believe a mere bullet could halt you entirely. I am not a stupid man, and I know that at the first chance you are given you will bolt. I needed to slow you down a bit, and bullets are very successful in that endeavor. I also knew that the task of elimination would be a challenge to you both, and your conscience would hinder you from following through.

131

You and James Taralock together are poison to me. I don't need you to have consciences, or to fight for each other. I need you to fight for The Jailer's Way, and understand its mission and the importance of helping the world go around." Felix sounded like he was purposely trying to be pathetic. "You need a little more time in my hands, to be molded and convinced that we work towards the good of all men. The world needs to be cleansed of the weak for human life to carry on and exist. Where would the world be now, how many mouths to feed, crops to grow, water to purify if certain events in history had gone any other way. One small act and human nature takes over and fixes the problem of too many weak."

His twisted, hateful mind saw no bad in what he did. He had no heart or human feelings. He killed without reason and justified it. I tried to stop rummaging through my mind digging up terrifying realities and hoping that I had nothing to do with them. I could not bear to accept that I hurt people. I rummaged through what I should have left alone in my mind and questioned every mission I had fulfilled for Felix. What had I done? I turned my eyes out the window towards the musical clouds and tried to drown his existence out.

"I am impressed. I have seen how you are strongest when James is in jeopardy. It's a side of you I admire. It's your strength," he admitted. Why couldn't he just shut up and stop talking to me, his voice was criminal, and his philosophy was poison. I hated hearing the hissing of his stupidity.

"But Miss Jailer our strengths can sometimes turn on us and become a weakness. I have brought you here to Russia to start your next series of tests. You will be brought to your weakest without your other half."

So he was separating us, and I would be handed over to Arlo. The plane landed, and we were politely invited by Felix to exit. Someone had put clean, unstained clothes on me, and bandaged my side tightly. I had a dark, loose sweatshirt and a pair of dark blue jeans on. Felix's men were near, with concealed weapons that made our escape impossible. It was over, we wouldn't get away now. I heard Jace behind me being maneuvered from the plane as well.

We were escorted to a parked SUV with the familiar blackened windows. I was starving for eye contact with Jace. As soon as he was in the van, I wanted to look in his eyes and try and read his thoughts and plans for escape. I wondered if he had a plan formed or if he was still feeling the despair and entrapment of the plane ride.

The air was crisp, and the smell of fresh snow was in the air. The blueish gray sky was depressing and felt like it would cave in on you at any moment. Cars flashed by splashing slush against the SUV. I was finally seated and waiting anxiously for Jace to sit beside me, but the door was slammed, and through the dark glass I could see Jace struggling as he was led down the street and put into the back of a black van. My dazed state made my mind jump and clamber for clues, license plate numbers, the surroundings, anything that would expose where they were bringing him. I hadn't expected Felix to separate us so quickly. Why hadn't I thought five steps ahead? Even two steps would have been helpful. Felix was sitting in the passenger seat of the SUV. He had sensed my panic and was eager to expose me.

"Miss Jailer. You cannot depend on another for your strength, that in itself is a weakness. Blood is thicker than water, and your Jailer DNA will overcome the weakness that your heart feels for that boy. You have much potential, and you're smart. You will see why you must be separated. You must have known you would not stay together forever. I cannot have 'pairs' of agents work together. Loyalty, sympathy, pity...and love, are all weaknesses. You worked together long enough to bring out your strengths and weaknesses, and now that I have a clear picture, you no longer need each other. Don't fight it. The quicker you submit, the easier it will be."

I wanted to fight, scream and tear my way free. Felix knew that, and that is why I had to be shot, and Jace was bound merely with zip ties. I had every intention of fighting to the death, but the pain in my side stopped me in my tracks and reminded me that I was still alive and just beyond my reach being driven away, was my reason to live. I couldn't push away what was happening. I would rummage and dig up whatever I could and plan. I would find a way to escape and find Jace. I would find a way to kill Felix and destroy The Jailer's Way, ...as soon as my body healed and caught up to my brain.

Each morning for the next two weeks, I was escorted from my prisonous Saint Petersburg hotel room by Nico and brought to Felix's lair two floors above me. I sat in a chair with a small table in front of me. The lights were always dim, and my wrists were bound and hooked onto a latch bolted to the table. My exposed wrists were forced upwards displaying my mysterious tattoo of symbols. I clenched my fists, knowing what was coming next. Felix pulled up his chair opposite me.

"Good morning Miss Jailer, let's see what progress we can make today." The sweet smell of Felix's cigar clouded the table and tightened my lungs.

"Your father..." Felix continued, "A memory...Where? Where did he take you? Come on now, you know how this works. Think...a *simple* memory..."

I looked into his eyes. Felix was coldblooded, like a venomous snake, and you would expect him to have soulless indifferent eyes, but they were not. They were warm umber with a twinge of caramel. His distinguished brow also hinted of congeniality. His face was so hard to understand. He repeated his request.

"A memory Theorie Jailer...Your father..." He was looking at me with his forehead raised in expected anticipation. "So far...let us review..." He pulled a small black leather notebook from his interior suit pocket and held his cigar in his right hand as he turned the pages.

"We have...Kolkata, Mumbai, Delhi, Egypt, Morocco, Ireland, France, Canada, Brazil, England, Italy...These are common knowledge, I could have gotten this information from flight records. Where did he take you and Mr. Taralock that I do *not* know about?"

I was silent because I honestly had no idea what he wanted from me. He knew everywhere I had been. So I began making things up. I would convince myself that I had been places that I had never visited. In the evenings as I tried to fight sleep, I closed my eyes and imagined streets, sounds, people, and smells. Details, and simple memories created out of nothing.

In the morning, as I sat strapped to a table, I would claim with impassiveness a real believable travel adventure. It was enough to convince Felix for the day, and he would release me and send me on my assignment.

"Berlin, Germany," was today's apathetic answer.

Whether he believed me or not, I knew what would happen next. He would nod his head, and take his pen from his lapel, jotting the location down in his journal. He would place the pen and notebook back into his suit coat, and puff deeply on his cigar, stoking the end and brewing the heat.

In the next moment, he would look into my eyes, and stare down my fear as he maliciously pressed the fiery coal onto my wrist, directly parallel and slightly overlapping my tattooed markings. Today's branding made four times he had punished me. My wrists pulsed and stung but I didn't break his gaze or satisfy his hunger for control by flinching.

After the first two weeks, I was not brought to Felix any more. I knew he wanted to know about my father. I knew that he didn't trust him. I knew Felix needed to understand what my tattoo meant, and why I had been marked. I was alive just in case I was needed or of use to him someday in his neurotic search for the answer. Perhaps I was alive because by blood I bore the name Jailer? My father and our trips around the world were a threat to Felix, and I knew that he would haunt me from now on, until he solved the mystery of me.

For the next year, my days were filled with assignments throughout Russia. Simple assignments, and only what Felix knew I was capable of accomplishing. Felix knew that I was hunting for a way to escape. My room was stripped of the phone, television, microwave, and anything else Felix deemed too much comfort for his prisoner.

Felix did not allow me to eat in the hotel dining room and kept me in a small single room at the Lourdes Hotel in Saint Petersburg. I was not allowed to explore as I was in India, and when I refused an assignment or purposely misplaced a delivery, I would be punished by being left to starve in my room for several days, until I complied and moved along with the mission. Many nights my stomach rumbled and throbbed begging for nourishment.

In Kolkata, when I disobeyed my orders, my human companionship was held from me. Now I was alone, with no humans to talk to, so all Felix could punish me with was depriving me of basic necessities. My bedding would be stripped. The heat would be turned off in my room, and I had to sleep exposed, shivering to the cold Saint Petersburg winter.

Nico was left in charge of my care and would drive me here and there on supervised missions. I studied him and without a word from his mouth, I could tell he was his most comfortable among the streets in Moscow. He would not speak to me, but I would talk to him about Jace, and Tobin, and Africa. He didn't respond and acted like he was alone in the van, but I didn't care, I just kept on talking out loud. I wanted him to see me as a human.

I spoke of Tobin and how kind and gentle he was. I told Nico how much more of a heart Tobin had than me, and I spoke of his cackling laugh that I missed so much. I told him that even though he was my twin brother, I always felt like I had to protect him and make sure people treated him fairly and with kindness. I told Nico how Tobin had been taken away by Felix and sent to a school in New York. I chatted on about the fun we had as children on our farm in Africa.

I knew Nico must have family or some connection in Moscow or Saint Petersburg because many times I saw him leave after I was locked in my room for the night. He felt free enough to adventure from the hotel, leaving behind his assistant to keep me captive.

I changed that year, in that way Felix was right. I became angry and pushed aside emotion. I would not smile, which was typical in Russia and not questioned at all. When I was in my hotel, my thoughts would drift to planning an escape. I knew I was asking for trouble planning and plotting, but I was careful. I came up with ideas as I sat and read through book after book. History books, geography, fiction, nonfiction. Nico would bring me books from the library in Saint Petersburg which was not far from my hotel prison. Felix approved of this one leisure because he didn't see any harm in reading about events in history. It helped pass the lonely days that I was captive in my room.

It was in these history books I first started to piece together my identity. I was reading one of the many books Nico brought on the Romanov's. I happened to read a section on Rasputin and his effect on the royal family. I learned of his infiltrating the family under the disguise of a healer to the young heir Alexei who suffered from Hemophilia. Rasputin reminded me of Felix. He was placed there in that family as a vice, as someone who would cause upheaval and damage socially. In the end, it was blamed extensively on this relationship that brought down the monarchy, resulting in the tragic, unnecessary deaths of the royal family. This subject fascinated me, and I devoured my study of it. I should have left it alone, but it hit a chord with me, and I dug deeper.

I found in my reading, diaries of Olga Romanov that shed light on the relationship the family had with Rasputin. I found different commentaries on why this man was allowed to be so close to the royal children. One word stood out. "Linchpin." This word repeated in my mind and left me buzzing for more information. How could one man take down an entire monarchy?

When placed ingeniously among naive, innocent people, at specific times, all it takes is one linchpin...One Rasputin. It made sense who Felix was when seeing him in this way. Understanding this mystical man Rasputin, who weaved through the Russian Monarchy at the beginning of the century helped me figure Felix out and understand his mindset. I saw him not as the God he promoted himself as...but as a man. A man with connections, and a domino line up of assistants. Still...he was just a human man, and I refused to be frightened and manipulated by him.

Felix was pleased with my successful jobs. I heisted what he assigned, and delivered what was given to me, all while remaining anonymous and invisible. He saw me grow and change into an adult and expressed his wisdom in giving me a second chance. My hatred for The Jailer's Way grew with every mission, as my conscience chipped away, and I became numb. I often botched missions intentionally, if I had any suspicion that it would directly kill a human being. I knew Felix saw this and was keeping track of what I was failing at.

Several times I believed my actions were directly related to the banks and money flow of Russia. Several communities were taken down, and many factories closed their doors. I justified it in my mind, unless I followed orders, I would never be free.

People were suffering, families were desperate for aid, there were no jobs. The suicide rate was up, blamed on the economy. It bothered me deeply to think I had been the linchpin that added to the stress of the economy. I mechanically obeyed Felix and his commands. I used the training I had received in India to prove every day that I was progressing as the next Rasputin...The next linchpin.

I balanced my need for food with my need to sense my moral compass again. Felix knew he was breaking me, and he wanted me to feel every bit of bitterness growing in my heart. I put on blinders and kept going.

Arlo was occasionally involved in my lessons on combat. Whether or not I defeated him didn't change the pleased arrogant smile on his disgusting face. He made comments on what we could have been, or what his plans were for the future, but I would turn my attention and refuse to give him acknowledgment. It was his fault Jace was gone, and I hated him with a burning sourness. I was stuck in my situation, and this was my life now. Battling Arlo in strength training was a relief of frustration and anger, and I enjoyed taking the first swing and beating his arrogant face into a bloody pulp.

He competed with me in combat, and target practice. He flirted and tried to flatter me, even pushing me into awkward corners trying to Lord over me and make me fear him. I would not cower and let him intimidate me though.

"The only reason I don't just make you my partner is because Felix forbids it. He doesn't like his people to have relationships, it weakens his force," he threatened.

"And the only reason I don't turn my weapon on you and blow your face off is because it would mean I don't get dinner," I replied spewing hate from my eyes.

It was during this time I searched my room for anything I could use to make a weapon or means of defense for myself. I was limited. I was not even allowed to have a razor. No phone, television, nothing. My room was stripped of all comforts and basic amenities. Felix was suspicious of me, and I was watched closely.

I did manage to make something. It was tiny, and probably couldn't even injure a squirrel, but it was something.

I didn't know when I would need it, but it was small enough to dismantle and conceal in the batting of my pillow.

I had used the plastic cap to a bottle, and two 5-inch pieces of metal I had snapped from the lining of the drapes. I managed to swipe a sturdy rubber band and fastened a miniature crossbow of sorts. I unscrewed several screws from the metal bed frame and kept them as ammo. It was tiny and almost ridiculous looking, but I had nothing else.

Each day it became slightly easier to shut my feelings off and push away memories of my father, Gideon, Joseph, and Emma. I even pushed away Tobin. The memories refusing to leave me were of Mahtap, and of Jace.

Dreams haunted me. I hated sleeping. I would wake myself up from my dream where I was back lying under the acacia tree having a picnic, or the repeating dream of Jace walking slightly in front of me on the way to Mahtap's cottage. Many times I would see Mahtap's smile and her eyes, one black like ink, one milky gray. She would be smiling, and a moment later her mouth would distort into an angry disapproving grin, and she would push me away and shun me. I would wake up screaming in pain. My chest hurt, and my heart panicked and raced.

My combat skills were put to the test against an opponent other than Arlo, when a mission caught me off guard, and triggered a fight or flight response in me. I had crawled through the HVAC system of the Marlina Theatre and had left a listening device in the dressing room of the Tenor, Kristov Sokolovich. I succeeded in ghosting my way into the room but was unexpectedly interrupted by a guard on my way out.

A dense man with deep, cold eyes, dead stared into mine. I read his face and knew that he would kill me without a second thought. He blunt force slammed me into the mirror, shattering it. I knew better than to underestimate his strength, so I allowed myself to be thrashed and beat so his inborn arrogance and morale would swell. He swung, and I would move in a split second to protect my face but allow him to still feel like he had hit me and was overtaking me.

Just as a smirk of narcissism creaked his mouth, and I was feeling weakened and tired, I retaliated with all my might, strength, and ingenuity. I released my built-up rage on this Russian guard. I had no time to allow my conscience to weaken me and allow me to check for a pulse. If I wanted to live, I needed to leave him incapacitated, and breathless. I battered and thrashed him, and used my smaller size to my advantage, until he was down, maybe for good. I had no time to allow my conscience to weaken me and allow me to check for a pulse. He lay on the dressing room floor with a broken jaw and the glass from the shattered mirror embedded into his cheek.

I became a ghost again as I left the theatre. This incident made a bitter taste fill my mouth any time I recalled it. An inhuman fierceness was buried deep inside of my Jailer veins, and it wasn't the last time it surfaced.

The day came however, that I had to turn my conscience back on and be courageous. I had to fight to keep my soul, and not sell it to the devil. I had to fight hating the people I saw living typical oblivious lives. I hated them because I was trapped, and they were not. I was in pain and lost and lonely, and the sight of friends playing in a park, or a couple having tea at a cafe burned like scalding borscht soup.

I had not planned on things changing so quickly again. It was September, and I was instructed to go to the library. I was fond of the assignment at first because there were some books I was interested in. I sat in a quiet corner and waited for a man in a brown suit. He was going to give me some flowers. I was to accept them, and pretend to be flattered, but leave hastily and out of the way of any cameras.

The table I sat at was safe, I knew the cameras were faced in the opposite direction. After ten minutes or so a scruffy man in his 40's approached. He had a brown tweed jacket and was sweating unnaturally. If he was to play the part of a nervous lover, he was nailing it. He skittishly sat across me and wiped his brow with his cuff and tried pathetically to make eye contact with me. He smiled nervously and handed me the red carnations. I accepted the flowers and remembered I had to be shy and hasty. I forced myself to kiss this stranger on the cheek.

"Spasiba," I thanked him. I would blush and look like a flattered girlfriend. I held the flowers close to my chest and hurried from the library. From there I was told to go back to my room, and the next phase of my mission would be explained.

In my hotel room I unwrapped the flowers and within the stems was a thin wooden tube, about four inches long and only as thick as a dime. I pulled the tiny cap off and pulled out a small paper with my instructions. In the tube was a glass vial. My heart sank. I knew it was poison, and I had held it clutched at my chest just moments earlier.

The mission was to break into an office in the early hours of the morning, before the sun was up. The office was owned by an insurance agency, and with gloves and a mask I was to cautiously cover the mouthpiece of two specific telephones with a swab of the poison. The Insurance agent as well as the phone used by his secretary. I was to deliver this poison at 3 am, so that by morning when the workday began, tragedy would strike the unknowing victims.

So far, my assignments had been theft, and deliveries that had only led to fraud charges, and various investigations. There *were* several assignments that got too close, and the weight of the outcome weighed heavy on my heart. I pushed them away every time they popped up in my mind.

I couldn't live with this reality though, and the assignment I held in my hand proved to push me over the edge. It was too direct and inexcusable. Clearly, Felix was driving me to the next level and was testing me. He was checking to see how much of my conscience and honor he had destroyed.

That was it. What would Jace think of me, and where he had been for the last year? Was he struggling with the same inner war, or was he dead? I needed to put into motion the plan I had been working on. I needed leverage to force Nico to tell me where Jace was.

I held in my hand military grade poison, and it was the only piece of control I had. Nico, my guard, was waiting to drive me as close to Moscow as was safe, and then I was to go on my own to complete the mission. I had this power in my grasp, and I was prepared to use it. Nico was a quiet man, reserved and protective of his true identity. I knew nothing of him other than when I first met him several years earlier on the night Jace and I were taken from Taralock estates that when he answered a simple question from Felix, there was a slight Russian accent. He had a connection here, and I needed to know who it was.

I knocked on my locked door, and my brute captor opened it. I didn't want to hurt him, but I knew I had to take advantage of his weakness. I put faith in my success in making him see me as a human.

"I'm ready," I stated.

The neurotoxin was safely in the wooden tube, capped and tucked into the gloves I needed to use to distribute it. As we made our way to the car, I searched for the most strategically placed street lamp, just in range, only about 4 feet above my head, and very close to Nico's car. I had one chance to create a distraction that seemed like an act of God. I could not be seen as the culprit.

From my jacket sleeve, I shimmied the miniature crossbow I had crafted from my hotel room treasures. I slid it down my wrist and placed the 3/4" screw into position. I knew it was a long shot, but I had to try. With my left hand I pulled the rubber band back as far as I could to make it fly, but with just enough leverage to be accurate. It worked! The tiny screw sped through the night sky and pinged the street light hitting the corner. A shard of glass shot off and shattered a section of the lamp creating a few sparks to fly.

Nico instinctively ducked, and I cowered behind him protecting myself from the assumed attack. In the confusion of the moment, I slipped my hand into his pocket and pulled out his cell phone. I slid it into my jacket sleeve.

Once Nico realized it was a blown light bulb and not active gunfire, he eased up and put me into the back of the car. As we pulled away and headed to Moscow, I searched through his recent call list. A certain number had been called frequently and within the last few hours. I memorized the digits and slid the phone with my foot under the driver's seat.

We continued the journey from Saint Petersburg to Moscow. I was not going to go through with my assignment. I would not be killing an innocent man and his secretary, and I knew I would be punished by Felix for being weak in his eyes. I would rather pour the vile of neurotoxin down my own throat.

I left Nico's car and made my way across the street. Nico would park and wait for me just in view of the insurance building that I was to leave the neurotoxin at. I turned down the side alley of the agency's building, but then quickly ran down the back of the building and went through the adjacent lot. I climbed two fences and went down one more dark path between the premises and made my way closer to Red Square. I found a payphone and dialed the number I had memorized from Nico's phone. A woman answered, and a young child could be heard whining in the background.

"Mama...Mama," It's sleep deprived cranky whine got more piercing.

"Is this Anna Petrovka?" I inquired in Russian.

"No this is Sophia; can I help you?" She sounded irritated, and I assumed I had woken her and her child up. The child in the background started to gripe louder demanding its mother's attention. She began to scold the child, "Roman. Stop! Go back to sleep!"

"I'm sorry, I have the wrong number." I hung up.

I had hoped to get one name, and now I had two. With two simple names, I had my leverage. I waited another half an hour and then returned to Nico's car.

"We can go, it's done," I assured him. As we pulled away to return to Saint Petersburg, I untucked the vile of neurotoxin.

"Sophia and Roman say hello," I said in perfect Russian, leaning into him closer.

He froze, his breathing stopped. I knew he had a weapon on him, so I watched his movements closely. He was cornered, and I knew he would react.

"I have a confession. I did not obey Felix tonight. I was supposed to place some of this neurotoxin on several surfaces of a certain office. But I went somewhere else. I went to a certain kitchen and placed just a drop on two surfaces that I'm sure will be of use in the early hours of the morning. Especially with a little one running around wanting breakfast."

It was time to use my training as a weapon, not against others but for myself. Every moment I breathed on Nico's sweating jawline, I grew bolder and more confident. I continued,

"I will tell you where the poison was laid if you bring me to Jace."

Nico could have turned on me, he could have driven the car off the nearest bridge, he could have seen through my lies and recognized that I was not really a threat and reported me to Felix, but he didn't. He was a man of size and strength, and only known as my captor, but his reaction to my threat proved to me that my ability to see through a person was on point. Nico folded quickly. He reached for something under the radio and for a second, I tensed. He pulled up a wired device.

"There are two of these in the car. I will erase them and put them back," he said, as he collected the tracking devices. In a gentle believable tone, he said in Russian,

"I know you did not plant the poison. If you could not obey Felix tonight, then you could not harm my family. I was not trained as a human weapon like you. I was given a job at a time when I was desperate. I've never agreed with his philosophies. I'll tell you where Jace is, but I will *not* take you to him. That is a death sentence for my family and me."

"Nico, do you believe that the weak should be destroyed? The poor, the old, the ill, the handicapped?" I asked.

"No. My brother was blinded as a boy falling from a tree. He is one of the strongest people I know. His weakness made him powerful, self-reliant, and brave. The world needs more people like my brother, people like you. If you are willing to fight for it."

"Why doesn't Felix just kill me for not following through with missions? Doesn't he see my conscience as a weakness?" I asked.

"Felix can't understand you. He knows there is a mystery behind those marks on your wrist, and he is obsessed with finding out who you really are. He keeps Jace as leverage on you. I overhear things, and I know Felix needs to keep you in his sights. He has many agents, but you are special for some reason. I am certain it has something to do with your parents."

Nico could have been lying to me. He could have been manipulating and plotting to turn me in to watch me die slowly at the hands of Felix, but inside I knew he wasn't.

"Jace is being kept in the Hanover, here in Moscow," he divulged. He pulled the car off the road and into a darkened empty parking lot.

"I can let you out here, you will have to walk the half mile back into Moscow. I will wait here for two hours before I call and alert Felix that you have escaped. It's all I can afford before he becomes suspicious and locks down the Hanover. Once in Moscow you go to see the man who owns the antique book store. Tell him that you are looking for a first edition copy of "The Count of Monte Cristo." He will help you get visa's and any other papers you need. You have to be quick, and you must leave right away."

"Thank you, Nico."

"One more thing. If Felix knows I let you escape, I am a dead man." He opened his door and got out. Opening my door, he asked me to step out.

"I need you to take my gun and shoot me," he stated pragmatically.

"What? No!"

"I put a bullet in your side at one time, I have it coming to me. A tooth for a tooth. It will buy you some more time. I can say I blacked out, and when I woke up, you had taken my phone, so I couldn't alert Felix, and I had to call when I could get to the next payphone." He searched his back pocket for his phone...

"It's under your seat," I admitted, looking at him apologetically.

"Nico, I can't shoot you."

"I'm a dead man if you don't." He handed me his pistol. I took the safety off, and in the darkness of the

149

parking lot, I aimed and shot my savior through his right shoulder.

My feet were tired, and I was so thirsty. It took an entire hour of walking and weaving through streets, but I finally made it to the back door of the Hanover. I knew the doors would be watched, so I ducked in with a crowd of delivery men bringing in the supplies for the mornings breakfast. They hustled to unload the crates of fresh eggs and cream.

As they communicated where to put things near the walk-in freezer, I methodically poured the bucket of cooking oil across the path of the entryway into the dining room. With one spark the flames rose, and people jumped into action to pull alarms as they tried to put the fire out. I flew by the crowd. Sprinklers were erupting, causing a huge commotion and distraction.

The voices rose and mingled together as urgent calls to evacuate were ringing out. They were getting the fire under control, but it had caused enough of an upset that sleepy-eyed pajama wearing guests flooded the lobby entrance wanting to know what had happened. No sign of Jace though. They had contained the fire too quick to justify a total evacuation, so my plan of having Jace run from the burning building had failed. Felix had to know I was here now.

One of the waiters called to an usher and assigned him the task of bringing tea to room 47 Specifically mentioning, "the Piano Player" had requested it.

That was it! I had to take the chance that the piano player was who I was looking for. I had nothing else to go on. Strategically avoiding camera angles, I made it to the fourth floor just as the usher stepped off the elevator. The housekeeper's master access card was an easy pinch since it was just clipped to her waist. She was stocking her cart for the day and didn't even notice me reach for it. I bumped her cart and spilled a bottle of cleaning fluid to distract her, apologized without looking in her eyes and continued to follow the usher around the corner. After several more newspaper and tea deliveries, room 47 opened its door, and my heart stopped.

It had been a year, and I knew my friend would be changed, but what stopped my heart was how he had not. It was the same man who had been torn from me the year earlier. He was in jeans and a dark green shirt, and just wearing socks. His hair was messy, and he seemed taller. I wished he would look my way as I peeked around the corner. How would he know that I was here? I knew I could not just go up to the door, anyone else could be inside, and I was sure Jace was under surveillance. He had no guard at the door though, which could mean his captor was in his room with him, or maybe Felix had turned Jace and was confident that he would not try to escape?

When all was clear, I took a chance and knocked on the door to the right of Jace's room. No answer. I slipped inside. It would have been too easy if there had been an adjoining door to Jace's room, but no such luck, and this room was clearly being used by a newly married couple who would be returning soon. They were probably in the lobby questioning whether or not to evacuate. I had to find a way to get Jace's attention quickly without anyone noticing. I ran through options but was coming up blank.

All of a sudden, my heart raced, and I froze in place. Someone knocked at the door in three distinct clearly timed taps. I had been caught despite how careful I was. I refused to open the door. If Felix wanted to catch me, he would have to break it down. A paper was slid under the door. I cautiously picked it up and pulled back towards the window. It was on hotel stationary and had no ink stain, just the imprint of words. I turned on the nightstand lamp and held the paper up to see the embossed message.

"Bakery, 3 blocks North, 1 hr."

It could be Felix trapping me, it could be Jace. Either way I had to get out of this hotel and find a place to think of my next move. I knew where Jace was, and if I had to burn down the hotel to get him out I would. For now though, I became invisible and escaped into the streets of Moscow.

I could not just walk into a trap and sit like a target at a bakery, so I waited outside in the alley of the Thai restaurant. Maybe it was Jace, and maybe he would turn me in to Felix, and it would be over. Felix would kill me in a minute if I were found. I decided to disregard the message and stay here at the alley of the Thai restaurant that was literally in the opposite direction from the bakery. I had relaxed against the brick and mortar wall. I was so tired that I started to drift off, when a figure curved around the corner and silently sat beside me. I straightened my posture and moved away instinctively.

It was Jace. He was wearing a dark gray hoodie and kept his head low. Neither of us could think of anything to say, and just sat there frozen in time. We didn't attempt to look at each other or even to move. The elation in my heart was bursting through, and I just wanted to hug my friend. I had missed him so much. It was all I could do to control my impulsive urge to grab him and hold him tight.

"Where were you?" he finally asked without looking at me.

"Saint Petersburg. I needed to know you were safe. You can turn me in now that I've seen you," I lamented.

"Turn you in? I've been waiting for you. I knew you would come. I knew it was you who set the fire downstairs, so I had a message sent that I knew you would understand. I saw you peeking around the corner down the hall when I opened my door."

"The piano player?" I acknowledged. "So it *was* you that left that note under the door of the room next to you?"

"Yes. I quickly kicked it under the door, so the cameras wouldn't catch me."

"How did you know to come here? It said to meet behind the bakery," I asked.

"Because I thought like you. You wouldn't obey and sit waiting to be caught at a bakery, and you didn't know who else was behind the door with me. You would go in the opposite direction. Plus, I know how much you really love Pad Thai."

"Jace, how are you not dead?"

"Felix was holding onto me to draw you out, and to test your loyalty. He knew you would look for me, he just didn't know when."

"I know. I am sure he knows I'm here. I know that he's done with me. I haven't given him the information he wants about my father."

"Your father? What did he want to know?" Jace asked.

I pulled back my sleeve and exposed my scars from the burn marks.

"He wanted to know what these meant, and where Dad had taken us? He thinks I know of other locations that Dad visited, but I don't, I don't know anything, and I disobeyed an order to kill someone. He will kill me now. I'm weak, *and* I rebelled. I can't stop him."

"What happened?" Jace asked referring to my cigar burned skin.

"I got hungry and started to eat my own arm...or it's cigar burns from Felix."

"That's bad, either way..." he teased back. He ran his finger over my tattoo and scar looking at the damage. It made me blush and pull my sleeve back down.

"I was worried that Felix had turned you into a follower and you would hand me over." I replied.

"That's not like you Theorie. You really think I would turn you in after everything we've been through? You're all I've thought about every day. I was so scared Felix killed you or gave you over to that pig Arlo. Arlo broke my leg last year after I tried to escape. I couldn't get away to help you. I felt useless. I've been held up in this stupid hotel as leverage just waiting for my execution." His voice became more frustrated.

He finally turned to look at me. In the light of the night sky, his eyes looked tired, but the smoky gray color transfixed me, and the familiar gaze refilled me with hope and life. He smiled at me with the corner of his mouth on one side creasing up. I remember that smile, I had missed it.

"You...ah... have changed," he said, watching me. It all of a sudden felt strange being with him. He was looking at me differently, but I couldn't help to look at him differently too. He was the same man but so much older. It had been a year but seemed like ten.

"I haven't at all changed. *You* have changed," I disagreed, "You need to shave, and your hair is darker. You're different, I don't know how though."

His smile changed bluntly, and sadness gripped his eyes. I was scared I hurt his feelings with what I said.

"I'm sorry, it's not a bad change," I apologized.

"No that's not it. I know it's none of my business but, were you handed over to Arlo? Did Arlo hurt you?" he choked out. I knew what he meant.

"No. I would have killed him first."

His smile returned. "I assume you have some kind of adventure planned for us?" he inquired, still smiling shyly.

"Well, I was thinking of going shopping for a first edition copy of The Count of Monte Cristo, and maybe some orange soda and waterproof luggage," I suggested.

"I still...walk into it every time," Jace remarked.

Chapter 9

Meghalaya

Our escape was unusually smooth, and with all we had dealt with to get to this point, it seemed unreal. Nico's help with securing ID's and visas was a life saver. We were able to pay a sizeable sum of stolen money in order to score believable new identities.

We knew that Felix would be watching for us to take flights out of any of the major Russian airports. So our plan was to get over the border into Kazakhstan. We switched transportation and snaked through streets and alleys. We got on and off buses to throw off any trace of ourselves. We had stolen enough money to take the train as far as the border. It would take a day and a half, but we needed the rest, and we were happy to be in each other's company again.

We slept in peace on the train, knowing we had each other to keep watch. I had missed the safety of Jace's friendship. He had been beaten and broken by Felix and made to feel useless and without purpose. Felix had tormented him with stories and lies of me and bragged about missions I had fulfilled and gave me credit for events that made Jace question if my heart had turned.

We talked about how to hide, and how to remain under the radar. With all my training in human nature though, it came to me by the second night on the train. Felix had an ultimate plan that he stands by no matter what the cost. He lives by The Jailer's Way of human manipulation. He always has a reason for everything...He let us go. He may not know *exactly* where we were going, but he would find us somehow.

We got off the train near the border at Troitsk, and had no problem crossing over. It was a small border crossing with nothing to welcome us into the country but a bus station and a small outside eatery. We got piping hot Baursaks at the eatery before boarding the bus and heading for the nearest airport. A flight to Nepal was easily booked and we were in the air leaving behind our past and hoping to make our way to New York to find my brother.

Nepal at night was busy. The streets were still lit, and people were headed to clubs and bars. We were getting more and more tired, but our adrenaline pushed us on as we journeyed through Nepal and headed into India. We used our skills as pick pockets to get money and food, and walked the streets blending in with the commotion of people.

We left the crowd and again jumped on and off busses, and cabs, eventually ditching transportation and walking along overflowing rivers and paths farther out of the city. We didn't want to chance staying in a rented room or hotel because we were still feeling anxious about Felix being on our tail.

As night fell and we were outside on the border of a jungle, I did wonder if we had just walked right into a death trap. The tree canopy darkened like a cave, and the sound of nocturnal beasts began scurrying and snapping branches in the black of night. The jungle was terrifying at night, but in a few moments, Jace took the lead, making us a shelter off the ground, between two sturdy trees. He used vines and thick branches to make an A-frame cot, sort of like a reclining hammock chair. We had nothing to tarp or cover it, but at least we could sleep off the ground away from snakes. I collected firewood and kindling, and before long the sparks whispered upwards through the thick forest roof, and the bugs took off for damper air. I stoked the fire and got it blaring to ward off curious tigers or leopards. We fell asleep tucked together, and with the serenity of sleep, I dismissed my fears of imminent death by jungle.

The morning woke us up. The sounds of the frogs barking and creatures prowling transformed into birds singing and monkeys screeching as they looked for breakfast. I woke up nuzzled into Jace's arm, grateful to be alive.

We started on our journey again and headed towards the nearest village where we got some food and caught a bus that took us down route 206 for about three hours. We walked the rest of the way towards Mawlynnong. It seemed like we were unable to relax and drop our guard, and there was no time at all to take in the sights or even acknowledge our surroundings. The whole escape was smooth, but anxiety driven and exhausting.

"Out of anything you could have right now, what would it be?" I asked Jace after three hours of walking. He looked right at my face dumbfounded, and unable to speak.

"What? It's an easy question. I want a shower with soap. And, I want to shave my legs and have clean clothes, *new* clothes." I reveled. "What would you want? Right now?"

"I don't know. Maybe a camel, so we didn't have to walk anymore," he laughed.

"We can at least get showers though, look…"

We had entered the tourist area of Mawlynnong. The welcoming sign was in several languages boasting that this was the "Cleanest Place on Earth," and "God's own true Garden." It invited people to stay in their village and drink their spring water. Nothing sounded better in the whole world. It started raining heavily, and we hid under the thatch roof of the tourist center looking over the brochures.

"You need place?" A tiny copper man spoke in broken English. He was an older local man with only one tooth dangling over his bottom lip. Two little boys about seven or eight years old accompanied him and helped him walk with his crutch.

"My daughter owns nice huts for travelers. Very reasonable." He handed me a professional looking brochure boasting of clean huts and showers, hot meals and tours for visitors. It sounded terrific, and we were both so tired from a night in the jungle and walking that we followed him to his cart and let his donkey pull us down the path onto a winding road. It became more and more muddy with every step, and it seemed impossible for people to live and survive this far into the jungle. We lost all sense of suspicion because we needed help, and in reality...Who would follow us out here?

We arrived at a thriving village with thatched roofs and pristine walkways. Flowers lined the fences, and women with babies strapped to their sides smiled at us as they swept puddles. The air was crisp and fresh and as the rain subsided the sun beamed through the tree line creating a fairytale scene. It was a beautiful place, unlike any we had seen before. The trees were so healthy and green with a variety of ivy and moss climbing through the rope branches.

There was a magnificent living root bridge made entirely by the twisting of limbs and vines that entangled together, and a breathtaking view of Bangladesh Valley known as the Sky Walk. The sounds of birds and monkeys chirped in the trees. People were smiling and nodding to say hello. Men with bright red stained teeth from betel nut smiled huge grins, welcoming us. Tea shops and souvenir stands lined the streets boasting of the best betel nut, and richest tea flavors. We both liked it here. The atmosphere was musical and relaxed.

The village was run by the matriarchs. Possessions, and the land was handed down through daughters. It was executed in perfect order and grace, making it a popular destination for tourists. It would be an excellent place to stay for a while to collect our plan and get some rest. There were about 250 villagers, and they spoke mostly Khasi, but also English and Hindi. We didn't speak Khasi, but we were quick learners and eager to fit in and understand these people and their ways.

We were brought to a small hut with posters listing all the rules of the village. Many laws were on keeping this destiny clean and unblemished. Our driver's middle-aged daughter, Bindi, stepped out and welcomed us at first with a smile, but seeing how filthy we were, changed her face and soon looked as if she had swallowed a rotting fish. She would not show us our lodgings until we were shown the showers.

Beautiful, clean tiled walls surrounded the shower with hibiscus and other perfectly manicured flowers cascading over the tops. Each stall had a teak bench with fresh clothes laid out, and a woven basket holding items a lady would need, including a razor. In all my years of life until that point, a shower had never felt so good.

After we were clean, we got a hot meal of pork and chilis with dal and rice from the village restaurant. It was a tropical style eatery, with open aired sides tucked into the brush of the forest. The bar and tables were filled with excited tourists. Bindi owned and ran the restaurant with the help of mostly her young daughter, and father.

Bindi, the owner, was a petite woman in her forties. She had a tight round face with several dark moles speckling her bottom eyelids. Her Asian features were tiny and sharp. She did not mess around, and was always in a hurry, scurrying about.

Jace and I, along with the other guests were shown our rooms. Many people were there for hikes and tours. Many were there for honeymoons or anniversaries. Our homestay was located only about two hundred feet from the open-air restaurant and bar. It had a clay fire pot and chimney, a mosquito net over the bed, clean linens and a basket with local fruits and treats. There were an electric hot plate, tea kettle, and a miniature sink basin making up a small kitchenette.

Bindi did not understand Jace when he asked for two separate homestays. She laughed and threw up her hands, walking away.

"Wait," Jace protested. "There are *no* other cottages?"

"It's fine Jace, it doesn't matter, this is fine, and they're so nice here. Don't make her mad," I pleaded. He looked nervous and uncertain.

"What's the matter with you? We got exactly what we were asking for. You got your camel...sort of, to pull you to the village. I got my shower and clean clothes. I love it here," I admitted as I looked over the homestay and settled in. He made a fire in the clay stove and laid on the floor.

"You can't sleep on the floor," I complained. "What if there are ants or scorpions? What's your problem? We've slept in the same bed before. It's just me. I won't bite you, but the fire ants might if you stay down there." Jace sighed and climbed into bed next to me, turning his back to me.

"Not since we were kids," he grumbled.

"We were in a cot together just last night," I reminded him.

"It was more of a chair, and it was all we had."

"Well...So is this." I didn't know what his problem was, but for the first time in a long time, I felt clean and safe.

The next morning I could tell something was wrong with me. Jace was already up getting dressed, and I wanted to ask where he was going but I couldn't get the words out. I knew what I was saying in my head, "Where are you going?" However, what was audible to him was mumbled speech. Jace quickly realized something was seriously wrong with me and came to my side, feeling my forehead.

"You're on fire." I heard the panic in his voice but couldn't understand what was happening. He left, and I was scared. Why did he leave me? I couldn't move or see clearly. The walls seemed to be floating behind water. Was I in pain? Yes, my head. I felt a pain creeping up in my skull like an arrow had pierced my temple. I grabbed for the back of my head and at the base of my neck and skull. A deep penetrating throb shot through my head. Whatever was happening was going to kill me, and I just wanted Jace to come back to be with me. I tried to scream for him, but I had no power. The pain stopped me in my tracks and grabbed hold of my brain. I knew it was bad, and I just wanted to sleep. If only this pain would leave my head. Sleep won, and the next thing I knew I was listening to the sound of a strong thunderstorm overhead when the lights went out.

"Jace!" I screamed throwing the blanket off me. I was still in our rented hut, but I was attached to a tube and wanted to be free from it. I started to pull out the tubes when Jace sat beside me, grabbed my wrists and held me tight to his chest. I fought it until I realized who it was and that I was safe. Jace held me until I settled and laid me back down gently.

"Theorie, You're sick. The doctor was here, the village called for him. I'm going to get him, don't move. I'll be right back."

He pulled away, and I felt scared. I wish someone would explain what was happening. My head was still pounding and piercing through my right eye like a spear was lodged in me. I was going to be sick. The doctor came in just in time to hand me the trash can to throw up in. I couldn't bend my head down far enough to reach the can and made a mess everywhere. Jace got a cloth and helped me clean up.

"I'm Dr. Tanabu. You are very sick with encephalitis. You've been sleeping for five days now, and we had to quarantine the area. Just as a precaution, but your husband here is not sick, so I'm quite sure whatever gave you this infection is not catching. We gave you fluids and antibiotics, also anti-malaria medication as a precaution. You're going to have to sleep and rest."

I was so confused. The Dr. gave instructions to Jace and said he would be back in a couple of hours. Jace sat on the bedside and helped prop me up a little.

"I have no strength. I'm so tired. What did he say? That man? Am I sick? Did he say I've been asleep for five days?"

"It's okay. You're going to be okay. It will be alright. I'm not going anywhere."

It would be another two weeks before the villagers were allowed to return, and I would gain enough strength to walk about the gardens. People looked at me like I had the plague, which technically was possible. The Dr. assured them that my sickness was isolated and most likely encephalitis brought on by a mosquito, but their superstitions had already set in.

Jace, however, was a hero to them. I woke up to a world where everyone knew his name and would greet him with smiles and nods. They brought him baskets of food and clothes. When I was at his side though, they ignored me and gave me nasty looks. Girls giggled and blushed as they walked by him. It was all so frustrating, and I was so mad I had gotten sick. I had ruined everything.

Jace took care of me and helped me regain my strength, which was taking longer than I wanted it to. I could walk but only for short times before becoming breathless and having to have him carry me back to the hut. I could talk but felt so confused on words, like the words in my head didn't match the ones coming out of my mouth. He was so patient with me though and didn't leave my side unless I was sleeping, and even then, would watch me closely. The headaches and dizziness persisted on and off for weeks. My frustration at how long it was taking for me to feel better was boiling. My stupid body was not cooperating as quickly as I wanted it to.

It was two months before I had the energy to join the village and travelers at the restaurant with Jace. The tourists new to the area didn't know my story and went on with their vacations, but the villagers and especially Bindi were uncomfortable with me. I tried to be friendly and thankful for all they had done, but she was angry with me for the two weeks quarantine and the scare I had given the village. People don't forget things like that. Jace assured me that they were kind and generous and because of their care and quick response I was alive, but I felt embarrassed and shunned. When I had nearly all my strength back, I walked to the stream where Bindi was washing linens, and I offered to help.

"You have a curse on you. I do not want your help," she snarled.

"What do you mean? Because I got sick?"

"You brought darkness here, and you destroy what you touch," she claimed.

"No harm was done," I defended myself. "We have paid you for your expense and lost money from the quarantine. Jace told me he compensated. I can't get anyone sick. Why does everyone hate me?"

"You came here filthy and diseased. The Doctor said you would die. You made your husband mourn you. He cried many nights and would not leave you. We tried to offer comfort, and we offered our daughter to take your place. You were to die, and she would be his wife. She formed an attachment to him and was happy. Then you get better. I say you are cursed. You have strange symbols on your arm. The village believes it is a symbol of heartache wherever you go." Her words were short and intense. She had so much dislike for me, her disgust spewed from her pores.

"My husband? And wait, you're upset with me because I didn't die?"

"Our daughter is heartsick, she was to be his wife, your spirit had already left, you had no voice, no movement, no thought," she yelled again.

"This is crazy. I don't see the point in speaking to you anymore."

I wasn't welcome and needed to be on my way. I packed up the clean clothes laid out for me and found Jace by the restaurant.

"I'm leaving!" I scowled.

"What? Wait! What happened? Wait!" He followed me to the root bridge. I was mad, and on a mission and didn't want to be bothered with. He stopped me at the bridge and caught my arm abruptly.

"What is happening?" he raised his voice.

"You were going to marry Bindi's daughter, and now she has an attachment to you? Everyone treats me like a villain because I lived. I'm just in the way, and you told them you were my husband. Everyone hates me, and now Bindi says I am cursed. So I am going! If I am cursed I have nothing else to lose, and I'm doomed anyway, so I'm going to stand on the top of a mountain and wait for Felix, or a lightning bolt to kill me!"

Jace looked at me puzzled and started laughing. It was so irritating I wanted to knock him into the stream below.

"Yes, I told them you were my wife. The doctor needed me to speak for you, to choose how to treat you, and I knew that it would be easier if I were your husband. And as far as marrying Bindi's daughter? She's Thirteen. I made it clear that it was not happening because you would recover, and she's THIRTEEN, but I will talk to Bindi," he laughed.

I hit his chest weakly and went back to the hut. I wish I had all my strength. That night, Bindi came to me to apologize and explain that Jace had talked to the family. They said they understood who his heart belongs to, but ended with a sharp,

"Even if she is cursed." She was wrong, about everything, I didn't have Jace's heart. He deserved better than me but arguing with her was like trying to catch a fly.

We were given a homestay to rent further into the forest closer to the Root Bridge. It was tucked away from the business of the restaurant area and tourist huts.

Jace and I could stay, and he would teach music and play with the little band for the tourists at the bar. Bindi offered me a job in the village school. I would be the English teacher. I hated English and asked if I could teach French or even Greek because I knew a little. But, it was English they wanted. So I was introduced as Mrs. Lock, and started work the following Tuesday.

The school was a large cement slab with a thatch roof and open sides. The wet season pounded down on the roof like a waterfall, and all my thirteen little students huddled underneath and chanted songs and rhymes about the English alphabet.

I enjoyed teaching. I loved the little students, and even though it was only three days a week, the rest of my days were filled with inventing ideas that would catch their attention and help them learn. The two other teachers instructed math and a combination of history and science.

Jace came over on Wednesdays to teach them how to read musical notes and about different instruments. There were steel drums and an electric Yamaha keyboard, a recorder, a ukulele, a violin, and a guitar. Jace shined the instruments up and even had the kids come up with musical inventions of their own. The children loved music and were the happiest on Wednesdays.

Our little friends ranged in age from five to ten years old. Their bright tawny faces with enormous smiles and shining eyes, eager to learn made me happy every day. In the late afternoon, I would stay and help the other two teachers reset the classroom and wipe down the wooden desks. Jace would meet me, and we would walk back to our homestay. The children would mock our footsteps and pretend to be Jace and I. They would scamper off barefoot to their huts, but only after I gave each of them a gumdrop.

We could place orders and have deliveries every three months, and we were paid a fair amount for our work. We spent all our extra money on treats for the children. I would get deliveries of gumdrops, and stickers and pencils and paper. There were many days I felt like forgetting everything that had brought us here. I wished we could stay forever and watch our little students grow. Every day was filled with games and songs and making new friends.

Most days I forgot that a dangerous criminal was after us and that I needed to find my twin brother. Most of the days we were normal. Our conversations transformed from plotting how to ruin Felix, to what child had been silly or naughty that day. Jace would listen to every detail, and I would listen to him practice the guitar or keyboard. He composed songs in his head, and I loved seeing his face light up as sounds clicked into place. His mind connected the musical notes, and only he could hear his beautiful chorus.

He wrote songs for the children and came up with fun projects to get the kids interested in music. He had ordered piano sheet music from America and perfected catchy popular songs. He would play them for the tourists in the evenings at Bindi's restaurant.

We stayed almost six months until the weather brought a change of season and made our internal clocks realize that it was time to go. We hadn't intended on staying so long, but my sickness and the overwhelming kindness of the villagers made us put off our hunt for freedom. We stayed two more weeks to refill our positions, but Bindi finally told us that the posts were being eliminated and the children had learned enough English. She abruptly told me I was no longer needed, and she was going to dismiss me anyway but affectionately said her goodbyes to Jace. I knew she was sad to see us go. Many of the villagers and students came to wish us well.

We had all our forged papers that we hoped would get us through the border and we passed with no trouble. It wasn't long before we were on a plane to New York.

After a long thirty-two-hour flight and sheer exhaustion, we arrived by cab at the doors of a Holiday Inn. Not fancy, but it was clean and comfortable. It had two queen beds and a much-appreciated private bathroom.

Jace made an appointment with a detective at the Federal Bureau of Investigation, on Federal Plaza, in the city. He used a false name, and we slept sound until the morning when we would finally talk to the police and make a deal. We wanted them to help us find Tobin and get out from under Felix's grip in exchange for all we knew about The Jailer's Way.

Chapter 10

Ol' Pal's & Linchpins

Diane Lecari was a strong-willed, big boned woman. Her hair was waist length, black and curly, tied in a ponytail hanging down her back. She wore a comfortably fitting pantsuit and a pair of black crocs. It was not exactly who we were expecting when we asked to speak to the head of the missing person's department of the FBI. She was gruff and no-nonsense. She did not live to impress, or please but to get the job done and to get some answers. I immediately liked her.

"Woohoo," she whistled as we sat down opposite her desk. Her office was painted Cerulean blue, and the clutter reflected the light slicing through the dusty mini blinds.
"Look at you two. I'm usually a good reader of people, but you two have me stumped. Why are you here? I'm not one for wasting time, and I'll be pissed off if you're here to sell me something."

"I'm looking for my brother," I said plainly.

She gave me a blank stare knowing that was not the whole story. "Let's start with your names."

We hadn't thought of that. Quickly we came up with a fumbled, "Sara, and Leo."

"Uh Huh," she said, knowing we were lying. We couldn't trust her yet though. "What is your brother's name?

And, his real name, a fake one like Sara and Leo isn't gonna help me find him."

"Tobin Jailer," Jace said blankly.

"Okay, that's a start. How long has he been missing?" She was moving her mouse around filling out info lines on her computer.

"He went missing in October almost four years ago, just before our 14th birthday. He is my twin brother. My parents were Rose and Morgan Jailer."

Diane Lecari stopped typing and looked over the top of her computer, staring right into my eyes. "Call me Wheezie on account of my asthma. We're going to be spending a lot of time together." My instinct was to get up and run, because I was reading on her face, that she knew exactly who we were, and we were busted, but Jace grabbed my wrist.

"There's no point in running. We have no one else to help us. It's this or nothing." He looked so solemnly into my eyes and my trust in him was enough to settle me back down in my chair.

"I need you to know something," Wheezie stated. "I know who you are, I know the name Jailer, I have for years. I investigated the death of your father, Morgan. It was deemed suspicious, but never proven as a homicide, it's a cold case now."

"Do you know anything about my brother?" I inquired. Again, her gaze startled me.

"One step at a time," she coolly replied.

"Are you going to turn us into Felix? Are you working for him?" I begged. "Just do it. I'm sick of the unknown, I don't care anymore."

"Felix who? Look, all I know is the case of your father's plane going down never seemed right. Your family's name is attached internationally to many unusual activities but can never be proven. I know of at least twenty-five cases here in the US, and I know that there are many overseas investigations we have been collaborating on. There is a department investigating the US side of incidents, but if this is as deep as I think it is, I feel it's wise to keep you two to myself for now, until I know more. Your brother Tobin, where did he go missing from?"

"Tanzania, Africa," I replied.

"What the crap were you doing in Tanzania?"

"We lived there, but we were told Tobin went to a school for the deaf here, in New York. He was born deaf."

"Okay. Excellent. I'll look into it, any other names he could have been enrolled under?"

"Not that I know of. Toby maybe. Sometimes we called him that," I remembered.

"And you?" Wheezie yelped, pointing at Jace. "What is your connection to this family?"

"Do you have an hour?" he answered.

Wheezie had coffees ordered up and took out a notebook and pencil. She sat back in her chair and listened to the tale of three little children being born in New York to a photographer father, and a demoralized mother. When caring for her children became too much, and Rose Jailer slipped into a deep depression, the three Jailer children were brought by their father to Tanzania Africa to live on a coffee plantation. Joseph and Emma Taralock would be their guardians.

Jace spoke of his farm driven father, and a cold, mysterious mother. He told her that our whole lives revolved around Mahtap and each other. He spoke of the trips to faraway places that Morgan Jailer would take him and I on, especially India, and Russia. He told her how my father taught us about the world, insisting we learn the culture and the language of the people, both literally and physically. It all seemed to have been for a reason, but there were still so many questions unanswered.

I was more reserved about dishing out all our life's secrets, but Wheezie knew just what questions to ask that made you *want* to tell her the truth. I even spoke of when I found out my mother had killed herself in her New York apartment after my father's plane went down. Emma had told me and my brothers very little, but it had always been tragic to me that she had suffered such depression, and that my father's death pushed her over the edge.

Finally we came to the fateful day we were taken away from the farm and carried away in an SUV. We divulged what we were trained in by Felix but held back details of certain drop-offs, so we would not implicate ourselves. We gave up all we knew of Felix. We detailed his appearance, mannerisms, and different cities he seemed to set up shop in.

Diane Lecari, or *Wheezie* sat writing ferociously. She occasionally went back to clarify certain statements. When there was no more to be told other than our experiences in Bangladesh and Meghalaya we stopped. Those were irrelevant because we had finally broken free from Felix and were on our own at that point. Besides I didn't want Wheezie to know that things were different now. I knew if I had spoken of my sickness, or how we stayed in the same homestay but were just friends, she would see through me.

I didn't want to give any sign that my feelings for Jace were more than friendship. I was fighting them, and I had to push them aside. They were ridiculous anyway, I was nearly eighteen, and he was twenty now. I knew we would find different paths soon, and as soon as we were at peace and Felix wasn't chasing us, he would not have such a hold on my heart.

Wheezie gave us her number, she didn't ask where we were staying, she said she didn't want to know. She did warn us to get out of the city though and to go somewhere quiet. The city was full of cameras and cops, and if Felix was looking for us, it would be too easy to find us here.

She said to call her in a week from a payphone, and she would look into it and let us know what she found. Before we left, she stopped us and once again asked if we had any form of proof to collaborate our story. Without thinking, I rolled up my sleeve and showed her a flash of my scarred tattooed marks.

"I was tattooed with this as a baby. I don't know why, and I don't know what the marks mean, but I am sure my father knew, and Felix is desperate to find out." I admitted. It caught her attention, and she froze for a moment.

"What is this scarring?" she inquired.

"Cigar burns," I replied without looking up at her.

She thanked us and reminded us to call her. We left unsure if what we had done was right or not. We didn't know if we could trust her, maybe she was calling Russia right now informing Felix of our whereabouts. Jace was not happy that I showed her my markings and was nervous about her reaction. He sensed that she knew what it was, or she had seen it before. We decided since it was us that had to call her, it could be from anywhere, so we got on a train and headed to upstate New York.

It was autumn, and the trees were in full color. We didn't talk much on the ride, we were too busy processing what was and wasn't said to the missing person's detective. The bus taking us upstate was packed with elderly leaf peepers and bird watchers. It smelled like bandages and Pepto Bismol. Overall our companions were amiable and assumed we were a young couple traveling to see the foliage. We played the part and felt pretty at ease.

"Your fella there is pretty nice to look at," chirped a tiny woman in her eighties across the aisle. She was leaning forward trying to catch Jace's gaze. He was drifting off to sleep though and was oblivious to his surroundings.

"Oh," I said, "He's not... Thank You." I quickly changed my response.

She grinned a plastic and resin smile and poked the belly of her partner who was snoring away.

"Been with this old goat for fifty-eight years." Her old goat snuffed and caught his breath scratching his tummy. She continued smiling until she fell asleep to the movement of the bus ride.

We rode several busses until we hit a little town called Whisper Falls at the base of the Adirondack mountains. It was tucked at the bottom of shale cliffs and tree-lined hills and mountainsides along the Erie Canal. It had clearly been a booming town in its day, and remnants of a once thriving population made the town look forgotten and passed by. It was such a beautiful spot, tucked among the hills, and you could tell hopeful locals waited patiently for Whisper Falls potential to once again be realized. There were large mills and brick factories with either broken or boarded up windows. The shops had "For Rent" signs taped to the windows along the Main street. A few local favorite shops had endured the economy and closed factories. The little town boasted a library, farmer's market, a one cinema movie theatre, and even a small hospital. It had a quaint family-owned hardware store, a Diner, and an antique shop with an above-shop Inn. All of the various town shops gave Whisper Falls an artsy, creative vibe.

Jace found us a room in the Inn above the antique shop called "Old Pal's." The old stone building overlooked the Erie canal and had the air of living a hundred years and seeing history pass by its hand-blown glass windows. The shops below smelled of basil and pine and felt like a well-hidden secret vacation spot. The antique shop had great coffee and a million books to peruse. We browsed the antique treasures throughout the shop. Tools, furniture, jewelry, and household trinkets. Each of the items for sale, had a story, a past, and they were still around on display as novelties and nostalgia. This place was fun and full of exciting plots.

For a week we walked and talked and pondered what the next few weeks would hold. It flew by in a blink, and I was nearly disillusioned again with the idea of being normal and forgetting why we were even in New York. We had to find Tobin, and to do that we had to call back Diane Lecari and find out if we had been turned in to Felix or see if she was someone we could trust after all.

Jace made the call from Old Pal's pay phone. It went to an answering machine. He didn't leave a number or message and hung up. Just a second later the payphone rang back, and Jace picked it up immediately.

"Is this Leo?" The voice on the other end was definitely Diane Lecari.

"Yes," he replied reluctantly.

"I'm only going to stay on this line for thirty seconds. I have info on the boy, a death certificate signed by your mother, two months after he was taken to the school in New York City. The cause of death was inconclusive. I Also found a photo of your girlfriend's father, it's VERY Interesting. Where do you want to meet me? I can be there on Saturday."

"Whisper Falls, I have an 'Old Pal' there," Jace answered. With that, Wheezie hung up. Jace hung up the phone looking like he had horrible news.

"What did she say?" I begged.

He pulled me outside, and we pretended to admire the bright yellow tree in the front by the gazebo. Families were enjoying ice cream and couples walked by not paying us any attention.

"Theorie," His eyes fell on me with so much compassion. He knew what he would tell me would hurt.

"We have to meet Wheezie here Saturday, she has a photo of your father that she said was of interest." He paused.

"That's it?" I questioned, "You scared me, your look, I thought…"

He cut me off, "Tobin is dead."

I had no response, I didn't feel anything in that moment. I had seen so much and been through so much that nothing surprised me anymore. Shouldn't I have that 'twin' connection, and have felt a piece of me leave my body when Tobin's life left him? But I did, the day that he was taken from the farm. I think I had known it all along and just hung on to the idea of seeing his floppy blonde hair again and seeing him skip over the hills as happy as could be. I felt lost in the moment and tried to harness exactly what emotion I was grappling with.

"If Tobin is gone what are we doing here? I asked. "I don't believe you. How did he die?"

"The certificate said 'Inconclusive.'" Jace's eyes filled with tears and he wiped them away with his jacket.

"It should have said…'Cause of death…The Jailer's Way.' Tobin couldn't possibly pose a threat to Felix. Why? When? Did Wheezie say anything about Felix? Has she found any proof of his crimes?" I inquired. My voice became more shaky thinking about the reality of my twin being gone.

"No, just the photo that she wants to show us. Wheezie said, Tobin died just two months after we were taken by Felix," he answered.

"Poor Tobin. He was just a kid." Sadness and anger welled up in me. "Felix can't get away with this. I can't think of anyone else on this earth that I hate as much as him."

"It also showed *who* signed the certificate and claimed his remains. It was my mother," he lamented, with a puzzled look of disgust and worry.

Saturday came, and we were anxious to meet up with Wheezie. Whisper Falls was buzzing with visitors. "We should find a safe place to watch, let's go to *her* instead of her finding *us,*" Jace suggested. We found a building across the street from Ol' Pal's that we broke into and watched from a window.

Around noon, a navy-blue sedan cut off another car that was waiting for a spot, ticking the other driver off and sounding off a horn war. So much for discreet. Wheezie pounded out of the car, slammed her door, and flipped off the elderly couple who were still waiting for her to move.

Wheezie didn't care. She walked to the coffee shop stand and after getting her order stomped back outside. We trailed after her a few minutes later, down a narrow alleyway between the antique shop and a second brick building.

She handed us an envelope while sipping her coffee. We examined the contents. Clearly signed by Emma Taralock, was a death certificate with Tobin's name on it.

Cause of death: Inconclusive.

"What does inconclusive mean?" I asked her.

"It means no one can agree on how the boy died. Too many opinions. Not a simple autopsy. But he was a young boy and was perfectly healthy, so it's inconclusive."

"But something killed him!" I snapped. "How hard is it to figure out what that was?"

"Harder than you think," she snapped back.

"Look at the photo," Wheezie proudly instructed. "I knew I'd seen those marks on your wrist before."

The photo was black and white. A group of men and women posed at a college on a field in the front of one of the buildings. The photo was slightly blurred from age, but it was apparent that it was a group of friends from their posture. I recognized my father right away, so did Jace.

"Look!" Jace exclaimed. "My mother!" Emma Taralock was standing next to my father wearing tight shorts, and a floral tank top. His arm was over her shoulders, and they looked familiar and cozy together. She was holding a flag with the college sports team, and a tattoo with similar marks as mine can be seen on her left wrist. They were so similar but were blurry and undefined. The same wrist we had grown up wondering about because it had a large scar at one time, had marks close to the ones I had on me right now.

"Can this be made any clearer?" I inquired.

"No," Wheezie answered. "Unfortunately that is the best we got. But, they are so similar to yours, I know it's not a coincidence."

"Do you really have no clue what they are?" she asked.

"No. I've had them for as long as I can remember though."

"Who else is in this picture?" Jace asked pointing to the three other people.

"This dark-haired man still remains a mystery. I am working on tracking him down, but I don't have much to go on. This blonde woman is Elizabeth something." The blonde looked familiar. She was slinky and tall with a trendy haircut.

The old man is Morgan's father, Theodore," Wheezie continued. "He was questioned a hundred times in connection with various incidents around the country."

"Incidents?" I asked.

"Yeah...thefts, deaths, and the sale pretty much of anything illegal. Your grandfather was a real creep," she exclaimed.

"I never met him...and Dad never mentioned him. Maybe that is where I got my name, from my grandfather, Theodore."

"Possibly. I can't explain any more here, but this case has intrigued me, and I love a good mystery. In a roundabout way, I'm going to inquire about the original case. I want to get to the bottom of this," she stated.

"The Jailer's Way," I blurted out. Jace grabbed my arm to hush me. "It doesn't matter Jace, if it's what we think, it *has* to be stopped somehow."

"The Way? What is that?" Wheezie implored.

"The Jailer's Way. It is a philosophy based on population control. Through history, things happen. They seem like accidents, but they are intentionally caused by linchpins placed all over the world. We were being trained as linchpins. We were told in the beginning that people have 'places' in the world and the weak should be eliminated. It's what Felix called 'Making the world go around,' or 'The Jailer's Way.'"

"Linchpins?" she remarked.

"Yes. They get assignments based on their skill level. They trigger events with seemingly insignificant, unseen actions. Small pins that tip over events that trigger further events, that trigger large scale events. Thefts, accidents, and sometimes assassinations, or, *eliminations of the weak* as Felix calls it. Either way...murder," I explained.

"So are you telling me I am standing in an alley behind an antique shop with two trained assassins?" She wasn't afraid, but more dazzled like a reporter catching a scoop.

"We didn't kill anyone directly, we wouldn't. We didn't ask for this." Jace became agitated and defensive.

I lowered my eyes, and Wheezie picked up on my avoidance. The shame on my face exposed that Jace may have a clear conscience, but the missions I fulfilled for Felix in Saint Petersburg were too often associated with loss of life, even when I didn't expect it to be. I knew I was indirectly responsible for the loss of lives, and I knew I could give Wheezie a list of names, that if investigated would expose me.

"Okay simmer down. I'm not arresting you. I think the marks on your wrist are significant and I want you to find a safe place to hide and spend the next week brainstorming on why. Why are you and loverboy's mother tattooed with these weird symbols?" I shot a quick glance at Jace to see his reaction to being called "Loverboy," but his face was expressionless.

"Why were you marked and not Jace, but both of you were groomed as linchpins? Why did you have to travel the world and learn a hundred languages while you were still in diapers crapping your pants? Why Africa? As a matter of fact, why India, and Russia predominantly? How can you find out more?"

"Finally!" I exclaimed. "Someone who wants answers, and I know how we can help. We need to go home," I resolved. "We need to go to the farm. Mahtap's letter said, 'When we break, we need to remember the stories and the music.' She said they were more than stories. Think about it Jace. All these years we've been away, how many times have we relied on her stories to help us? Even if the story was simple, it gave us enough hope to get through the day or flicked on our moral guide when we were falling. If Tobin is gone, we don't need to be in New York looking for him. The answers are at home. I'm going home," I insisted.

"I can have new ID's, and passports made up. So Jace, she's the one making all the decisions? Are you on board with that?"

"I'm not letting her go alone. She'll just barrel ahead and bust into my mother's bedroom demanding an explanation. We can write to Rubin, we trust him, he can meet us and get us into the farm secretly."

"Okay...You two baffle my mind. You're raised by an evil villain taking down entire nations but will walk right into danger to save the world."

"We weren't raised by Felix, Mahtap was our mother," I corrected her, "and I think she knew more than we realize. She protected us for years and helped us have a normal childhood because she knew we were being groomed for something, and I think she knew what these marks mean. We *can* just ask your mother, I don't know why we have to keep her out of this. She's got all the answers!" I blurted out.

"NO!" Jace cut the thought right out of my mind. "See...I told you," He looked at Wheezie. "My mother's absolute loyalty lies with Felix, or she would have fought to keep us. He has too much power over her. She can't know we are in Tanzania. We can't trust her or my father. Only Rubin."

"I can help you get a message to him that will not be traced. Tell me about Rubin... His ways, his job, his life. I will get a message there, and he will know what to do."

Wheezie's assurance was a relief. We had a good plan, and a lead, and we were going home. We would leave in two days on one of the US missionary planes. It was arranged, and no one but Detective Lecari/Wheezie and two trusted contacts knew we were coming.

Rubin had been sent a message to pick up some crates with a new coffee seed, a GMO from the United States. A program was devised to have fair trading between the United States and Tanzania to pass these coffee seeds to other nations, in exchange for authentic Tanzanian beans. If they cultivated the trees and produced, the coffee would be repurchased at premium prices. It was a testing ground for the rest of the world. It was a new program and just the right excuse to have a special delivery made to Taralock Estates.

We slipped in the cargo bay undetected and crouched under the canvas. Wheezie had made sure the plane was on its way, and that we wouldn't be disturbed for the nearly eighteen-hour flight. It sure was easier traveling and escaping when we had someone helping us.

"I'm happy to go home. I wish we could be on the farm again, working with the Maasai. I miss dancing around the bonfires and having fun. Don't you miss Bao? I love that game. It's been so long since I played. I wish it could be exactly the same as it was before." I pulled out a water bottle and settled next to Jace. The plane took off with ease, and in a few minutes, we settled in and set up our camp. We laid seed sacks out to sit on and ate some of the green apples from one of the crates.

"It can't ever be the same Theorie. Nothing is the same. We're not kids anymore. You'll be eighteen soon, I'm twenty. If this is all figured out and we don't end up killed by Felix or going to jail for what we did, then we will have to start a new life. We have to figure out who we are all over again."

"I don't feel different, I know a lot more, and I'm older, but I want to draw, reread my books, and lose myself in their pages, and I want to smell the coffee being roasted and take walks through the property. I won't even mind Emma, maybe she'll be nicer to me if we can help her get out of Felix's grip. I want it to be fun and happy again. It's been five years, not twenty. The farm couldn't have changed that much."

"Not the farm Theorie, you've changed. You say you haven't, but you were fourteen when you left home. You've had training unlike *normal* girls your age."

"Normal girls? I'm not normal?"

"No you're not," he said in an obvious tone. "Maybe when we get back, you'll find new interests. You say you want it to be the same as before and you'll be as playful and wild as you use to be, but you're seventeen, eighteen this month. Maybe you'll want to be more serious and grounded."

His words hurt me. He made it sound like I was a savage running wild through the fields as a child. I was pulled from my childhood at fourteen years old and made to see the reality of life and death at a rapid pace. Maybe I want to regress for a while and just run and play with the younger generation growing up in the fields with their Maasai parents.

"I don't want to be grounded, Jace. That sounds like Gideon. I'm not planning on knitting or baking bread all day, I can't, I'll go crazy. I need to feel some sense of the childhood I had, I don't want to go back home as a grown up. And...I wasn't a savage. I was just...busy."

"Theorie, I was just as wild as you, you know that. It's why we always had so much fun together. I knew we would have an adventure. I loved your imagination and your mischief. I don't think you should knit or bake bread all day. That's not what I mean. If you want to run around and play, then go right ahead."

"Than what are you talking about? I'm not going to go climbing trees like a monkey, I just want to feel young again." I couldn't hide the crack in my voice.

"I wish I was better with words. I am only saying that maybe you'll be more grounded and think more in the way of a typical seventeen-year-old. You haven't had a chance to catch your breath for five years now. Most seventeen-year-old women are thinking about boyfriends. I know right now it's still unsettled but maybe being home and figuring all this out will make you want to, you know…find a boyfriend."

"I told you a long time ago, men don't fall in love with girls like me. I'm not tame, you know that," I scoffed.

"Well, maybe you need someone who understands you and won't try to tame you."

"No man like that exists," I remarked.

"Really?" He said, unbelievably annoyed at me.

"Jace, I'm not going to change. I'm always going to want to travel. There will always be days I'm lost in a book or learning something new. I want to learn how to draw really well, or how to play an instrument, maybe I'll learn the violin...Or scuba diving. I have so many ideas and plans. Boys don't like that. I don't think they would let me be free to follow all my whims."

"So, you don't think you would be happy, even if the guy loved you with every vein in his body? What if he knew you well and understood you, and didn't want to change you? What if he was happy with exactly how you are right now. What if he *wanted* to be a part of all your adventures and whims?"

"That would be more than I deserve. I'm too much work, and he would lose his mind. I want to be someone's wife because that's an adventure in itself. Someday, but not right now. What about you?"

Jace's eyes opened wide like he was struck with a jolt of electricity.

"What?"

"What about you? Do you want to fall in love someday?" I repeated.

"Yes," he finally collected his thoughts and found his words. "I like the idea of belonging to someone and planning a life with one person. I already have someone I was thinking of."

"Who?" I asked surprised.

"I am not telling you. I was all messed up, I denied it, fought it. Some time went by, and I was determined to tell her, but I got scared." He cleared his throat and grabbed another apple. "Really?... You want to learn how to scuba dive?" he asked, changing the subject.

My heart hurt for a moment at the idea of him loving someone. My eyes pouted, and I had to look away before it was too obvious. Why couldn't I be happy for him?

"Did you meet her while I was in Saint Petersburg, and you were in Moscow?" I collected myself, cleared my throat and tried to understand my feelings and confusion.

"I'm not saying anything else," he replied.

I knew everyone he knew, he couldn't be talking about Andrea. Maybe they drew closer this past year, and she had worked with him as Arlo had battled me. I felt sick to my stomach suddenly at the thought. I wanted to run away and hide, but I was trapped in this stupid airplane with crates of coffee seeds and fruit. What did she have that captured the heart of my best friend, and why couldn't I just be happy for him?

"Andrea?" I bit my lip to conceal my snotty reaction.

"No, I have NEVER liked Andrea. I thought she was cute at first, but she's hollow. I would think you knew me better to know I wouldn't just go around loving empty people."

"Okay...than is it stupid Allison Cade? I swear, she's a shallow two-faced snob who thinks she..."

"It's not Allison!" He stopped my rant. "Are you kidding? I can't even look at you right now. When we get home, on the farm, I'll tell you. Really? Allison?"

"Do I know this person?" I asked.

"No!" he replied. "Maybe we need more studies on human behavior and how to read people. You can pick a target out of a crowd and know his story within moments but..." He trailed off and didn't finish his sentence.

I was getting irritated now, why couldn't he just tell me? It's not like I was going to tell anyone, we were in a cargo plane heading to Tanzania. I wanted to change the subject, but his comments consumed me, and I was worried. Worried that in the past year he had met new people and fallen in love with someone. I was afraid she wouldn't appreciate him or protect him.

I was worried this would change everything and he would go away, and I would lose my only friend. I reminded myself of all the bad things I had done for Felix, and that I was not beautiful, so I shouldn't be surprised Jace didn't see me as anything but a friend. I had to resolve to let him go I guess. He didn't belong to me after all. I should have known this day would come. It had to... We grew up.

Chapter 11

"The Music Will Set You Free"

In the five years since Mahtap's death, many things had changed at Taralock Estates. Joseph had resigned to overseeing production, but he had grown wrinkled and appreciated the youth of Gideon and Rubin. He put Rubin in charge of the trees and orchards, and Gideon in charge of livestock and hay.

Joseph felt quite at leisure on a regular day, but with the trees ripening and the inspections and quality control ahead of him, he grew more anxious every day. They needed this crop to sell at a premium, it had been a hard year. Civil unrest had crept in, and tensions were high. Poachers were putting pressure on the community and were trying to frighten people away. People were not coming for tours or safaris, and the economy was lulling. There had been war in the East for several years and globally the world was uptight and on the brink. It was felt strongly at Taralock Estates, and even with a bountiful crop, Joseph's mood was still unsettled.

Rubin Gambre was a married man now. He worked hard managing the farm and organizing the Maasai workers. Rubin took his responsibility seriously especially with a wife to care for now. They had been married two years earlier and had lived in Mahtap's cottage ever since. It had been painted yellow and Neemala his bride had taken every measure to make it her own, with new fabric curtains, and potted flowers.

Rubin's wife was a great manager. Her organizational skills and way with people made Rubin's job easier. She was proud of her husband and thrived as a wife. She had been raised several villages away and was from a humble family with many children. She was the second daughter, and much of the money Rubin earned went to helping Neemala's parents and seven siblings. He was happy to do it though because he was loved by a large family and it made him feel needed.

The coffee trees were getting bigger every day, and it would only be a few months before they were ready for pruning. Camps were being set up on the border fields, and Maasai families were arriving each day. Many extra people would start to arrive to help with the planting, pruning and eventually harvesting in March and April.

Rubin was expecting a shipment that he was unsure of. It carried seeds from the USA in an attempt at a fair-trade deal. He nor Joseph trusted the hybrid seeds though and agreed to take them only if they could plant them in a distant field. If they grew and produced well, a premium price would be paid for the processing, and they would make a few dollars. If the crop failed, the only loss would be the time and money it cost Rubin to pick up the crates from the airport.

Rubin had received a message about the crates that was unusual, but then again, they were coming from the USA, and he didn't understand their words entirely. He had received a message saying when and where to pick the crates up. That was expected. What was unusual was the message below that said,

> *"GMO seeds. Returning the babies. To be picked up Only by Rubin Gambre."*

It was strange that the US saw these seeds as babies, but it was a new program in its infancy, so he pushed it out of his mind until two days before the pickup.

He and Neemala got into a conversation about the future and their hopes for the crop and the price they prayed for. If all went well, it meant her family would be cared for and that they would have a little extra money, maybe to start a family of their own. Neemala talked of wishing for just two babies, a girl, and a boy. It would be all she needed and would feel content. More than two would be too many mouths to feed.

Rubin laughed his memorable grumble and agreed with his wife, that two babies would be just fine. He thought of his mother and how she would have loved to see her grandchildren, a boy, and a girl, just like her babies Jace and Theorie. She loved them so much. And then his mind stalled and he realized like a thunderbolt above his head what the message about the *"babies returning"* meant.

His mother's babies were returning. Theorie and Jace would be on that plane. For whatever reason, his mother's babies were in trouble, and it was not to be known that they were here. He understood, and knew it had to be serious, and kept quiet. He knew Joseph, Emma, and even Gideon had not been given this information, so it had to be treated with great caution.

He went to his nightstand drawer and pulled out the final letter from his mother and reread it. He took out the pocket watch that had been kept for Jace. He could finally give Jace the special gift his mother had instructed him to years earlier in her final letter to him! Two days later the shipment in Tanga was picked up. Five crates and two volunteers from the red cross to help deliver them and show the specifications for planting.

We waited for just a few minutes after landing when the gate doors opened, and we shuffled into Rubin's truck. The old jalopy I remembered had been long gone and in its place was a white pickup truck. I could not show any display of affection and had to hold back the urge to wrap my arms around Rubin's shoulders and not let go.   He spoke to the pilot and unloaded the crates while we waited silently in his truck. Just that jolly tone made me so happy. I wanted to jump up and reveal that we were home, but I had to stick to the plan. I wanted to be Theorie Jailer again. I wanted to run all the way to Taralock Estate, up the hill and down again. I wanted to smell the air and listen to the Maasai drums and bells singing in beautiful rhythm. I wanted to visit the villages and see how much everything had changed.

Once in the truck alone with our old friend, we drove away along the familiar road to our home. Rubin kept on the path and nearly drove off a dozen times, he was so excited and distracted. Rubin was the same, other than being bigger around the belly, he hadn't aged at all, and his warm eyes glowed with happiness to see us. His Swahili accent was thick and like a well-known melody.

"What happened?" he begged at first. Jace quickly responded, because we had already agreed, the less Rubin knew, the safer he was.

"We were taken to a school in India, and some people are chasing us. A detective in the US helped us get here," Jace answered.

"Aah. I thought you were in trouble. Don't worry I will keep you safe. You tell me what you need, and I will get it for you. Joseph and Emma do not know about this. I didn't tell them. I didn't tell Gideon either. You are much changed. If I saw you on the street, I wouldn't have recognized either of you. Theorie you're a woman now, beautiful. No more little wild child, huh?" He was finding humor in his shock at how we had aged.

"And, you James Taralock, you're strong! You're a man! You left as puny little ducklings and returned to us as swans." He grumbled his laugh and wanted to know all about our "schooling."

The ride was filled with catching up on the farm and all that had happened in five years. Rubin explained how he had concluded that the shipment would be carrying his mother's babies. He described his wife, Neemala as having the most beautiful eyes he had ever seen and such lovely brown skin. You could tell he was enamored by her and that they were very happy. I was so glad for him and immediately wanted to meet her.

We came to the peak overlooking the farm, and we saw our home. It looked so much smaller, everything did. The hill heading down wasn't even as rough or steep. Rubin drove as crazy as ever though and brought us directly to his cottage, Mahtap's cottage. What a welcome sight it was.

The truck was barely stopped before I jumped out and walked to the path, running my hands over the greenery. I wanted to run like a child soaking it all back up quickly, but the staircase roped me in. The wrap around porch was precisely the same, and I stopped in my track and put my hand on the wooden railing. I slid my hand along and went up two steps and stopped. The feelings of love were overpowering.

It was just a porch, but it is where Jace met me every day after school for a whole year. It was where we would prepare vegetables for dinner with Mahtap, and where I would sit and play Bao with Rubin. Tobin ran up and down these steps while we played tag, and it is where Jace held my hands on the day Mahtap died. I sat down slowly on the second step, and the reality of all that had happened came down like gravity on me. I just needed a few minutes. Jace left me to absorb my situation and went inside with Rubin.

A woman wearing a blue dress with silver thread stepped down onto the porch and sat beside me. We just looked at each other, and I didn't need to speak. This was Rubin's beautiful wife Neemala, and she knew exactly who I was. She smiled in such a way that it shook me, and I gasped, realizing I had been holding my breath. She was lovely, and just as Rubin had described her. Her thick, dark braids were long and shiny. The sunlight broke through the lush trees and made the silver thread of her dress sparkle. Her smile was genuine and honest. I didn't know her, but I felt like her kindred spirit.

"I'm so sorry if we are any trouble for you. Rubin is the only person on earth we can trust," I blurted out.

"Not anymore, now you have two people. I'm Neemala, but everyone calls me Neema, and you are Mahtap's daughter."

"Yes," I said tearing up. "This porch is very special to me, and you've made it so beautiful with flowers. Mahtap would have loved it."

"I never met Mahtap, but Rubin's stories keep her alive," Neema expressed. "I piece together a picture of a much-loved woman who always had a story."

"Yes, so many stories."

"Will you tell me about her? Only if you want to," she inquired, "and, only what you *want* to tell. I know some things are sacred between mothers and daughters." My smile said it all. Neema had won my love and trust the moment I met her, and I knew right away that we would be great friends.

Rubin and Jace came outside to meet us and talk about our arrangements. Jace showed me a beautiful silver antique pocket watch that Rubin had been holding onto for many years. It was kept hidden by Rubin until Jace became of age.

"Where did you get that?" I inquired. I had never seen it before.

"In her last letter to Rubin, Mahtap told him to hold onto it and keep it hidden until I was older, she wanted me to have it," Jace explained. Rubin filled in the details,

"Mama told me, that under no circumstances should I ever pawn it or give it to anyone but Jace. She was very firm. She did not want me to have it repaired, or looked at, she said to leave it as it was, exactly. For years now I have held it for you. I'm sorry, it is broken, I know a man who can fix it if you'd like."

"No, that's okay," Jace answered. "I'm grateful, thank you."

Rubin went on, "She also insisted in that letter to keep your piano safe. I was never to allow it to be sold or damaged. At all cost, I was to watch over it. She loved her piano, and I am certain that if I had let it go, she would have come back from the dead and scolded me. It hasn't moved though since you left. Emma has not changed anything in five years. It's like the big house is frozen in time."

Rubin and Neema explained that they had the barn we could stay in, because it was safer, and Neema would help us with whatever we needed. The cottage was secluded, so we had to keep low but not entirely hidden. Jace and I knew exceptionally well how to remain unnoticed and how to make sure it was safe to be out in the open.

"You will lodge together?" Rubin asked. I didn't see any problem. Jace and I were always alone but the question embarrassed Jace, and he stumbled through his answer.

"We can stay in the barn together if that's alright with you?" he cleared his throat.

"Of course, you are together, I assumed but wasn't sure. You are married?" Rubin pressed.

"No," I clarified. "We're not married. We're just…" What were we? I had no idea. Friends, pretend couple? Either way, Rubin looked at us suspiciously and said,

"Neema will help you get the barn ready. Jace and I will walk a little, down the old path. No one goes there, and we won't be seen." It sounded serious. I wanted to go with them. If they were talking about me, or Emma or Tobin, I wanted to be there. Neema insisted on me staying to help her prepare supper though, and I complied with my new friend. She scurried me off to the cottage as Rubin and Jace trailed down the path.

After a long while, Rubin and Jace returned, laughing and seemingly in some sort of agreement between men. Whatever they had talked about, they were clearly pleased with the results.

Our first meal back was typical Tanzanian comfort food. Ugali, bread, beans, and stewed beef. Followed by fresh mango slices and the best cup of coffee we had ever had. I decided from that moment forward, that if possible I would have coffee every day. We spoke about Neema's family and of the farm and its occupants. The Maasai were moving in. Camps were popping up, and it would be getting busier and more crowded each day as the plants needed pruning and the harvest neared.

Rubin and Neema were so happy together. They laughed and were not afraid to tease each other a little or show affection with each other. They were open and comfortable and happy. I envied their life a little. Maybe this is the *normal* Jace was talking about. If normal was this happy, then yes, I wanted normal. Rubin and Neema felt safe with each other, they didn't have anyone chasing them, they had children in the plans and hard work to keep them busy. I envied normal.

We were given a flashlight and said our goodnights and found our way to the barn. The loft had a window at each end and fresh hay.

"This is my window, that's yours," Jace said firmly.

"Why the serious tone? What's the matter with you? Are you afraid of me all of a sudden? We just spent fifteen hours in the back of a plane sitting three inches away from each other, now we have to stay on opposite sides of the loft?"

"I'm not afraid of you. Rubin said since we're not married that we have to keep a space between us. He said you're like a match, and I'm like tinder. He doesn't want his barn burning down, and I would jump off a cliff if Rubin asked me to right now, so I'm doing what he says." He smirked and settled in. I froze at night with only a quilt and some hay, but I didn't want to upset Rubin, so I stayed on my side of the barn.

The next morning Rubin woke us up, and I was so glad his inspection showed we were obeying his rules and keeping away from each other. He brought us cornbread and eggs and said to lay low because the farm would be buzzing with people that day. Jace had explained our need to find out about Emma's scar and that we wanted to search the main house for clues. Somehow Joseph, Emma, and Gideon had to be distracted so we could have time in the house.

Jace and I were allowed to go into the cabin once Neema and Rubin had gone to work and told to make ourselves at home. I was glad to have the cottage to ourselves, it felt like home. We made coffee and went over a plan, throwing ideas at each other.

"Remember Mahtap's last letter to us?" Jace asked me. "She always had a reason for her words. I think she meant something specific."

"I wish we still had that letter," I said with remorse. "I remember it said that 'the music would set us free, and that she wished the stories were just stories.' Do you remember any stories about music?" I asked.

"No. I remember her teaching me the piano though, and especially that melody. It's engraved into my memory. Rubin said the old piano is still in the house."

"We could go see, this afternoon," I offered.

"Rubin said it would be busy today. We should ask him to help us get into the house in the next couple of days. I want to play that melody again, maybe it will jog my memory."

"Ugh..." I groaned. "It will be fine. We can go through the trees. No one will see us," I whined.

"Sure, I'll just put on my loin cloth and scale the trees with my calloused fingertips. Then I'll miraculously grab on to perfectly placed vines and swing like a Vervet all the way to the house."

"I meant, we can stay low and go through the forest instead of the path, Tarzan," I snapped back.

He tightened his jaw. "When we were thieves, you had complete control, and patience. You could wait and follow through with the plan...What is so different now? Why can't you just *sit* and *wait*?" he asked, putting his hands on my shoulders and pushing me to sit in Neema's chair. His face washed over with a shade of dark coral. His words stuttered as he looked at his hands gripping me.

"This is...a mission...Follow the plan." He pulled his hands away and went to pour coffee into his mug.

"It's not the same," I scowled. "Before we were being watched and expected to perform. I couldn't mess up, or Felix would be disappointed. He isn't watching now. He is not bossing me around and demanding obedience."

"I'm not bossing you around, but I *will* tie you to the support beam of this cottage if I have to. Seriously...Wait for Rubin. If you want to run ahead and be stupid, I will do what it takes to keep you safe from yourself."

"Well, what do we do in the meantime?" I asked.

"I am having coffee, but I think you should be cut off." He sarcastically answered, as he sat at the kitchen table and slowly pulled my mug away from me.

The next morning Rubin found an excuse for Emma to leave the house. Neemala had to arrange the tables for the drying process and just couldn't do it that day because of an aching back. Emma was annoyed but agreed to help get the seasonal workers information and write it down. Workers lined up at the sign in tables. Entire families would stay on the land for the duration of the ripening and harvest, and younger ones were running around, babies were crying, and wives were getting anxious to get camp set up. It was an exciting time for everyone, and the farm buzzed with people. Gideon and Joseph were occupied with the menagerie of animals. It was the perfect opportunity to get into the house.

We waited for the opening and slipped in through the kitchen door at the back of the house. It seemed like the house *had* frozen in time since we had left. The pans and dishes were all in order, and the kitchen island I so often hid under remained in the same place. Emma's bread was rising on the counter with tea towels draped over them. We checked them and saw that they had barely risen so we had some time before we knew she would be back to knead them for the second rise.

The smell of the house shot memories through my mind. It was as if yesterday we ran through these rooms chasing each other. I felt so sad that Tobin would never be coming home, and memory after memory distracted me from our important task. Jace found the old upright piano. It was in the living room, backed up against the railing to the stairs. He sat and examined it while I looked for photo albums or pictures leading to some clue of who Emma was before she became the wife of Joseph Taralock.

Not a single photo was to be seen. No wedding pictures of any kind, no baby pictures of Jace, no photos whatsoever. I tried to remember if there had ever been photos in these rooms and I couldn't remember ever seeing any. Who doesn't have a picture of their newborn or their wedding day? It struck me as so strange. There was nothing to show Emma's style or personal touch. Then again, what exactly was Emma's style? If Emma didn't currently live here, I would not have known she ever existed.

Jace was standing at the piano, silently staring at the ivory keys afraid to touch them. He had spent hours upon hours playing when he was younger. If he wasn't running around the orchard playing, you could be sure he was at his piano. He played beautifully by ear but could read and write music like a second language. He understood the circle of fifths and had tried to explain it to me a hundred times, but it wouldn't click in my mind.

"I'm certain this piano holds a clue. Mahtap made me focus on learning to play. We played that melody a thousand times, and she made me memorize it. I have missed playing so much, I wish I..."

"I'll keep a lookout, just play the melody softly," I assured.

He looked at me earnestly hoping my suggestion was possible, quickly giving in and positioning his hands over the chords.

"They have to be played in sequence and timed perfectly," he explained.

With the first chord, I heard a sigh of relief like he had just come up from water. Twenty-one chords total, sounding deliberate but pretty. With the last chord played we sat in absolute silence waiting for a lightbulb to go off, but nothing.

"I'm going to try again. I played too quietly, I need to play the chords more forcefully, like they were meant to be played. Make sure you're on the lookout."

I returned to the window and scoped the yard. No one. Everyone was down in the West Orchard. Jace began with precision and perfection. He played the chords again one by one. With the resonating of the last chord, he held his foot on the pedal, echoing it into the room. We heard a faint click. I panicked and checked the kitchen, but it was empty. I was sure I heard a distinct crack though. I tiptoed through the other rooms on the first floor and went back to the living room. Jace had the piano pulled away from the wall, and his arm was reaching down, stretching as far as he could.

"Something popped inside with the last chord. I see something, a latch I think. I can almost reach, it's like a compartment. It must have been closed, and the last chord popped it open. Some of these gears and wheels don't belong in a piano. It's some sort of mechanism. Got it!"

He pulled out a small metal box. It was heavy and slightly dented with hidden hinges. We were good at getting into things, but this was going to be a challenge. The lock opening was awkward and thin.

"I have an idea." Jace pulled out the silver pocket watch from Mahtap and looked it over. It looked ordinary but had clearly been tampered with at the top. He inspected it for a moment studying its shape and uniformity.

He knew there was a reason Mahtap had kept it for him, and he knew it was somehow connected to the piano. He turned the back of the watch and twisted it in the palm of his hand. He held it to his ear, turning the clasp slowly and meticulously until...Click!

The fastener released, and the back popped off. A thin, slightly curved key was exposed laying in the watch workings. It was narrow but solid.

"Eight...ten pins!" I acknowledged. "And look at the engravings. I've never seen a key like it."

Jace inserted the key, turned it to the right, and it was a perfect match. The box burst open to reveal a thick wall of metal explaining why it was so heavy but also virtually indestructible. Inside was a folded stack of papers tied with twine.

"That's everything," he clarified, pulling out the last of the contents.

"What is it?" I begged. I was so anxious to devour the bundle. It had been hidden here for a reason, and Mahtap had hidden it well. Without the specific chords and timing that only she and Jace had memorized, and without this key, these things would have been buried forever. Jace untied the twine, and we went into the kitchen, double checked that no one was coming and laid the contents on the kitchen island.

Birth certificates, one for Jace and one for me. They looked to be the originals bearing the raised seal.

There were a couple of photos of us all as children. A picture of my father with his plane, an identical copy of the photo we had seen in New York with my father Morgan and Emma in their college years. The spot on the picture that would have exposed Emma's tattoos had been scratched away. Emma had been careful to obliterate any knowledge of what her marks were.

But, the photo at last that shook me and made me yelp, before covering my own mouth was a photo of my father and Mahtap. He is a no more than fifteen or sixteen and she is so young. They are standing posed in front of the Metropolitan Museum of Art, in New York.

"My father knew Mahtap as a teenager? I thought they met when we moved here or just before. I am so confused."

"Look!" Jace startled. Under the photos was a badly worn piece of paper. Yellowed and tattered with distinct fold marks as if it had been in someone's wallet for years. Jace held it open, and even with fading ink, it was clearly visible. Ten symbols in a row with the numbers zero through nine listed below them. My mind focused, and nothing else mattered but that paper. It felt surreal. Jace had no words either. We held the paper intently looking at the symbols that clearly identified the marks on my wrist.

"95.9915," I spoke out loud. I looked at my wrist and for the first time could read the message that had been inscribed on my body my entire life.

"It sounds like a coordinate," Jace guessed. "But, it's only one. If that's even what it is."

"Maybe it's temperature, or a radio station or an ID number, 95.9915. All along it's been normal numbers. What am I?" I wondered out loud. "When I was a kid I pretended they were the coordinates to Atlantis," I said with an ironic laugh.

In a flash of a second, my heart stopped dead with a sudden noise at the doorway. My view was blocked. Jace instinctively jumped in front of me shielding me from whatever had interrupted our discovery. Neither of us moved. The air was suspended, and nothing but the ticking of the grandfather clock could be heard. I wished I could see what was in the doorway because the unknown was killing me. My heart was beating fast, and I tried to damper the heaviness of my breath. I wished Jace would move, but at the same time wanted him to stay and shield me. The tension broke with one word from our captor in the doorway.

"Son?"

Chapter 12

Joseph's Place

Joseph Taralock stood suspended and dumbstruck. He had not seen his only child in five years. Standing before him was a man, not a teenager. Jace's jawline was distinguished, and his brow had depth to it now. His boy had changed in more ways than he could imagine, and the reality of seeing him in the unchanged living room brought him to a breakdown.

"You shouldn't be here. What are you doing here?" Joseph demanded. The natural warmth in his voice was pushed aside, and he forced himself to be firm and unmoving. "Your mother can't know you are here." Jace was immobile, not sure of his father's involvement in this whole arrangement.

"We are going," Jace replied coldly. He gestured for me to take his hand, and I felt obliged.

"Theorie!" Joseph howled as I walked towards Jace and hid slightly behind him. Joseph's eyes filled with tears and emotion. I had no idea how to react, and my only thought was of escape. I clutched the papers in my free hand and slipped them into my jeans.

"Are you going to turn us in? Or can we go?" Jace demanded of his father. He in no way was going to crumble to this man who had let him be taken away. He saw his father as weak and powerless.

"You stayed together?" Joseph inquired, with stunned uncertainty.

"Of course," Jace replied, confused at the surprise in his father's eyes. "Well, can we go? Or will you call Felix?" Jace's voice got more aggressive. He pulled me closer to him and started to edge us to the door. Joseph looked behind him and when all was clear replied,

"You can go, son." Joseph's hair had turned pure white over the years that we had been gone, and his face was more tanned and leathery, but his eyes still slanted on the sides slightly. Despite the weight of years past, and lines creeping in like ivy vines, his smoky blue eyes still matched his sons.

"I'm an old man now and I was never allowed to have a voice. Let me have a voice son. Let me help you."

"How can we trust you?" Jace pleaded.

"Nothing I say will convince you, but I do know you both are masters at reading people. Read me. Read me and know that I am tired. I am tired of The Jailer's Way. and I have no other moves in the game but to fall on my back and surrender what I know. You can run if you don't trust me, I would understand. You can hit me, or yell at me, or both, I would understand. But, you are my son by blood, and you have made it back here with Theorie. There is more to that than you realize."

"Tomorrow at Rubin's cottage. We will watch for you, and know if you've deceived us," Jace warned.

That night Mahtap's story grew in my head. I had so many unanswered questions. Why didn't she tell me that she knew the symbols on my arm were numbers? Did she know my father better than she led on? Who *was* she really? My mind danced with ideas and myths, and I fought these plots with the few facts I knew.

Mahtap was a mother to Jace and me, and she would have done anything to protect us. She raised us with stories and lessons that we listened intently to and shaped our lives around. Her love for people and understanding of human imperfection molded us to see the world with open eyes. She would tell us that "Laws change, but principles remain the same, so we could build our lives around principle." She taught us to use our conscience, to feel deep empathy and do what was right and honorable.

In all she did, I understood now that she had been molding us for what we would be thrown into. She knew that we would need the foundation she gave us. I fell asleep with swelling feelings of guilt. I recounted all the horrible things I did to people. Mahtap would be ashamed of me. I cringed at the possibility of hurting her and betraying all her training and honor. What had I become?

The morning came quick, and a thick fog had rolled in overnight. The Vervet monkeys and Woodpeckers chattered and knocked on the trees. They sounded louder with the fog insulating the forest.

I was up early and impatient to start watching for Joseph. He hadn't told us what time, so I was expecting him from the moment my eyes were open. Jace was sound asleep, and I didn't want to bother him. He looked comfortable on his side of the loft.

I shifted myself up and peered out of the window trying to look through the fog. No sign of Joseph. I took out the pack of papers and reexamined them. I looked at the code decipher again, and repeated the numbers in my mind, 95.9915. I tossed over in my mind what it could mean.

A photo of the boys and me made me remember warm summer days, and playful times. We were all in overalls, barefoot and arm in arm like a tiny gang. We were walking down the main road. Four little comrades off on an adventure. I looked like one of the boys in between Jace and Gideon. My braids had swung towards the front making my hair look short. We were young, only about six or seven. Jace and Gideon were around nine or ten. I don't remember who took the picture, or where we were going, but I know we were having a great day and were happy to be together.

I was happy to have this picture, I had so few photos of my childhood. With a photographer for a father, one would think there were boxes of photos, but his photographic interest was always in the people of the world, not his own children. We did not intrigue him like the bright eyes of a child on the streets of Kolkata, or a Russian Babushka. His true love was every other person on earth.

Mahtap had always been the one to show any particular attention to Jace and me. She didn't like that Dad would take us on trips. She would scoff when he showed up in his little plane and get frustrated. She would want to know where we were going and when we would be back. She kept track of all the places we had been, in a little journal, and would ask my father when she would expect us back. Right in front of him, she would mark a date in her book, looking at him with a threat in her eyes. Only a few times did he ever return us to the farm later than promised, and he would surely hear about it. She would attend to us quickly, and scuffle us off of the plane, and need to "speak" to him about keeping his promises.

My father respected Mahtap, and even though she yelled at him, he always kissed her on the forehead and gave her a smile. He would promise to be a better babysitter, and better at keeping a schedule. She would roll her eyes and smack him playfully. She wouldn't stay mad at him for long and would want to hear all about where we went, what we saw, and who we met. She cared and worried about us as a mother should, and we loved her for it.

Looking over at Jace, stirring awake, I was grateful I still had him and his friendship. I didn't' want him to love someone else and be taken away. I would be alone then. I was helpless against it though. He seemed to have his mind made up, and as soon as this mystery was solved, and we were free from Felix, I knew he would be leaving to pursue his mystery woman. I needed a plan for myself. I needed to have in place a strategy for when that happened. I needed to find my place in the world somehow, and I had to do it by myself.

Jace finally woke up. "Any sign of him?" he asked as he ran his fingers through his hair and rubbed his eyes with his thumb and forefinger.

"No. But the fog is so heavy today, I can't really see. I'm starving. Do you think we should go down to the house after Rubin and Neema leave? She said she would leave something to eat," I reminded him.

"Sure. If Dad turns us in to Felix, we're as good as dead anyway. We might as well get some of the cornbread Neema made yesterday. It could be our last meal," Jace said with a sly smirk.

"That is not funny," I said dryly. I was too hungry to joke around.

Looking back out of the loft window I could see the path leading to the cottage coming to life. Bugs whirled and sparkled in the morning sunshine. A trained ear like ours alerted us that we were about to have company. Joseph scuffed into the barn like he was looking for supplies. He played the part well. We met him at the base of the loft steps.

"I have to be quick. I have to do the walkthrough with the new Maasai workers this morning." He explained. "I wish I could say I can't imagine what you two have been through, but I can. The game is simple, Felix and his network decide who shall live, who shall die, and who will be left alone and be given a place. I can't leave this farm. I've never been allowed to leave this farm. It was decided a long time ago, that this is my place. Just like with Gideon. Felix allows me to live because I play a part in the game. This farm is a strategic location and easy cover for buying, selling and trading. All I have ever been is a game piece in the strategy."

"All along you knew this?" Jace questioned his father.

"Son, do you think I wanted this life? I was an engineer, I had a plan for my life, but The Jailer's Way took over, and I was made into a pawn. Your father Theorie, and my wife went to college together. They were 'very' close," Joseph squirmed uncomfortably. "They were members of

216

The Jailer's Way for two decades. They accomplished unspeakable things...If you only knew."

"We get it. We know 'The Jailer's Way' and what it stands for," Jace snapped.

Joseph continued, "I knew Theorie would be taken. You have the same type of markings that Emma had, and because you're a Jailer by blood, and the strongest of Morgan's kids, it was inevitable. But I didn't know until the day of Mahtap's memorial when you worked together to kill the snake, and Felix saw it all play out. I knew then that Jace would be your partner. It all made sense."

"What made sense?" I asked.

"Your father always brought the two of you on his trips. Never Gideon, never Tobin. I didn't completely understand why until that day. Your father knew Gideon would be the farmer, the pawn. But he knew *your* strength, and he knew that you and Jace had a special connection. Felix needs certain qualities, certain strengths in his game."

"We've heard all about that. But Felix split us up this last year. He didn't want us working together," Jace explained.

"Just like your mother and Morgan," Joseph went on. "They met in college. That's where we all met. The Jailer's Way was a program. The head of the group was your grandfather, Theodore Jailer. He was the leader before Felix took over. He arranged everyone's 'place.' At first, Emma and Morgan were a team. They trained and worked for Theodore.
Under his father's instruction, Morgan was expected to excel. But he fell in love, with Emma. They fell in love

with each other. Theodore saw it as a weakness and separated them. Morgan continued to run missions, but Emma refused. She was sent here. We both were. We were married and had you two years later James. Emma burned her tattoo markings off her wrist the day we were married. From that point on we lived normally, running the farm. We were not to question shipments, or undocumented deliveries, or crates."

"What was in the crates?" Jace asked.

"Weapons, money, Ivory, drugs, whatever would make a profit or be leverage over the players," Joseph explained.

"We ran the farm, and Morgan was married to a colleague in New York, your mother, Rose. It was years later that Morgan showed up and explained he needed a place for his three children. He had diverted from his father's control and wanted you all to be safe.

Things got worse after that. Theodore died when you were nearly four years old, and his brother Felix took over the position intended for your father. Felix was not willing to let Morgan get away free and clear. He had a hold on him and forced him to run missions. Most likely threats against you and your brothers, and mother. So your father continued to work under Felix's domain."

"Felix *is* my uncle! That's awful! Emma didn't lie to me. Our trips," I started. "They *were* missions, not photography assignments."

"Yes," Joseph admitted. "You were to live here and be raised by Mahtap. Your father trusted her like she was his own mother, but Felix requested that you go on assignment with him. You would begin learning at an early age how to live by The Jailer's Way."

"But my father took us to places and showed us how people struggled just to live. He believed in human kindness and taught us how to walk a mile in someone else's shoes, and that all people, no matter what race, religion, or disability, were worthy of love and respect. He didn't believe in 'The Jailer's Way'...I just DON'T believe that!" I howled.

Joseph watched my reaction, but I could tell he didn't believe in my father's innocence. "I thought the training was for you Theorie. I thought Jace was just a companion, but I know now that he was training the two of you as a team. Your father did divert from The Jailer's Way, but to keep himself and his children alive, he agreed to train you."

"That makes sense," Jace expressed. "We were told to watch people, understand languages, and cultures. We were trained to blend in from the time we were preschoolers. Theorie...He had to obey Felix and take us on assignments, but in the process, he was blatantly instilling in us the qualities we would need to survive The Jailer's Way. He was growing rebels right under Felix's nose."

Joseph continued, "You became the mission Theorie. Felix focused on your training and potential. You were sent to the Primary School as a testing ground, so Felix could observe your personality on the sidelines, away from the farm, and James."

"The tattoos on Emma and me, what are they?" I begged.

"I don't know. Honestly. But I do know, there are always *two* people at a time that have the markings. Emma had them, and your father had them."

"I don't remember seeing any sign of them on my father," I pondered.

"I know that when you came at four years old, you had them, and your father's were scarred over and removed like Emma's were."

"I don't think Felix knows what they are," I admitted, "Who has the second set now?"

Joseph looked at Jace but didn't answer my question. He just nodded and shrugged his shoulders.

"The day Felix came here, the night he threatened Emma, he asked her about her markings and if she remembered them. He sliced her arm and threatened her, but she refused to give him any information. She said it had been too many years and she had forgotten what the symbols had looked like. Felix wants to know what they mean. And from what I know of Felix, he runs on power and playing God. He may not know *what* the marks mean, but he believes it is significant in some way."

"Well he's seen my marks, he knows what they are. He just doesn't know Emma's."

"No, but I do," Joseph admitted under his breath reluctantly. "I remember them exactly. She wanted to forget them, but I have always known, that if Felix felt it was important, then it was the only bit of power I had over him.

Emma has done everything she can to erase the memory of those marks. She has destroyed all the photos of her as a young woman. But she hasn't destroyed my memory."

Joseph turned to check his surroundings, walked towards Jace and hugged him tightly. While still embracing his son, his hand reached out and gripped mine. His blue-gray eyes were so much like Jace's, yet so many years of regret pooled in them. He collected himself, adjusted his shoulders, cleared his throat and left quietly. I held fast in my hand the small piece of paper he had pressed into my palm.

"Come on," I said, as Jace and I climbed back up the loft ladder." I handed Jace the paper. Six symbols similar to mine with a decimal point, but they were different. It was the second set of numbers. Emma's numbers.

"Jace. We need a map."

He stopped and looked at me. "Why?"

"They *are* coordinates," I exclaimed.

"We really do have to go, it's not safe here anymore," he worried.

"Can't we stay to say goodbye to Rubin and Neema? I don't want to go just yet. One more night with them. Please?" I begged.

"Theorie Jailer wants to stay put for twenty-four hours? Are you ill?"

The evening came. The faint sound of tic toc drums and the rhyming voices of the Maasai workers and their children rang out in the distance. They were preparing their camps and making dinner on their fires. The melody echoed through the forest surrounding our hideout. Rubin and Neema arrived home together, hand in hand. Neema went into the house, and Rubin met with us. We asked to stay one more night and apologized for being trouble.

"You are my family. Family is always trouble. Come in the house, Neema is making barbeque and sweet potatoes."

We talked and laughed and ate as a family should. Rubin ate so much that Neema made fun of his growing belly, and he joked that it was happy fat, so it was okay. Neema's grace and gentleness reminded me so much of Mahtap. In the evening she brushed my hair and made a crown braid with a piece of gold ribbon woven throughout.

"What a beautiful girl you are Theorie," she stated. I disregarded her words and scoffed at her.

"Sure. That's what all mother's say. I gave up a long time ago on any hopes of me being beautiful. Even my eyes are ruined."

"What?" she asked.

"See...My eye is blueish green, but this is a streak of brown like mud. My eyes couldn't even make up their mind on what color to be."

"You see mud, I see Amber, and Amber is a natural beauty, that just needs polishing," she replied.

"Ever since I was little Emma has told me I was hit with the genetic wheel of misfortune."

"Well, she is wrong. You have a natural beauty. You just need polishing," she consoled.

I didn't know how to receive a compliment, so I just awkwardly pushed her words of as crazy. We sat by the fireplace and had tea and mangoes. Jace and Rubin spoke of music and all the songs that he wanted to learn from America and Britain. We talked about the countries we had visited and how cold Russia was. Neema asked about the spices of India and if the air really smelled of curry and cinnamon. We told them all we could without explaining that we were really trained killers, and that we were probably responsible for the death of innocent people. Even though I had a mission rolling in my head, and wanted to chase after these coordinates, I also never wanted to leave Mahtap's cottage.

Jace and Rubin went to take care of the goats and pen them up for the night, so Neema and I started cleaning up dishes.

"I'm sorry Neema if we have been trouble for you. I'm sorry you have had to hide us. I wish we could live here and have a life like yours."

"Nonsense girl," she smiled. "You would not be happy staying in one spot, working on a farm. You have too much spirit in you. You need adventure and movement. For me, Rubin is enough adventure," she groaned, rolling her eyes and smiling. "But you are still young and wild. You still have an amber streak running through your blue blood," she teased. "For now anyway. Maybe in a few years...you will settle and tire out and be ready for what you call 'normal.'"

"I don't know. Sometimes I am tired of running," I admitted.

"Are you happy?"

"Happy?" I questioned, not understanding what she meant.

"Yes, happy. Are you happy? You have questions and answers you need because of who you are. Your purpose has always been to find those answers. Are you happy searching for answers?"

"Well, yes. I guess so. I am happy traveling and learning and fighting for justice. I didn't like who I had become in Russia, but it has changed, and I'm here now. I am happy now."

"See. Even though you are on the run hiding from most likely very dangerous people, you are still happy. You still have a purpose, and you have someone to help you along. When you find your answers and figure it all out, what then? You will have to find a new purpose and find out who you are. Until then, you will not be settled enough to be 'normal.'"

"Jace says he's going to settle down and get married. I feel bad for making him stay with me. Bad things started with the Jailer family. It's all my fault he can't stay here and be happy."

"Hmm. I see. You are going to make this all about you?" she questioned. "Jace is a man who can make his own decisions. He was born into this life just like you were. You may bear the name Jailer by blood. But he bares it by love."

I wanted to ask her about marriage and love, and if she thought I was a lost cause. I wanted to tell her about how my friendship with Jace felt different now, but how I didn't understand it. I wanted to ask her so many things that a daughter would ask a mother, but we heard the boys returning.

I tried to hide my blushing face, but the awkward silence when they entered the kitchen made it worse. I was so sad that we would be leaving in the morning. I just wanted to go to the loft and pout.

I arranged the hay and blankets and settled down, looking out the loft window at the stars peeking from the tree branches. Jace came up as I was drifting off and the noise of him arranging his own blankets woke me up. Suddenly, I felt so awkward around him. He was truly a handsome man, and I didn't want to think about him in that way, it would just hurt more when he would walk away and love someone else. I adjusted my blankets to cover myself up and fixed my hair that was popping from the braid.

"What were you and Neema talking about tonight?" he questioned.

"She wanted to know if I was happy," I responded, pretending to be sleepy.

Jace paused arranging his bed. "Are you?" He seemed interested in my answer.

Laying there in the loft with Rubin and Neema nearby, in the farm I had grown up in and with the person I loved most in the world sitting across the room from me, I answered a definite,

"Yes."

Jace came closer to me, startling me. "I know what the coordinates are," he whispered excitedly. Sitting up, I smashed my forehead into his, making him jump back and press his palm to his head.

"Sorry! I'm sorry. How did you find out? Where? Where do we need to go?"

"The Middle of the Universe." he responded, still rubbing his forehead.

"Jace! Stop fooling around. Did you find out where the coordinates lead?"

"Yes, but someone just bashed me in the head, and now I have Amnesia."

"You're a jerk!" I scolded, flipping back down on my hay bed.

"Seriously, we have to go to the Middle of the Universe…or Kansas. It's one and the same."

I was so confused.

"I explained a little to Rubin, and he helped me find it on a cell phone that one of the Maasai workers had. It maps out to a strange place called the Middle of the Universe, in Kansas. We have to go to the United States," he stated.

"Jace?" I pleaded. "I'll go. You stay here."

"What?" He sounded so confused. "Why would I do that?"

"Because you're happy here, and this is all my fault...Felix is *my* uncle. It's *my* family's fault."

"That's ridiculous," he retorted. "Stop thinking like that." He turned away brushing me off and went to fix his bed.

"But it's the *Jailer's* way. My father and grandfather and goodness knows how far back are involved and are probably the masterminds of this whole awful philosophy. My family is no good, and you were dragged into it. You could have been killed. I deserve this life, I'm no good. It's in my blood."

He cut me off, "Yeah but you're in my… Nevermind. Whether you like it or not, I'm involved. Your father traveled with *both* of us. Felix trained *both* of us. You may have the same last name, but that's where it ends. This is not all on you. You're my best friend, and I have never let you jump into your life alone. I'm not going to start now…So we are *both* going to Kansas."

I couldn't battle him. He was not going to listen to me, and I couldn't understand why. I knew his stubborn refusal to let me fight this battle alone would get him killed, and that the weight of losing him was more than my heart could handle. I knew I had a death sentence and had to appreciate every breath I was allowed.

The next morning came quickly. Rubin met us at the bottom steps of the loft, hugged us and told us he loved us. Neema had packed food for our trip and began to hug us goodbye. I reluctantly left my dear new friend standing on the porch of Mahtap's cottage and promised I would someday visit her again. We would drive in the back of the truck, under the strapped down canvas, to Arusha with Rubin as our driver.

He had to pick up a shipment, so it was a natural assignment, and he wasn't questioned. When we arrived at the airport, Jace used a payphone to call Wheezie and let her know we were traveling to the USA and needed to be helped once we arrived. He used the code names Leo and Sara, and keywords to help her understand just in case anyone was listening. All I could do was hope she understood, hope she was still willing to help us, and hope that she wouldn't betray us and lead Felix right to us.

We used our faked passports and ID's so Felix would not be able to trace us, and we sat separately on the plane, so we wouldn't be photographed or spotted. It was a long flight, but it was uncomplicated and peaceful. We finally arrived at JFK airport in Queens, NY and slipped in with the crowd, looking like locals.

Chapter 13

The Middle of the Universe

New York City was a blur to me. People in every direction jotted and darted in sync in all directions, like schools of fish. The buildings shot into the skyline and seemed to go on straight into the heavens. It was loud and alive. We arrived in early Spring with people complaining of air quality and a lingering coldness. Compared to the mob of humans in Kolkata, New York was surprisingly better smelling. Other than a faint smell of old food and motor oil, the air was clean. The streets held on to the last few remnants of ice and snow. Blackened snow hills slushed and made a mess of the roads and walkways as it melted.

Different accents and cultures blended and melted into each other. I could hear random words in various familiar languages being pulled from the crowd. We walked two miles down 186th street winding through the crowd. We were able to get money exchanged and a change of clothes along the way. It gave us enough time to observe the speech and mannerisms of the people. We had been here before to meet up with Wheezie at FBI headquarters, but only briefly before we traveled upstate, so we paid more attention this time. My father had only taken us here a handful of times, and it was never for lengthy trips. He had always flown into the smaller Floyd Bennett Field in Brooklyn, so we didn't know much about this area. We knew nothing of the culture and trends.

Nearly everyone was drinking coffee or holding phones in their hands. People, for the most part, were friendly. Street vendors were not as pushy as in Kolkata, and most people were on a mission, storming to their destinations. We quickly adapted and walked in the same manner until we reached the doors of the Winstead Hotel.

Our room was compact and straightforward with only one bed, but I promised Jace that I would stay far to one side. We also had a television and a microwave. Two things we were significantly inexperienced with. A shower and clean clothes made everything seem alright. Jace went and got what the Americans called 'Chinese food.' We hadn't tried it before, but it was so good. The Winstead Hotel was a good starting point to be able to collect our plan and decide what to do next. I wanted to go directly to Kansas. Jace wanted to contact Wheezie and ask for her advice.

I turned the TV on, and a sitcom was playing that had an array of hilarious characters. People must really like this show because people were in the background laughing. I thought to myself *I may really like American culture.* The people seemed friendly and had more time to have fun and play. It was quick paced which engaged my mind and entertained me.

Jace was not interested in TV. He looked over the photos and documents again that we had stowed away from the box in the piano. He grabbed the pen and paper from the nightstand drawer and was calculating how much money we had. We promised that from the moment we were on American soil we would not pickpocket or swipe anything. If we were going to change who we were, we had to start to forget our training.

"We've got to find somewhere else to stay. This hotel will wipe us out in about two months. That's without food or anything else…Theorie?"

"Hmm? What? Sorry." I was so distracted by the banter and chemistry of the TV characters I didn't even hear Jace asking me a question.

"I want to call Wheezie. She can help us with a place, maybe some money just to get us through. Maybe we should get one of those cell phones, so we don't have to use pay phones anymore."

"No!" I disagreed. "Let's just go to Kansas. Tomorrow. We don't even know what is there. Maybe it's nothing. Besides I don't know if I trust her."

"She's our only option. We have no one else we can ask for help. Would you pay attention to me! We've got to figure this out!"

Jace seemed frustrated but knew it was pointless making me focus when something new and shiny was put in front of my face. He couldn't compete with the chemistry of American sitcoms.

"Fine," he surrendered. He kicked off his shoes, grabbed the Lo Mein and propped himself up against the bed frame.

The next morning I woke up early to the sound of TV fuzz. It wasn't light out yet, and I was glad I woke up first because I was semi-wrapped around Jace's leg and arm. He had been avoiding any physical contact with me since pushing me to my side of the loft and would not even look at me in the eyes, so I knew he would be uncomfortable if he woke up and saw that he was my pillow.

I carefully moved to get up and shut the TV off. I washed up and changed the channel instead though. I sat at the foot of the bed, turned the volume low and watched the news and goings on around Queens. A shooting, a heist on a gas station, a politician being exposed for a scandalous affair. Computers that were technical marvels throughout the world were household devices here in America. Commercials offered products and luxuries that I didn't even know existed. Jace stirred and realized I was already awake.

"What are you watching?" Jace asked.

"Advertisements. They have a lot of movie stars here and shows and plays. America really loves the movies I think. Computers and cell phones are a necessity. I think we need to get one. People must have a lot of money in this country. Anyway, what are we going to do today?" I smiled at him.

"Kansas?" he inquired, rolling on to his back, and stretching his arms behind his head.

It would be a long trip, but we would switch transportation and change up our appearance. Jace bought us both sunglasses, and himself a baseball cap. I changed into my newly purchased jeans and a white button-down blouse. I bought a navy-blue sweatshirt that had a baggy hood.

I used the gold ribbon I still had from Neema to braid my hair up. Jace didn't shave and was scruffy making him look even more like a New Yorker. We jumped on the subway, taking it as far as Manhattan, where we used our fake

IDs and gave the man two hundred dollars to rent a car. We had all our documents hidden away and tucked into our clothes just in case we ever had to get away quick.

For the next two and a half days we took turns driving straight through to Kansas. Our little white compact sedan darted through state after state. Traveling before always involved walking through filthy streets or mosquito-infested jungles, so sitting in an air-conditioned compact car felt too good to be true. We used the time on the long drive to figure out our next move. Coffee became a necessity, and we figured out what a 'Drive Through' was. There were so many conveniences in America. We stopped only to get gas and grab food or to use a bathroom. Hours went by talking about what we would do when this was all over.

The radio sparked life into Jace, and he was absorbed with the variety of voices, and instruments. "I can't wait to write my music down and get onto paper what has been in my head. To play my music out loud,… and maybe even sell some of my songs. It must be amazing to have someone else love something that you created," he mused.

"Oregon," I admitted. "I want to see this country more. I want to go and see the Rocky Mountains and the Grand Canyon. When I was in Saint Petersburg, I read a lot about this country's history. The Desert, and the Rocky Mountains, and the Grand Canyon. There's a lot of museums and Oh! Niagara Falls, I want to see that. There's just so much to see here."

"There's the Appalachian trail, and some beautiful mountains I'd like to see too," Jace admitted as he switched lanes and put on the cruise control. It was nice to think of forgetting all of this. I really hoped that the coordinates that were marked on my and Emma's arms led to an answer and would end my chase for justice.

"What do you think is hidden at the middle of the universe?" I asked.

"I don't know. Maybe money? Felix wants it, so it must be valuable. Theorie, what if Felix goes free? What if we never find out?" Jace asked.

"I can't think of that, it makes my stomach knot all up. Tobin deserves justice. All the lives Felix took, all deserve justice. I will just keep trying until Felix is gone, or I'm dead I guess. What about you? What about settling down? Are you still wanting to find your girl, and be 'normal'?" I sarcastically taunted him.

"Someday," he answered.

So he still had feelings for her, whoever she was. I really did hate her. I didn't even know who it was, but I didn't like that *she* had Jace.

"You told me you would tell me who this person was when we were at home, at the cottage. You didn't. So you have to tell me now," I demanded. I wanted to put an identity to this girl who had bewitched my friend.

"No. Not now. We'll have to wait until we get back to Africa."

"Why?... It's Allison isn't it?" I grumbled "It has to be. You said it isn't, but I think you're lying. She's back home in

Africa. Neema told me that she had visited not long before we got there. She's definitely uncomplicated and normal. I wish I was not so complicated and was like other girls and didn't have trained killers in my family line dragging me to Hell...Well, I hope you're happy with her. She's good and boring and just the right amount of brainless. And you can live in peace without feeling like your being chased by a psychopath." I was irritated now and had worked myself up into my own little fit. I was mad at him, and he didn't even do anything.

"Theorie...it's not Allison. I promise. I will tell you, I just... You're....you're not going to hell. Mahtap taught us that hell is just the dirt of the earth anyway, remember?"

"Well, when Felix kills me, that's where I'm going, so I'm right, I *am* going to Hell."

Jace rolled his eyes at me. "Besides Allison is boring. I would spend my days chasing snakes away from her and bringing her lemonade. She's spoiled and pampered. I would never want to be married to someone like that."

"I want a marriage like Rubin and Neema's," I admired. "They have such a beautiful way together. I like that they tease and laugh, but you can see that they entirely live for and need each other. I want to not have to worry about loyalty or if my husband would get tired of me when I got fat or old. Or that would make fun of me if suddenly, I wanted to learn how to...be a Glass Blower, or a Sailor. I want every day to be an adventure and to be more in love every year that passes. Oh, ...And I want him to be my best friend, and have red hair," I concluded.

"Red hair? he spat. "You want him to have red hair? I'm done talking about this."

"Why? I like red hair. What is important to you?" I demanded.

"In a wife?"

"Yes. Why do you love this mystery woman, if it's not Allison? What makes her so special?" I picked at him.

"She's fascinating..."

"Ok? What's so fascinating?" I questioned further, mocking his words.

"When I'm with her there's never a dull moment. When I think I have figured her out, she surprises me with how smart she is, or how kind she is. She is beautiful in a real way, and it doesn't matter *what* color her hair is."

"It's Andrea...You liar...She's the only one I know that dyes her hair..."

"Oh My God...Your brain makes me dizzy," he replied.

"You really love her, don't you?" I confirmed, feeling so sad inside. "You light up when you talk about her."

He stopped answering my questions. My will power sank realizing his heart was already taken. A weight fell heavy deep in my body knowing that he would never love me like he loved this woman. She was beautiful and captivating, I was just someone he had to take care of because he was a loyal person. The guilt I felt because I was keeping him from having his normal life with the woman he loved was too overwhelming for me. I didn't want to ruin his life. I knew my fate. I knew Felix would catch up to me at some point. I don't know why I imagined for just a moment that Jace could have loved me that way. There wasn't anything fascinating or beautiful about me, and he loved this woman because she was kind to people. I had callously harmed and killed, there was nothing kind about me.

The rest of the ride into Kansas was silent. I pretended to sleep with my jacket rolled up under my neck. I turned to look out the window and told him to wake me up when we got there, and then I cried to myself in a self-contained pity party.

I would refuse to think of him as anything but my friend and partner through this trip. I set in my mind that as soon as I knew what was at the middle of the so-called universe, I would leave Jace. I would run away and get a new identity without him. I would let him go.

We crossed into Kansas and eventually pulled into the parking lot of the Gallant hotel. It was a beautiful Art Deco style hotel with checkered floors in modern styles and geometric shapes. We were able to get a room with a kitchen and two queen beds. I was glad for the space.

"They have a rooftop restaurant. Do you want to try it out?" Jace asked.

"Sure," I surrendered, still wallowing from the car ride conversation.

"What's the matter?"

"Nothing." I brushed him off and washed up. I had nothing but jeans and a clean top to put on, and I felt totally inadequate for the atmosphere and my company.

Jace shaved and cleaned up attempting to look the part and blend in. I carefully entwined the gold ribbon through my freshly done braid. My hair was such a mess all the time, Neema was right, I did need polishing. It had darkened slightly looking more of a rich cinnamon brown but was still wild. I looked in the mirror getting ready and my nose scrunched up just looking at myself. My freckles had faded, but still made my skin look blotched, and it sunk in deeper that Jace deserved better than me anyway. I had a burn scar on my wrist, and a bullet scar on the side of my waist. I was a mess.

The weather was a perfect 64 degrees, and slightly breezy. Overlooking the night skyline the city looked so peaceful. We ordered a couple of drinks. Jace was old enough now, but we still had to rely on our fake IDs'. They passed without question, and I ordered what the lady behind me had, and tried a margarita.

"Why do you look so harsh and grumpy?" he asked.

"I'm completely pleasant. What are you talking about?"

"You have been quiet since Illinois. What did I do?"

"Nothing. You did nothing. I just…I don't belong," I pouted.

"You look pretty tonight, you look like you belong. No one is looking at you like you don't belong here."

"No... You have a plan for after all of this is over, but if I survive, I'll be alone. I don't have any family other than you, and you'll be going away. I hate being alone."

I wouldn't look up at him, but I could tell he was looking at me, and I felt stupid for admitting my weakness out loud.

"Nevermind, I'll figure it out, just forget I said anything. So tomorrow we finally figure this all out," I said, changing the subject and ordering another drink.

The morning was rough. The night had dragged in a reluctant storm. We had overslept and even though we were on our own time, we had gotten used to the idea of hurrying because someone was always on our tail. The day was gray and stagnant, and the air smelled thick. We took the bus line to Paulo Ave., towards the "Middle of the Universe." It was not what we were expecting at all.

We found a metal plaque explaining that the location had once been a vehicular bridge connecting downtown to the rural district. The bridge had burnt down in the '30s, and when they rebuilt it, a circle was placed on the expansion route. The circular stone boundary pattern was added, and it was declared a tourist destination and brought in thousands of people each year.

A gray brick path led us over some railroad tracks and towards an open paved area. A one-foot diameter circle was in the center of a large bricked area. The pavement and bricks spanned out towards a hip high planter wall that surrounded the "Middle of the Universe." It seemed quite unremarkable.

There were several tourists and their children running around exploring. Several street musicians played and collected coins. We waited until a crowd of school children cleared and approached the center of the circle to investigate why this place was so significant. Standing on the center ring looking down at this unimpressive piece of pavement baffled us. The noise of the street musicians was drowned out, and an eerie silence echoed. Jace spoke first.

"What is this place?" His voice echoed and returned to us, leaving us confused.

People were walking around, and children skipped about outside the ring of the circle we were in, but all we could hear was Jace's voice. Like children, we raised our voices and howled and whistled to get the full effect. It was our own private amphitheater. The precise placement of stone barrier walls turned the acoustics in this mini arena into a deafening dome of silence. We could not hear anything beyond the border wall, and no one could hear us inside. It was fascinating.

But why were this location and its coordinates stamped onto my arm as a baby? There had to be more than an echo, and a stone wall. I kneeled to examine the center circle. The rust paint and etchings on the cement had worn away from weather and foot traffic, but a dull engraving of a creature was still visible. It looked like the head of a Lynx. I ran my finger along the arc of the circle, and something that would have been insignificant to others caught my eye. A keyhole.

Not a normal keyhole. A one-inch diameter circle, with a sliver of an opening. It was slightly curved, but it was definitely a unique keyhole of some kind.

"Jace! Look!"

He squatted onto his feet and ran his finger over the slot. "It's so small. How did you even notice it?"

"There is something inside, underneath. We need to open it," I announced.

"We can't. Not right now, there are too many people," he warned before I immediately tried to tear up the heavy cement.

"Do you think the key from the pocket watch would fit?" I asked excitedly.

"Not sure, it doesn't look like a match, but you never know. I can look over the watch when we get back to the room...Theorie…. Promise me you're not going to go ahead and do anything stupid."

"What? Why would you think that?"

"Because you have a puzzle right at your feet and you have to wait until tomorrow to try and solve it."

I wasn't giving him the satisfaction of accepting his words. "Fine," I hissed.

Back in our room Jace examined and reexamined the pocket watch that we had pulled from the piano. "I don't think it's a match," he ascertained. We ordered Kansas tenderloin from room service and turned on the TV. There was news of a fear gripping the nation that the world's infrastructure would soon be crashing and turning the economy to chaos. A massive bomb dropped on a camp of refugees. One hundred men, women, and children were killed. I couldn't help but think Felix was involved somehow. I couldn't stand it.

"Those poor people," I stammered. It hurt my heart to imagine the families just trying to survive as refugees and thinking they were safe.

"We will end it Theorie. And we don't even know if Felix caused that attack...It will be okay."

Four hours later I woke up and instantly went into mission mode. I didn't want to wake up Jace, he was sound asleep from such a heavy dinner. I snuck silently and got my shoes on, grabbed the key from the pocket watch on Jace's nightstand and threw on my blue sweatshirt.

The streets were eerie, quiet and cold. It was still damp out, but not raining, and even though it was dark, I could tell the sky was dull and thick. I had the key tucked deep in my pocket. I walked several blocks and finally made it to downtown. I walked the path we had taken earlier that day and crossed the railroad tracks. The musicians were gone, and tourists were packed away in their hotels. I had the Middle of the Universe all to myself.

I knew something was buried beneath, and most likely it was what Felix was desperately searching for. I was not going to let Felix get his hands on any riches or treasure hidden below the cement. I would collect it and use what I needed to free Jace and me, and then hand the money over to the FBI so they could help the families that Felix tore apart. I would ask Wheezie to set some aside for the families of the insurance agent and his secretary, some for Emma and Joseph, Gideon, Rubin and Neema, and for Yuri and Nico's families.

Money couldn't replace their loss, but maybe it could help them have one less thing to worry about. And it had to be money. Felix would not be so eager to find it if it didn't empower him in some way.

I knelt beside the circle, and the acoustics made me feel like I was in a dome. The breeze even seemed to avoid entering this circle. I took out the key and tried every which way possible to maneuver it into the keyhole.

It just wouldn't fit. I lay on my stomach on the damp ground to get a closer look. I flipped it, turned it, and angled it in every way possible. It just didn't work. The key was too thin and just floated in the keyhole not catching anything.

After ten minutes of trying everything possible to get the key to fit, I surrendered to my frustration and pounded on the pavement with my fists. My aching hands throbbed, but I didn't care. I slammed my hands down again, beating the ground over and over. I wanted to scream on the top of my lungs. Why couldn't I? No one could hear me.

A frustrated cathartic explosion of a scream tore out of me. Years of trying to beat Felix at his game... and I had failed. I failed everyone. I just wasn't smart enough. I bent over myself in shame. Complete and total helplessness overpowered me. I cried from deep within my stomach, burying my head to my chest. I was useless to everyone I loved.

A panicked shrill went down my spine when I looked up and saw a figure rushing towards me. A silhouette was approaching, and I had nowhere to go. Felix had found me. I should have known.

"Theorie!" Jace yelled as he came into view.

I crumbled once more and fell back to my knees, breathing deeply, relieved it was him. I sat on my feet crying and disappointed in myself. All of the tears I had held in when my father died, all of the tears belonging to Mahtap, and Tobin. They all spilled out uncontrollably at this moment. I didn't want Jace to see me, I didn't want him to see me break but I couldn't contain it.

He lowered himself to me and helped me up, pushing me back to the stone border, lifting me slightly and sitting me on the waist-high wall. He saw my bleeding fist and used the bottom of his shirt to wipe away the pebbles embedded in my flesh.

"I didn't know where you were!" he barked. "Do you know what that's like to wake up and instantly panic? I thought Felix found you. I told you not to do anything stupid. Why couldn't you just wait for tomorrow?"

"I did!" I yelled loudly. "It is tomorrow, and I am stupid," I sobbed.

In the light of the street lamps he was able to see my pain and realized my sudden release of emotion was enough punishment for scaring him. He went into repair mode. He put his arms around me and pulled my cowering shoulders into his chest. I crumbled and buried my head. I couldn't look at him.

"I'm sorry. It's okay...It's okay. What happened? ...I didn't mean to yell at you...Theorie, why did you come here without me?"

"I wanted to come and find the money, and I wanted to bring it to Wheezie, and I wanted to keep you away from it, away from me," I wailed. "I'm sorry Jace. I'm sorry I'm not smart enough. I failed you, failed Tobin, failed Dad and Mahtap. I can't figure it out! Why doesn't the blasted key work? It was supposed to work! Please go. Please go, and I'll just wait and let Felix find me. At least I'll know you're safe. I'd at least have that. Please just go!" I sobbed louder.

Jace pressed closer to me taking my breath away. I looked into his eyes, not fully understanding what he was doing. His hands moved to the small of my back and the crook of my neck as he pulled me as close to him as he possibly could. Before I could protest, his mouth met mine, and the gentle sweetness of his kiss was melting all other feelings whirling inside of me. It was stirring in me something new. It was the truest most genuine feeling I had ever known. I yielded to his embrace. I stopped crying and dissolved into his strong arms. Every breath I could catch was a warm inhalation of him. At that point, he could have asked me anything in the world, and the answer would have been...Yes.
It felt so natural to have his arms around me, that the chemistry scared me. It took me by surprise how much I

loved him, and I didn't think I would be able to let go of him. The pounding of my heart was loud enough for me to hear, and a spark of fear jolted me. I felt like I didn't have control of my arms. My heart wanted to stay lost in his grip, but my mind was forcing my fists to clench and burrow between our chests to push him away.

He pushed back the strings of hair from my cheek, wiped the tears from my face with his thumb and kissed me lightly right below my eye. With one hand on my face and one wrapped around my back he looked at me with such endearing care and love. His blue eyes. made it nearly impossible to turn him away, and I could hardly refrain from pulling him back to me.

"I'm not going anywhere. I can't convince you that the weight of the world's future is not on your shoulders. The key doesn't fit...alright...So we move on to the next clue. We keep trying. I will NOT leave you to do this on your own. I am physically incapable of doing that. I have fought this for so long, but I surrender. I do not want to fight loving you anymore."

"Me?... You love me?... You said you had someone...All those things you said... That's not me."

"Yes Theorie, it has always been you. I know you see me on the same level as Tobin and Gideon, and I probably messed everything up, but I stopped seeing you as my sister before I reached double digits. I tried to stop but pretending to be a couple and seeing you every day and just living with you. I can't. I can't stop. I don't want to love anyone else. You consume me. I have had to fight my eyes from giving me away every day. You run through my veins, and I can't just tear you from me. Please tell me, if there is *any* chance at all that you would see me as more than *just* a friend."

I was genuinely stunned.

"Me?" I muttered again. He laughed under his breath.

"Why do you keep asking that? Yes...you." His eyes were so full of hope that I would reciprocate.

"I can't," I replied. "I'm not beautiful, or smart, or kind. I'm not even a good person. It wasn't supposed to be me. I'm not all those things. I don't know what to say to you. When you talked about who you loved, it wasn't supposed to me."

"Well, it is....so, you can't what?" His demeanor sank. " You can't love me?"

"No... yes...I can."

"But, you love me like you love Tobin and Gideon, and I've ruined everything," he said with a disappointed tone.

"Felix will kill you. He separated your mom from my father when he found out they loved one another. He set them up with other people, and they couldn't be together."

The words coming from my mouth were not the ones I wanted to say. I was confused and frustrated at myself that I couldn't just be honest with him and fall back into his arms. He had pulled his hands away and withdrew into his jacket.

"Theorie...Felix will always try and destroy what he doesn't understand. He will always destroy what he judges as weak. He already knows how I feel. He's not stupid. Rubin saw it, Neema saw it. It's hard to hide. Felix will separate us and try to kill me either way."

"I can't let you get hurt," I pleaded. "If Felix or anyone else were to know, he would hurt you, and you would be targeted like he targeted my father. I ...I don't see you like Tobin and Gideon, not since Saint Petersburg," I stuttered the words out. "But I can't. I shouldn't. It will get you killed. I'd rather you be alive."

"I wouldn't." His voice echoed, as he walked away.

I followed a tails length behind him back to the hotel, and neither of us spoke to each other. The next day we boarded a train bound for the East. Jace had called Wheezie and notified her that we were in the United States with information and needed help.

Chapter 14

Wheezie, Gia, ...& Michael

Jace was cold-shouldering me for the last three days. He bought train and bus tickets to avoid a rental car where he would be forced to sit for hours alone with me. I had hurt him, deeply, and he avoided all eye contact with me. The few times I tried to get him to talk about anything he gave me short answers. He didn't agree with my reasons for pushing him away. I didn't know how to fix this, and I knew he would take off and leave me as soon as we met with Wheezie.

Wheezie wanted to meet us in Boston, Massachusetts. She was working a case and staying near the city for a while, and if she up and left to back to her office in New York, it would draw too much attention. Neither Jace or I had ever been to Boston.

It was early spring, and the city was still defrosting from a colder than typical winter. We were to meet in Quincy Market at Faneuil Hall.

Families ran through the cobblestone walkways taking pictures with the bronze statues. Peddling carts sold jewelry and candles in a thousand scents. A man playing the violin was gracefully bellowing his music. People walked in and out of shops looking at souvenirs and treats. The food court seemed to have every type of food on earth. Carefully we wound through people that were lined up ordering food.

We waited at the standing tables and watched people eating eclairs, cannoli and gyros. It smelled so good, my stomach grumbled. I was starving, but I didn't dare tell Jace that I wanted to stop so we could get something.

With our jackets and dark glasses on we turned to avoid security cameras as we waited in the busy shopping area. The large stone building pulsed with history. The vendors and crowd reminded me of England and Paris. The people were here to enjoy their day and explore the shops and historical landmarks. A happy chatter echoed through the building.

We spotted Wheezie heading towards us, and as she came closer, she made eye contact with each of us and swiftly walked past us. We followed her all the way to the waterfront near the aquarium several blocks away, where historical guided tours took off from.

Wheezie, Jace and I waited in the empty line. A boat had left just minutes before, so we had some time before more tourists arrived for the next scheduled departure.

"I'm glad you could meet me here. It won't draw suspicion," Wheezie confirmed.

We looked out over the water and felt the sea air blowing through the little overhang. Seagulls squawked and landed looking for handouts. The tide was out, and the smell of dethawing mudflat pooled near the water.

"Why the bristles? What happened with you two?...Nevermind," she changed the subject. "I don't want to know. I have information. I dug up a photo from about 1923, '24." She handed me the picture.

Jace inched closer but not too close. It was a vintage black and white photo of a woman in a flapper dress, and a feather pinned to the side of her short haircut. She was smiling but had a mischievous grin. On her wrist were markings. The same markings that were on my own wrist. They were exactly the same, symbol for symbol.

"I don't understand." I was puzzled.

"My theory is that there are always two people at any given time that have the marks. This woman knew what they were."

"That is what my father said. He said two people were marked. It used to be my mother, and Theorie's father until they burned the marks off. We know that they are coordinates," Jace admitted. I shot him a look of wrath. He really did want to be done with me now. He was handing over all our leverage.

"I figure as much but coordinates to where?" she pleaded.

"We can't tell you," I cut in, "We don't want the information to fall into the wrong hands. If money or anything else that would empower Felix is hidden there, then we can't give the location away."

She could tell that Jace and I were not on the same page anymore and something had changed between us.

"Look…. I don't know what the heck is up with you two, but I need to know right now if you're in or out. This is a symbiotic relationship, and if you're not going to help me, then I'm not going to waste my time pretending to be a tourist waiting for a history lesson. I have more. I have a box of things I found in evidence belonging to your father. I found the contents of his plane on the day he crashed. I'll make a deal with you. You don't have to give me any location. You don't have to tell me where you've been or what the crap is up your butts. I'll give you a place to stay, while you figure out your next move."

"In exchange for what?" Jace demanded.

"Names…I just want the names of any linchpin you have ever worked with, any contacts you know that Felix had. Employees, henchmen, and… I want to know what missions you were a part of, any *incidents* you may have assisted in…Are you in? Or not?"

I looked at Jace and knew this was his chance to leave me in Wheezie's hands and be done with me. I didn't want it to end like this, but I nodded in agreement. It was the first time he had looked at me in three days, and I felt like it was all I was going to get as far as a goodbye.

"I'm in," Jace insisted quickly. What was his game? Why wouldn't he just go and leave it to Wheezie? I could give her the names she wanted. I had clearly turned him away from me. Why was he staying with me?

Diane Lecari was called Wheezie for a good reason. By the time we skirted through streets and highways in her SUV she was huffing and puffing like a locomotive. Her blood pressure was spiking, and she lost most of her lung capacity within twenty minutes of our car ride. It took nearly an hour before she pulled in to the historic seaside community of Gloucester, Massachusetts. We passed a chocolate and candy store, pet groomer, and multiple companies offering Whale Watches. The town was cleaning up from winter and opening shops. We drove slightly out of the Main Street area and into a more rural setting.

She pulled in to a one car garage down a rural back road. The garage door shut, and we got out and followed her. She stomped and grunted for air coughing and wheezing as we winded through a field stone path and into a dethawing garden. We entered a country style home kitchen.

"Sit," she wheezed as she moved papers from a cluttered oak table. She picked up sweaters and crocheted scarves from the back of the matching chairs and threw them into a pile on the floor. The TV was on in the background, and we could hear someone laughing and talking to it like it was a person.

"You tell him, Judge. That's right. Trash people. They're all lying." The voice bellowed from the living room.

"Ma? Is that you?"

"Yeah!" Wheezie coarsely yelled back, with only a half a lung left. She shuffled through a junk drawer and found her Albuterol, puffing it five or six times and inhaling deeply. "Stupid thing, I can never find it when I need it."

253

"Gia?" Wheezie hollered, with newfound lung strength. "Where is my back up puffer thing?"

"What?" The voice yelled back even louder.

"Get in here!"

A woman in her thirties and no taller than five feet stomped into the room holding a mug and abruptly slammed it on the counter. She had small pretty blue eyes and a tiny little nose. Her hair was matted mouse brown and pulled back in a tight bun. She looked a lot like her mom, just smaller and younger.

"Ma! What is this? Come on!"

Gia poured more coffee in her floral mug and nodded in disappointment at her mother like she had brought another set of homeless dogs' home.

"Gia…. Jace and Thea. Thea and Jace…...Gia. My daughter. This is her place. She's got an extra room upstairs. Gia, you know the deal. No one knows they're here and I'll move them as soon as I can." She dug through a duffle bag on the chair and pulled out another inhaler. I didn't question the shortening of my name to Thea, I didn't question anything.

"I'll stay on the couch if that's okay?" Jace muttered. Wheezie and Gia raised their eyebrows in sync.

"I assumed you were together," Wheezie sighed, "but, what the crap do I know?...The couch it is."

"I'll get some blankets." Gia winked at Jace, making him blush and clear his throat. She scurried off enthusiastically to get sheets and pillows.

"Oh, and this is Michael," Wheezie stated.

There was no one else in the room, so I was pretty sure that Wheezie was insane and we had made a *big* mistake coming here. She pulled out one of the kitchen chairs and hollered as if speaking to someone that was hard of hearing,

"Come on Michael, I know they're scary people. Don't be a jerk, come say hello."

I didn't know what to expect. I glanced at Jace and realized he was as confused as I was. I stood there wide-eyed. I swore, if a grown man crawled out from under that table I would pick up my bag and walk into the surrounding forest. Hopefully, it was a kid. That's it...It must be a kid, or a dog maybe. Named Michael?

All of a sudden from under the table an uncontrollable amount of sneezing began. Clearly, it was not the petite sound of a child or the gruff sneeze of a dog. The idea that a full-grown man was hiding from strangers under the kitchen table was absurd.

"Great!" Wheezie yelped. "He sneezes when he gets nervous. Gia! Michael's sneezing and he won't come out from under the table, you're going to have to come down here!"

I stared at the table waiting for an answer. Wheezie went to the pantry and brought out a large cardboard box.

"Michael!" she yelped. "Get out from there, and let our guests sit at the table. I am NOT ordering pizza if you do not come out here and show your ugly face."

The box was abruptly plopped onto the kitchen table which frightened Michael, and he finally decided to be social. A peachy pink round 200-pound Pot Bellied Pig wearing an argyle sweater vest shuffled out from under the table. He ignored us and walked into the living room. Michael sat politely watching reality court show reruns while Gia came down the stairs and set up a bed for Jace on the couch.

Wheezie ordered a pizza, and we opened the box labeled Jailer, Morgan, case 1244. In between bites of sausage pizza, Wheezie tossed through papers and files pulling out the contents of my father's plane on the day he crashed. She handed me a photo, it was of me when I was about two. My hair was redder, and my freckles brighter. I'm smiling and sitting on someone's lap. It's a man because it's clearly wearing a suit, but the top was cut off, and there was no way of telling who was holding me. I looked so innocent and unaware.

Another photo she handed me to look over was of my mother smiling. It caught my attention. It was a small 2x3" black and white photo. She has the costume of a dancer, with bells and fringe, and the lighting was professional. She was smiling, and she had a sparkle in her eye. I placed it in my hand and aligned the two photos trying to find a resemblance.... maybe the eyes, but it was black and white, and I couldn't really tell if I looked like her at all.

"My father had these on his plane?" I asked.

"Yup, found in the cockpit among the wreckage," she replied as Michael pranced into the kitchen and lifted his snout. Wheezie put another slice of pizza in his mouth, and he contently went back to the livingroom to watch TV with Gia.

The files in the box were inquiries about the plane crash. I was about twelve years old when I remember getting the news from Joseph and Emma. Seeing the items, he had carried with him on the last day of his life made it seem like yesterday. The plane had been tampered with, and someone had jammed the fuel gage making is stick on full. He ran out of fuel over the Mojave Desert in Arizona.

His plane had flown out of the small airport in the Bronx, so the case was referred to the NYPD. When the name Jailer was noted it was instantly handed over to the FBI. That is where so many years ago Diane Lecari had come across the path of this unusual family. The fact that an experienced pilot would fly over the Mojave Desert on a hairline of fuel never made sense. The investigation proved foul play and had always lingered in the back of Wheezie's mind. So many investigations and incidents were associated with the Jailers in some way. There had never been solid proof. Witnesses would disappear, evidence would burn.

File after file of fires, poisonings, riots, murders, and even kidnappings filled the box in front of us. I shuffled through them looking for one thing. A key. I was sure my father knew the marks were coordinates. He was a pilot. He knew about the middle of the universe, and he knew what was buried beneath it. The key had to be among his things.

I felt every inch and shook each file. I found no key. But I did find a partially burned copy of the exact same Atlas he had bought me as a child. The very same Atlas that was at home in my special box in Tanzania. I held it in my hand knowing my father had held this Atlas at one time. It had tally marks just like mine but far more. Some pages were burned, but it was still filled with information.

"Can I look at this for a while?" I asked.

"You can. Just let me know if you figure anything out," Wheezie insisted.

I was shown to my little room to the right up the stairs. It was cluttered but homey. Wheezie gave me a set of fresh clothes. They were baggy and soft and so comfortable. It felt good to get out of jeans. They even found a baggy sweatshirt for Jace, and Gia threw our clothes in the washing machine for a much-needed wash. It was nice to feel human again. I curled up in bed and looked through each page of the charred Atlas. My dad had traveled so much. India, Asia, Russia, each European country, the United States, Ireland, even Australia. However, the page marked most frequently was New York. My father seemed to have traveled all over the globe.

The page was filled on the margins and overflowed onto the map itself. Hundreds of visits to New York, yet Jace and I had only gone to New York a few times. Kansas was not marked at all, even though I know my father had to have gone there.

Who was this man? It seemed like I didn't even know him. Did he work for Felix all those years? What was he responsible for? How many lives had he ruined? How could my father knowingly make Jace and I a part of this? It's not what a good father would do.

I fell asleep with the Atlas on my chest wondering if Jace was okay downstairs with Michael. I didn't wake up until ten o'clock the next morning. Everyone else had been awake for hours, and no one bothered waking me. I could hear voices coming from the kitchen.

Michael was curled up in Jace's blankets on the couch, watching cartoons and smiling. Jace and Gia were sitting at the kitchen table having coffee. They were talking about mothers. Gia was loudly explaining how her mother was impossible and stubborn, but if anyone needed a kidney, she would be the one to ask for it. She would either give you hers or find someone else to volunteer that same day. She got the job done and was efficient and responsible.

Four padlocks were lying on the table and a few bobby pins and handmade picks. Gia was fidgeting with them, and Jace was observing her and correcting her movements.

"I give up!" she yelled, "This is impossible, and these are simple locks you said?" She picked the lock back up and looked into the keyhole. "Nope!" she dropped the lock back onto the table and noticed me in the doorway.

"Good morning, princess." She threw at me as she sipped her coffee. "Jace says his mother doesn't like ya much," she accused in a thick New England accent.

"That's a shame. I'm truly devastated," I replied as dryly as I could.

"Oh Boy Jace, we've got a real live one here. Keep ya panties on, I'm just getting to know ya. Ma went downtown, she had work. She says to lay low here today, and she'll be home for three o'clock. I have to go to work in about an hour. You're welcome to anything in the fridge," she offered.

"Thanks," Jace said appreciatively.

"I am a house cleaner, not that you asked, princess. It's not glamorous, but it buys the pizza."

I nodded apathetically. I really didn't care what Gia did, but Jace was attentive and gushing with personality this morning, taking an interest in her life and hobbies and opinions. And there were a lot of opinions. She had something to say about everything for the next hour. From children's cartoons to how pedestrians should never have the right of way.

She explained that she had inherited Michael from one of her house cleaning jobs, who's little girl changed her mind about wanting a tea-cup pig as soon as he passed fifty pounds and ate her Barbies. Gia was as abrupt and crass as her mother, but there was also a side of human compassion and sarcasm that I admired.

She and her mother had a way about them that was sassy and fresh but never crossed the line. They got away with picking on and hollering at each other but neither ever got their feelings hurt or took it to heart. It amazed me, and I wanted to watch them like a television sitcom.

It was jovial and fun and sometimes downright inappropriate and mean, but the love they had for each other and the mutual respect for what each of them had endured through life poured from their banter. Jace fit right in, blending in with their show immediately. He rolled with the punches and even braved throwing it right back at them sometimes. They could take it just as good as they could dish it out. I didn't dare try, because I knew the sarcastic banter would be received differently from me. I knew what to say to really cut them, and I liked them too much to bite that hard.

So I kept quiet and watched from a distance and took all the throws and accusations of being too serious and solemn. They would sometimes get so mad at each other that they would accuse the other of playing 'Expose a fault.'

"Great Ma! So you're gonna tell them that story? … What is this? Expose a fault? You wanna go there?" Wheezie would huff and puff and tell her to hush up and go on with the funny story. By the end of the week, they had cracked my crispy shell and had me laughing. Gia's telling us about her list of precisely 97 pet peeves ranging from the letter 'C,' to people with moist hands had me belly laughing.

The light-hearted week passed, and the thick air of a disappointing love story started to lighten. Jace was not avoiding my gaze anymore and would tease me along with the girls. We helped with household tasks and tried every form of American 'Take out' that was available. We watched TV and organized and read through the files of my father's case over and over. Jace and Michael bonded over a bag of cheddar cheese popcorn, and Michael would sit next to Jace wherever he went. Jace would talk to him like he was a person and Michael seemed to appreciate that.

One evening Wheezie sat drinking a cola, while Gia sipped her herbal tea. Jace was sitting on the couch reading out loud to Michael. He was reviewing one of the files detailing the planes exact location. It was a file he had memorized by now. The pig was intently listening to him run through scenarios and map locations.

I decided to tell Wheezie about the Atlas. I explained that I had a matching one at home, and how the tally marks were different. I told her that it did not match where we had been as children. I didn't mention Kansas and the 'Middle of the Universe,' but I explained everything else I possibly could.

"Are you telling me that you can show me the differences? Do you remember your tally marks and where your father took you, and how it differs from this Atlas?" she questioned.

"Yes. I have a good memory for stuff like that. I know every mark I made in my copy."

"That…. Miss Jailer….is of great interest to me."

We spent two hours going through each page. Wheezie sat with a pen and paper writing down all the contrasting travels. In the end, it was New York that she had circled in red.

"So, what is in New York? Does it mean anything to you?" she inquired.

"No… Dad only took us there a few times, but he had been there more than a hundred times according to this book."

"We'll see…We'll see." She took her pen and drew an exact copy of my tattoo marks neatly on the paper.

"So we know your symbols. But there's always two. I know you aren't willing to tell me yet what the location is or how you were able to decipher the code, but that's okay. Unless you're willing to let me just take it from here? I can free you from all of this," she suggested.

I looked at Jace who was sitting on the floor now with his new trusted pork friend, leaning against the couch watching TV.

"No," I answered.

The next morning Wheezie was gone by the time we woke up. Jace was still out cold on the couch, and Gia was making her tea, and wiping up where she spilled. She was still in her red striped cotton pajama pants and a baggy sweatshirt. Michael trotted past her wearing a bright red hoodie on his way to use the garden.

"Ya getting sick of being cooped up in here?" she bugged.

"No. Not really," I responded. Then I instantly questioned if she had been asking the pig that question.

"Michael!" She yelled at him in a whisper interrupting herself. "Don't you dare pull up those tulips. I swear I'll sell you to the Chinese restaurant, and don't talk to Mr. George, he doesn't appreciate your cynicism," she warned.

She ignored the confused look on my face and continued her conversation as Michael looked back at her and snuffed.

"Don't you swear at me," she barked. Michael grunted and went outside to the garden.

"What a jerk," Gia said turning her attention back to me. "From what I can tell you are itching to go. You are not someone who likes to stay put, are ya? So why don't ya go?"

I looked over at Jace asleep on the couch. "I don't have anywhere to go. I need your Mom's help."

"No, you don't. I know you want to go to New York, to see what's so important that ya father stopped there so many times. It's driving ya crazy isn't it?"

"No. I can wait."

"Wait for what. Wait for my mother to hold your hand all the way there? Or are ya waiting for him?" She nudged her head towards the Living room.

"No!" I protested under my breath, so I wouldn't wake Jace up.

"So what happened? Ya, turn him down?" How did she know that?

"No!... I told him to go," I whispered under my breath even softer. "I told him he didn't have to fight this with me and he could go, and he could get away from my name and who I am."

"So you make all the decisions for him?"

"No," I disagreed.

"Well, seems that way. Seems to me that you are an impatient person who likes to be in charge. You don't appreciate what you have. You've been running, and hiding, and lying and whatever else crap your life is, and you aren't seeing what is right in front of you. You can't decide for him. Just like he can't decide for you. Seems to me you've been fighting a certain battle for so long, you don't remember why you're fighting it."

"I know why I'm fighting The Jailer's Way. I want it destroyed," I barked.

Gia sipped her tea and held her stand…"That's not the battle I'm talking about." Her one eyebrow raised, and she grinned at me with such a coy expression. "You could lose something mighty important, all so you can be the hero and solve the mystery of your last name. Your brain has run away to New York ready to chase justice, but you're hanging around here because your heart is sleeping on that couch." She sat down at the table to read the newspaper, acting like she hadn't just thrashed me and made me feel even worse about myself.

Later that evening Michael, Jace and I had the house to ourselves. Jace was still cold and distant, but I could tell he was warming up just a little. I heated up pizza in the microwave but just melted it into lava, so Jace just ate his cold. I sat at the table with a piece of paper and a #2 pencil that I pulled from Gia's junk drawer. As Jace watched TV, I sketched away.

I worked on remembering Arlo and Andrea's face, so I could get a sketch description for Wheezie. I finally brought them to life with a few flicks of eyelashes, and I used the eraser to pull the color out to leave the white light reflection in their eyes. I knew these eyes, they were so familiar. Something about seeing them again, even on paper made shivers go up my spine. Jace overlooked my paper as he grabbed more pizza and a cola from the fridge.

"It's good," he praised. "But Arlo has a more despotic brow."

I spent the rest of the evening blending and adding detail while Jace watched TV and showed the pig how quickly he could open the padlocks that Gia had been working on.

Wheezie didn't tell us where she had been the entirety of the day. It was nearly midnight when she finally shuffled into the kitchen. She was such a clutz she knocked over mugs that were drying, crashing them into the sink, waking the whole household up and drawing everyone to the kitchen. She startled Michael who was asleep at Jace's feet, making him thrash himself onto the floor, skid into the kitchen, sliding on the linoleum, finally skidding underneath the table for safety.

"Geez, Ma! What the crap? I nearly whacked you with the lamp upside the head."

"I broke the Tasmanian Devil mug. The handle chipped off. Stupid place to stack dishes!" Wheezie grumbled.

Jace was propped up now, lights had been turned on, and I moseyed down the steps curious.

"I have information," she stated frankly while picking pieces of the mug from the sink and throwing them into the trash. "You might want to sit down." Jace shot me a look inviting me to sit by him on the couch. "I went to New York today," Wheezie started.

"I'm making tea." Gia bounced back and loafed to the kitchen to turn on the kettle. I straightened my back and sat at attention with wide eyes.

"I spoke to an individual, that had been frequently visited by your father. There was a case surrounding a well-known psychiatric institution in New York. It came up in *more* than one inquiry. I had my suspicions but when I saw from the tally marks the overwhelming amount of times this city was visited I was intrigued. So I flew out this morning. I know it could have triggered an alarm, I was careful," she insisted.

"Geez, Ma. Thea, see you and Ma have the attractive trait of impatience in common."

"Hush up!" Wheezie spat. "I was able to match dates of admissions and certain trigger years, and I found a patient. A patient that your father visited at least a dozen times a year. I spoke to them. Or at least they spoke at me with a medicated smile and a constant rocking back and forth. They just kept saying over and over...hold on I wrote it down. It was a pattern of statements on repeat..." She pulled her pocket-size notebook from her jacket.

"Okay...'I was given a place...Thank you...I have three jailbirds... I have to find them... I have to give them their bookworms... I have three jailbirds... I was given a place,'...

and so on, and so on. This person walked into the psych ward and checked herself in after she admitted to aiding in the murder of two college professors. Two professors that were already retired and living off campus. They had been professors at the same campus where the photo of your father and Emma was taken. The college is where recruits for The Jailer's Way were found. Smart kids, engineers, professors, chemists. She was also a student, but instead of being a Linchpin, she was apparently given 'a place.' Do you know what that means?" I was processing everything and couldn't answer.

"Yes," Jace choked out. "It's part of Felix's game. There are Linchpins, and there are Pawns. The Pawns are placed strategically to make the lives and identities of the Linchpins or the agents blend in. My father Joseph, and Thea's brother Gideon were all given 'places.' The places are checkpoints for illegal trade, but many of the Pawns, like Rubin and Gideon, don't understand who they are working for.," Jace quickly defended.

"So when the professors were shot and killed, this individual was institutionalized, and given 'a place' for some reason." Wheezie paused and cleared her throat preparing herself for her next statement. "This person turned themselves in and refused to leave. She begged for medication. They questioned her repeatedly over the murders and how she was involved. She took responsibility for the crimes and wanted to be locked away here. Whatever her 'place' was, whether she was a Linchpin, or a Pawn, she was scared and saw no other way out than to beg for Lithium-based medication and be put in a straight jacket. The interviews went cold when she started this repetitive sentence loop. That was fourteen years ago."

"So, Tobin and I were four. The same time we went to Tanzania," I surmised.

"I was four years old, Jailbirds?" I muttered.

Wheezie knew precisely who this woman was, despite rocking back and forth to comfort herself, thin and frail from years of powerful medication, and a voice so fragile it was hardly audible. Despite having been on record as taking her own life fourteen years earlier. Wheezie knew the moment she saw the woman's eyes. They were a pretty blue-green, with an amber streak in the right one, breaking the ocean blue with a mudslide.

Chapter 15

Hidden in the Pages of Untold Stories

Wheezie had dropped a bombshell of information on me, and I had no words or questions. Jace sat beside me just as stunned.

"All these years. Your mother has been alive," Jace projected. "Theorie, do you remember the day Felix came to the house, and you overheard him say to my mother that "It was the coward that got him killed?"

"He was talking about my mother. The assignment that she refused eventually got my father killed," I agreed.

"My theory, if it matters, is that when you were four, your mother was assigned a task. Felix wanted her to kill two college professors, and she refused. She put herself in the hospital and admitted her involvement, ensuring her a life of Lithium-induced prison. She found a 'place' for herself before Felix could." Wheezie surmised.

"And then she sent you and your brothers to us," Jace added.

"But, why did Emma tell us that she took her own life just after my father's death? If she had been hiding in the institution for years, why did Emma make up how she died, and who found her? Emma said, 'she had taken her life and her flatmate found her in the bathtub.' So many details and they were so real."

"Probably because you asked so many questions, and she needed you to forget your mother," Jace concluded.

"I want to see her." I blurted out. "Tomorrow!"

"Well, I'll see what I can do. Probably not tomorrow but I head back to New York in three days. If we let the events just flow it will seem natural and won't draw attention," Wheezie offered.

"Fine," I snarled sitting back on the couch.

"Don't do anything stupid!" Jace blared at me.

"I won't!" I bit back as sarcastic as I could. Wheezie and Gia muttered under their breath mocking my inability to stay put.

"That's it!" I threw up my hands and left the room. Instinctively I wanted to pack my things and leave, but I wouldn't let them be right. I wouldn't be stupid, and I wouldn't do anything irrational. "I need to go for a walk or something." I hurried to get on my jacket and scarf. Jace shot up from the couch and started putting on his own jacket and boots.

"I don't need a babysitter Jace, I'm just going for a walk. I'm not going to be stupid. Leave me alone, and don't follow me!" I shouted as I slammed the screen door and walked through the garden to the road.

I walked the whole length of the tree-lined New England road four times. There were only a few neatly manicured homes along the way and no traffic. The evergreens smelled fresh, and the maples were just sticks this time of year with little birds hopping to and fro. Spring was in bloom and tulips, and crocuses shot up from the damp leaves and frosted trenches.

How could my father tell me that my mother was living in New York and was depressed, and too ill to care for my brothers and me? Emma and Joseph have lied to us all these years and told me she died right after my father's plane went down? I had asked them so many questions about my mother. Emma always said to me that she had not known my mother and could not answer my incessant questions. I was desperate to know little things like, what her laugh sounded like, or if she hummed while she baked? Strange and random questions would pop into my mind ever since we came to Tanzania. Both Joseph and Emma had gone to college with my mother, they knew her. Maybe they couldn't answer *all* of my questions, but they could have told me something...anything!

I had only ever seen black and white photos of her. What had she been a part of? Why did she break and fault from Felix? Why didn't Felix just kill her? I had so many questions. I pieced together memories and conversations that were all clicking into place. I finally collected myself enough to walk back peacefully to the house. Jace was waiting by the fence. He had not followed me, but he had stayed within earshot of me.

"Wait," he pleaded, holding on to my arm before I could walk by. "I just want to say I was sorry."

"For what?" I sneered.

"Just pipe down and let me get out what I need to say." His tone was serious, and it scared me. "I'm sorry I rushed you and tried to make you see me differently. I thought that I could forget, and it would go back to how it was. I thought I could, but it's not that easy." He paused and looked at me with the same look of hope I saw in his eyes the night he first kissed me. "I'm sorry about your mother, and that my parents lied to you."

I didn't know how to respond. Part of me wanted to run into his arms and forget the universe around me. Part of me wanted to yell at him and make him hate me so that he would leave and be free.

"Jace. I am afraid."

"Of your mother?" he asked.

"No…I'm afraid I'll lose you. But, no matter what I can't prevent that can I? If I push you away and you leave and start a normal life, then I'll lose you. If I accept how much I love you, I *will* push aside all reason and unreservedly be your other half. But, then Felix will find out and separate us or even kill you, and I will lose you. Either way, I can't think of a way to keep Felix away from you, other than to push you away and fight this battle alone. Jace, you could get a new identity, and disappear, and you would be safe, and I could breathe knowing that."

"You would know that *I* was safe. But, I wouldn't know that *you* were. You've been my other half since you came to the farm. You tell me just to stop hearing your heartbeat in my head, or to forget how your eyes get brilliant teal when you are thinking of what to do next. You can't expect to destroy a decade long attachment in one day just like you can't destroy a century-old network all on your own. You are the bravest person I know, but you are fierce and impulsive, and you're going to get killed doing this alone. To protect you is instinct in me, and you can't stop it."

"I don't know how to be anything else, or how to fight for anything else. Why can't my mind figure out what to do? "I will get you killed. You have to get away from me. I'm not a good person!" I pulled away with a pain in my chest and quickly sped back to the house, and into my room.

I hated myself even more. I knew deep down that if Jace stayed and waited for me, Felix would hurt him. I knew that I could not have him, but I also could not hold the burden of losing him in my hands. I forced the images of Arlo beating him to death out of my mind. I fought the images of searching for him or seeing him on Mahtap's path a few feet ahead of me, but never actually reaching him. I resisted the pictures painting my brain of being in his arms and seeing how much he really did love me overflowing from his eyes.

I tried to sleep to pass the daylight, but I would barely sleep for the next two nights. Jace was no longer angry at me. His expression had changed from the first time I had turned him away. He wasn't cold, or distant, or angry. He went through the next couple of days as if we had not spoken at all. He was trying to maintain a poker face because he knew I could read his body language, and he was not willing to let me see the consequences of my refusal. We went on like this for two days as we waited for Wheezie to bring us back to New York to meet my mother.

The New York Central Psychiatric Institute was a compound straight out of Mary Shelley's Ingolstadt. The exterior was eerie and cold, but passing through the entrance and lobby, I noticed that the first floor was cheerful and pleasant. The room smelled like soap and pine needles. The walls were bright lime green and outdated with artificial ficus trees placed in corners.

People sat randomly in rocking chairs or wheelchairs left to their own disoriented reasonings. Wardens went about their duties, as patients on the low-security level wandered about. Some were playing cards, some were aimlessly looking out of the big front picture window.

One man in gray sweatpants and greasy hair was talking to the plastic pine tree in the corner of the room that still had remnants of Christmas decor strung about. He laughed occasionally and leaned in to tell the pine a secret, while cupping his mouth, and cautiously looking over his shoulder. A woman in a blue skirt and thick tan stockings sat in a chair and ferociously rolled her clothing over with a lint remover. She frantically removed the furry dulled layer, exposing a fresh sticky new one. Then began the whole process over again.

Each one of them at one time had been someone's baby, or someone's brother or sister. Each of them was here for a reason. Some smiled, some sat crying, some stood lost and confused. Each face had a story but was unable to tell it. Not many of them would make eye contact with Wheezie, Jace, and I as we walked past the common room and got security passes for the top floor.

Level three was reserved for the severely ill and dangerous. Either to themselves or to others. Stepping off the elevator with our armed guard, the atmosphere changed and became much grimmer. The walls were grayish blue, and the windows were barred. The air turned to an aroma of metal and chlorine. The feeling of a sunny common game room two floors below changed to a prison ward, where sectioned padded rooms with small barred windows were all we saw of the individuals living on this floor.

We went through two more security checkpoints, and Wheezie escorted me to an interrogation style room. There was an observation window that could be viewed from a secured office, where Jace and Wheezie watched as I sat anxiously waiting for my mother's company.

An armed guard finally broke the silence, entering the room escorting a small figure wearing a white hospital robe over a gray jogging suit. She had hand crocheted pink slippers on, and her hands were bound with a cord. Her hair was cut short and was unkempt but was the same color as Gideon's, a dark rich brown with a jet-black tone. Her nearly closed eyes were set deep at the bottom of encompassing dark gray circles. She stared at the ground, rocking slightly from one foot to the other.

"Do you want to sit down?" I pleaded. She didn't answer. I started with idle chit chat about the little garden and park outside that residents could exercise and walk on. Then I realized she was on the third floor, and probably not allowed to walk the grounds freely. "There are a lot of little birds in the park," I started.

The word caught her attention, and she perked her chin up in a slight pinching motion like she was smelling the air. Birds...I needed to ask about the Jailbirds.

"The park has many little birds...Jailbirds.... Three... Little... Jailbirds," I continued.

The words disturbed her, and she started to become anxious. Her rocking was evolving into a swifter pace from one leg to the other.

"Jailbirds," she mumbled without looking at me.

Her appearance was so sorrowful and pathetic, I wanted to grab her and hold her and call her...Mom. I felt so much pity for what she had been through. I knew she was forced to be my father's wife even though he loved another. I knew she had given up her children after a failed mission, and she had been in fear of her life. I knew she deliberately brought herself into this state of confusion and ignorance.

"I was given a place." As she said this she briefly looked aimlessly around the metallic interrogation room, rocking her head awkwardly. "Thank you...I have three little Jailbirds... I have to find them... I have to give them their bookworms," she muttered. Her rocking was much more intense now, and the guard stood erect to steady her and gave her a warning with his body language.

"It's okay," I motioned to the guard. "I'm going." I didn't want to instigate a problem by causing her any upset.

I walked closer to her, just to look into her eyes. I would most likely never see my mother again, and even though she was gray and puny, she was beautiful still. Her eyes met mine, and for a moment, I saw a twitch of mental clarity. Her rocking steadied, and she calmed, looking at me like an adoring mother naturally would look at her newborn daughter. Her eyes *did* match mine, blue with an Amber streak. She had a look of hope on her face and excitement for just a few seconds before the medicines circulated, and she was brought back to a glassy-eyed lost soul. She leaned in rocking again slightly and whispered,

"My little Jailbirds need their bookworms. If they are to get away, they need the key. They need their bookworms." In an instant she became panicked. Her body trembled, and the rocking intensified.

"I want my medicine!" she yelled at the guard. "I want my medicine! Now!"

The guard led her to the third-floor infirmary, and Wheezie and Jace met me in the hallway.

"What did she whisper to you before she flipped out?" Wheezie begged.

"She said the Jailbirds need their bookworms." I left out the bit about the key for the moment.

"Can we see her room?" I inquired. Wheezie tried to connect dots in her head, but I could tell she was coming up blank.

"Sure, I'll ask the guard."

My mother's room was about ten square feet with one barred window that had been taken over by the film of weather and age. The walls were the same gray color as the rest of the third floor. Her bed was neatly made and tucked in. A small nightstand table had a Bible and some crayons of various colors laid out.

Wheezie picked up the Bible. Passages had been highlighted throughout with the crayons. Most of the markings were from the book of Samuel. I took the book and flipped through quickly reading what was of interest to my mother.

It was the account of Hannah who was barren and prayed to God for a child. The high priest Eli believed she was at the temple drunk because her prayer was so intense. I remembered this story, Mahtap had read it to us. Hannah promises that if she has a child she would give him over to the temple once he was weaned and the child would grow up in the service of God.

Hannah is blessed with a little boy and she names him Samuel. She honors her promise to God, and after Samuel is weaned, she delivers him to the temple where he will live and grow up. It's a story about honor and sacrifice and a mother's love. I placed the Bible back on the table and arranged the crayons precisely as they had been.

The room was plain with a chair bolted to the floor, and a small bookcase also attached to the wall. The bookshelf held all that was important to my mother, all she was allowed to entertain herself with. She had several classics. Robin

Hood, Anna Karenina, and Dickens were lined up neatly in a row. I knew these books well, they were favorites of my own. A basket full of socks rolled into tight balls sat on the bottom shelf, and a blue crochet hat was placed next to them. A soft-bristled hairbrush and a leather-bound journal sat on the second shelf. The journal had nothing but blank pages, and there was no pen or pencil, but it was placed perfectly on the shelf. Her words about her Jailbirds needing their bookworms ran through my head.

"Alright, I don't see anything of importance here. We can go so they can bring her back to her room," Wheezie suggested.

"Wait!" I pleaded. "I just want to look at her books." I looked over the titles. Emma, Sense and Sensibility, The Secret Garden, Robin Hood, Uncle Tom's Cabin, Our Mutual Friend, Little Dorrit, Anna Karenina. My first instinct was to pick up Tolstoy, but then a thought jumped into my mind. My mother was precise and deliberate in how she laid her items out. She would have been deliberate in her words to me. Jailbirds?

What book was about a jailbird? I knew several secondary characters here and there were criminals or considered to be jailbirds, but for the most part, they were love stories or childhood adventures. Other than Dickens. Those stories were in-depth and encompassing, and the reason I always loved Dickens was that in most of his classics, the bad guy gets it in the end.

I thought about jailbirds...Little Dorrit! I knew as soon as I realized that I would find something inside the pages of Dickens famous book about a father and daughter living in debtors' prison as 'Jailbirds'. I lifted the book and carefully skimmed through the pages looking for a clue, or maybe a code or message written, matching the marks of my tattoo. Nothing. There were no tally marks, no letters circled, no pages creased, it was just a standard copy of Dickens.

I was wrong! I really was stupid, and all my hopes of figuring my life out were about to fly out the barred window when a page stuck, and I carefully pulled it apart to reveal a thin sliver of metal. It was many times thicker than the paper and as stiff and unbendable as titanium. I peeled it from the page it had embedded itself into. Jace and Wheezie drew closer to examine my treasure.

"The Ke…" Jace started to spit out before I cut him off.

"No! Not here."

I tucked the metal strip into my sleeve and replaced the book, straightening and perfecting its exact spot. I knew that was important to my mother. I gave the lonely room one last look and turned my back on my mother and her life in that isolated sanctuary. I hoped I'd see her again someday, but not like this. I wanted to see her again as she was in that small black and white photo that was on my father's plane when it went down. She was smiling and playful and had mischief in her eyes. I would have loved to know those stories.

We flew back to Boston immediately after our visit and drove the hour trip back to Gia's house in Gloucester. Back at Gia's home, Jace held the metal treasure in a cloth and sat at the table examining it. It was sharp and detailed. It had been explicitly cut and forged by a master. Wheezie poured all of us a scotch and plopped herself into the chair.

"Should I leave?" Gia inquired.

"No," I replied. "It's okay...Stay. You've let us live in your house for weeks now and never made us feel like we had to go. It's your kitchen anyway."

Jace looked at me, I could tell he was bursting at the seams to explain that we knew what this piece of metal was. I just smiled gently, and he knew I wouldn't mind if he told them and brought Wheezie and Gia up to speed.

"It's a key," he divulged. "We do have a decipher, and the coordinates led us to a spot out West. We had never been there with Morgan, but we believe he went there many times without us. We found the spot Felix has been looking for, but we couldn't open it. There was a slim keyhole with strange grooves and twists. Custom made and impossible to pick...This is the key."

Wheezie looked like she had just been handed a shiny diamond. "Are you telling me that all we have to do is go unlock this spot and untold treasure and wealth will be found?" She lightened up.

"It's not that easy. Felix has been looking for this place. He wants whatever is inside. He will kill for it," I warned.

"Well, we have a better shot at exposing him if we know what is inside." Wheezie offered. "I have some following up I'm going to do tomorrow. We have resources that can help unwind this. I've looked into the case of the murdered professors, and I have an open case right now regarding a missing diplomat. I have reason to be looking into specifics on the name Jailer, so I won't draw attention. My concern is how high up Felix has contacts. We can't trust anyone outside of this circle. Is that clear?"

"We are well trained in the art of distrust," Jace consoled.

"You trusted me, you trusted my daughter, Why?" Wheezie asked.

"Because we don't have a choice," I admitted. "If it's not you, then there is no one we can trust so, either way, we are dead. But you brought us here, to your normal life, to your daughter and her pig. You knew we had targets on us and yet you still took a chance and believed our story. What choice do we have other than to trust you?" Jace looked at me surprised by my words, and I felt confident that what I said was true...for a moment.

"Okay." Tomorrow I'm going to double check and make sure I haven't set off alarms. I can set up a reason to go to Kansas."

"Wait...How did you know it was Kansas? We never said it was Kansas?" I panicked. I jumped from the table and startled everyone. "How? How Wheezie?"

Jace was suspended, and the air froze. Gia held her glass to her mouth.

"What's happening? Ma?"

"Simmer down. I'll tell you. I've known all along it was down route 66. The Middle of the Universe. I had written down your markings, I had the photo of Emma at the college. It was blurry, and we thought it was illegible, but I have resources and access to the newest technology available. I was able to clarify the photo, and have it enhanced. With two lines of intersection, I just needed to have the marks deciphered."

"Let me guess...resources?" Jace suspiciously asked.

"No... I checked your clothes while you were sleeping. I found the decipher folded up in your pocket. Hey, if you didn't want it to be found then don't leave your pants on the floor...Just saying."

Jace was visibly irritated and disappointed in himself for not being more careful. He shot me a look of apology.

"Don't judge me. I'm not just going to let anyone know where my daughter lives even if she is a pain in my crack. I needed to do some digging, any mother would, let alone an FBI agent," she justified. She was right, I didn't blame her. We were dangerous, and she had taken a chance with us.

"Why didn't you tell us that you knew?" I asked

"Clearly, when we met, you didn't want me to have the information, so when I found the decipher, I cut off that lead and pinned it for another day. I let you think I was still looking, that you had a bargaining chip. It was like I said in the beginning... You give me names, and I give you pizza and clean clothes. I'm not after money or any treasure hidden in the Middle of the Universe. I'm after the faces behind this whole diabolical operation."

"So I will set up Kansas, and you will give me names?" Wheezie asked.

All sense of suspicion was useless, we did need her as a confidant, and friend. I handed over the sketches I had made of Arlo and Andrea without hesitation. Jace cooperated in giving a detailed description of their appearance, specialties, and where they had been seen last.

I asked Gia to fill my glass and sat down at the table. I began to explain the missions in Saint Petersburg while Jace and I were apart. I told my friends that I had killed a man. Jace was woken up by these words as I broke down. With a trembling voice, I explained what had happened to a target that I was assigned.

"I was told to break into a pharmacy and switch out a prescription bag with a man's name on it in the pickup bin. I knew I should not have done it, but I had declined three assignments earlier that month and had a threatening visit from Felix. I went to the pharmacy in the dark of night, shutting off the security system and picking the lock carefully, so it did not look tampered with. I replaced a prescription for the intended victim and completed the mission.

Two days later there was a train derailment. The train engineer had failed to slow at a junction that he had driven a thousand times before. It derailed and slid off the track hitting a building head-on. There were forty-five people with injuries and two deaths including, the engineer.

The engineer's name matched to the prescription bag I had switched. The news stated that his blood came back clean, so he wasn't drinking, or high. His wife explained that he had a disorder that blurred his vision due to ocular blood clots but that he was on glaucoma medication for it and took it religiously. I knew it was me that had caused his death. I didn't understand why this man was significant, but the accident was deemed sabotage.

The engineer was Croatian and rumored to have been working with a group of extremists. Later that year genocides and senseless bombings took innocent lives in retaliation. It just escalated…."

I was unable to finish my last few words. The pit in my throat choked me. "See Jace…see why you should leave me alone…I have to answer for that. I'm, sure there are many more 'incidents' that my actions are linked to. I'm sure I was the linchpin that tipped so many things over. I have no right *not* to trust you because you should *not* trust me. I am dangerous, and I was hiding it from you. I understand if you want to take me into custody," I confessed.

I burrowed my chin into my chest in shame. I couldn't look and see their disgust and rejection. I was exposed, and I felt alone and doomed. Gia poured another shot into everyone's glass, and I drank mine down instantly. I was trembling and felt exposed and raw. They saw me now for who I was. My entire childhood I wanted people to like me, I tried to fit in and be accepted. I would lie about who I was and make up stories about magical childhoods. I wanted attention, and I wanted to have a fantastic story.

Now sitting here I hated who I had become. I hated everything about my story and who I was. I didn't want anyone to know my story, I wished to hide it from the world. I awaited my sentence, slightly relieved to have gotten that secret out. I knew it was my burden to bear, but just admitting my despicable behavior felt like a step in the right direction.

"Theorie. I'm going to be honest with you," Wheezie admonished. "I work for the FBI, I chase down international criminals. Especially the ones who impress and train MINORS to run tasks that end in economic shutdowns or genocide." Her voice raised, but not at me...She was fuming with anger and it burned in her a need for justice. I understood her urge.

She spoke with a fierce determination. "Felix will answer for his population control schemes, and Felix will pay for using children and training them to be linchpins. Felix will pay...but I can't stop you from living with guilt."

"But *I* should pay for what *I* have done!" I intensely damned myself.

"Look at you!" Wheezie shouted back at me. "You are running and hiding. You have had everything taken from you. Your parents, your brother. You are punishing yourself for being Felix's victim. You and Jace were children when your father started your training. You were molded and pressed into fearing this man and forced even at gunpoint to run his evil errands. You were shot for crying out loud. Stop punishing yourself. Stop punishing Jace."

"I'm not punishing Jace. He chose to stay, I'm not forcing him..." I looked over at him. He sat intently observing my scolding. "I'm not punishing you…" I murmured softly, searching my mind for any truth in her words.

"Woohoo." Gia whistled out. Anyone got a knife. The air in here is waaay too thick. Want another?" she implored, holding the bottle to my empty glass.

Jace held out his cup for another. I didn't know what I wanted right then. But my head pounded now. I got up slightly dazed and went to my room while they finished the bottle.

The morning came, and everyone's head was pounding for various reasons. I showered and then joined Wheezie at the kitchen table. She pulled a mug from the drying rack next to the sink, and I sat with my left-hand holding up my forehead, still unable to make full eye contact.

I unwrapped the cloth and reexamined the key. I hated this key. I hated Felix, I wanted to see him executed in multiple ways. Death wasn't enough justice for what he had done. I was scared to imagine what Jace thought of me. Maybe now he would easily be able to move on and let me go. I didn't deserve him. I had lied about being honorable and good and hid my actions. I wished I had never gone to Tanzania when I was four. I wished my father's plane had crashed with me in it.

Wheezie poured me a cup of black coffee. "Stop it!" she snapped. I looked up confused. "Stop wallowing in thoughts and what-if's and wishes. There's no sense in it," she insisted.

"I *am* punishing myself, and I *am* punishing Jace. I am punishing him for loving me. I don't mean to…Seeing my mother and how damaged she is scared me. She's so alone. She may be technically alive and breathing, but she has no purpose or love. When I saw her, I understood that she is punishing herself for her past. She decided to punish herself and lock herself away, but she punished me and my brothers as well. We grew up without her."

"Alright now, no sense in this wallowing. It is what it is. This is your life, and you can be one of three things: A die-hard seeker of justice, taking down international war criminals like a woman crazed with blind hatred. You can lock yourself away like your mother, and blind yourself to the world and the people who love and need you, or you can hand over your death wish and appreciate what you have. Let yourself be loved, and live."

"That's not an option. Why even bring that up? It puts everyone in danger."

"No," she continued. "I have an alternative suggestion…You lay low for a while somewhere. Wherever you were before Kansas maybe. I'll keep looking and digging using my resources. I give you my word that I will not give up until Felix is caught. I will dig into every case and every incident. I will find people he has worked with, and this will end."

"It's too dangerous, he would find you and have you killed. He could kill Gia. I couldn't throw it all on you, and if Felix knew Jace and I were…he would kill Jace."

"Don't you know who I work for? I have been with this agency for thirty years. I have a pretty good idea of what resources I need to use, and a darn good nose for laying low, and you and Jace are masters at hiding and being unseen."

"Why would you do that? Why would you let me go?" I pleaded.

"Because *you* are not 'The Jailer's Way'. You're just an eighteen-year-old kid. If you go now, you could still have a life. You're young enough to find some sort of happiness. Now...I'm not saying you're not scarred...physically, and emotionally. And you'll have to mend and heal, but this is your chance. Start new. Try shopping. Try going to the movies. Try normal everyday things. For God's sake, you don't even know how to use a microwave. That's a real problem." I couldn't help but smile. I looked over to the couch at Jace...but he wasn't there.

"If you're looking for Michael he's not there," she teased, "He went with Gia for breakfast stuff. Like normal people do. Don't worry, he'll be back."

"I'm pretty sure I burned that bridge with my confession last night."

"Look, lady. You still think it's all about you. We polished off that bottle and Jace had a few confessions of his own. You both are no angels. I have been sharing my house with a couple of trained assassins," she mumbled under her breath teasing me.

"Wheezie?" I implored.

"Ya?"

"I really am sorry. For everything. I need to fight this to the end. I need to see my last name and all it's tied to go up in flames."

She cleared off the glasses from the night before, putting them into the sink as Jace and Gia returned with bags of food. "I know, and I understand," she comforted. She put her arm around my shoulder, and half squeezed me without showing too much of her tender side.

"Who's up for pancakes?" Gia announced cheerfully.

Michael flew into the kitchen at the speed of light. Pancakes were his favorite food, and he barreled in, plopping himself on his bottom as soon as he reached the stove. He waited patiently not taking his eyes off the preparations.

In the next hour, the day's plans were made. Wheezie was going to the office to set up a reason to travel to Kansas and to double check for any leaks or reasons to think she had gotten the wrong kind of attention. She didn't want us to leave with anyone catching wind of this part of her investigation.

Gia had a cleaning job in the morning, and we would all meet back at headquarters/ the kitchen at 1:00. Wheezie told us to be packed and ready to go at any time, so I washed our clothes and repacked them tightly. I had the key wrapped in the handkerchief and tucked it deep in my bag. We had our documents, and ID's all set.

Jace was quiet all morning, and I was anxious to read him, and how he felt about the last twenty-four hours. I washed up the dishes and changed the sheets on my bed and anxiously ran through scenarios of our trip to Kansas and the dangers we might face. I debated over Jace and how I could fix it between us. But the more I thought of him the more confused I became.

"I'm going to go for a walk," I announced.

"But we are supposed to wait for Wheezie." Jace sat up concerned.

"It's just a walk. I'll just go down the road, I'll be fine," I promised.

"Can I come with you?" he asked.

"If you want to."

He tied his shoes and jumped from the couch to join me. We made it out the back door and walked through the garden. It had sprung up in the last few weeks, and buds and weeds were intertwining in a wild and unkempt way. It kind of reminded me of the foliage along Mahtap's path. I ran my hand over the hip-high weeds and wildflowers. The sweet smell of lily of the valley and lilac swept through the light breeze. It was such a beautiful day, with the noon sun glittered on the green buds and tall grass. Michael pushed past us and went to roll in the shade near the big evergreen bordering the yard.

"Theorie?" Jace stopped me at the gate. "If you're going to bolt for Kansas with the key… I'd like to go with you."

"What? Why? No, I swear I wasn't going to bolt. I'm waiting for Wheezie. I honestly just wanted to go for a walk so I could think," I defended myself. Both of us silently stood awkward wondering what to say next.

"You would run with me?" I pressed.

"Yes...If you really need to go, and it's killing you to stay here and wait for someone else to direct us, then we can go. I just want you to know that if it's between you and Wheezie, I will go where *you* go. We could take the key and leave right now before they get back."

"My confession last night didn't shock you? I sort of thought you would take off as soon as you could get away from me."

"Really? he said sarcastically. "You still don't know how this love thing works do you?"

He smiled at me, and his warm gray-blue eyes melted me. Why he loved me made no sense, and I fought accepting it, but an overwhelming need to begin that adventure pushed me towards him. Wheezie's words about laying low, going home, and being normal filled my head. Jace was willing to leave behind the safety of Wheezie and the FBI's resources to chase after a death wish with me. Clearly, he wasn't going anywhere no matter how much I pushed him away and deep down inside I was so grateful. Why couldn't I just let him love me? All of a sudden, I didn't want to be a hero anymore, I just wanted Jace.

I inched closer to him. His look of confusion made me smile more.

"What?" he asked. "What are you smiling at? Theorie, what do you want to do? Where do you want to go?" he pleaded, getting frustrated.

I moved closer to him picking up his hands in mine and sliding them down the curve of my sides as I pulled him closer to me, compressing the space between us until I was pressed up against him.

"Here," I softly assured him.

He pulled me to him with a hold on my waist that would have taken a tsunami to separate. Years of frustration and want cemented us together. An urgent force pushed my body backwards against the garage wall as his arms held me in a protective grip. My racing heart beat so fast I felt like it was burning within my chest. I knew from that moment on that my adventure tides were changing, and the hate I stoked for Felix was no match for this wave.

I stood with my eyes closed, feeling the softness of his dark hair in my fingers, and in an instant, I couldn't imagine being anyone but his other half. Nothing else mattered, and I would have married him right then and there if I could have. There was no one else I could marry. I could never love anyone the way I loved him, and there was no way I was going to live my life without him. I had belonged to him, and he had belonged to me for years before I appreciated it or understood it.

The electric garage doors rattled and brought us back into the realm of reality. Either Gia or Wheezie was home. Michael trotted to the gate to greet his family. Quickly Jace and I crept from the garden, back to the house and tried to gather our composure. Jace started rewashing clean dishes, and I ran to the living room, turned on the TV and combed my hair with my fingers and pretended that I had been sitting there alone for the last two hours waiting for her return. It was Gia.

"What kind of lunatic sits watching infomercials?" she murmured. She shuffled in with her pig and flopped her bag on the kitchen table, grabbed a cola from the fridge and snatched the remote from my hand, changing the channel to a reality court show. We were unmistakably quiet, and it was awkward and torturous.

"Okay. What the crap? Did I just walk into a massive argument or should I leave and give you the place to yourselves?"

We didn't have to answer because Wheezie broke through the screen door and threw her bag on the table. Jace sat at the table adjusted his chair and tried to act natural, but it wasn't working. We had been trained to behave naturally and to not draw attention to ourselves, but everything I was feeling was new, and I didn't know how to hide it.

The relief of not fighting or punishing myself and just loving Jace the way I wanted to was glowing from my face. I tried to tone down my happiness and act stressed and anxious about our traveling, but it wasn't working. I couldn't help but look at him with a hidden smile and wish that our friends hadn't come home.

"So…Hi…Isn't anyone going to ask me what happened today?" Wheezie pleaded.

Gia chuckled while she sipped her soda. "That's an excellent question," she mused, as she went to watch TV on the couch.

"Okay…So I had an interesting…Is someone going to tell me what the crap is up with you two?"

"Nothing, we have just been waiting for you. We're all packed. So what did you find out?" Jace asked, deferring the attention off us.

"Alrighty then…I arranged for Kansas, and we can leave in the morning. I found some information about your father, Theorie. I started tracking his movements from his flight records. They're all a mess, and big patches are missing but I mapped it out, and it seems like annually your father would visit this 'Middle of the Universe.' The only reason I know about it was because I looked up specific flight manifestos from the airport." She pulled from her bag a pile of documents.

"He did *not* fly into Western International. That airport log had nothing on him. A small operation, a Francis T. Macintosh Airport had all the flight records. Felix would have had no reason to look into this area, and your father manipulated the dates to have it coincide with missions he was on for extended periods of time. I believe whatever is in the middle of the universe, your father put it there."

"Why did the old photo of the woman from the twenties have the same marks as me? She must have known about the hiding place, and whatever is inside," I surmised.

"I… agree," Wheezie stated as a matter of fact. "I think your father was not the first to be visiting this location. I think Felix inherited The Jailer's Way from your grandfather Theodore, and your father inherited the knowledge of whatever is hidden in that hole in the ground. I don't know who from yet, but I'll find out. Your dad believed in you Thea, he knew you were clever enough to figure it out, and not just ignore the 'writing on the wall,' or your wrist."

I remembered my father's look of approval, and how happy he was when he found a face that spoke to him in a crowd, a face with a story that he wanted to know. I thought of how proud he would be when his photos would come out just right, and he would beam with a satisfied, "There you are, you amazing soul," as he held his photo up and studied the lines of their eyes, and the brightness of their teeth. Each portrait was his masterpiece.

In the moment of opening the hidden world below the middle of the universe, I could just for a moment, be my father's masterpiece. Even though he was gone, I still wanted to make him proud. I wanted to vindicate my father and prove that he had fought the Jailer's Way and was not a callous linchpin.

I could for *my* moment in the spotlight be the hero that exposed an evil man and brought justice to so many people. I would be loved and admired and accepted. It was all I had ever wanted...Until today.

"So tomorrow we go!" Wheezie exclaimed with excitement.

"No!" I erupted, startling her and Jace. I stood and carefully took the key from my bag. I handed the wrapped treasure to Wheezie. "Here... You offered to take this for me?"

She reluctantly reached out her hand and laid her fingers over the cloth. She was unsure of my intentions at first, but then she looked in my eyes, and she knew. She saw the resolution on my face to hand all of The Jailer's Way over to her. Without a word, I told her I was ready and willing to leave behind the purpose that tenaciously moved me, and the knots of justice that bound me had been untied and surrendered for a new cause.

"Yes, I did…" she accepted with a respectful grin. "What do you need from me?"

"A way to escape, so we can stop running, and just...live," I answered looking over at Jace who seemed stunned at my willingness to relinquish my fight.

"Are you sure, Theorie?" he asked looking intensely into my eyes for any regret or second guessing. My smile of contentment and determination was evident.

"You will need money, and tickets, and a way you can get in touch with me. Use payphones for now. Don't use cell phones, I don't trust those things. Too easy to hack and track." Wheezie jumped into action plan B. "I want you to call me on the 9th of every third month, at nine in the morning exactly. I'll expect it. Use false names and don't call from the same area that you are staying at. What else will you need from me...ID's?"

"A marriage license," Jace answered. He came closer and stood in front of me. "We have been the truest of friends in sorrow, in pain, fear and laughter. If we're going to stop running, stop fighting, and we're going to...live, will you live life by my side? As my friend *and* my wife?"

"I will. I think that is where I have belonged all along."

"I knew it!" Gia yelled. "Ha! See Ma, I told ya."

"All I did was go to work...and all of a sudden we're having a wedding," she said, enamored with the sudden change of plans. "I'll have everything ready by morning." she agreed with a smile from ear to ear.

Chapter 16

A Keyring & Bits of Chewing Gum

Wheezie arranged for us to take a private flight. It was full of Red Cross donations, and we would pose as Red Cross volunteers. We had the necessary papers forged. We had chosen the names Ben and Hannah for our documents, but fortunately only had to remember to use the names as far as Katmandu, Nepal. Wheezie had all the paperwork we needed including our marriage license, which was made out in our birth names.

Sitting at her kitchen table, she laid out our paperwork and told us of all our instructions and contacts. We were shown our tickets and ID's and presented with a certificate of marriage, as Wheezie said,

"Sign, here James, and Theorie, you sign, here."

"All set," she exclaimed. "You got rings?"

"Oh...I didn't even think of that." Jace seemed embarrassed.

"I don't need a ring," I quickly responded.

300

"Oh no... What is wrong with you? You need a ring." Gia stated. She began rummaging through her junk drawer, tossing things aside. "I got nothing..." She finally gave up.

Wheezie sighed as if she was the one who had to fix everything and grabbed her purse. She tore her keys out and tossed the bag back to the chair. She untwisted a small aluminum key ring from her key chain.

"Here!" She shoved it into Jace's palm. He looked at it and didn't dare criticize the generous offer. It slid onto my finger and fit perfectly. He held my hand, and we both smiled looking down at this impromptu wedding band.

"Congratulations! You're married." Her matter of fact statement threw me off guard.

"Wait…. That's it? We're married?" Jace looked just as rushed and bewildered as me.

"Yeah. It's just signatures I needed…You know it's not complicated, right? Anyone can get married. It's the divorces that take months."

"Oh," Jace replied. Wheezie shuffled through more papers abruptly.

"I'm going to look for some champagne. I must have some somewhere…" Gia announced as she kneeled on the floor and reached into a lower kitchen cabinet. "Nope, that's Balsamic vinegar…That won't work. Oh, wait!" She hustled over to the fridge, pulled out two beers and filled four glasses. "Congrats!" as she chugged hers down. "You make a very *complicated* couple," she added.

Still not quite sure how to react, I felt a sudden intense embarrassment. I was Jace Taralock's wife, in the flick of a pen. It was what I wanted most in the world, but the rush of the preparations and the wild company in the kitchen prevented us from showing any excitement or affection. I could see the look on Jace's face, wondering, what next?

Wheezie helped put all our paperwork in our bags, and Gia put essentials like granola bars, soap, and extra socks tucked neatly inside. She went back to rummage through her junk drawer, looking for something specific.

"Here! Found it. Every newlywed needs these." She pulled out a half-eaten roll of wintergreen breath mints and shoved them into Jace's bag."

"Those *are* important," he joked. Wheezie was still sifting through her satchel of work files and papers.

"Ah here!" She handed me an envelope with a thick wad of cash.

"Wheezie...No. We can't take this. You've helped us so much already," I protested pushing the money back to her.

"I just got the low down on you two. You came clean with me, and I owe it to you. Besides, I won't have you pickpocketing or snatching to survive. You can get money exchanged as you need it, wherever you end up. Consider it a wedding present. Get a microwave, shop for lingerie. Heck... buy a cow. Whatever you want to do with it, it's yours."

I hugged her and thanked her from the bottom of my heart, and even though she was not a hugger and straightened her shoulders, I could tell she was hugging me back.

"Alright...no more sap...We've got to get to the airport," she added.

Gia hugged both of us." Keep in touch okay? Be safe. And, keep an eye on that one...She's wild," she toyed, as she hugged Jace goodbye.

Jace laughed softly, "I will... Thanks, Gia... For everything."

Saying goodbye to Wheezie and Gia...and Michael, was harder than I expected. Maybe because I was saying goodbye to what had been my life up until now. I was excited, nervous and happy all at the same time.

As we boarded the plane and took one last look at our friend who had risked so much, and would continue to risk so much, I felt uneasy and worried that she and Gia would be safe. I was handing over a mega-sized battle with so many unknowns. I felt selfish as I boarded the small Red Cross plane and sat beside my husband.

"They'll be okay," Jace comforted. "She knows what she's doing."

"I know. It's just the unknown and the waiting bit that I need to get used to."

"Well Mrs. Taralock, we are technically on our honeymoon starting now. I mean, yeah, we have an uncomfortable thirty-hour flight in a cramped cargo plane with four other people sitting right over there...one of which...just threw up in a bag, and I'm not allowed to kiss you because we're just Red Cross volunteers, but still...we're on our honeymoon," he sighed as he settled in for the long flight.

It had been six months since we had left India. We had gone from Mawlynnong to New York, to Tanzania, to Kansas, to Boston. We found a long-lost mother, made new friends including a pig who didn't know he was a pig, and handed over a battle of justice to a worthy confidant. We were eager to start our new life.

We landed in Kathmandu with the Himalayan mountains at our backs. We aided in unloading the crates for the Red Cross using the names forged on our temporary papers. The city was colorful and lush with activity. Tourists and locals intermingled in happy confusion. It was much like India but with an Asian flare. Ten thousand pigeons peppered the streets and flew from rooftop to rooftop. Monkeys randomly caused mischief and begged for crackers. Colorful flags were strung from building to building.

People surrounded shrines and idols and made offerings of incense and oranges. Candles were lit in the hundreds, and deeply religious people scampered to have a moment to pray or offer a sacrifice. The fragrance of patchouli, and frankincense filled the air and engraved stone sculptures decorated the architecture. I wanted to explore, but Jace was eager to get to Mawlynnong village.

We headed towards our new home. It was the winter season, so the jungle and valleys were dry and lush green. We stopped at the Mawnok Damper Valley Overlook that was only visible during these winter months. It was breathtaking! It was a paradise with crisp green hills and deep valleys. The cold breeze hit us as clouds swam by at near eye level. The last time we were here we were on the run fearing that Felix was on our trail. Now it was different. We could stop and see all the sights we had not appreciated before. Jace could hold my hand, and we no longer had to hide that we loved one another. For the first time, my life made sense.

We arrived in the deep, dense forest of Mawlynnong village. We were back in God's True Garden, and the emerald trees and manicured pathways looked the part. The villagers meandered about sweeping brush into handmade bamboo baskets, and booths were set up selling bracelets of colorful beads, small local baskets and cloth. It was prime tourist season and searching for our old friend Bindi proved difficult.

We finally heard her sparky voice as she was busily herding a group of children into a section of the village. Many of the children recognized Jace and me and immediately broke from her corral and ran to us chirping in Khasi that they were excited to see us again. There were many new faces among them, and I was eager to learn all their names.

"You!" Bindi snapped in her short yelping tone. She had not changed, and even though she scowled at me fiercely, I was glad to see her. "You are not full of the disease, are you?" she barked, as she moved closer pulling a child or two away.

"It's good to see you Bindi," I smiled. She inspected me from head to toe with her judgmental eyes.

"Give me your hands," she insisted, examining them closely for dirt or rashes.

"I have NO job for you. There is a new school teacher for English. We no need you." It seemed my history of walking into this village with a deadly disease, even though non-contagious was still whirling around the community.

Her grouchy personality and hostile welcome were comforting to me. She was much more pleased to see Jace, and he wasn't subjected to the inspection I was. She smiled and welcomed him into the restaurant chattering away in Khasi about all that had happened in the last year. Business was booming, and the population had grown.

Jace inquired about a place to stay, and Bindi offered a small homestay near the trail to the Living Root Bridge. She was apologetic in her tone with him when she explained that there was no work available right now. Jace assured her that we were not looking at being a burden and we were willing to pay full price.

"You have a place, Jace. Bindi will take care of you," she assured. She looked over his shoulder and sneered at me.

"I guess *you* can stay too. But you keep it clean. How long you stay here?" she asked.

"Awhile. I can rent the homestay for a few months to start," Jace clarified as he handed her an American fifty-dollar bill. The prospect of American dollars put a smile on her face. "I knew you would be successful in your life. Is your music liked in America? You famous yet?"

"No. Not famous. We just have good friends," he admitted.

"You will be famous. I will see about finding the keyboard for you. It is still in good shape. Those filthy tourist children play with it, but I can have it fixed up. You like that?" she admonished.

"Yes, Bindi. That would be perfect. Here... for any repairs." He handed her another fifty, and she grinned from ear to ear.

"I can order a new one for that price!" she beamed.

"Ordering...can we put some things on your list for when you put the order in for the month?" I inquired.

"You pay cash!" she barked at me, turning hostile again. It was clear I would have to get used to being spat on by this tiny woman, but I didn't care. I was back in Mawlynnong, and this time I really was Mrs. James Taralock.

For the following months, I got used to Jace in a whole new way as we integrated into the Meghalayan village. Nearly my whole life, I had known Jace as my truest friend. I knew him as the only person I could spend every day with and not get tired of. Now I knew him as the other half of my heart. He was a part of me now.

This was a new adventure, and I often slipped into thinking that I was not good enough for Jace. I hadn't been raised to have a particularly positive view of myself and my past haunted me, but with just a single look in his eyes, I could tell that my insecurities were senseless and that he unconditionally loved me for me. It was too great a gift for me, and I was so overwhelmed at times imagining what I would do if I lost him. I would have no one.

Jace played his music and was free to write and compose. He played and practiced on his newly purchased upgraded keyboard. It even had features on it that could make it sound and resonate like a baby grand. He was able to pick up his work with the restaurant band, and he learned new music from the USA and Britain to play for the guests.

Through the winter tourist season, we lived off tips, and the generous pay Bindi allowed for entertaining her guests. We helped clean the village and obeyed the strict rules about hygiene and water preservation. We got used to the temperamental electrical system that would flicker on and off at random intervals especially during storms.

I was never offered my former position of English teacher, but I spent hours with the village children, having them at my feet, eagerly listening to my stories and drawing sketches with them. I still ordered gumdrops and stickers to entertain them and to keep them coming to visit me. After the first six months, we were no longer seen as transient, and the villagers accepted us as friends.

Jace was often invited to fish with the men and young boys on the crystal-clear waters of the lakes and pools. I would offer to help the women with their children, entertaining them as the women went about their business of weaving and beading souvenirs.

The living Root Bridge was a favorite spot of ours, and many times Jace and I would escape from the village and explore. It was a magnificent bridge that had been growing and entangling for a hundred years. Made from the roots and weeds of the vast forest, it was a bridge that got stronger and stronger each passing year instead of man-made bridges that rust and deteriorate. It attached Mawlynnong to the rest of Meghalaya in a roundabout way and was popular with visitors from all over the world.

When tourists filled the area, Jace and I would sit on the moss-covered rocks below the bridge and watch the activity. We made up stories just like when we were kids about the lives of the visitors. Sometimes the stories would be so funny, we would belly laugh so loud that the visitors would stop and throw angry glares at us.

In the rainy summer months, we were more isolated to our little home tucked away deep in the forest. It was about half a mile walk to the main area and had only three other family homestays nearby. We enjoyed the rainy season, just as much as the dry winter, and filled our days writing, drawing, dancing and reading. It was all new to us, and the freedom we had was overpowering sometimes.

An older couple two homes away became our dear friends. It began with a fishing invitation from the husband, Solar, and grew into a friendship and a role model that Jace and I both needed and cherished.

Solar was a short little man in his fifties with only four front teeth. He had spent years chewing betel nut and lost most of his teeth, until his wife banned the product from their household. His eyes smiled with his rosy pink cheeks, and his skin was the color of a shiny new American penny. He seemed always to be friendly and jolly.

His wife Tripura was as sweet as her voice. She was so gentle in nature with big brown eyes and a bright full-toothed smile. She wore her hair in two long dark braids with a red chord woven through. She was a hard worker and had inherited her home and little stand where she sold jewelry and other souvenirs.

Tripura and Solar had been married for twenty-seven years. Many times I asked Tripura for advice and many times she reminded me that marriage is like learning a new language. The longer you speak it, the more fluent you become. They had two children, a boy about fourteen named Mumtaz, and a daughter who looked exactly like her gentle mother, named Grace, who was twelve.

The family invited us into their home and helped us many times with the local customs and language. They laughed until they cried when Jace or I would misuse a word or say it entirely wrong and embarrass ourselves. Solar and Mumtaz were fishermen and knew everything there was about canoeing on the lakes and rivers. They taught Jace how to fish, salt, and dry his catch. They spent their lives working hard and enjoying each other. They valued each other and showed the highest amount of respect I had ever seen in a family circle. One evening Jace started telling Mumtaz and Grace stories of our childhood.

"Thea got me and Tobin in so much trouble. She convinced us that dinosaur bones were buried under my mom's garden. We pretended to be Archeologists and dug up all of her potatoes? She nearly killed us. Why, out of four hundred acres did you have to dig in her garden? And, use her basting brush to clean off the bones...which were actually all of the potatoes."

"You were a funny child Thea," Mumtaz laughed.

"I was a *terrible* child. Why didn't anyone tell me?" I asked. "No wonder why your mother hated me."

"She didn't hate you...She just didn't understand you. But then again, not many people did," he joked.

We enjoyed spending time with Tripura and her family. They could play and have fun in a genuine lovable way that for the first time made me think of having a family of our own someday. Tripura would invite me along with Grace and her to sit at the souvenir stand, and even trusted me to watch over it occasionally. The other women allowed Bindi's nasty approach to me influence them, but not Tripura and Grace. They disregarded the taunts and teasing that Bindi would throw at me and accepted me as their friend.

Bindi still would not warm up to me even after a full season. She enjoyed taunting me and putting me in my place every chance she could get. I would get so frustrated and angry at Jace for not sticking up for me and teasing along with her. He would tell me to pipe down because they were just joking.

"I can't help it," he admitted. "It's just too easy to get you all riled up. You're cute when you're angry." I glared at him like a viper, and he would wise up briefly, but still smile with his little Asian sidekick.

Bindi did not want to be my friend and didn't appreciate my presence at all. After several months her attitude had not improved, and since she saw that it wasn't knocking me over and I would let it slide, she upped her game. She decided to revamp the rumor that I was cursed. She bled the fears and superstitions in the women of the village and told them that I had a curse on me and could *not* have children of my own.

The fable grew until it escalated to accusations that I was out to steal the women's husbands and take their daughters away. I had let all the relentless teasing and jeering slide off my shoulders, but this time it had gone too far.

A few of the children that I had befriended were no longer allowed to sit with me to hear stories. Bindi had succeeded in spooking their parents. Tripura, Grace and I were at the booth waiting for customers, and Grace revealed what the community was saying about me. Her sweet twelve-year-old innocence spoke with such concern for me.

"Is there truth to these words Thea?" she pleaded. Her usual pretty smile had softened, and she seemed a little afraid of the answer.

"No, Grace. I am *not* cursed, and I do *not* want to take other people's daughters."

Tripura interjected, "Bindi is bitter. She punishes Thea for her own hurting. Her own daughter no longer wants the restaurant and property. Her daughter goes to the big city. She goes to New Delhi. She saw the world, and now *this* place is no good to her. Bindi is full of anger. Anger makes people do bad things."

Grace seemed relieved at this explanation. Her gentle smile returned. "Why *do you* not have any children Thea?" she innocently questioned.

"Hush child. It is not for us to know," her mother scolded her. Grace frowned and looked as if she had been thoroughly rejected.

"No, it's okay Grace. I don't mind the question."

Both she and her mother were looking at me inquisitively waiting for a solid reason as to why Jace and I hadn't had a baby yet.

"We just…it just hasn't happened yet." They seemed satisfied with this weak explanation and were soon distracted by oncoming tourists.

The streets were wet and running like small creeks as I waded and shuffled my feet slugging along. My sandals and my pants were soaked through by the time I got back to the restaurant. It was the start of the rain season, and fewer tourists were lurking about. Most of the winter rental properties were empty, and a peace was coming over the village. The rainy season would last six months until the air would dry out and we would see bright sunny skies.

A local mother holding her child's hand swooshed by me. As they approached, I smiled at the little girl which made the gullible mother pull her child inward in a protective stance. She glared at me, like I was a threat to her family.

That irrational, unjust movement enraged me, and without thinking, I marched myself to Bindi's restaurant and started hollering at her in Khasi.

"Bindi!" I projected loudly through the small crowd of locals and leftover tourists. She whirled around and stood her ground. It was a showdown, and I wasn't losing.

"No More! I have come here from a world that terrifies you, and you have NO idea who I am. I am no more cursed than you are. I may not have a child, but you do, and yet, she doesn't...want...you! You are brutal and vengeful because you are unhappy. The chance of you having a child at your withering age that will want your legacy is ZERO! Stop telling these people that I want to harm them or their families. Your own bitterness is making this village rot like garbage. You are making it FILTHY with your lies!"

By now a crowd of onlookers and suspicious mothers gathered cautiously. I stormed home and sat in my soaking wet clothes trying to register in my mind what I had just done. I was still sitting on the bed, dripping wet when Jace walked in slowly. He was tiptoeing and purposely acting like he was approaching a venomous snake.

"Stop it!" I spat. I was in no mood for his antics.

"Sorry?" He apprehensively approached.

I started crying and yelling at the same time. "Where were you? I shot off and ruined everything. I don't know why I can't shut up and let stuff go. We have to move now! Where are we going to go?" I burst out sobbing. I capsized onto the bed and put a pillow over my head.

"I heard what happened. Pipe down, we don't have to move." He started getting a towel and opening my drawers pulling out dry clothes. "Come on...you're soaked." I let him baby me because I felt pathetic. I was ashamed of my behavior, and I was embarrassed for Jace. The whole village saw now what a maniac he was married to.

"We do have to move. I can't show my face in the village ever again."

"Yes, you can," he retorted patiently, as he helped dry my hair. "I'll make us some tea."

The electric hot plate was heated up, and the kettle was filled with fresh rainwater from the reserve cans. The power had been intermittent with the heavy rainfall, but it lasted enough to heat the water to a boil. Somehow tea makes things better, especially if someone else makes it for you. Jace wrapped me in the quilt from our bed and put my clothes over the chair to dry.

"You really are something, Theorie Taralock. I leave you alone for one minute, and you demolish the dignity of the village matriarch," he sighed.

"Did you hear what the people are saying?" I whimpered.

"Yes…. It hit a nerve? Huh?"

"Bindi thinks I am no one without a baby. I don't want a baby. What if I *can't* have a baby? Maybe I want a baby."

"I swear, your mind is like a firecracker, shooting off in every direction. You just have to wait. The answers and everything that we are going to live to see and experience can't be laid out right now, today. One day at a time…Thea."

I nodded my head. I *did* want a child, but I really loved just being a wife for the time being. I loved this new adventure and our life here, despite Bindi's biting poison.

"Where were you anyway? Were you with Solar and Mumtaz?"

"No," Jace answered." I was finishing up a project. The shipment of supplies arrived, and I needed one thing to finish what I was making. Here…" He handed me a small embroidered pouch.

"My Necklace! How?...Where? ...I lost this back at the ship yard in Bangladesh years ago."

"It's a duplicate, I had it made. Tripura and Grace helped me. I ordered the beads, and I had to use fishing wire, but the last of the beads came in this morning, and I wanted to put it together. I was going to get you a real ring, ...I still can if that's what you want, but I wanted to give this to you first. Is it okay?"

I didn't even have words…."Yes," I choked. "It's perfect, the stones are exactly the same."

He put it around my neck, "Not quite, but real close. It still looks like chewing gum pieces to me but…"

"It does. I love it, thank you" He pulled me close to him. I gripped the strand of black, teal and pink beads tightly and held his stubbled face in my hands. Seeing in his eyes, how much he loved me, still made me blush. It was the most beautiful gift I had ever been given. He had remembered the pattern exactly and had known how much they meant to me.

The rains picked up that night and filled the roads and paths of the village. The power was unreliable and had been flickering on and off for hours. The villagers had retreated to their homes and gone to bed in hopes of a better tomorrow. Jace and I were listening to the pounding rain on our thatch roof. In the distance, we heard the faint shrill of the Vervet monkeys. They usually weren't out in heavy rains like this, but it soon became clear that the noise was *not* from monkeys.

The village stirred into a panic. We hurried outside and met a growing crowd. A village mother of three named Larna was on her hands and knees in the mud with pellets of rain smacking against her back. Her toddler son was missing...

He had been put into his basket, and the family had drifted to sleep. His mother had been awoken by the heavy rain to find his basket nest empty. The door to the home was ajar. She ran for help, and the villagers went into search mode. They gathered flashlights and began searching the forest and rapid streams.

Every mother has a great fear in Mawlynnong. It is the terrible possibility of drowning. Heavy rains made deepening pools this time of year. Small creeks were brimming with rapid waters. The lack of fencing and barriers made caring for a wandering toddler especially tricky.

This poor mother lay frantic and hysterical. She was yelling gut-wrenching screams at the earth. Several mothers, including Bindi, knelt trying to comfort her and bring her out of the rain, but she would not cooperate.

Jace joined the crowd in digging through the dense jungle and scaling the moonlit lakes and creeks. I couldn't accept the horrid reality. I had to do something, but I was useless in aiding this boy's mother. Why? Why such a little child?

That's right!... Why? Wait...Why would a two-year-old brave the pounding rain and growling thunder? Why would a two-year-old leave the safety of his basket, and not climb into the security of his parent's bed as they slept? Why would he scurry into the thick darkness? He wouldn't have...

"Grace!" I commanded" Come with me!"

We went to the empty dark home. The door was open, and water was pooling at the threshold. The light began to flicker on and off. Grace held the flashlight and guided our path through the dark room.

"What are we looking for?" Grace inquired.

"THAT!"

The home was a duplicate of mine. A metal bed frame was pushed to the far end of the room against the back wall. Several cots and the toddler's empty basket were strewn with bedding. From the far end of the parent's bed, nuzzled against the back wall was a tiny white sock barely poking from its den. The light flickered on, and in a second of flashing light and the crack of thunder, the sock wiggled and disappeared deeper into its lair.

"Help me...I don't want to scare him." I lay on my belly, and Grace held the flashlight. In Khasi, I gently spoke to the little boy and asked him if he wanted me to take him to his Mama. He was scared and curled into a tight ball. I finally lured him out of the damp hideout with a blanket I pulled from his mother's bed. I wrapped him up and told Grace to fetch his mother.

His eyes were so wide and frightened, and he looked at me with utmost trust and complete dependence in that moment. I cradled him in my arms hushing his whimper as he clung to me through the thunderclaps.

The speed at which the panic-stricken mother flew into the room and ripped her child from my arms was impressive. Her love and relief smothered her sleepy boy. She couldn't speak words, and as the villagers began to enter to inspect and verify that their little friend had been found, she pulled me close and squeezed her precious bundle between us in a grateful embrace.

Within minutes Grace had told the story of how I had known the mind of a child on a dark, stormy night...I knew right where to find him, and Grace was my brave accomplice who shined the light on the little boy. The villagers patted our shoulders and hugged us in thankful gestures.

By the next day, the women in the village had a change of heart and seemed to realize the silliness of Bindi's words. I was smiled at more than I ever had been before, and the children were allowed to associate with me again.

It took another week though for Bindi to approach me. She came to me in the evening and asked Jace to step out. She spoke curtly and deliberate.

"You…are no longer cursed," she said frankly, and turned to leave.

"Bindi?"

She turned to face me again. "I'm sorry Bindi. My words were harsh and cut too deep. I am sorry I said those things about your daughter."

"Your words were true," she surrendered. "My daughter is in the the big city now. Your words were like a storm. But it takes a storm to make a lightning bolt." She turned again but stopped at the door. "Mrs. Lock?"

She lingered, "Will you tell me of this *other* world you come from? The City? I know nothing other than this village. Maybe then I will understand my daughter, and maybe then she will come back to me."

"Sure, Bindi."

Three weeks later Jace and I traveled to Nepal to make our scheduled phone call to Wheezie in New York. I munched on Lakhamari, and Jace found a payphone tucked away behind the Dragon Dust Market in Kathmandu. Wheezie had been anxious to hear how we were and to give up some news.

Jace held the phone to his ear, and I pressed closely trying to hear. She spoke in code where she could, but her excitement slipped out, and she was bursting to tell us of what had happened in the last six months. The key had worked!

She explained that there was no money, which was upsetting, but assured us that what was inside was better than treasure. A large metal box was unearthed deep from within the center. It held a century of secrets. Document after document and hundreds of photos were securely packaged and stored. Photos my father had taken and secretly placed in this location. Proof had been stored here from before my father's time. It was Information exposing The Jailer's Way going back to the year 1914.

"You got a pen?" she asked excitedly.

"No." Jace searched his surroundings looking for anything to write with. "Can't find one, just tell me, I'll remember," he assured.

"Ok...On the top of all the documents, the first thing to hit our eyes was a postcard. It had a nasty looking dragon coming out of the sea and attacking a ship. It was an old postcard, maybe from the 1930's. On the back there was a handwritten message. It said, "Revelation 12:9... 1914.

It took a crap load of research and trying to figure out *why* that Bible verse was written on the very first document we pulled out of that box, but I figured it out...Like I said...I'm good at my job. Anyway...the verse in the Bible describes a dragon being thrown to the Earth. Since the year marked on the back, things on the Earth escalated...globally. *'Incidents'* and manipulations of society...internationally. That's when The Jailer's Way began. Growing from Theodore Jailer's family line, a hatred for people grew. The world was thrown into its first World War, and since then it's just been one thing after another. Sparks of hatred and fear. Trigger after trigger, war after war."

We listened intently without taking a breath. "All the photos, all your trips, both of your mother's, everything. Damning and concrete video footage, and recordings. Hundreds of cases. This is huge...too huge for me alone. I brought in who I could trust, which is precious few, but within the next few weeks we will have it pieced together, and we WILL take this whole thing down!"

Her voice beamed with excitement. Could it be true? We set up the date for the next phone call in three months, and hung up stunned and shocked, not fully believing that we had heard it all right. We had three months until we would hear anything else. Three months to wait and worry about our friend and if she was capable of pulling this off. She was clever and had the upper hand, but Felix was conniving and had contacts in high places. All we could do was hope. We returned to Mawlynnong perplexed and weary.

"So, your father all along was making drops and putting this proof of guilt in the Middle of the Universe. All this time he had a plan. He must have been who tattooed you!" Jace roared.

"That's why Felix wanted to know what the marks were. He couldn't decipher the code, he had no idea *where* my father hid the evidence against him," I added.

"Felix must have known your father was plotting against him. He must have had him killed. Do you think my mother knew how to decipher the markings? Do you think she knew they were coordinates?" Jace asked.

"If she knew, then she stood her ground and didn't hand that information over to Felix. Despite us being taken away, despite Tobin being taken away, and despite him cutting her arm that day on the farm." I defended Emma, which I had never thought possible.

"Or she didn't know what they meant, just like you," Jace offered.

"Our parents all along went against The Jailer's Way. They tried to destroy it…" I lamented.

"They just needed us."

Three months past and we anticipated our next phone call. We were in the thick of rainy season, and water streamed down the streets pooling in the front lot of our house. I was excited for winter to come, I was tired of all the rain. For a couple months I had felt so sad and glum and suspended. I was eager to know how the investigation was going. Jace would try and cheer me up with his music, and even Bindi came to check why I had not been to the restaurant lately. Tripura and Grace brought me news of the community trying to lure me out. Grace told me a batch of puppies had been born and Bindi wanted to drown them because they brought fleas and filth into the village. Even that couldn't motivate me though. I was just glum. Jace said I had Mawlynnong blues from all the rain and gloomy days. He jotted across the room gathering things for the trip to Nepal, and I lay on my bed just watching him go here and there.

"Jace, why don't you just go to Nepal. I'm so tired, I really don't want to make a trip, it's so long, and it's awful out." Rain beat on the thatch roof proving my point.

"What? No, I can't go without you…What's wrong? Are you sick? Do you have a fever?"

"No, I'm just tired, and I don't feel like making the trip. I'll be fine here. If you go than you can be back in two days, I'll just slow you up."

"I don't know…I don't want to leave you. You do feel warm." He felt my head. "I'm not going…forget it," he decided.

"You have to go! Wheezie is expecting it, and we have to know what has happened in the last three months. Really…I'll be fine. I do *not* have a fever. Look, I'll stay with Solar and Tripura, or I can have Grace stay with me."

"I don't like this. I don't want to leave you."

"You have to because if you don't leave in the next thirty minutes than you will miss the bus, and we will not know if Felix is around the corner trying to kill us…And, I'm not moving from this spot," I insisted.

"You are infuriating. Why are you so stubborn?" he demanded.

"I'm not stubborn," I stated, even though I was lying.

"Fine. I'll go, but you have to stay with Tripura…I'll go talk to them."

Arrangements were made, and I packed a small bag and made the 200-foot journey to my friend's house. Jace only agreed to make the trip after fretting and questioning me a thousand times if I was going to be okay, and made Tripura promise to call the Doctor if there was any sign of a fever.

"Promise me Thea. Promise me that you will stay here," he pleaded.

"I promise...Why are you so worried?" I asked

"I haven't left you alone intentionally...ever. If something happened to you while I was gone..."

"Don't think like that." I held my hands on his face and looked into his worried eyes. "I love you...I'm not going anywhere." I kissed him and wrapped my arms around his neck, breathing in the smell of his hair..."Can you bring me back some Lakhamari?" I whispered.

He couldn't help but ease up and smile. He finished packing, hugged the family goodbye and rushed to the bus.

"That boy worries about you," Solar smiled a big four tooth grin.

"He really does." ...I returned his friendly smile.

It wouldn't be bad, it was just 48 hours, but as soon as the bus pulled away and was out of sight, a deep loneliness set in. I sunk in spirits and wished I had gone with him. I regretted my decision and insistence on staying behind. If I wasn't so tired, I could have run after the bus.

Grace let me have her cot, and she squeezed in with her parents that night. In the morning Tripura made grilled fish for breakfast. I woke up to the smell of what frequently was a pleasant meal, but my insides turned, and I quickly grabbed a large mixing bowl and threw up. Grace's cot was closest to the kitchen appliances and cook stove, and the heat from the breakfast and the humidity in the air choked and gagged me.

"Tripura?" I wiped my face and sat back on Graces cot. "Can you call for the doctor? I think I *am* sick. Jace was right. Bindi will never forgive me for bringing sickness into the village again. I need medicine."

"Grace. Get Thea some fresh water," Tripura ordered.

Grace scurried off, and Mumtaz followed her out the door. Tripura shot a look at Solar only a wife could, and he quickly got the message and exited as well. I assumed she wanted her family at a safe distance from me, who knows what I had this time. She got me a cloth and wiped my brow, as Grace scurried back in with the fresh water.

"Grace, don't come near me...please. I'll get you sick, and you will die, and your mother will hate me," I murmured, and dry heaved into the bowl.

"My friend, Grace cannot catch what you have. You are not dying," Tripura assured.

"Please just get the doctor, and Jace. He left yesterday. He'll still be gone a day or two," I fretted. "I can't die without him here...He will be so mad at me."

"He will be back in plenty of time. You settle down and have some more water. Grace! Take this fish outside, let the house air out, then she will feel better."

My stomach was about to come up again. "I just want Jace to come home," I wallowed.

"Patience. You need to be patient my friend."

"I'm not though," I protested.

"Well too bad...you will *have* to be...for the next six or seven months."

Chapter 17

The Living Root Bridge

Three days past and I was agonizing about Jace. He should have been back yesterday. The rain pelted the roof of Solar and Tripura's home. I sat waiting for any sign of the caravan. He would be traveling back with the monthly shipment truck. The villagers were also anxious to get their supplies. Tripura and Grace kept busy organizing shelves and ignored me. Solar worked on nets, and Mumtaz tried to distract me by asking me to teach him more types of knots. We practiced what I had taught him, but my mind was elsewhere, wondering what had happened to my husband. The whole village seemed frozen in time waiting for the rain to stop and the fresh supplies to arrive.

Another day passed, and I was imagining every possible scenario. I hadn't slept at all. Tripura made green tea and kept the home relatively odor free for my sake. Only Tripura and Grace knew about my situation, and I knew they would not tell anyone. Grace wanted to tell Bindi that I really was *not* cursed, and she would have to respect me now, but her mother forbid her saying, it was "not their news to tell."

I was so tired, and my exhausted brain was imagining the worst possible outcome. I would make myself sick, thinking of Jace and the supply truck upside down in a deep valley, or trapped in a mudslide. I became frantic at the thought that Felix had caught up with him and had hurt him or worse. Not knowing was torture.

Finally in the evening and nearly four days late, the supply truck arrived. Villagers ran from all directions to see what had delayed them. Men helped unload supplies and quickly scurried them off to get them out of the rain. I walked as fast as my exhausted body could and found Jace collecting his bag and some other supplies. I took him by surprise by jumping into him and pulling him to me. I couldn't talk or say hello, I was just so happy to hold him again.

"I'm so sorry. You must have been panicked. Are you okay? You're not sick?" he worried.

He wiped my wet hair out of my face. "I was so worried about you. The men tried everything they could, but the truck got stuck, and we had to wait for help. We lost half the supplies in a ravine; the roads are flooded completely."

"I'm so glad you're here," I muttered, falling into his arms again. "You can never go again. Forget Wheezie and the investigation. Who cares about it. I don't want you to go to Nepal anymore." I buried my head into his chest.

"Well, it may be a while until we need to." We walked home, and he started the kettle.

"Jace, I've decided that I should absolutely never be in charge of decisions again. Don't ever listen to me again. I'm not sensible." I stated.

"No... You're not. You are stubborn, but that is ridiculous, you have to make decisions. That is how this being married bit works."

329

"No... I've decided. I'm not," I insisted stubbornly.

"Well, we will see how you feel about that tomorrow. You are very good at changing your mind from one minute to the next."

He sat me down in the chair and kissed me on the forehead. My stomach was turning, and I was exhausted, but I didn't want him to know that yet. I had planned on telling him our news that evening.

He opened his backpack and pulled out a plastic bag holding a newspaper. It was partially destroyed by rainwater, but the headline was clear. A photo of Felix was on the front page. In Hindi, and in bold letters, it declared,

"International Criminal Will be Held Responsible!"

"What?" I implored.

"It's true. Wheezie explained everything. The photos and evidence that your father left was concrete. He had been thorough and so descriptive that Felix had no possible way of denying his actions. Wheezie said, so far 143 people have been incriminated. The prosecution has enough to call for the death penalty. Felix is being tried for war crimes and genocide."

"Jace! Have we been named? Are we exposed?"

"No. There is a man who the FBI has called Daniel Mills. A phantom scapegoat made up. This made up engineer, allegedly uncovered the information while surveying and excavating the site for renovation. He's the scapegoat, we were left out of it entirely."

"I don't fully believe that it was that easy," I uttered.

"Read the article. It's all there. Whatever your father hid there was all the FBI needed. Wheezie said it was incredible Thea. She wants us just to stay where we are until it's all over. She's not sure how long. Maybe a couple years at the most. Just to be safe."

"Of course, I'm sorry, I don't know what to say. I'm just trying to process everything. So Felix is in custody?"

"Yes."

"How can it be over? Just like that? It can't be over, Felix would have had a backup plan, or two, or three back up plans. He wouldn't just surrender," I lamented.

"Felix was not counting on your father being *so* strategic and naming the names he did. He didn't count on your father's photos through the years or the video recordings. Your dad knew Felix. He knew all his moves. He knew what had to be sacrificed to do this."

"I'm just unsure, I guess. It seems too good to be true."

"Actually. There is something that will sound even more farfetched," Jace affirmed.

"There has been an account set up, a finder's fee of sorts. Within the files was a vast fortune in bonds and the locations of multiple storehouses filled with stolen goods, gold, artwork, priceless artifacts and even arsenals of weapons. Whoever your father inherited the evidence from going back to 1914 had maps marking locations where things have been stored for the last century.

The finder's fee for these lost treasures was extensive because so many parties were involved. Wheezie said that the UK and United States alone had a combined total of over a billion dollars' worth of goods that they were hunting for. We were given one percent of the finder's fee."

"Wheezie already gave us money, and we're okay with what you make from the restaurant."

"No, you don't understand...One percent is two million dollars. $2,345,000.00 to be exact. It's in a secure account in our names that we can access at any time. If you want to help Yuri's family, and Nico's, we can now."

I had no response other than shock. My heart began racing, and I ran to the sink. I threw up for the next two minutes.

"That's not the response I was expecting," Jace exclaimed. "Are you sure you're okay?"

"We can stay here though right?" I ignored his concern and wiped my mouth and rinsed it out. This random barfing had to stop.

"Yes. It's safer that way, at least for a while. You like it here right?" he pleaded.

"Yes! ...Jace...are Wheezie and Gia alright? And was your mom implicated at all?"

"Wheezie and Gia are fine, they say hello. Michael says hello. Wheezie said when this is all over, and it's safe she wants us to visit and stay with Gia again."

"That would be nice."

I spent the evening still processing what Jace had handed me and running down scenarios in my head of what Felix could be plotting. The next morning the village restaurant was swarming. A mini-convention of villagers and a handful of tourists had congregated around the bar to admire the new arrival...One of the items on the shipment this month was a television. The first one the community owned. It was small and static, but when it was plugged into the power outlet at the restaurant, it lit up and instantly gathered the children and many curious adults. It got only two channels, and they were barely visible through the fuzz, but it bewitched people.

"Piece of crap!" Bindi squawked. "All that money, for a piece of crap."

The rain slowed down in the next few days, and the streets were mush. Bindi was furious this time of year. The constant flow of rain slowed and was not enough to wash the streets, and people mucked mud all over the place. She was continuously cleaning and washing off mud and debris that swam in from the forest. She was grumpy, and I avoided her at all cost. Tripura and Grace worked to clean their little stand, and I tried to straighten up and be helpful. The village smelled of new growth and earth and it made me sick to my stomach nearly every day. It had been three days and I still hadn't found the right moment to tell Jace that we were going to have a baby. Tripura asked me every day and was getting upset with me because I had delayed telling him.

Jace and I spent several days talking about my father and Felix and piecing together memories. Trips we had taken, and my father's incessant need to photograph certain people made sense now. The equipment we helped carry, was all to record and document Felix's activity and agents in action. It baffled my mind how the pieces fit together and distracted me from telling my husband he was going to soon start a new adventure. I just hadn't found the right moment, and I was just reveling in the fact that he was home and explained over and over the terrible stories that went through my head when he was late coming back. And, I was slightly afraid of how he would take the news.

I knew I had to tell him soon though. In my mind, I was trying to work out the right words, and how to explain to him how afraid I was. This little life had no past, no story yet. A brand-new person was growing inside me, and the overwhelming fear of ruining its life was too much to worry about.

After throwing up my tea, I could tell Jace was uneasy. "I am NEVER having green tea again. It tastes like pine shavings and grass," I gagged.

"Maybe you have a parasite or something. Did the doctor come and look at you? You still don't seem back to yourself."

"No. Tripura took good care of me. I'm fine…"

"Thea, you're sick all the time and you're tired, I can see it in your face."

"Well, I told you, I didn't sleep much while you were gone. Grace's cot was small. It was right in the kitchen, so Mumtaz's snoring and having so many other people in the same room...I just didn't sleep good."

"I just wish the doctor could help you with your stomach. What if it's something serious? It could be the water or something you're eating."

"It's not the water."

I started getting dinner ready and heated up the electric skillet. I was hoping I could hold down some rice. Jace walked up behind me and put his arms around me in a bear hug. He nuzzled his face into the hair covering my neck.

"I missed you." He held me tight, and I leaned back into him. "Do you want help?" he asked, kissing me on my jawline. He started reaching for the typical spices and chilis we would use to season our dinner.

"No... I can't deal with the spice...Let me just make this plain and then you can add whatever you want," I started crying.

"Okay?" The corners of his eyes crinkled suspiciously. "What? Why are you crying? What did I do?"

"Nothing! I'm going to Tripura's." I ran out the door towards my friend's house. Jace followed at a safe distance, waited for me to go inside, and knocked reluctantly on the door. Tripura opened the door looking angry at him. I was still crying, and I didn't know why.

"What did I do?" Jace begged.

Solar nodded his head sending husbandly advice to back away and let the hysterics just happen.

"Nothing!" I cried, "I just don't want spices or chilis on my rice tonight." I knew that I sounded ridiculous, but I just needed to cry over something, so why not rice?

"Okay...No spices...I am completely fine with plain rice," he replied.

"No... I should at least be able to make you something good to eat." I got up and went to him and wrapped my arms around his neck and he tightened me into him. I sobbed like a baby with my head on his chest. He looked so confused but just kept on holding me.

"The female brain...It does not work like a man's...Don't try to understand," Solar explained to Jace. Tripura shot a look of fiery spite at her husband, and he quickly added to his statement... "It is on a higher level than a man's." Nodding at himself in agreement, trying to stay on his wife's good side.

"Okay...You go now...The rice is fine Thea...It will be perfect," Tripura consoled, as she pushed us towards the door.

"I am sorry," I apologized to this poor family that had been a victim of my hormonal attack. Tripura smiled accepting my apology, but I knew that I had to tell Jace that night.

We walked back through the door of our home, and I stood at the stove looking at the pan of plain rice. Jace cautiously and silently got the plates ready. He didn't complain or question my irrational behavior.

"Jace... I'm going to have a baby...I'm pregnant.... I'm not sick," I spilled out.

He didn't move or respond, and I couldn't look at him. He put his hands on my shoulders and turned my body to face him. He stared at me dumbfounded for a solid two minutes, fixing his eyes on mine. Without a word he drew closer to me and pulled me towards him. He pulled me to his chest tightly. His smile crept up and was uncontainable. He was glowing from ear to ear.

"I'm sorry, I didn't tell you right away. When you were late coming home, I panicked, and then all the news about Felix...I wanted to tell you right away, I'm sorry."

"Rice," he said, as he connected the dots and now understood my uncontrollable crying.

"Rice..." I nodded. "Sorry."

His smile grew wider, and he hugged me. "Are you sure? Really sure?"

"Yes," I maintained. "I'm sure."

"You need to see a doctor." He instantly began fretting about the room picking things up and moving them around. "It's a girl, I know it," he alleged. "We can put a basket over here for her, and a rocking chair over there...We need a rocking chair and blankets, and when? When?" His excitement grew.

"In about six months. Tripura said the doctor comes next week to give the village children their immunizations, and I can find out for sure then, but it should be just at the end of winter or beginning of summer."

"You're sure?" His smile beamed.

"Yes! I know how these things work, and I looked at a calendar."

"How are we going to wait that long? Six months...What will we name her? I wonder if she'll have blue eyes?" he anticipated.

"Well, we both have blue eyes, so that's a likely scenario."

For the next week, he walked around the village announcing to anyone who had ears that he was going to be a father. He ordered a rocking chair and became adorably attentive. My morning sickness started passing, and now I was sleeping all the time. Jace continued to play his music and even started composing a lullaby for the baby. He wanted it to be perfect.

"You keep saying *her*...but, what if it's a *him*?" I asked one morning.

"Then it's a boy, I really don't care, either way...but it's a girl."

The last few months dragged on forever. I continued to wake up having night terrors of things that could go wrong. Irrational, impossible things. I would toss and turn and have to be woken up to be settled. Jace would do what he could to calm me, and Tripura assured me that bad dreams were a normal part of this process and told me to put a knife under the bed to drive the nightmares away. I knew it was ridiculous but wondered if there were any truth to it because the dreams were so vivid and real.

I would wake up physically traumatized, and I was desperate. I clearly saw Felix around corners and alleyways and drew a picture in my mind of my baby that was dark skinned and Asian, missing from the basket. I dreamt that Jace was searching for the baby and destroying the room in a frenzy yelling for his child. I dreamt that I felt rolling and slithering in my belly, and when Jace placed his hand on me to feel the rolling motion, he shrieked from being bitten by a venomous snake.

"Jace, the dreams are getting worse," I confessed one evening. "I'm afraid to go to sleep."

"I know, you woke up a lot last night. It will be over soon. You're really afraid, aren't you?... Come here." He pulled me to sit on the side of the bed. "Tell me each fear that you have. I want to know them all."

I felt stupid for being so scared. Tripura had consoled me when I told her of some of my worries and told me that many women gave birth in the village each year, and that I would be well cared for. She knew what to do. But that wasn't it. I wasn't afraid of giving birth. I wasn't afraid of pain. I was afraid of the after…

"I'm scared that I won't be a good mother," I poured out.

"Alright. That's a big one. It sure is horrible to have a bad mother." I knew what he meant. "You will be a good mother…I mean you'll probably make some real rookie mistakes, but so will I."

"Do you know 40 percent of child deaths in this area are from drownings. What if we turn our back for a second and the baby falls in a puddle and drowns? What if she gets too close to the electric stove? What if her legs are on backward? What if she doesn't like me?"

He couldn't contain a humorous grin.

"Stop laughing at me! You don't understand. I don't know how to be a mother. It's too big of an adventure. I don't want to do it," I whimpered.

"I'm not laughing at you, and It's too late now. I can't stop you from worrying Thea. I've never been able to make you do something you don't want to."

"I don't want to worry so much!" I burst.

"You do! You *do* want to worry over EVERY. SINGLE. THING. POSSIBLE. Worrying makes you feel better. You think that as long as you worry about every random possibility, then there's less of a chance that it actually comes true. You want to cover everything just to be safe. So if you want to worry and imagine everything that could go wrong all day long, then all night your mind will try to process it, and you'll be a zombie during the day because you don't sleep." He was right, but I wasn't going to let him know that.

"That's ridiculous, you don't know anything," I argued. He knew better than to rile me up anymore. He knew he had hit a nerve.

"Here's what we *should* worry about...What are we going to name this baby?" he asked.

Each day, I walked a little more like a penguin and felt increasingly onerous and completely useless. I tried to help at Tripura's cart as tourists flooded the area. The clouds had broken up, and the paths cleared, winter was here. This was my favorite time of year here. I loved the activity of the village and the uplifted spirits. People occupied each rented hut and the restaurant buzzed with activity. Honeymooners and young couples dotted about exploring.

The Living Root Bridge was famously visited and given attention. People gawked and awed over it. This bridge was my favorite spot in all of Mawlynnong. The roots intertwined and twisted into one another over the creek below and connected the paths throughout the village. The strength and endurance of the roots impressed me. It was a combination of Earth's natural wonder and a little bit of guidance from man.

On that bridge, Earth and man cooperated in creating a marvel that enamored visitors. No steel beams, no metal plates. Just vines and roots that mingled and were coerced into natural ropes that made a bridge strong enough to hold a family of elephants.

I came here almost every day, and me and my enormous belly would sit stationed below on the moss rocks, with a big glass of ice tea, watching people.

The vibrant greens burst from the trees, soaking up the sunshine. Monkeys and birds chirped drawing the attention of people with binoculars. People were enamored with the beauty of this place, and many times I heard visitors remark that they wanted to live here, in this paradise. It was such a pleasant time of year, yet I was as irritable as a wet cat.

I could hear the keyboard resonating from the village. I waddled over to the restaurant to beg Bindi to have mercy on me and make me some dumplings. Jace had stopped playing and was sitting on a barstool at the tall table.

"Are you alright?" He stood and met me.

"I'm fine, just starving." I rubbed my pinched side. "This baby definitely weighs fifty pounds and will rip me in half on its way out. Gravity is super strong today!" I sighed.

Jace pulled out a chair and motioned for me to sit down. "You thirsty?"

"No. I just drank a tank of ice tea. I'll explode. When can you come home?"

"An hour or so."

"Tripura says to walk a lot, to make this kid evacuate. I'm going to walk laps around the entire village. If I'm not back by dinner leave me to die in the forest. Let a jungle cat eat my carcass."

"Okay...that's good, I'll do that...and you're not walking way out there alone. If you want to walk, you have to wait for me, give me an hour."

"I can't wait that long… All of my body parts are hanging between my legs and I'm dying."

"That's disgusting" He ignored my drama. "Sit here and wait for me," he demanded, grinning. "Bindi? My wife is grumpy. What do you have that is delicious?"

"She needs papaya and pineapple," Bindi exclaimed. That sounded perfect. "I have none! All I have is spiced fish," she then barked. "Pineapples are for visitors only!"

Jace gave a lopsided grin, "I'll get you some pineapple."

That night the dreams were horrendous. I tossed and flopped and curled my body up in a ball. I dreamt I was trapped, and someone was pressing down on my lungs. I saw Felix standing over me, looking at me with his wicked eyes. The panic I felt next as he plunges a knife into my stomach, made me moan and gasp for air. Jace shook me awake finally, and the relief that it was just a dream overwhelmed me, and I just started crying.

"It's okay, it's okay," he comforted me. "It was just a dream. You're safe. I'm right here. I've got you." He sat up and propped me against his chest.

I settled and let my body relax into his embrace and felt drunk with sleep until an instant replay of the intense pain shot through the lower half of my body.

"Uuuuhhh!" I moaned and clenched upwards to release the pain. But it wouldn't go away. It tore and ached in a deep throb. I felt my stomach, and the soft round rolling baby inside was as hard as a rock. "I'm in labor!" I cried.

"Oh My God!" He jumped up. "What do I do? Tripura! I'll get her!"

"No! Wait! Just wait…. I can't...don't leave me!" as another pain gripped my body.

"Okay." He paced, running his fingers through his hair, and rubbing his eyes. He sat beside me and tried to prop my pillows. I relaxed and took a deep breath.

"Your water? Did your water break?"

"No. I don't know. Maybe. Go get Tripura and Grace."

"I'm going! Don't move!" he instructed. I glared at him, and he rushed out.

Tripura came quickly with an enormous smile on her face, followed by an apprehensive Grace. We had talked about it earlier. Tripura would be my midwife and Grace would assist. It would be Grace's first birth, and I knew right away; she was nervous now that it was really happening. Her mother took charge though and with a few confident instructions put the whole group at ease. She did not want Jace to be in the room, but he refused to leave, and I was glad. I wanted him there.

The pains increased in length and came quicker each time. Jace fretted and tried to comfort me through each contraction. I had been scared the first half hour of contractions, but as the pain and pressure worsened, I felt no fear, just sheer determination to push this enormous human out of me. Tripura gently coached me and assured me that everything was going naturally. Grace handed her mother supplies and wiped my forehead. Sometimes even wiping Jace's brow and smiling. His anxiety was showing, and he winced in pain every time a contraction flowed over my body.

Towards the end, as each contraction slipped away, I trembled uncontrollably and felt so cold. "I'm freezing," I shivered. Jace wiped his teary eyes and nose on his shirt and laid close to me with his arms wrapped around my shoulders and his head in my neck. His warm body and tight hold steadied and warmed me, calming the tremors.

"Is she alright?" Jace begged Tripura for reassurance. She promised him that the searing pain was normal, but his anxiousness twisted his brow.

As the pain crawled up my body again, I pushed him away and clenched the bed sheets at my side. I was quite sure that the bullet I had taken through my liver several years ago was less pain. It took a half hour to finally feel the relief of my body pushing my baby into the world. Like a train barreling through a tunnel, at that point nothing could stop it.

I gasped for a refreshing breath and immediately worried about how the baby was. I forgot the world around me. My brain zoomed in and locked on that child. I steadily watched its small frame change from a bluish to pink tint.

"It's a girl!" Grace yelled happily.

"Is she okay?" I begged.

"She's fine Mama." Then the sound of her squeaky voice hit the walls of our home and instantly broke my heart and filled it at the same time. I heard her. I heard her little helpless sound crying for me. She was scared and needed me. She was placed on my chest, still attached to me. I covered her and held her to me, calming her down.

Jace wiped his eyes and kissed my forehead "You're okay. See...I knew you had to be alright." The whole moment was in slow motion and surreal. In the second that baby came into the world...the world changed.

"Here Papa. You take your baby, let me make sure your wife is okay. Jace held out a terry cloth towel and bundled the baby up, tucking it under her chin. I had never seen a father in the moment that he first met his child before. I watched Jace's eyes pour over with pride, anxiousness, worry, and unconditional love. I felt such a sense of accomplishment that I had been able to be a part of making him incandescently happy.

Tripura had Mumtaz bring the scale from the fruit stand, and my fifty-pound enormous baby ended up being seven pounds exactly. As the morning peeked into the village,

Jace and I sat alone examining every little feature of our baby girl. She had so much hair for a newborn. It was long and soft, golden ginger, with blonde highlights. Her little nose and chubby cheeks captivated us, and we couldn't get enough of this tiny being. Jace changed her diaper and swaddled her in the little blue blanket we had picked up in Nepal. He let me sleep as he held her and watched her little face, as he swayed her in the rocking chair.

The days that followed were flooded with emotion. The village had provided us with delicious meals and many gifts for the baby. Jace would play at the restaurant and anxiously push through his day so he could come back home to us.

He was spellbound by his tiny daughter, and I loved seeing his love for her. I was tired but healing and getting stronger each day. The doctor made his rounds and deemed her a very healthy baby. He praised Tripura and Grace for delivering a healthy child.

"I can't wait to tell Wheezie," Jace beamed. "We need to name her."

"Not Wheezie!" I quickly retorted.

"No... How about...Bindi?" he teased.

"I have no idea what to call her. I knew if it was a boy I wanted to name him Tobin, but I've got nothing for a girl."

"What about Indira? It means beauty," Jace offered, "and she is the most beautiful baby in the world." He kissed her gently on the forehead.

"I like that...Indira Grace maybe?" He smiled and kissed her forehead again, "Indira Grace."

We stumbled our way through the first few months of parenthood and found our footing. I tucked my little girl in a handmade sling tied around my waist and took her everywhere with me. When I needed to rest or get laundry done, Grace watched over her like a perfect big sister. We filled our days with walks through the forest and sat telling stories to the other children in the schoolyard. I was asked to join the teachers at the school one day a week to help the children with their English. Indira clung to my chest and slept peacefully as we recited the English alphabet. I liked having her right at my heart, I could kiss her delicious little head any time I needed to.

Three months later we were busy planning our trip to Nepal and reveled in the memory of my pregnancy and how even though it seemed like the gestation of an elephant, it went by quickly. We packed a larger than usual bag and made the journey to Kathmandu. Jace fretted and hovered over the baby and me. He was more nervous than usual.

"Relax Jace, she's attached to me in her sling. She's pretty much still a part of me," I assured.

"I know, but she's so small, and there are so many people everywhere. Here sit here, it's not as crowded," he insisted, corralling me into the back of the bus.

Kathmandu was chaos. People ran to and fro. Tourists had flooded the area and caused a frenzy of peddlers and merchants into a frantic state of competition. Jace held onto my arm and led us, pushing through the crowd until we reached the payphone.

The baby seemed unstirred, and I adjusted the sling and Jace got me some bottled water. We called Wheezie at the scheduled time, and before we let her speak, Jace blurted out his news. He couldn't contain himself. He spoke to Wheezie and spilled out praise of how brave I had been and what a beautiful baby he had.

"Oh Wheezie, she looks just like her Mama, she's so beautiful...blue eyes, and blondish ginger hair. She's so perfect...I wish you could see her." I pressed my ear to the phone and heard Wheezie yelping,

"Woohoo! That is good news. I knew it. I knew it wouldn't be too long. Wait until I tell Gia. Congrats! Did you name her Wheezie?"

Jace beamed and then calmed enough to remember why we were in Nepal, and it wasn't just to but tiny socks.

"Everything on this end is going well. We have 275 people in custody, and the list keeps growing. Did you see it? The television interview with Ed Lancaster?" she inquired.

"No. We only have two channels," Jace admitted.

"Two weeks ago, they interviewed Felix from the maximum-security prison. The interviewer questioned Felix and asked him if he felt accountable at all for his actions, and he had no remorse. Complete devil. He spent the next ten minutes trying to JUSTIFY The Jailer's Way, and its philosophy. The interviewer was so stunned that he could hardly contain his infuriation.

The interview ended with Felix coldly stating that The Jailer's Way was right and honorable, and that the world would see. He said the population would explode with weak mutant humans and we would be sorry that this method was interrupted. The journalist was so shaken, that he ended the interview early and left shattered.

They did a follow up on the emotional state of the interviewer, Ed Lancaster. The world can only be told a fraction of what Felix had his hands in. This was deep, a CIA analyst and three MI6 agents were exposed. The Linchpins are coming out of the wood
work wanting to make deals for leniency."

"Has Arlo or Andrea been on the list of accomplices?" I questioned.

"No... unfortunately they are on the run and haven't been identified yet, but I'm not giving up yet. Let's just say, anyone attached to Felix has been cut off, all his assets have been seized, even the ones he was confident were hidden well. I'm going to tell you right now, I've gotten to know this creep really well, and I am certain he has a plan and other resources that we have not fully opened yet… but I'm still looking. The media has helped in keeping it relevant and active. That helps keep him under wraps. Remember, he's a man who worked under the radar, his weakness is the public. He's losing friends every day because money and power is no longer a motivation. One name did pop from your list though. A Rohit Dara. He cooperated and will be tried. What was your run in with him?"

"Rohit?" I gasped. Jace and I looked at each other not believing what we were hearing.

"He was the uncle of our friend Yuri. We thought he was innocent."

"Not so innocent... among other things, he ran a money laundering operation from the cellar of his Kolkata restaurant."

"The Balan Sings?" I questioned.

"That's the place...He admitted to having his nephew killed for helping two defectives...I'm assuming that was you."

"That's awful," Jace said with a heavy heart. "Will he be tried?"

"Most definitely. Rohit Dara is in custody, being held in Mumbai awaiting his trial. The money laundering will put him away for life. Felix is going to be executed for his crimes against humanity...by the end of this year. He has no appeals, and his defense team exhausted itself looking for loopholes but came up with nothing. Do you know what that beast's statement was at the last appeal when his sentence was handed over?... He *asked* to be executed. He has so much faith in his philosophy that he says it is '*his time*.' He said he was weak and no longer deserved a '*place*.' He has no remorse, no fear. He is just ready to die."

"That's not surprising," I affirmed.

"The bad news is that his philosophy has begun sparking riots. Psychopathic racists are rearing their ugly heads and creating a movement. Then, on the other side of the bridge, you have human rights groups fighting for honor and justice. It's chaos. I gotta tell you...The human race never ceases to amaze me. I'm astonished we're not extinct.

"So what's our next move?" Jace asked.

"You love that baby, and live."

For the next two and a half years we continued to live in Mawlynnong, Meghalaya. Indira filled our days with adventure. Watching Jace with her, and how gentle and protective he was made me love him more than I thought was possible. He would pretend to eat her toes, and she would belly laugh in the most addictive way. He played music and sang the lullaby he had written before she was born. She toddled happily through the village, learning to walk on the forest path and over the Root Bridge.

The older children always watched over her, and Grace was like an adoring big sister. Mumtaz, Solar, and Jace fished every day, and Tripura taught me how to cook local recipes with pork and bamboo. Our two families collided and bonded. I felt a sense of acceptance and friendship that I had always yearned for.

In the evenings we would tell Indira about Mahtap and all her stories. She would lay on her back and play with Jace's scruffy face or wind my hair in her little fingers. She loved to laugh and play and was always looking for things to keep her busy. She would watch our faces trying to match our expressions, and giggle when we kissed her cheeks.

She had a little stubborn personality, and there was no making her do something she didn't want to. She would stomp her feet and cross her small arms with such a dramatic scowl. We tried not to laugh or to give in, but she had both of us wound tightly around her finger. Her blonde hair had grown more ginger in color and long enough to put in short braids. It would end every day with it all falling out and being unkempt. She was a happy, energetic little girl with her mother's hair and freckles, and her father's gray-blue eyes.

She adored Tripura and Grace and often ended up staying at their house playing with handmade toys and being tucked in for naps in the large wicker basket used for transporting souvenirs. When she was with our family, Jace and I would sneak away to the Root Bridge and sit below on the moss-covered rocks. We would watch people and make up stories about visitors.

"You know we have to head to Nepal next month. How did two years go by so fast?" Jace spoke solemnly.

"I know," I frowned.

"I don't want to go, I just want to stay right here, watching people...watching you," he smiled. "This is what I have wanted for as long as I can remember...Just you." He pulled me close to him, tucking me in his arm.

"We have to go. It could all be over, and we could travel again. We could go to see Rubin and Neema. And Wheezie, and Gia. Your parents and Gideon could meet Indira. I wonder how Indie would like Africa and the farm?"

Jace mouth curved into a crooked smile. He leaned his head on mine, kissing my forehead.

"She has so much of you in her Theorie. She will find adventure in every corner.

Chapter 18

Emma's Porch

Carrying my hollering toddler like a surfboard in my arm, I stomped the two hundred feet from Grace's cottage to ours. We were scurrying to get everything packed for Nepal, but in her two-year-old mind, she was dragged from helping Mumtaz repair his fishing net, and I was tearing her from all happiness.

She had wrapped and knotted twine around her bare feet and was working her way up to her knees. Mumtaz let her play with the ball of string to occupy her and told her what a big help she was being.

"We have to go Indie...Come on." I went to pick her up. She twisted and pushed her tangled feet at me. In a Khasi lisp, she hollered,

"No! I Not! I Not At All!" as she turned onto her belly and tried to squirm away across the floor like a baby seal.

I dragged her wiggling body home and plopped her into the basket of clean laundry. She was still crying when Jace came back from the village stands with some fruit and crackers and bottled water for the bus trip.

"Your daughter is being very stubborn," I announced.

Jace handed me the food and picked up his little girl, making her cry louder and in a forced dramatic whelp.

"What are you doing to your Mama?... We're going on a trip...Are you ready Indie? Where are your sandals…Uh? Oh no!" He gasped…" Where did they go? … They ran away..."

He started muddling through the laundry basket and in the bed blankets and got on his knees pretending to be very concerned with finding the shoes that were *clearly* sitting on the mat by the cottage door. Indira perked up and instantly smiled and looked under the bed. She waddled over to the door and triumphantly squealed,

"Juti!"...." Shoe, in Khasi.

Her little cheeks were pink from her tantrum. They shined making her freckles stand out. Jace put her sandals on while I brushed her hair quickly and put it in two braids. She pushed my hands away and made my task more difficult.

Tripura had made us dinner the night before, and she used papaya, which never sat right in my stomach. I wasn't feeling well and was feeling rushed and anxious. We had not been to Nepal for over two years. This day had been marked in our calendar for a long time, but still came quicker than I was ready for.

We had heard of Felix's execution from the chattering of visitors and an occasional update from the news station. But the village television was so unreliable with its sporadic power shortages and infuriating fuzzy screen, that we were unclear on the details.

We traveled by bus, and Jace held Indira close to him as she slept for most of the ride. It was winter, and the roads were dry. Many tourists filled the bus this time of year, and at first, Jace had to stand and hold the baby. It finally cleared at the first scenic overlook, and we were able to all squash together into the third row. I fell asleep against the window and woke up only when we arrived.

The streets were packed as usual, and Indira clung to her father, taking it all in over his shoulder. We stopped at a vendor and got some food and water and found our way to the payphone. Jace had found a hotel for us that was cleaner and just up the street. The phone booth was located about five blocks from the hotel. We had to wait to use it. A short line had formed outside, and Jace grew anxious that we would worry Wheezie if she had to wait too long to get the call. Finally, it was our turn, and the three of us packed into the booth sandwiching Indie in between us.

"It's been too long Wheezie…we have missed hearing from you," Jace mourned.

"How's little Wheezie?"

"Good…Say hello to Wheezie." Jace held the phone to Indira's mouth.

"Kumno," her squeaky voice giggled.

Wheezie went on to tell us of Felix's execution. His case had been tried in the United States because the prosecutors sought the death penalty, and the US is one of the only countries still allowing it. He was killed by electrocution just three months ago. Wheezie was present for the execution. He had no last requests and his only words were "She will prevail...She always does."

"We don't know if he was talking about a female specifically or The Jailer's Way in general. But, if it goes above Felix, we will find who this 'She' is. It didn't seem like enough justice, watching him fry. It was over too quick. I wished he had suffered more for what he did to people. But that is just me," she bragged.

405 people were in custody and being tried in various countries. Not to mention the radicals that wanted to revamp The Jailer's Way, because they boiled with shallow hate-filled minds. People were on edge and anxiety ran thick. The world was gripped by terrorist attacks and unspeakable cold-hearted bombings and shootings that shook normally peaceful nations to their cores.

She still warned us to be cautious in certain areas and to stay away from certain countries where security alerts were high, and we would be questioned. Other than that we were free to go where we pleased. Our names had never been brought up, and she reminded us that our finder's fee account was still waiting for us.

"It's sort of a bribe I guess. To eventually get you to come to New York so I can see that baby of yours. Live your life, don't be strangers. Give Itty Bitty Wheezie a kiss from me."

With that, we ended our multi-annual visits to Nepal. It was over.

"I don't believe it...I don't believe it's over. For all we know, Felix could have tipped a domino somewhere that ignited terrorism. It's all connected, I know it is," I said.

"You heard Wheezie, he's dead."

"I know that...but he's dead because he *wanted* to be. Felix was the weak link, and It doesn't shock me that he would eliminate himself in the name of his cause. He had a plan... He always had a plan. Whoever he was talking about, '*She* will prevail,' there is someone else, higher up than Felix. Maybe Felix was just one of *her* pawns. Who could it be?"

"We have no way of knowing that. We can't feel responsible for all the lives Felix and The Jailer's Way has destroyed throughout the Earth. We can't spend our lives chasing an invisible woman."

"So we are just supposed to move on? We go home? We forget all of our life up until now? What do we do? Where do we go?" I asked.

"We go back to Mawlynnong," he replied.

Back in Mawlynnong, we went back and forth with the idea of returning to Tanzania. Jace wanted to show Rubin his daughter and tell him that he had been right.

"Right about what?" I inquired.

"Nothing...never mind. You would just get mad at me."

"Too late," I smiled. "We could go...for a visit. Summer is coming, it will be so wet and dreary here. We could go for a few months," I offered.

"Maybe we can stop in Europe. We can call Rubin from there, so Mawlynnong always remains our safe place. Just in case." Jace popped with anticipation and happiness that I agreed to go back to Tanzania. "Thea! I can't wait to see Rubin and the farm. Indira will love it there." He was so excited. I was more apprehensive. I thought of all the goodbyes we had to say here, and I choked up thinking about it. I was excited to see Neemala and even Gideon and see how their lives had changed in the last four years, but my heart felt so sad thinking of leaving our cottage and family.

We said Goodbye on a Friday, with watery eyes and sad hearts. Our promises to Grace that we would return failed to comfort her. She held Indira tightly, and we had to pull the two of them apart. Indira loved her big sister and didn't understand why we were leaving home. We hoped to be back before the next winter, so our cottage was closed up.

Solar and Mumtaz bravely told us that they would watch over our little home and fight off Bindi and her craving to rent it for an extra profit. Jace paid Bindi for the cottage for the remainder of the year, just in case we were delayed. Bindi was surprisingly emotional over our departing. I had told her that I was nervous and feeling nauseous at the prospect of leaving everyone, and as a parting gift, she brought a bag of her dried pineapple slices.

"Thank you, Bindi." I warmly embraced her stiff little body. She pat me on the back and said curtly,

"Six months… then you come back." She seemed to be reassuring herself.

Tripura packed us a bag with Indira's favorite crackers. She pulled her from me, and held on to her, kissing her plump little cheeks. She couldn't say goodbye, she hugged me and smiled warmly with water filled eyes,

"See you soon," she said with hopeful confidence.

I cried the entire flight to London. Jace held Indira, asleep in his arms. We arrived at Heathrow airport, UK on a rainy day. Nothing like the rains of Mawlynnong but still a nuisance. I was sick to my stomach as soon as we arrived in London, but was in denial, and trying to push through it.

Jace brought us to The Lancaster Square Hotel. It was on the corner of two streets and had little shops below. The rooms were more like small apartments, so we planned to recuperate for a couple days and adjust to the time zone. The room had a separate bedroom suite and a small kitchenette with a sitting area and television.

Indira had never seen a television that didn't have fuzz, let alone a cartoon. She was instantly magnetized and planted herself in a TV coma eating cheese crackers that Jace picked up from the shop below. She and I fell asleep cuddled on the sofa with the TV still on and didn't wake up until the next day around 9 am. Jace had left a note on the table that he had gone a half hour earlier to pick up some food and supplies, and to make a call to Rubin.

Indira and I took a shower, and I brushed her hair. She was much more cooperative if I plopped her in front of the TV. I would have to get her some more clothes, all she had was the typical Khasi clothing. Brightly colored shorts and top, with a little knit sweater and sandals. It was raw and colder here, and she would need something more to keep her warm. Jace returned with gyros, and something called a corn dog for Indira. She nibbled away at it as she watched cartoons.

"Rubin will pick us up in Arusha. I told him about us getting married, and about Indie, he can't wait to meet her. You should have heard him, he was so happy we are coming," Jace relayed.

"It will be strange being there as your *wife*."

"I think we can stay on the same side of the loft this time," Jace teased.

We were able to go out that night to get some clothes for Indira. I was not use to so many choices and styles. I tried to see what was popular among the locals and tourists and finally found some tiny pants in three colors, socks, underwear, and five tops with different animals on them. I also found her a little green jacket with big pink buttons and a pink knit hat just in case it got colder. I bought small blue shoes, and pajamas with purple flowers on them. Jace didn't care about clothes shopping, he was interested in finding Indira a doll. He went in and out of stores carrying her and asking if she liked this one or that one. She came close to picking a large plastic horrendous looking dinosaur with red teeth that she found fascinating, but Jace quickly diverted her attention to more loveable creatures.

She turned her head at all his suggestions. After the fourth store, she finally found her first beloved toy. It was a small bean-filled white kitten. She cuddled it and cradled it in her arms and stroked it making meow sounds. Jace was satisfied with her smile, and we could move on.

We got ourselves some fresh clothes and supplies and headed back to the hotel. We made a little bed for Indie with the reclining chair and edged it with pillows to make a nest for her. She was exhausted and put to bed in her flannel pajamas with purple flowers, and tucked in her arm was her little kitten, that she named Grace.

The next day, we took another twelve-hour flight from Heathrow to Arusha with a layover in Casablanca, Morocco. Finally, we arrived in Arusha, and the familiar warm breeze filled our lungs. We were not hiding in cargo ships or Red Cross deliveries this time. We were met openly and freely by our dear friend Rubin. His cheerful and excited welcome home drew us into his big bear hug. He nearly squashed Indie who was hiding her eyes from the blaring sun.

"My heart! Indie… My child, you are magnificent!" he triumphantly announced. She tucked her head into her father's neck and squeezed her kitten. "Ah…you will love me baby girl…by tomorrow… I love *you* already…*you* and your kitten. Come let's get your bags." He laughed that well-known belly laugh of happiness all the way to the luggage pick up.

The truck ride to the farm was a welcome moment in my life. I had dreamt of the day that I would freely return to my childhood home. My fears of Felix and any diabolical plan he may have, faded with every mile. We bumped and jostled and dug our feet into the floor of the truck as we made our way to Taralock Estates.

"The whole house is in an uproar about you coming. They are cleaning and preparing food. Emma has hired extra help to get the rooms ready."

"I thought we were staying with you and Neema?" I worried.

"I did too, but Emma was not having that at all. She wants you at the big house."

"Was she happy to hear about us returning, and about Indie?" Jace asked.

"Well…I will tell you, I told her and Joseph that you were returning, but I left out the being married and having a child part. It is your news to tell your parents Jace Taralock. You know Gideon has a wife as well?"

"Really?" I happily expressed.

"Yes. Kateri, but they call her Katie…from Arusha…and you know what?… She has skin like mine! They have a boy. Three years old now, named Toby. They live in the big house also. I tell you…this family is growing fast!" he chuckled.

Once we peaked the hill, the house became visible. Rubin took the main road and avoided the shortcut for the sake of Indie. The house had not changed, and the farm looked as plush and thriving as we had left it. We arrived in a dust cloud by the large acacia tree.

A little boy with chocolate milk skin dotted with freckles stood at the stairs. A puppy nipped at his shorts as he called for his mother. Katie came from the kitchen screen door to greet us. She was a plump woman with glowing brown skin. Her hair was neatly tucked into a bandana, and she wore jeans and a baggy red short sleeve shirt. She looked about my age and had the prettiest dark chocolate eyes and long eyelashes. Katie swatted at the puppy's behind and came to meet us. She introduced Toby who hid behind his mother's legs, lowering his blue-green eyes to the ground. Indira tucked tightly to her father's chest and buried her head in his neck.

"This is your cousin Indie." Jace lowered her, but she just clung tighter and pulled her legs up, refusing to be placed on the ground.

"It's fine...they will be friends...once we get you all settled," Katie consoled. She was a cheerful, lively woman with an encouraging, confident manner. I was genuinely happy that Gideon had found such a personable wife.

Neema came from the path and sprung into a sprint as she got closer. We embraced like long lost beloved friends. She hugged me tight and kissed my cheeks.

"Theorie…Jace…My family…You are here." Her smile beamed.

Jace turned his shoulder exposing his bashful little girls face. She was scared and unsure, but Neema had known that...She gently held out her hand to the little girl and smiled.

"Hello Indie…I'm Neema." She came closer and kissed Indie's clenched hand, and with one finger stroked her little stuffed kitten. "Hello little kitten...you must be scared...it's okay…you are okay little kitten." Indira's face softened, as she watched Neema pet her cat. She uncurled from her father's shoulder and looked at Neema wide-eyed and smiled.

Neema instinctively reached out, and Indie climbed into her arms and cuddled her. It astonished Jace, but I understood. I knew that Neema would love my daughter as her own and the warmth between them was instant and true.

Gideon and Joseph came from the barn and hugged us. My brother had grown into a man. I had not actually seen him in ten years. The last time we were here, Jace and I were in hiding. He was robust and healthy and was excited to introduce his wife and son. Joseph hugged Jace and pat him on the shoulder.

"It's good to see you son… Good to see you."

Gideon and Joseph simultaneously looked at the child in Neema's arms and halted their salutations.

"Who's this?" Joseph begged.

"Dad, this is Indira… my daughter…Our daughter."

"Well, I could tell who her Ma was just looking at that hair." He smiled and grabbed hold of his son for a second time. "She's just beautiful son…Theorie…she's beautiful…like her Ma." He wiped a tear from his eye and patted his son on the back again smiling proudly.

"I knew it!" Gideon exulted.

Katie chuckled at her husband and alerted us, "Come on…Emma's waiting inside for you."

We went into the kitchen and Gideon, and Rubin brought our bags to our room. Emma came from her back porch and was smiling but subdued. We weren't expecting much of a welcome from Emma, she wasn't the warm hugging type, which was fine, because we were really here to be home with Neema and Rubin. Emma' s hair had frosted over to a near complete white. Her upper lip was cracked with lines and her eyelids looked heavier, making her expression seem kinder and wiser. She had gotten older, and I hoped that meant she would be kinder to me.

"Mom." Jace walked right up to her and embraced her naturally. She weakly patted him on his back.

"James...It is good you are home, and Theorie...you as well."

She looked at me with less enthusiasm. You had to be impressed with Emma's ability to hide her emotions. She knew that we could read her like a blueprint and she knew exactly how to remain poker-faced. She hugged me lightly.

"I had your rooms kept just as you left them. Katie helped me get them ready for you…Toby has your room now Theorie, but we put him in with his parents, so you can have that room for now. I hope they're suitable."

"Mom, well, we…we can stay in one room…" A look of sharp disagreement swelled her face. She didn't know.

"I'm sorry I couldn't contact you to tell you...I wanted to...I did...Toby doesn't need to give up his room, Theorie is my wife," he uncomfortably stated.

She blankly stared at Jace, awkwardly sizing up the situation. I didn't think she understood what Jace had said, or maybe she was going to yell at me and kick me out of her house. I felt about two inches tall and wanted to hide under the kitchen island again.

Just then, Neema walked through the kitchen screen door joining us carrying our ginger haired daughter. She handed Indira to me, and promptly left sensing the tension.

"Mom...this is Indira." Jace introduced his baby girl. I clung to my daughter protectively not wanting Emma to be cruel or indifferent to her. I couldn't bear if she treats my child the way she had treated me. I would have berated her until I choked the last bit of dignity out of her and left her feeling like an ashamed child.

As my maternal protection flared, Emma looked back and forth between Jace and I and welled up. Seeing this child brought her to tears. She was calm but clearly shaken. My mind raced with explanations as to why. My first thought was that she hated me and was disgusted that I had married her son and had his child.

I speculated that maybe seeing Indira reminded her of Felix, and she worried about Indira's future. I worried that she wouldn't love my little girl, and I wanted her to so badly. She calmly collected her emotions and forced a fake smile.

"Well, she's probably tired from the truck ride. You remember where your room is I assume...I'll have dinner ready in an hour."

Jace admitted defeat in winning over his mother, and we retreated to the sanctuary of Jace's room.

"Ugh. Why can't we stay in the cottage? Why did she want us to stay here?" he whispered.

"She didn't know about us, or Indira...It's all new to her...She's just processing. Remember how overwhelmed I was when I learned it was all over and we could be free to do what we wanted? It's like someone blew air into her lungs forcefully and didn't let her catch her breath on her own."

"If she is mean to you...or God forbid to Indie...I swear..."

"Jace I'm an adult now, and Indie has us...We will be fine."

"So many memories Thea... Mom is right, it is exactly the same in here...My shelves, my guitar, my twin bed," he stated annoyed.

"Well, we will just have to sleep very close to each other," I teased. He smiled and started showing Indira around his old room.

Dinner, that night with the family, was awkward. Katie focused on the children and making sure their food was adequate. Emma fretted over place settings, and Joseph and Gideon told Jace all about the farm. It had been a good crop, but civil unrest was rampant. Land disputes had started, and poachers had moved into the area destroying properties trying to force farmers South. It had been quite a challenging year keeping alert to the local troubles. The whole economy had started to whirlwind downward shortly after we left due to corruption in the government and starving people. That affected tourism and trade which created a domino effect of tension and desperation.

"People just aren't thinking right," Joseph lamented. "They can't think right when they're hungry."

There was no mention of Felix or The Jailer's Way even though I knew they were all aware of the state of things. I wasn't sure how much they knew, or if they knew how involved Jace and I were in the exposure of it all. Either way, Felix was a name that was not spoken of at the dinner table.

Joseph watched Indira interacting with her cousin Toby and smiled contentedly. The children had warmed up to each other, and by the end of the night, Indie even let Toby hold her little stuffed kitten. Just for a moment, but long enough to let him know she wanted to be friends.

That night after Indie had fallen asleep we pulled out Jace's dresser drawer and scrunched up the clothes that no longer fit him into a makeshift mattress. We laid blankets down and made a cozy mini bed for her, and she slept soundly.

"Come on..." Jace lead me eagerly down the stairs to the piano. He pulled his sheet music from the bench and sat down at his old friend. He played softly, closing his eyes and tilting his head to the sound. He was taken away by the sound of the keys and played louder.

"Shhh," I whispered smiling at him. "You'll wake everyone."

"Sorry." He played softly, and I moved to the couch and drifted off to sleep listening to him play the piano like it was his first language. I didn't know what time it was when he finally woke me up, and I trailed behind him back up the stairs to his room.

"Jace? Are you asleep?" I asked after trying to fall back to sleep.

"Hmm?" he acknowledged half asleep.

"I'm going to have a baby."

"We already have one," he mumbled with his eyes closed.

Several minutes passed, and there was no response, he had fallen asleep. I would have to wait until tomorrow to tell him.

"Huh?" he gasped a second later. "A baby?"

"Uh-huh. I wanted to tell you once we got here. I don't know how, but..."

"Um…I'm pretty sure you know how."

"I'm saying, it's not exactly expected...I know we weren't planning on it. Two kids are a lot, and Indie's still so little."

"Yeah...but a baby…." His smile overpowered him.

"You're happy? I pleaded.

"Are you joking…Yes, I'm happy. I want four or five kids. At least. When?"

"In April... And four or five? How will we feed them and where will we live? Four or five...Really? No…nope...two is good."

"April, so five months." He ignored my statement about not wanting that many kids and was on cloud nine thinking of his new baby, that he insisted was a boy.

The following week we visited Mahtap's grave and showed Indie where we had grown up. Jace played the piano like it was a breath of fresh air to him. He reveled in it remembering the sound and feeling of his beloved instrument. He polished the keys and tuned it to perfection. He sat Indie on his lap and helped her little chubby fingers find the middle 'C.'

"I'll teach you Chopin first, then Mozart," he boasted.

We also had several visitors come to see Jace and me, and to meet Indira. Some of the Maasai that had worked seasonally for years and knew us as children made their way to the cottage yard while we were spending the day with Neema and Rubin. They were happy we had returned, and we reminisced about Mahtap. It was healing to speak of old times in a positive way, and hearing Rubin's belly laugh while talking of how much trouble I was as a girl was contagious. It felt so good to laugh.

He told Neema about when I was six years old, and for five days, I decided to live my life as a dog. I would only drink out of a bowl on the floor and pretended to chase my tail. Mahtap had humored me, allowing my imagination to grow.

It was only when she told me that I was a smelly dog and needed a bath that I questioned my decision to be a canine. She filled a basin with warm water right in the yard of her cottage. My brothers and Jace were playing ball, and she told me to strip down and get into the water, so she could get my fleas off. I quickly changed my mind and decided to be human again, since it was in my best interest.

Neema laughed so hard and warned me of the things to come, and that having two children, I was doomed to have one just like me. "Are you ready Jace?" Rubin teased. "Great adventures await...Two puppies will keep you busy!" Rubin chuckled sporadically as the day passed. We drank mango juice on the porch and Neema showed me how to tame and braid Indie's hair.

Toby and Indie played on the porch with her little kitten whose white fur was already turning gray from love. He had brought his stuffed elephant from his room, and they made them chase each other.

One visitor I was less than excited to see was Allison Cade. She drove up in her decked out fancy crossover and pranced into the barn, speaking to one of the workers looking specifically for Jace. Joseph, Gideon and he had been patrolling the perimeter on the quads checking for signs of poachers or damaged fences. Neema and I were walking from the barn after fetching a crate of apples.

"Well...Theorie Jailer...I never thought I'd see you again." She pushed her sunglasses to her forehead, pushing back her perfect silky blonde hair. She was tall and had an hour-glass figure. I looked at her puzzled. For a split second,

I saw someone other than the Allison Cade I had known as a child. Her eyes seemed familiar in a frightening way. It was the same person, but a biting chill crept up my spine, and I didn't know why. What was wrong with me?

"Where did all your adorable little freckles go?" She spoke like a baby asking the question.

Indie waddled closer to me balancing several apples in her little arms. They rolled away, and she grabbed for them, making more of them fall to the ground. Allison looked at her like a creature crawling from the swamp.

"Oh...they seem to have spit out onto that." Her tone changed, and her lip went up making her nostrils pull back.

"Allison…. What brings you here? I knew you missed me. Have you felt a hole in your heart, longing for our endearing friendship to rekindle?"

"I actually heard through the grapevine that *Jace* was back in town," she replied in a snarky tone.

"Oh really? You didn't hear, I was back as well?" I picked up my daughter and wiped the apple sticky from her face. Allison stared at the child, instantly realizing who its parents were.

Jace and the others pulled up to the back of the barn and parked the quads. They chatted away about a fence needing to be fixed and that it should be done as soon as possible. Jace came over scooping his daughter from my arms, kissing her whole face, and making her giggle.

"Uh, ppt, you're all sticky baby. Are you eating all the apples? How will Neema make us a pie?" He whirled her around and then noticed the blonde wearing tight blue jeans and a shirt two sizes too small standing at the door to the barn.

"Allison! Hi."

"Jace...I heard you were back in town." She flirted, ignoring everything that she had just pieced together. She walked past me and put her arms around my husband like she owned him...or would someday.

"Yeah...Wow...It's been awhile."

She cringed realizing how close she was to his sticky child. "So, you've been busy I see," she snarled.

"A little...This is Indira." He handed her back over to me.

"I guess there is an audience for *every* medium," she stated as she looked my body up and down like I was painted over with manure.

"So what have you been up to?" Jace politely asked, looking at me to read my irritation level.

"Me? Oh, a bit of everything...I'll tell you, I have not had an easy time of it. Dad lost a lot in the market crash, and he had to sell THREE of his properties. We lost the Paris apartment," she pouted.

"That's unfortunate," I mocked sarcastically.

She didn't acknowledge me and continued, "I am here supporting my father, and helping him manage the Ranch now...Until we head back to Dubai next month."

She sneered at me. "I'm not married...yet, I've had plenty of proposals, just haven't found the right one. *You* broke my heart James Taralock when you left so quickly without saying goodbye to me."

"Uh, I'm sorry about that...I guess...I didn't know I meant that much to you," he replied in a confused tone.

"Look at you…acting like there was nothing…I get it, it's the wrong company to admit that in front of," she sighed dramatically. I was standing right there, and she didn't care one bit.

"What's your…" I began before Jace cut me off abruptly. I was about to rip her to pieces verbally. I ran through insults about her manicured body and how people like her couldn't even begin to understand the real world or love of any kind because she was made of plastic, and that at least when she dies it will be easy to find her body because she will be swimming with the fishes in the shallow end.

Jace could see my mind swirling with insults and distracted my spite by speaking louder.

"I'm sure you'll find the right person." He literally bumped into me to shut me up.

"Well, I hope you're around for a while… I'd love to catch up," she flirted.

I sarcastically giggled under my breath, "Sure you would."

I stomped into the house carrying Indira, ahead of Jace. Emma startled in the kitchen as I swooshed by her and went upstairs. Jace followed behind on his way to do damage control.

The next week we broke the news of the baby to the rest of the family. Joseph assured us that we were welcome to stay as long as we wanted, and Katie teased that it was because we were given only a twin bed. Even Emma softened towards me and made little gestures of affection and attention towards Indira. For the next few months the children filled the days with hope and laughter and we began to heal as a family.

I was going on my seventh month when Emma invited me to sit on the porch with her. She offered me her rocking chair and moved to the bench. I had never sat with her here, and I knew it was a huge step forward in our relationship. We sat looking towards the sunset as it peeked through the tree line. Looking at the horizon, I finally understood why she had chosen this porch as her special solitude. The view was spectacular, and aside from the cottages tucked among the forest, most of Taralock Estates was in view. The evening sunset painted the sky in deep maroons and coppers. As a child, I would have never appreciated this spot, but as a mother and wife, I now saw Emma's porch as a place to ponder and appreciate.

"I want to give this to you." She handed me a small white silk pouch with a snap.

"A ring? It's beautiful!" I gushed.

"It should have been your mother's," she solemnly stated. I looked at her puzzled.

I rubbed my rolling belly and watched the gliding motion push out a gentle bump. I smiled at the little foot that was trying to be a part of this conversation.

Emma looked down as well and cracked a smile. "I see so much of your father in Indie," she admitted. It was the first time any mention of our past had come up. I held the ring looking closely at how beautiful it was. It was platinum with three sapphire stones. The one in the center was slightly larger with a smaller square sapphire on either side. Tiny diamonds bordered each stone.

"Your father gave me that ring when we were in college. Before…all of it. I didn't know who he was. I didn't know who your grandfather was." Clearly, she knew we were involved somehow, and she knew that I would understand what she was talking about.

"I know you may think your father was an accomplice to Felix, and to Theodore before him, but he wasn't. It was your father who was trying to destroy what Felix was."

I knew she didn't know how much Jace and I already knew. I let her go on and listened to her confession. She was finally talking, and I was anxious to hear her story.

"We were so young… So in love…We had plans." She looked so sad and full of regret. "Theodore, your grandfather, was the head of the organization then. But, what your father somehow unearthed was that there was a second organization fighting against 'The Jailer's Way.' It is called the 'Order of the Lynx.'" Emma sat on the porch bench and looked off in the distance at the sunset.

"They were good people that gathered what they could to expose the crimes that were committed, and they were the revealer of many secrets. Many members of this opposition were within Theodore's realm, traitors that were trying to destroy and expose The Jailer's Way. They prevented many terrible events, but Theodore's operation was growing and becoming more difficult to contain.

They held a safe with information in a secret location. And they marked the location with a secret code of coordinates tattooed on their arms. Only two people at any time through any generation knew of these symbols.

Your father lead the double life of a Linchpin while he gathered proof. For years he made drop-offs at the safe as often as he could, without being found out, and he was good at what he did. He tattooed the coordinates on my arm…and his. He didn't tell me the code to decipher the numbers, he thought it would be too dangerous."

"If I am marked, who is the second person? Your marks are burned away," I interrupted.

"It was supposed to be my son...But I couldn't do it. Your father asked me to stain the symbols onto James after Felix burned my arm, but I wanted to forget everything. I didn't want James targeted by Felix, and I knew the symbols would lure Felix in and put him into a situation that he was not mature enough to handle. I refused to involve him, but Felix took him anyway."

"Felix burned you?" I asked, remembering the torture Felix put me through trying to find out information.

"Yes. He believed I had information about your father and the organization trying to take him down."

I pulled back my sleeve and revealed my scars from Felix's cigar. Emma's eyes pinched in painful reminiscence, as she looked away.

"Theodore found out that your father had been gathering this proof and tried everything in his power to get your father to give up the information, and where it had been hidden. He wanted to know *who* was leading the opposition and tried to force your father to betray his contacts. The only reason Theodore allowed him to live was because he was his son and because he was desperate to eliminate these threatening documents.

Your father was forced to run missions in exchange for my life, and we were made to marry other people in Theodore's network, ordinary people who had been given 'a place.'

When children came along, Theodore saw them as leverage and threatened to take them and make them master linchpins. He threatened to make them everything your father had been fighting against.

Your Grandfather Theodore died when you were about three years old, and his brother Felix inherited the organization. He had no mercy, and your father knew that he and his children were in danger. He tattooed your arm knowing that Felix would soon have him killed and hoped that someday you would be curious enough, and courageous enough to unearth the truth. He knew you would be brought into the organization. Your parents knew from an early age that you would be taken. It drove your mother mad.

Rose loved your father, even though it was an arranged marriage, and she loved her children. She deserved better than the life she was given. Your father brought you here, so you could have the chance to grow up free and happy, and in the care of someone, he trusted, someone who understood his plight ...Mahtap.

He made a deal with the new leader of The Jailer's Way and told Felix that he would train you in languages, and cultures. He brought you around the world to prepare you for what he knew was coming in order to spare his life and have time to train you. He was determined to open your heart to empathy and compassion. It was his only weapon against Felix. Morgan knew that if you felt people's stories, you would never be swayed by hatred and prejudice."

I sat motionless watching every word spill from her mouth.

"Why are you telling me all of this now Emma?"

"Because for ten years I have wanted to explain why I let Felix take you that night," she explained and continued.

"When you were twelve years old, your father no longer was necessary, he was seen as a weak threat. Your training was complete, and Felix had you in his sight. He knew you had the markings and assumed you were a whimsical child, that he could manipulate. When I was told that my own son would be taken because Felix deemed it necessary, I knew there was a chance.

I couldn't stop Felix from taking you that night, and I didn't want to. It was my only chance that you would fulfill your father's work. I had one opportunity to let you go so that I could save Morgan's children. *All* of Morgan's children..." she stated looking at me intensely to read my reaction.

"I trusted that you were what your father had created. A strong, stubborn fighter with an aptitude towards empathy and compassion. I don't know if it *was* you and James that took down The Jailer's Way. I don't know if you found the decipher to the markings on our wrists, and I don't want to *ever* know. I want this to be over. I want to watch your children, that are a part of Morgan and a part of me, grow up and be happy and live a beautiful full life."

I rocked in the chair and watched the sun lower. Emma had unloaded her burden on me, but I could bear it. I knew her plight. I put her ring on my finger, up against the keychain ring from Wheezie's purse that I still wore. My father had given Emma this ring a lifetime ago. It was a ring given in honest, true love, and I knew she was handing over to me a piece of her heart.

"Thank you for this Emma. It means...so much." I clenched my hand to my chest and watched her expression change to satisfaction.

"Emma, do you worry that even though Felix is gone, The Jailer's Way will live on?"

She sighed and leaned back on her bench. "I have a hard time accepting it too...We've met a great many villains along the way...But, we've also met honorable and genuinely good souls. It's the classic tale of good versus evil, and only time will tell."

The conversation pooled in my mind, and the more I thought about her words, the more turbulent my mind became. Who was involved? Who could I trust? My entire childhood had been plotted and manipulated.

Two nights had passed since Emma opened up to me. I had told Jace what she said, and for the first time, I saw a twinge of forgiveness in his eye towards his mother.

I lay trying to go to sleep up against the safety of my husband's chest, but I couldn't rest my brain enough to drift off. I nudged and adjusted the blanket and pillow. My eyes closed, and I swayed into sleepiness only to thrash awake panicking a moment later. My breath was heavy and suffocating.

"Thea!" Jace sat up grabbing my arms and steadying me. "What? What's the matter?" he pleaded. Indie started to stir awake, and I tried to settle my anxiousness.

"Jace..." I tried to catch my breath. "Jace...It's the eyes. We have to leave. Please!"

"What are you talking about? Calm down…It's just us…No one else is here." He held me tight, but I was so cold I couldn't stop trembling.

"Her eyes…" I repeated.

"Whose eyes?" he begged, whispering so not to wake Indira.

I calmed my shaking and took a deep breath. I looked right into his eyes so that he could see the seriousness of my fright.

"Allison…Cade…Allison Cade's eyes are the same as Arlo's, and Andrea's," I finally pushed out.

"That's impossible…We have known her since we were kid's and she is an *only* child."

"No…No.." I tossed in fear again trying to break away from him, so I could pick up my daughter and run. "I spent an entire year staring into the arrogant eyes of Arlo as he beat me and forced me into a defensive rage just to survive. I fought him and read his body language, I read his eyes to see what his next move was so that he wouldn't have the chance to overpower me. His eyes gave him away every time. It's her eyes…She knows we are here, and she is part of Felix's next move. I want to go…Now…Please…"

"Okay, In the morning…Shhh. It's okay. Right now you are safe, Indie is safe. Look at me…"

I looked into his gray-blue eyes and searched for security. I found it. His intent gaze was promising me that my daughter...his daughter would be alright and that we would be safe.

Jace sat up and adjusted the blankets and pillows. He went to the dresser drawer that was our little girl's nest and scooped her up. I shuffled my back up against the wall and Jace placed Indira in the tuck of my arm. He covered us with the blanket and lay on the other side of the bed facing us, barricading us from the dark room and the unseen. I could finally sleep.

The next morning as the sun barely began to rise, Indira looked so peaceful still sleeping in the bed. It was still very early, but I quietly packed our things and set the bags poised and ready to go. Emma was reading Toby a story in the living room, drinking her coffee, letting his mother sleep a bit more. We wanted to say goodbye to Rubin and Neema. We planned on leaving right after breakfast. We would take Rubin's truck as far as we could and find a phone to call Wheezie, we needed her help more than ever before. I had no ideas or plans...I couldn't think straight because the possibility of loss was too great to factor in, and my emotions were all over the place.

Jace and I went to the cottage early. Joseph, Rubin, and Gideon had already left to work on the fence that needed mending in the West orchard. Neema was cleaning up dishes.

"Ah...what brings you out here so early?" She smiled, and instinctively pulled out two coffee mugs from her pantry.

"We came to say goodbye," Jace announced. Her demeanor changed, and she became sorrowful.

"I knew you could not stay forever...When will you go?" she asked.

"We want to use Rubin's truck...as soon as possible...but we wanted to say goodbye first," Jace explained.

"Rubin will not be back until lunch. Poachers were in the fields. Tracks were found. Joseph is very anxious to repair the barrier. The farm is on edge. Several Maasai camps were robbed at gunpoint last night. The workers are uneasy and want to leave the farm until the danger passes. Must you go today?"

"Yes," I sorrowfully announced.

"Well, I will see if I can find him. Sit... Have coffee..." Neema went to the door, and from a hook that had hanging jackets, she pulled down a small rifle.

"Neema, I'll go." Jace jumped up, anxious that she was putting herself in danger.

"I know how to use this," she stated as she checked the barrel and made sure she had ammo. She hung it over her shoulder.

"You stay...or go to the main house, I'll fetch Rubin."

Neema opened the screen door just as shrills and screams echoed and piled into the forest. We instantly became panicked, and all three of us stepped onto the cottage porch to see if there had been an animal attack or if the poachers had been spotted. We surveyed our surroundings and tried to focus our ears to figure out where the hollering was coming from. In the direction of the path to the main house, and just above the thick tree line, the morning sky was rust and blood orange. Robust clouds of thick gray and black began emanating into the morning wind above our heads.

Chapter 19

"You Will Break, & When You Do..."

"The House!" Neema screamed.

She dropped everything and ran. She ran up the path towards the main house, and Jace and I ran as fast as we could behind her. The first floor of the main house was engulfed in flames. Toby was standing by the acacia tree screaming hysterically, and his mother ran from the kitchen porch screaming on the top of her lungs to get help! She scooped her son up and held him to her body in a smothering grip. The heat from the fire blew out the kitchen window overlooking the porch, shooting glass at us and hurling Neema back several feet.

In a frenzy, I failed to think like a rational person facing a wall of fire. Jace was blocking me like a brick wall and yelling at me to stay where I was. I twisted and wrenched against his defense and the burning house pushing my way and breaking my arms free. I ran towards the house to get my baby girl.

Katie yelled from the safety of the tree like a Banshee...

"Emma went back in...She went back in...to get Indie...They're both inside!"

I screamed a guttural holler and threw myself with all my might towards the inferno. It had not reached the second floor yet...and I WOULD get my baby out.

Jace lost his grip on me, and I ran to the door jetting past the kitchen island, through blasts and sparks. I choked and coughed and covered my mouth with my elbow. The heat burned my eyes and made them water. I couldn't see. In an instant the panic and inability to see what direction the stairs were in disoriented me.

Suddenly a mighty force pulled my shoulder back, and in a flash, I was shaken abruptly and yanked from the house and thrown into the yard.

Joseph's powerful arm threw me against Jace. "HOLD HER!" he yelled at his son!

Neema joined Jace in trying to hold me back. Jace ran forward joining his father trying to get through the door, but I broke free from Neema again, and ran towards the glowing house, following my husband.

Rubin came running from the orchard and pulled Jace away by the back of his shirt just as he hit the threshold of the burning door, and a beam from within the house crashed to the floor. He pulled him back throwing him towards me at the steps.

"Hold your wife, James! Stay back!" His aggressive tone threatened Jace and forced him to submit to containing me. He had to let Rubin and Joseph rescue Emma and Indie. Jace held me in his arms like a straight jacket. My legs flailed and kicked, but I was weakened and was choking on my own lungs.

Rubin ran inside dodging flames. The acacia tree began to burn above us, and the Maasai workers started flocking in, bringing water in buckets from the well. I remember that I was struggling, and would try and inhale deeply, but the pain in my lungs shot jolts through my body with every attempt. Jace was holding me so tight that I couldn't fully expand my lungs.

I was only seeing the house and the tree above in motion picture shots. I think I was screaming, but no sound was coming out. I kept having waves of a strong motivating force telling me to get up, fight Jace's embrace, push him away so I can get into the house…but why? Why was I struggling? Why was I in pain?

I was so tired, and groggy. I felt like I was drunk. I was not in pain anymore, in fact, I felt numb and weak. It was so bright, and I blinked to clear my eyes.

A hospital? How did I get here? I tried to sit up, and the comforting face of Neema gently told me to relax and to lie back down. She rang for the nurse as I scanned the room. Jace was there, sitting across the room in a chair with his head in his hands. He didn't look up when I called to him.

"Jace?" I choked out. My voice was cracking, and there was no power behind it. A tube ran from a machine at the bedside and clung to my nose. I pulled it away to clear my face. An IV was taped to my left arm and bandages covered my left shoulder.

Jace still did not lift his head. Rubin sat beside him watching him closely. A bandage wrapped along Rubin's right arm and hand. I was so confused. Why was I here? The baby...Had I gone into labor? I felt my stomach. I pushed and rolled my palm over my belly. It was swollen but felt empty and soft. I had bandages along my lower groin area. My heart began to pick up speed as the nurse entered and spoke to Neema.

"The baby! The baby... Where's the baby?" I croaked.

The nurse injected medication into the tube hanging from the pole and attached to my body. Neema called Rubin over to help her control my aggression. I didn't want medicine...I wanted to see my baby...I want to see Indira!

"Where's my daughter?" I screeched out loudly..."Stop...Please... Jace...Stop them...Indie?...Stop them!"

I woke up again to Neema sitting very close to me. She was the only one in the room, and I was nauseous. I stirred and tried to sit up, leaning over the bed and vomiting a mango colored liquid all over the floor. She clambered to find a basin and rang again for the nurse as she tried to calm me by holding my shoulders. The nurse came in and checked my IV bags and asked me questions about the pain. I didn't answer, who cares about me...

"Where's my baby, Neema? Where's Indie and Jace…" I cried.

"Theorie, you must lie back, your body is still healing."

For the next three days, I intermittently seesawed between sleep and waking in confusion. Every time my eyes opened and filled with the white of the ceiling, I would hear voices, and then all would go black again.
    The fourth day I gained enough strength to sit up for a moment or two. The nurses were weaning me from the pain medication flowing through my veins, and an aching throb deep within my core grew slowly. I didn't want to be numb anymore. I wasn't afraid of the pain.

Neema never left my side, and I begged her to tell me where my family was every ten minutes. She consoled and comforted me physically, but I wanted answers, I wanted my family.

"Where is Jace, Neema?" My voice seemed clearer, and I no longer had to wear the tube shooting air into my lungs.

"Jace is with Rubin, he is home at the cottage."

"I want him...please call for him. Please?"

"I will call for him."

Jace didn't come though. I tried to stay awake so that I would not miss him, but I couldn't keep from dozing off.

That evening Neema and the nurse helped me to get washed up, and a bowl of broth was brought to me with some bread. I had no appetite, but Neema insisted and held it to my mouth. It trickled down my dry, cracked throat and felt so soothing. I was able to sip it slowly and keep myself calm enough to swallow.

"Theorie, I must tell you something. And you must remain calm, or the nurse will put medicine in your arm, and you will go back to sleep. Do you understand?"

I looked at her beautiful face that was now exhausted and tormented, but still strong, and I knew in my heart the words she would speak…I didn't want to hear them…I needed to speak the words first.

"They're gone…aren't they Neema…They're gone…Emma, Joseph, the baby in me? Indie? Jace?" My voice trailed off in a tremble, and I lost my voice again. My body shook uncontrollably, and I vomited again all over the floor. The nurse came in asking if I needed medicine and began cleaning me up.

"No, she is fine for now," Neema answered.

"You have been here for nearly three weeks Theorie. Your body was burned on the left side, but it will heal."

"The fire," I began to tremble again, "Rubin's hands were bandaged."

"Yes, but he will be alright. He pulled Emma from the fire. She was on the stairs, and the smoke was heavy. It made her unconscious. She's burned, and it is serious. She is also here in the hospital. Katie has stayed with her. After Joseph pulled you back, and Rubin pulled Emma from the staircase, Joseph went back in to get Indira. He tried to go up the stairs, but the fire was so intense. The staircase gave way beneath his feet."

"Joseph is gone," I whispered…" and Indie…is …" I choked and became frantic.

"No!...No!...My baby girl, No! She's not! She didn't cry...I didn't hear her crying! Why didn't she cry? She's not gone!" A mean hatefulness erupted from my chest.

"No! I hate you...You lie...She is NOT gone!" I screamed with crackling lungs.

"Shhh." She steadied me. I felt my stomach.

"The baby...they cut it from me…" I sobbed. I pushed her away with my fists clenched but gave up and finally crumbled into her grip. Neema sat on the bed and held me tight, tears streaming from her warm eyes.

"Yes, my dear girl. He was too small. The doctors tried, they took him from you, hoping his heart rate would rise and his lungs would open. They really tried…Jace stayed with him until the end when he lost his fight."

"A boy...Jace was right." My body started to panic, and my stomach was about to heave again. "Jace? He's gone too.

"He's alright… He had smoke in his lungs, but he is okay." She tightened her grip.

She wiped my face with the sheet. I looked in her eyes. She was so full of empathy, feeling my pain right along with me.

"No Neema...He didn't come. He didn't come...I have lost everyone."

I was in the hospital for another two weeks. I had repeated mood swings of anger, violence, uncontrolled crying, and numbness. I begged to stay and be medicated. I begged them to take my life. Instead, they discharged me with grief counseling appointments and a broken soul.

Through it all, Neema never left my side. I was released into her care when my stitches healed, and infection had passed. She brought me back to the cottage via a back road so that I wouldn't see the house and all the damage.

I imagined riding up to the cottage and seeing Jace on the second step-up of Mahtap's porch, waiting for me. But he was not there. Neema settled me into her own bed and made me as comfortable as possible. I would never leave this spot again...I would stay here and ignore the world. I wanted medication to numb my brain. I understood my mother and why she admitted herself into a psychiatric facility. She had the right idea, and I envied her.

Wherever Jace was, Rubin was with him. Neema said Rubin would not leave Jace alone and was his shadow. I lost all sense of time in the following weeks. I put thick quilts over the windows to block out the life outside. Neema would pull them down and try to refresh the bedding and air out the room, but I fought her.

Her patience was tested, and her kindness abounded as I spit cruelty at her. She never raised her voice to me, and never once told me to pick up and move on...because she knew I couldn't.

After a month of stank darkness, I finally felt brave enough to wash and face the kitchen. Neema jumped on the opportunity and washed bedding and floors, and even the walls as I sat at the table in fresh clothes and ate Mugali. There was a bowl of mangoes on the table that turned my stomach, but the hot meal and a clean body did make me feel like I could breathe a little. Neema brushed and braided my hair and encouraged me to eat.

Gideon and Katie came with Toby, but the visit was cut short when I trembled and became frantic as I remembered the events of the fire, and how Katie had run to the tree and clung to her son. I hated her for not losing her child too. I hated that she and Gideon and helpless four-year-old Toby would continue to be a family.

They explained to Neema as I zoned out that they would be selling the farm after the funeral services and moving to the United States. Gideon bought farmland in Upstate New York and would plant hay and keep beef cattle. They would be taking Emma with them as well.

Good, I didn't want to see Emma ever again… I despised her for not saving my child instead of Gideon's.

The funeral services were set for the next weekend and Gideon, and his family would leave the following Monday, to find their place in another country far away from the fire of the African sky. The day before the services, Neema prepared food and helped me get ready for the next day. She was tender and patient with me as I spat hateful words about having people here and hating everyone. People didn't really care and could have no possible way of understanding my pain. Indira was *my* daughter, not theirs. Her voice haunted *my* thoughts. I could hear her giggle when I would tickle her. I could still feel her soft ginger hair between my fingers as she fought me brushing her wild hair. I could still smell her sweet breath as she tucked her head into my neck as I rocked her to sleep. She was mine, and she was gone. Not seeing her anymore was a nightmare that sent an uncontrollable fight against reality that would shake me to the floor. My little boy was *my* son. No one else felt his little feet kick within them. No one else imagined the softness of his wrinkly newborn fist gripping my fingers to feel safe. I refused to cooperate with Neema and would not get ready to go.

"I can't go to the funeral...I will not go," I wallowed.

"But, you will regret it in the following years if you fight this Theorie. You will always have a hole in your chest, but it will be larger if you do not bury your children," she admonished.

I agreed to go but told her I would refuse to speak to people, and that I would kill Allison Cade if she appeared. She didn't ask why I wanted to kill the neighbor's daughter, and let my hateful speech pass her ears.

I was sure Allison Cade had given us up to her brother Arlo, or someone else in The Jailer's Way network. I knew no one would believe me, and even Jace hadn't fully believed my epitome about their matching eyes the night before the fire. But I knew I was right. In my bones...I knew she was a pawn in The Jailer's Way.

Neema had placed my beaded necklace at my bed stand. It had been wound around my wrist the morning of the fire, and she had kept it with her from the moment I had been carried into the emergency department. I sat on the bedside, thinking of having to stand and watch my children go into the ground.

I slammed the small table, picked up the necklace that Jace had so perfectly matched to the one my father gave me. The necklace he gave me the day I attacked Bindi with my words for saying I was cursed because I did not have a child of my own. She had been right.

I tore the necklace apart with all my strength. Beads of teal, black and pink shot across the wood floor and bed. I stomped and kicked any bead that caught my eye and broke down sobbing. What had I done? I dropped to the floor and tried to gather the few visible tiny rolling beads. I cried deep and heavy, pounding my fist on the wood floor.

Neema ran into the room and cradled me in her embrace, and I crumbled. The crying didn't make me feel better, but my soul needed to erupt and release. I had lived through a gunshot, beatings, the pain of encephalitis, and childbirth, but nothing compared to the pain I felt aching through my body right now. It was deeper than anything I had ever experienced because it was something I could never heal from. I was broken.

Rubin came that afternoon with Jace trailing closely behind him. Jace...I wanted to see him. I wanted to tell him how sorry I was that I had not been able to get Indira out, I wanted to say sorry that my body wasn't strong enough to heal our infant sons' lungs. The feelings of guilt sank in my gut.

"Jace needs to talk to his wife, Neema," Rubin stated as he walked up the stairs and pulled his wife behind him into the cottage. I stood on the porch, and Jace came two steps up and paused.

We stood silently for a moment. "Jace, I'm…"

"We have to choose a name, Theorie." He spoke coldly and with emptiness.
It took me by surprise.

"A name?" I questioned.

"For the baby. The services will be tomorrow and... he has to have a name."

"A name… what do you want to call him?" I choked.

"It doesn't matter...It's not up to me."

"What do you mean? He's your son… It *is* up to you."

"No!" He snapped sharply..."Just name him."

What do you name a child that lived just a moment in this world? A child I had felt cuddle into my body, but never laid eyes on? What do you name a child that had no story, and never would?

"Can't we name him after you?" I asked, hardly able to steady my voice.

"Fine," and he walked away. Rubin came from the house and followed him down the path.

The day was sunny and warm. Birds chirped, and monkeys chattered, as the wind sighed through the trees. Neema helped me get ready in a simple black dress, and I walked with her to the burial site arm in arm. People had just begun gathering and flowers, and small gifts and offerings of toys and trinkets surrounded the acacia tree on the hill like a shrine.

The air should have smelled like roasting coffee and earth but all I had swirling at my nose was a faint smell of cigar. I knew I had to be imagining it, but it distracted me and made my eyes search the tree line for a man I knew was dead.

Gideon and his family stood close to the freshly dug dirt mound. Emma sat in a chair beside Gideon and just stared at the grass in a daze. From a distance, I made out the figures of Rubin closely walking behind Jace. As they approached, Rubin came near to his wife and kissed her on the forehead and grabbed hold of her hand.

Jace stood on the other side of Rubin and made it impossible for me to make eye contact with him. He despised me. I held back the intensely swelling feelings inside of me and turned my mind off for the duration of the services.

Rubin led the service and spoke about Joseph first, and all the kindness he had hidden behind his masculine mannerisms. He spoke of his fair and just treatment of his workers, and his great bravery.

Gideon welled up with tears, and Katie held her husband's arm tight. Gideon's little son clung to his mother's skirt and looked anxiously at his father's hurting face.

Rubin cleared his throat and spoke of Indira and the baby...

"A parent should never outlive a child...It goes against all reason. It goes against nature itself. The little ones that we say goodbye to today cannot be gone forever. God is not heartless and cruel. Their stories have been put on pause, and we will have to wait to turn the pages of their lives until another day. We will see them again, and we will watch them play, and laugh, and grow. One must dig and search for hope when the heart has been so shattered. My mother Mahtap spoke of hope. A hope that we will see those we have lost again. Just as they were, in body and soul. We will hold them, smell them, hear them, and love them just as they were."

He ended by asking God to remember Joseph, Indira, and baby James. I disagreed with his words that God was not cruel and heartless. Right now I felt that he was as conniving as Felix. I didn't understand how a loving God would allow an innocent child and a baby still growing in a womb to die and leave this world.

Neema took me back to the cottage as the three boxes of ash, carrying my two children and their grandfather was placed into the earth. They had been buried on the hill overlooking the farm next to Mahtap and her lost husband and son. A cool breeze blew making the grass look like waves rolling onto the beach. It was so peaceful and calm on the hill, and I hoped that all the memories I had up here, would cradle my children and keep them safe somehow.

Neema explained that poachers had been blamed. They had set the fire in an attempt to force Joseph from the land. They wanted the farmers out of the area so there would be less regulation and areas for them to hunt their illegal game. I didn't believe it was poachers though. I knew somehow The Jailer's Way had killed my children.

I sat in the yard of the cottage, with my mind wandering on possibilities of where I would go. I started feeling bad that Rubin and Neema had entirely upturned their lives to care for Jace and I. Neema told me not to rush into anything and that making decisions right now while deep in the throes of grief was not a good idea. I thought about going to the United States as well. I felt so alone, even with Neema's company. Alone in my thoughts, and alone in my hurt.

Jace came up the path being followed by Rubin. I was surprised to see my husband and ran through my mind what to say or do to try and keep him here with me. Rubin went inside with Neema and left Jace and me on the porch.

"I'm leaving. I just came to tell you and to say goodbye to Neema," he stated.

I was lost for words and just looked at him dumbfounded.

"Without me…"

He didn't answer me.

"I'm going to New York City. I can't stay here anymore." He turned to go, and fury of anxiousness pulled me up and towards him. He couldn't go. How dare he leave me here alone. He really did blame me and hated me. He wouldn't even look at me.

"Jace!" I hollered making him stop, but still hiding from my eyes with his back turned.

"You can't go. I'm sorry, I'm sorry I couldn't get her out. I'm sorry that the baby's lungs were too small."

"You didn't have to run into the house," he mumbled. "They would still be alive."

"What?" I gasped.

"If you stayed with Neema and didn't try to rush ahead and be a hero. If you didn't fight me *so* fiercely. If you didn't run into the house. If you had stayed and let Rubin and I go...My father would be alive, and my son would still be growing inside of you. I could have gotten to Indira. I could have gotten her out." His words cut my heart open, and a shiver crawled up my legs and into my neck.

"I wasn't trying to be a hero," I whispered because my voice trembled so intensely I couldn't push sound out. "I needed to get her, I'm her mother, no one would have fought harder or gone through a wall of fire like I would have to get her out. *You* stopped me... *You* stopped me from getting her! You held me back and let Rubin go in. I would have left your mother burning on the stairs and climbed past her to get to my baby. But *you* stopped me, and Rubin saved *your* mother because he saw her first, lying there, useless. My baby was just up the stairs!"

"How dare you!" he screamed…"How dare you blame this on my mother and Rubin!"

"I do blame her…It's her fault that we were handed over to Felix. If she had been stronger and fought for you, and for me, and stood up to Felix, then it wouldn't have gotten this far."

"You think Felix is behind this? WAKE UP! …It's not about 'The Jailer's Way' anymore…It's not about YOU anymore. You are not the *only* one who fought him and his ways. You are not the *only* one who suffered at his hands! I want nothing to do with this anymore! No more Felix, No more Jailer's Way. No more…"

He threw his hands and turned to leave quickly. Rubin flew out of the cottage door and followed Jace down the path, hustling to catch up to him.

I collapsed onto the bottom step. Neema gently sat beside me, and we didn't move or speak for two more hours until the mosquitos started buzzing and the sky turned fiery orange and deep purple.

That night is when the nightmares began. I woke up screaming and tearing at my clothes and blankets. I imagined I was burning, and I could hear Indie crying for me. The nights became more unbearable than the days. I dreaded sleeping. I swore I smelled the faint whiff of Felix's cigar coming through the window and it sparked tremors of fear and panic. Neema would come to me at the instant sound of me stirring to try and cut the dream off before it began, but it was of no use.

It was all my mind tormented me with the moment my eyes closed. I would scream Indira's name, and search for Jace out loud. I was going mad. I needed to escape. Everything here reminded me of the fire. I fought a battle between dwelling on memories forcing myself to feel the deep cut all over again as a punishment, and zoning out and turning off my brain, ignoring the smells, and sounds of the air surrounding me. I had to get away…

Chapter 20

"Remember the Stories, the Places, the People, and the Music..."

Three months had passed since I said goodbye to Neema and Rubin and the ruins I had grown up in.

Neema worried that I would be alright. It had only been six months since the fire, but she and Rubin understood why I had to go. Jace was gone. He had left a month before me and moved into an apartment in New York City, not too far from Wheezie.

I had contemplated going to Colorado, and seeing the Rocky Mountains, or visiting the different places I had always wanted to explore, but I settled on the East coast of the United States, in a small waterfront village overlooking the Atlantic. There wasn't anything in particular that made me choose this place, other than an idea that I would start on the East Coast and travel through to the West Coast over time. I would see everything in between, and in solitude try to piece my heart back together. I was lonely, but my own thoughts and emotions were all I could handle right now.

I had purchased a cell phone and promised Neema that I would call once a month at least to check in. I phoned Wheezie and let her know I had settled in Rockport, Massachusetts, only about a half an hour from Gia's Gloucester house. I had found a small dilapidated rental property that was only six blocks from the waterfront and shops. Wheezie helped me access the account waiting for me so I could use some of the money to get started. I didn't want to use any of it, but I was desperate.

Wheezie was eager to offer her apologies for the loss we suffered, but I brushed her aside and changed the subject. She had been in touch with Jace in New York and had news that he was writing songs for a record company and was successful in selling a few. It must have been enough money for him to get by on because I was the first one to bite into the multi-million-dollar account that had been set up for us. I felt terrible about that and needed to find a job as quickly as I could to earn my own way. I didn't want to have to touch the account ever again.

The area I stayed in was beautiful. My little New England wood sided beach house was only three rooms and had a small carport with a tiny fenced yard, just big enough for a garden table and two chairs. The kitchen and living room were an open concept, with a hallway and bedroom off to the side. It needed a lot of work, but I planned on fixing it up bit by bit. It was brand new to me, with no memories attached, so I could clear my mind and breathe the salty air free and clear.

I had rented the property in the spring and the days were getting longer and warmer. People started filling into the summer rentals, and the town came alive. Rockport was an artsy town with retirees, authors and actors frequenting as vacationers.   I was told that most people fled for Florida during the harsh winter months, but if I planned on staying, I would need to stock up for the winter and prepare to be bunkered down, buried in snow and salty storms. I hid any trace of an accent and spoke clear English. I didn't want to sound local because people would ask questions, so I pretended to have a flat New York tone and when asked where I was from I would tell them Upstate New York.

On the first of May, I walked five blocks to the town library and asked if they would be hiring any time soon. A tall thin woman in her sixties, with pointy features, and French braided snow-white hair warmly introduced herself.

"I'm June...It's nice to meet you. So you're going to be in town awhile or would this just be through the summer?"

"I'm here for a while," I explained.

"Okay. Well, fill out this application and write in this box any special skills you may have. I'll be right over there, bring it over when you're done."

I sat at the solid maple table that had several computers being eagerly watched by patrons. It was a large building broken into sections for fiction, nonfiction, a video department, and a children's department. I worked out the application filling in the address of my little rental.

Skills? I knew hand to hand combat, lock picking, and theft would not be taken well and struggled with what I could write down about my life…What could I write? I could be honest and tell her I was a trained Linchpin that had aided in the death of an unnamed amount of people, or that I had traveled the world and brought down an international war criminal.

I finally settled on writing down the many languages that I could interpret. I could read people and pick out a thief or a victim, so I put…. "Great with customer service and human resources." Two days later June called me and told me I could have the job. I met the staff of the library and was given a tour.

My boss was the director of the library. Her name was Jenny, and she was very petite. She had dull gray eyes and long stringy salt and pepper hair that parted dead center down the middle of her head and cascaded to her lower back. She was older, in her fifties and was an organized perfectionist.

There was a mousy brown-haired sweet woman named Betz who had two teenage sons whom she adored and spoke of as if they were her entire world. She continuously apologized humbly for things that were not her fault. She was timid and meek, and always had a warm welcome for me.

Within the tight-knit library family, there was also a tough love heavy set, black woman who told me I could call her Mrs. Augustus. She greeted me with a gruff, "How ya doing?" She was in her sixties and demanded respect from anyone younger than herself but had a soft side when it came to storytelling. She collected small porcelain dolls with various ethnic costumes and lined them up on a shelf behind her desk in the children's department.

The children could not touch them, but she had developed a story program that she organized. She wrote short stories about each of the seven-inch dolls and would have the children sit at her feet in a circle. She would hold the specific doll and explain its attire and tell the story of its heritage. She filled the stories with historical facts and humor, and the children looked forward to the program very much. I found myself sitting right along with them and listening intently.

Jenny's brother Christopher also worked at the library several days a week. Christopher was full of himself, and since spending all his father's inheritance and failing to go to college, was hired by his sister in an attempt to make him grow up and take life more seriously. He was in his early twenties but acted like a fifteen-year-old.

The position of assistant to the director had only become necessary in the last few months because more locals had decided to stay through the entire winter, and computers had invaded everyone's brains. The library had the most up to date equipment, and people were always waiting for their turn to research and take advantage of the technology. I made phone calls, scheduled, and organized lunches for Jenny. I typed her notices and in general, helped her day go easier.

On slow days when Jenny was away at a conference or had little for me to do, I would help organize the books or straighten the stuffed animals in the children's department. A large porcelain clawfoot tub sat in the corner of the children's room, with pillows and oversized plush creatures. The kids visiting would occupy themselves in the bathtub reading a book or pretending to be pirates while their mothers searched for what to read to them that week.

It was in this room that I first exposed who I was. I was helping Betz and Mrs. Agustus move a table to get a projector set up. The old film, Gulliver's Travels was going to be shown that day as a special program for the children. Parents started gathering, and children's voices began yelping. A mother scolded her son, saying "James. Let your sister play with the dollhouse too… James!" she yelled louder, trying to get his attention. With those few words, a swell of pain shot into my throat, and I choked up. My eyes filled with tears and I began gasping for breath.

I dropped the table and felt foolish for looking so fragile in front of all these people. I ran off to the bathroom to throw cold water on my face. These mothers must think I'm crazy. And I probably was. Small things each day from then on started triggering memories that would make me instantly become a fountain and humiliate myself.

If I was shopping and saw the grocer's white cat who had just had kittens, I would grip my mouth and try to hold back the gasp of sorrow, but it came so quickly, and without warning, I had no control over it. Even in my home that was a million miles from Mawlynnong, if the rain pounded on the rooftop, I would cry and sob until I fell asleep. Once Just the sight of a woman who was heavily pregnant and waddling sent me into hysterics. The sound of piano music on the speaker at a gift shop forced me from the store. The smell of cigar sent tremors of panic up my spine. It was random, and I felt foolish.

I tried to control these episodes at work, but many times had to run to the bathroom or lunchroom and regroup. The friends I was making tried to help me, and their kindness was so appreciated.

Betz offered to be a listening ear any time I needed. Jenny pressed for information in a more direct insistent way. She was no-nonsense and married to her job. If my crying spells interfered with her organization and direction of the library, then she would not tolerate it. I promised her that it was nothing, and I did my best to control my emotions especially when working in her office.

I hated exposing myself to these people. They didn't deserve my baggage, but at the same time, I yearned to tell someone about my children. I wanted them to know what a beautiful girl Indira was, and how her giggle sounded like bells chiming. I wanted them to know how cheeky her smile was, and how she loved her daddy more than anything. I wanted to tell them how I had carried my baby boy safe in my belly and felt him move and kick, and how I knew he would have looked like his father. I wanted them to know that I was married and missed my husband and his embrace.

I occasionally heard from Wheezie. She traveled a lot back and forth from Boston to New York and saw a lot of Jace. She always wanted to update me on how he was. I was happy to hear he was selling his songs, but hearing how his life was moving ahead, would sometimes trigger a crying attack.

"He's doing alright, he sold a song to that band...you know the one with the guys, and the lady singer...I don't know names, anyway, he wrote the lyrics and all, made a fortune. Some people have all the talent I tell you. He's gotten attention he doesn't quite know how to deal with," she explained.

I knew what she meant. He had women throwing compliments and pining after him like Allison Cade used to. He was good looking and had an accent that women could not figure out. He had a mysterious rugged look of having seen things, and women loved that.

"Wheezie, please don't tell him where I am," I pleaded. "He seems like he is doing better. I don't want to ruin anything for him.

"I most definitely have already told him where you are. I update him, just like I update you. And he's not okay. He writes music and lyrics to try and let the hurting out, but then crumbles everything and throws it across the room and loses it. It's like the Jace we knew is gone, he's either angry, or empty. He's been staying at an apartment on East 34th street, and we have dinner every Sunday night. Sometimes he talks to me, many times he's just quiet and lost. But I still go."

I was so glad he had Wheezie to be a listening ear, but It hurt me to hear he was suffering internally like I was. He had cut me to the core with his hate-filled words towards me. I hid from the fact that he blamed me and my stupid impulsiveness for killing his children and father. If my mind dragged me back to the day on Mahtap's porch and the words we yelled at each other, my stomach would instantly turn, and my pulse would become rapid.

My property was coming along, and my job was giving me enough to do some much-needed repairs. I bought a bicycle, and on warm nights I rode to the point and watched the sea. Couples would take photos and teenagers would make out. Parents would scamper after their children darting in and out of gift shops. Seagulls hovered waiting for a toss out. It was peaceful and calming to sit and watch people. I no longer saw stories of long-lost princesses or heiresses in disguise. The stories I saw on faces now were filled with the realities of life. I saw the enthusiastic young lovers, the exhausted but proud mothers, the infidel husbands. I could tell who had lost a husband or wife, and I could tell without a mistake which had lost a child. Facial expression and people's mannerisms were a blueprint to read, and I spent hours in the fresh sea breeze overlooking the sea, watching the passerby's while sipping a perfectly roasted coffee, and filling my mind with other people's stories because my own was too much to bear.

It was clear to me now that my father had known exactly what he was doing when he molded us to see the stories, and not just the faces. We have no right to judge another person based on their race, appearance, or status, because we can only see the parts of their story that they are willing to show. Any sense of judgment or superior attitude exposes the cowardly and ignorant as scared fools. But human nature blinds those fools. It's the sad tale of humankind.

One day midweek, I had gone to work early, and I sat at the maple table reading over Jenny's itinerary for the New York benefit that was coming up. I turned the rings on my finger round and round. I still wore the sapphire ring and the thin keychain that Jace and Emma had given to me.

It didn't seem to deter Christopher though. As winter approached and the library had become hollower, he became more and more persistent in getting my attention. He was exactly my age and had blonde hair and green eyes. He had far too much confidence in his appearance and attractiveness. He had pestered me for several days about where I had moved here from. He said I intrigued him, and that if I didn't go to dinner with him, he would die.

He wanted to know how I learned so many languages, and why my eyes were so pretty to look at. His attention was irritating and immature, and I cringed every time I saw him coming near me. I wanted to scream at him..."Don't you know who I am? Don't you know *what* I am?" But it would only get me fired.

His sister noticed the attention he was throwing at me and warned me that he had plans to be a doctor, so to stay off his radar. I had no intention of flirting with him or leading him on, but she thought it was necessary to keep me away from her brother. She gave him way too much credit, and I wanted to tell her that he was too stupid to pass medical school but definitely had the arrogant doctor part down. Despite his sister's threats and disgusted looks, he continued to reach for my attention.

"You're so serious Theorie Taralock. Right now...from this moment forward I'm making it my life's mission to make you smile," he stated.

"I really do not think you can comprehend the depth of impossibility in those words," I dryly replied rolling my eyes at him. I focused on my work, which is what he should have been doing instead of flirting with me.

I dressed like my goal was to blend in with a swamp, and I barely wore makeup. Nothing about me said, come and get me, I'm available. I cried at random moments and kept to myself on all my breaks. It had been seven months since I had started working here, and a year since the fire. I wanted to be left alone to heal, but he was such a pest.

My emotions were raw getting through all the firsts. The first anniversary of the fire, the day my little girl would have turned 4, and my son would have been a year old. The first time I spent an anniversary alone, and the first time I held someone else's baby in my arms. All these firsts were milestones and hurdles for me, and I battled them alone.

The loneliness was the worst part. I had no one to talk to and tell about my children, and I would randomly fear that they would be forgotten by the world. I would wake at night going over every feature of Indira's and Jace's face. I had one photo of my little boy that the hospital had given me and a handful of Indie and her father. My emotions were like a rollercoaster.

Occasionally I would meet Gia for coffee at Rockport Point. She lived less than an hour from me and offered to help me with home repairs. Sometimes she would help me paint or bring Michael along to help manicure the yard. She never pushed or asked how I was. She focused on the task given her and worked to move ahead. She let me be silent and brought attention to the little things that I had forgotten to care about. She would bluntly call me out for leaving my front door wide open or for leaving my house looking unkempt and sloppy. I was grateful for her company and was even building up the courage to mention my heartbreak and speak of my lost family.

One afternoon Gia and I went shopping in the town for cleaning supplies. "We're getting you some lip gloss," she insisted.

"I really have no need for that."

"No... but *we* are the ones that have to look at you," she teased.

As we shopped, I picked up soap and toothpaste, and meandered into the deodorant section, as Gia examined the makeup. I'm not sure what on earth prompted me to start searching for a particular smell, but I began opening and sniffing each and every men's deodorant. A manic mission started moving me. I knew it was insane and if anyone saw me, my crazy would be exposed.

Gia joined me, instantly understanding the manic workings of my mind, and not questioning me at all. She assisted me in opening every brand. We went through at least twenty-five scents until finally, a connection was made deep within my brain. Page after page of days and nights in an instant woke up my heart and unveiled memories that I had been skipping over. I had found it... Gia took the antiperspirant from my hand.

"You sure it's him?" she asked.

"Yes...I know it's silly. I'm going crazy Gia...This is so stupid." I took it from her hand and went to replace it on the shelf.

"Shut up...Come on...I found lotion for Michael, lip gloss for you, and you are getting this." She picked the deodorant up and went to the register to pay.

When the first winter had passed, and I had worked for Jenny for nearly nine months, I was asked to go along with her to a benefit in NYC. It was a librarian's conference with a black-tie gala the following day. I was to help her with her schedule and in making key contacts with certain people that she was interested in asking for grants and other donations to the Rockport Librarian's Society.

"You'll have to wear something nice to the dinner. Christopher will be coming as well. Nothing brown, or green…No colors found in nature…AT ALL!. It's black tie…do you know what that means?"

"Yes," I lied. Later that day I snuck off to the computer department and searched what "Black Tie" meant. I instantly knew it would be a horrible trip, not just because Christopher was coming along but because I had to buy a dress that I would only ever wear once.

Two days before the trip, I packed and realized I was in big trouble. I needed a dress that would stun investors and entrepreneurs but would hide the scarring on my left shoulder. I had to go shopping…I called a taxi, drove into Boston and spent the entirety of a day looking for something that would be acceptable to Jenny, but would hide the broken parts of me.

Christopher drove us the nearly four hours to New York in his black SUV because Jenny said it looked more dignified than her little gray station wagon. Jenny had her agenda set. She fretted over her speech and worried who she would be seated next to at the gala.

Once we checked in, I stayed in the suite, and she went downstairs to the conference room for her first lecture. She would have hours of lectures, and I was free to do what I pleased. I made it my goal to hide from Christopher who had already started using a fake Bronx accent and acting like an idiot. I sat on the balcony of the hotel room and called Wheezie.

"You're in town?" she exclaimed excitedly. "This is excellent. Let's have dinner tomorrow night."

"I wish I could, but I have to go the gala for the Librarian's Society. My boss can't play nice with others, and I need to help her make contacts and beg for handouts."

"Sounds like fun."

"It's not going to be...It's black tie, and I have to dress up."

Wheezie laughed hard. "You?...Ha... I'd love to see that. Well maybe in the morning? Breakfast?"

The next morning, Wheezie met me with a manly hug, and we sat in a small café that had a sticky floor and loud waitresses. We ordered horrible coffee that I had to choke down without breathing.

"You look good, Wheezie."

"You look like pig crap," she returned bluntly. "You ever think of trying *to not* look like death rolled over? You're twenty-four, not eighty-four."

"Thanks, I missed you too. You sound just like Gia. Is Jace around? " I reluctantly inquired.

"No, he's not… He went to California, headed out last week. He had a contract he had to work out. His music is really taking off."

"I was just wondering. I didn't want you to tell him I was here."

"Sure you didn't." She paused…"He's doing better Theorie. There are bad days, but they're not as fierce."

"Wheezie…Does Jace talk about Indira? And the baby?"

"He didn't…for a long time," She sipped her awful coffee. "but now, yes a little," she confided.

"He blames me, hates me…"

"He did…He hated himself at the same time, and you hated him. Maybe in the moment he blamed you. But you have to remember. He's your husband, and if I know anything about Jace Taralock, it's that he lived, and breathed to protect you and that little girl. Ultimately in his mind, he failed. He failed you, he failed Indie, he failed little James, and he failed his father. Maybe he couldn't look at you because he felt guilt and failure, not because he hated you and blamed you."

"He said it was my fault, and he was right."

"He was wrong…and he knows it. He feels the guilt of those words, just like you do with yours." I thought about what she said, and my heart ached to tell him how sorry I was.

"I told him I didn't believe it was poachers, I blamed his mother and The Jailer's Way."

"And, you weren't entirely wrong in that speculation...I have a question for you." The waitress brought our breakfast and filled our rancid coffee to the brim, we paused our conversation until she left.

"In the interrogation, I came across a face. It seemed so familiar to me, but I couldn't place it. We interviewed a young man in his late twenties, early thirties who would *not* cooperate. Wouldn't give us his name or anything. Instead, he insisted on his innocence, and said he just had a common face and had been mistaken for someone else. But I knew I had seen him before. We had nothing on him other than hearsay from other Linchpins, and in a lineup, he was overlooked and not identified, so we let him go. But just last week, I was going through interviews and buttoning up loose ends, and I found it."

"Found what?"

"A sketch...that you drew when you stayed at Gia's. You sketched me a man and a woman's fa….."

"Arlo!" I cut her off.

"That's it...I knew it began with an A. So many papers went through my desk in the course of this whole thing, I could punch myself for not remembering it when I had him in the interrogation room."

"Do you think he had something to do with the fire?"

"I have my suspicions. I kept tabs on him, and he did travel overseas in the timeline of the fire, but I can't prove it. I lost track of him...but I'll find him," she stated.

"That will be difficult. He was trained to be invisible."

"Well, we found him once even without a name...I'll keep digging. The CIA and FBI are all a part of this process now, and it's still unraveling like an avalanche. But I want you to know, I've got your back. Both of you...and If I sense even the slightest sign of danger, I will let you know."

"He has another sister," I whispered, leaning into the table and checking over my shoulder.

"Other than Andrea? We haven't seen anything of her at all."

"I have no idea where Andrea is or if she is even alive. But I know that right next to Taralock Estates is a Ranch. It's owned by a wealthy entrepreneur who owns many properties. He has a daughter Allison. We grew up with her pompous face, but I know that her Ranch and her father's enterprise are all 'Places' Felix used. I don't know why, maybe they were put there to keep track of Taralock? Whatever the reason, it's involved somehow. Allison came to the farm just a few days before the fire. She exposed us and had something to do with the fire. It was *not* poachers."

"Allison what? What's the Ranch's name?" Wheezie pulled out her notebook.

"Allison Cade. Cade Ranch. I never met her father, but Joseph did, and Emma may know more. I think her father's name was Ivan?"

"Ivan Cade? You're kidding..."

"Why?" I asked, wondering why the name intrigued her.

"The school for the deaf that your brother Tobin was sent to is owned by Cade Industries. I went there and met with the headmistress. She was hiding something and was startled when I questioned the death of Tobin Jailer. She was visibly shaken. I asked her for any information that would explain *how* he had died. She told me to ask Emma Taralock. It took me by surprise because I hadn't mentioned Emma's name. I stirred her enough that as I pressed for information and wanted his files, she misspoke and said...'If you want to find him, ask his mother.'"

"What? What does that mean? Did she mean Emma, or my mother, Rose?"

"I don't know...She closed up after that, and I couldn't get anything else out of her. But Ivan Cade owns that school and owns about a dozen other medical facilities and just as many hospitals throughout Europe and Russia. He is not just a Ranch owner in Tanzania. His name came up in the evidence we unfolded, but he's been missing since around the time Felix was executed and we don't know what he looks like. I'll keep digging. I have something to go on now."

The gala was beginning, and Jenny and I were picked up in the lobby of the hotel by Christopher who would be our driver. He wore a tux and wore so much gel in his blonde hair, he looked like a department store mannequin.

"Woohoo," he whistled as he came to greet us.

"Christopher, really!" his sister scolded.

Jenny's burgundy dress was painted on her, revealing that she had the figure of a ten-year-old boy. She looked unnatural in heels and uncomfortably pulled her dress down as it slid up her lanky body.

I had taken Wheezie's advice and tried to look alive. I wanted to look pretty, and not so sluggish. It had taken an hour and a half, but I managed to put on makeup, and twist my hair into a low loose bun. Pieces hung from the sides of my face already though, and I knew taming it would be an all-night battle. I put a thick band of silver bracelets around my wrist to hide the tattoo marks and cigar burns. I wore sapphire blue teardrop earrings that complimented my ring and a matching sapphire dress that gathered at the chest and swam over my left shoulder. I had found a near match to the color and fabric of the dress at the craft store and altered the shoulder to cover further down the arm, just enough to cover the damaged tight skin. It was the first time I wore an elegant gown, and I felt awkward as I walked through the lobby and drew the attention of passing men.

"You *do* have a body under all that moss and foliage," Christopher declared. I scowled at him, and his sister shoved him forward.

"Focus...Move on," she scolded.

Once in the SUV, Christopher turned the radio stations and settled on a newer song.

"I love this song!" Jenny announced.

Its lyrics sounded familiar, and it took me one verse to recognize it as Jace's work. As the tune played and Jenny softly mumbled the lyrics hiding her monotone voice from us, I listened to the chorus. I had seen Jace writing a hundred songs. He would tap the paper, erase marks, and quickly scribble and jot sounds that pounded and flowed in his head. I had only ever seen his facial expressions and movements while orchestrating a new song, now I could hear it. I could finally hear what had been beating harmoniously in his head. Its words spoke of an 'incomplete heart, and loss.' It spoke of 'the girl with an amber spark in her eye, and how words can cut down something that should have been eternal.' It was a beautiful song that made me miss him and wonder what he felt when he was writing it.

The gala was stressful. Jenny was sweating, and it showed how nervous she was. She was also out of her safety zone and made it known on the ride over that she was here to make money for the library, and then we were leaving. Christopher meandered around scooping up champagne where he could, and I stayed by Jenny's side helping her maintain composure and from not wholly embarrassing herself.

She was starting to be at ease, and I could lower my guard. Gentlemen came up introducing themselves to me, thinking I was important. Apparently, all it takes to get attention was a pretty dress and some mascara. I hated the compliments and flattery when caddy wives would comment on how 'lovely' I was, and 'where did I get that dress?' I would answer that I was just a librarian from Massachusetts and that I got my dress at the mall and they would laugh and call me a tease. The champagne flowed, and the compliments got bolder. Christopher had managed to find some blonde to dance with, and I followed Jenny like an obedient comrade.

Jenny drank champagne and looked for the next beneficiary to hit up for funds by giving them a sob story of how desperate the Rockport community was for programs and educational classes.

"Don't look…but at 9:00 there's a very nice-looking man that has NOT been able to take his eyes off of you," Jenny mumbled under her champagne breath. I looked at my 9:00.

"Not your 9:00, My 9:00 you dope. And don't look...he's looking over here," she scolded.

As I turned inconspicuously to see who was watching me, I was stopped by a tall man that had a faint smell of cigar lingering on his skin. He approached directly and gallantly introduced himself to Jenny and me as Mr. Japp from London. His debonair manner captured Jenny's attention and she became putty in his hands as his broad shoulders blocked my view of Mr. 9:00.

"I've been eager to meet the two most beautiful ladies in the room all evening." His voice was deep and smooth.

Jenny giggled like a teenage girl and held her hand out to him. I was mustering up the boldness to make eye contact, but I already knew who this man was. The air in the room had given it away before he even approached us. I took a deep breath and raised my eyes in a cool, collected dominating glare.

"Hello, Mr. Cade." I stared him down, unafraid of whatever threat he was trying to convey. After all that had been taken from me, I would have no conscience about killing this man right here. I knew why he was introducing himself, and it was not to donate to the Library Foundation. I knew in that moment that I had one chance to either cater to his control and let him dominate my life or take a stand and end this right now. Jenny stared in silence at my sudden confidence and cold manner towards this deep-pocketed tycoon. I looked up into his light brown eyes with determination and a callous heart.

I reached to my ear and in an audible tone, gave the camouflaged agents the positive ID they were waiting for. I had never seen this man before in my life. I didn't need to...Wheezie had confidence in my ability to hunt down an evil story, and I didn't fail her. His eyes gave it away, just like his son Arlo's. His craving to confront me with his dominance in a setting that he would seem the most powerful was the weakness we exploited. Wheezie knew that I was the bait she needed to draw him out, and that I was more than capable of fulfilling a mission with accuracy.

He and I kept a steady hold on each other's eyes as he was forcibly taken into custody. He was escorted by the FBI throughout the crowd of entrepreneurs, business men, and their plastic wives who seemed only slightly stirred by the activity. He didn't fight their grip. He looked straight ahead with an arrogant charm. Two of his assistants approached to intervene but I stood my ground and blocked them from exiting. I smiled and nodded my head, exposed the gun I had hidden in the fold of my dress, and said with firm control,

"Three o'clock, FBI. Six o'clock, MI6. Twelve o'clock, Russian FSS. I would think twice before causing a scene in *this* studio."

The two men backed off, dropped their weapons to the ground and cooperated with the agents that surrounded them as they were cuffed. I collected the weapons pointed them to the ground and released the magazine unloading the cartridges. I handed them over to the FBI as the music picked up and voices resumed chattering.

The guests continued on with their evening as the gossip began of who the man had been, and who the mysterious woman in the sapphire dress was. Christopher and Jenny stood looking at me as if I had a monkey sitting on my shoulder. I knew that I had to leave, and my life at the Rockport library was over. Wheezie had already arranged a place for me, and I was glad to be moving along.

"The languages, the too wise for your age look...I get it now," Jenny concluded.

"I have to go... Jenny, I'm sorry...Christopher will have to help you. I won't be back to work."

"You can't go, you just became very interesting," Christopher pleaded.

"By the way...Mr. 9:00 is still watching you," Jenny exposed. "Go talk to him…If you don't, then I'll drag you over."

"I can't Jenny."

"Why not? He's beautiful. Are you not seeing what I am seeing?" Her champagne was making her friendlier than I was used to.

"Because he's my husband."

Jace stood near the piano in a tux, watching the room.

Jenny spit her champagne back into her glass. "Your what? Your husband...You are not serious, right? He is not *your* husband. He's so...tall."

"He is..." I admitted.

"Why didn't you say anything. You never said that you were married. Never mind, you never told us you were a... whatever you are, either."

"No one ever asked. I wear a ring." I showed her my hand baring the keychain and sapphire rings.

"Unbelievable"...Christopher finally caught up to the conversation.

"You're married! That explains a lot. Oh My God," he stated, "I bet he's some hippie, earthy, smoothie drinking poet. Oh, wait...is he a spy too?"

"I am *not* a spy, and he is a musician," I admitted, watching Jace across the room. I wanted so much just to run into his arms and escape to a mysterious place with him. Then a second later I wanted to hide from the shame of my words and the pain I had caused him. What do I do? Run to him, ignore him, hide behind a plant, escape, stay, run to him? What was he doing here?

"You've got nothing over him you dope." Jenny degraded her brother. "You are not in the same caste as Mr. 9:00. And all along I thought you were trying to catch my brother...Hah! Theorie Taralock, I should have known. What other secrets are you hiding?"

I couldn't answer her. She had no right to know me. She was my employer and *not* my friend. She wouldn't be able to comprehend even a day of the life that I had lived. People could not *ever* know who I was. I would have to carry on with my existence and forget the first twenty years of my life. I would have to be ordinary.

"Goodbye." I smiled and left the two of them baffled and full of plots. I hurried past Jace and left the gala.

"Wait, Thea...Please." Jace said, following me out. "I didn't mean to scare you. Wheezie wanted me here as back up."

"I thought you were in California?" I asked, biting my quivering lip.

"I got back this afternoon, Wheezie called me."

We stood on the street with cars buzzing by and pedestrians pushing past. The gala was mostly over, and the older couples were exiting the hotel and calling for their valet's. I didn't know what to say to him.

"Wheezie told me to pick you up and bring you to the airport in an hour," he stated.

"I'll be fine, I can get a cab, or I can walk, it's not too far."

"Not in that dress, at night, in New York City, four minutes after you exposed a master criminal. I'll bring you. We need to talk anyway." His protective tone made me hope that maybe his hatred for me had lightened. At least he was willing to talk to me. His car wasn't far, and it would feel safer than walking the streets exposed and alone.

"You look beautiful Theorie…" He broke his gaze and looked at his feet as he opened the door for me.

"You look good too Jace, not beautiful, but…good," I smiled back at him. He was blushing as he took my hand and helped me get into the car. It took me by surprise and feeling him touch my hand instantly transfixed me, and I didn't want to let go of him.

"I heard you sold some of your songs." I said once we were on our way. I tried to lighten the atmosphere by diverting from any deep conversation.

"Yeah…Did you hear them? …It doesn't matter…Never mind. I have papers I need to give you. We have an hour, how about some coffee?"

431

We drove several miles, double checked that we were not being followed, got coffee and parked on a hill overlooking the night lights of the city. I thought about what papers he was talking about, and I was certain he was filing for divorce. Wheezie would have helped him draw the papers up, and she wouldn't have told me because her affection had always leaned towards Jace. I withdrew into my thoughts and tried to fight the intense pull he had on my heart. If it was what he really wanted, I would have to let him go. I knew it would tear my heart open again, and I wanted to get it over with quickly so that I could get to the airport and go on with the plan Wheezie and I had arranged. I would be given a new identity and live my life as an entirely new person...alone. He handed me a manila envelope.

"I was wondering if we could open this together."

"Okay Jace," I surrendered. "I'll sign it and be done with it."

"What are you talking about?" he asked.

"I assume they are divorce papers, and you want to be done with me," I admitted.

"I don't know *what* is exactly in this envelope, but I know it's *not* divorce papers. Neema sent this to me, a month ago. I haven't opened it. I couldn't without you. She told me to wait and open it *with* you."

"You don't want to be free of me? For all those things I said?"

He looked baffled, his eyes pleaded to understand my thoughts..."No," he gently replied. "Theorie we said things...both of us said things... I am *so* sorry for yelling those words at you. My words beat you when your heart was already shattered." He started to crumble in his voice.

"A month ago I got this in the mail from Tanzania." He cleared his throat and pulled a note from the large envelope.

"It's from Neema." He handed it to me to read. In Swahili and in her flowing handwriting her note said...

"Jace, I have no words to fix or even comfort you, and I can't say I know how you are feeling because I have never lost a child. I found these among the things in the house, and they belong to you and Theorie. Open it with her, when you are ready. Your father and children will not be forgotten or left behind, Rubin and I check on their resting places every day. You are broken, but not destroyed. Remember the music you have made and the stories you wrote along the way. Every day of your lives was another page in the epic story of a boy who played piano for a girl with an Amber streak in her eye."

I unsealed the envelope and pulled out a stack of photos and a small leather pouch. Photos of Indira and Toby playing with Toby's puppy, a picture of Jace and I on Emma's porch with his arms around me, his hands on my round belly with our growing son inside. A photo of Mahtap and us as children picking coffee cherries. A group of dark-skinned Maasai wearing red Shuka cloth beside a little ginger-haired girl with her arms wrapped around her blonde twin brother.

The last photo in the pile was of a young man about seventeen or eighteen. Behind him was a waterfall, and he was leaning back on the guard rail. He was smiling and wearing jeans and a maroon t-shirt with "NYC" printed on it. It was a recent photo. His floppy blonde hair was thick, and his blue eyes were carefree and innocent. They were familiar and had my father's sparkle. I thought for a moment...*" Could it be?"*

In the small leather pouch was the pocket watch that Mahtap had saved for Jace. I pulled it out and handed it to him. He ran his finger over the engravings. Lose beads dropped into my cupped hand from the pouch. They were beads that Neema had collected from the cracks of her bedroom floor. Pink, teal and black beads that looked like tiny bits of chewing gum.

I broke down and swelled with tears, trying to catch my breath and not make a scene. I ran my finger over the loose stones and glass beads and then carefully placed them back in the pouch. I held it clenched to my chest and tried to wipe my face. Jace pulled me close to him, and I tucked into his enveloping embrace. It felt so natural to be in his arms, like he was the binding of a book and I was the loose pages that needed holding together.

For a year since the fire, tears would overtake me, and pain would pour down my face. It never made me feel any better though, it just allowed me to feel something other than numb. For the first time, crying felt like it was a step towards forgiving myself, a step towards healing.

We undeniably needed one another. We knew each other's pain and understood it like no one else possibly could. We knew the scars that our bodies wore. We knew the stories that filled the pages of our lives. We knew how to heal and mend one another. *We had been training for it our whole lives.*

"Our life is not so simple, not so normal, is it? I have always chased tomorrow and tried to jump ahead to the unknown. I overthink and over-complicate everything, and I am so tired of it," I admitted.

"Surviving doesn't have to be complicated. I love to write music, and you love to tell a good story. A chorus can stir a heart, but it needs lyrics to complete it."

"I still don't understand *why* you love me Jace Taralock. But I'm so thankful that you do."

"There will be bad days...A lot of them. It may take another two decades to make you see why my heart is attached to yours like the Root Bridge in Mawlynnong," he whispered, pulling me closer and putting his hand on my face, wiping a tear away from my cheek with his thumb.

I reminisced about the Living Root Bridge, and its entangled strength. Year after year it grew stronger and more beautiful despite thousands of people stomping over its path. It took time, and patience to get through the days where it endured nothing but beating rain. I was ready to slow down, I was ready to let time strengthen and sew back together the broken parts of me.

"My heart doesn't know what to do without you beside it," I confessed. "Mahtap lost her baby boy *and* her husband, but she told a story of 'hope'. She spoke of holding him and hearing his voice again and being able to watch him grow up. It gave her strength and healed her. We need that hope, we need it like we need air in our lungs." I dropped my head and leaned on his shoulder.

435

Jace put his hand on my lowered chin and tilted my face upwards toward him. "Then let's start a new story. Let's find what made Mahtap smile."

THE END

Made in the USA
Middletown, DE
27 September 2019